By the Mast Divided

DAVID DONACHIE

Allison & Busby Limited
12 Fitzroy Place
London W1T 6DW
www.allisonandbusby.com

Hardcover published in Great Britain in 2004.
This paperback edition published in 2005.

A CIP catalogue record for this book is available from
the British Library.

10 9 8 7 6 5 4

ISBN 978-0-7490-8260-4

Typeset in 11.5/15.5 Adobe Garamond Pro by
Allison & Busby Ltd.

The paper used for this Allison & Busby publication
has been produced from trees that have been legally sourced
from well-managed and credibly certified forests.

Printed and bound in the UK by
CPI Group (UK) Ltd, Croydon, CR0 4YY

DAVID DONACHIE was born in Edinburgh in 1944. He has always had an abiding interest in the naval history of the eighteenth and nineteenth centuries as well as the Roman Republic, and, under the pen-name of Jack Ludlow, has published a number of historical adventure novels. David lives in Deal with his partner, the novelist Sarah Grazebrook.

CHAPTER ONE

'Somethin'll turn up, lads, something always does.'

Charlie Taverner tipped back his battered tricorn hat then waved his tankard to add sincerity to the statement, aware that the jug in his hand was more than half-empty and there was no money for a refill. 'How many times have we been in a spot and somethin' has happened along to ease matters? Time and again, lads, and damn me if that ain't the truth.'

His cheery voice did not carry far in a crowded wharf-side tavern like the Pelican. Nor, judging by the expressions on the faces of his three companions, did it do much to lift their spirits, which made Charlie Taverner question – not for the first time – a fate that had bound him to them. Ben Walker, furthest from Charlie and never much given to talking, was staring fixedly into the smoke-filled room, lost, as he always seemed to be, in private thoughts and concerns that creased the forehead above his smooth oval face.

Abel Scrivens, the oldest of the group, was slowly shaking his head at the folly of such cheerfulness, his hooded dark brown eyes sad in a tired, lined countenance made sharp-featured by years of dearth. Taverner reckoned Scrivens an awkward cove, but he had also to allow that Abel was no misery-guts – just a man who could see the world for what it was, for he had seen it the longest.

Only Rufus Dommet looked as though he had any faith in the confident assertion. But then the red-haired freckle-faced youth, the bairn of the group, was such a simple fellow he would believe any statement made by the likes of Taverner – only three years his senior in age, but a dozen ahead in experience. Rufus would have been helpless in London without someone or other to mind out for his welfare, which his trio of companions did with varying degrees of tolerance. In truth, Taverner was working hard to sound hopeful in the face of the naked reality that was mirrored in the expression on old Abel's face – the four of them were right on their uppers, and with no place to go for a good three hours. Their bed space was still occupied by those who had a turn in the tiny hovel that was all this quartet could call home, night-soil workers who would roam the streets of London lifting other people's filth. In the crowded Liberties of the Savoy, the few streets and alleys bordering the Thames, any place to lay a weary head was at a premium, and hot-bedding was the order of the day. Two, sometimes three shifts of sleepers occupied the same small room, some sunk so low they were forced to share shoes and topcoats as well as a straw-filled, flea-ridden mattress.

The casual riverside labour on which the four depended was slack at this time of year, with nothing but winter greens and root vegetables coming in for unloading on good days. A week of hard frost in the country had meant no produce for the nearby market at Covent Garden, and without work and a day's pay they had little to live on. It was freezing outside, turning to night, and if they could not see a way to keep their tankards topped up, then the tight bastard who ran the Pelican would toss them out on their ears.

'I hear they're takin' in volunteers for the army at Chelsea Barracks,' said Walker, without looking at anyone in particular.

'Now why in Christ's name would you want to go fighting the French?' demanded Charlie. 'What has they ever done to you?'

'They's chopped off King Louis' head,' insisted Rufus, with an air so serious it seemed a personal affront.

'Good luck to them, I say,' Abel Scrivens growled.

'That ain't right,' Rufus protested.

'Why ever not?' the older man demanded, eyes opening in surprise, for he had little love for anyone of means, soundly based on his having to deal with them. With age on his side and a placid manner, Abel Scrivens was the one who sorted out the work they undertook, the fee for their labour and the time they were given to complete the task – that followed by the inevitable haggle over payment.

'They're chopping the heads off all and sundry,' the boy mumbled, now sounding uncertain, for he had learnt to be cautious when arguing with the older man. 'An' it stands to reason there will be good folks among them.'

'Would that be the same good folks who pass along the Strand, not two streets distant from this very spot, and step over the bodies of those dying or forced to beg? Or would they be the same good folks who are forever trying to rob us of our dues once the work we've engaged for is done?'

Scrivens shook his head in wonder at what he saw as the boy's innocence. Charlie Taverner knew Abel would want to put young Rufus right, to let him know that the boy was a fool for his view of the world, but he also knew that Abel's manner would add nothing in the way of cheer. Rufus, likewise, would resent being hectored, so Charlie, with another sweep of the tankard, adopted his usual ploy when dispute threatened the mood.

'Talking of kings and the like, did I ever tell you about the occasion I got myself carried round London in a coach and four?'

'Not above a dozen times,' groaned Ben Walker, the lilt of his West Country drawl taking the sting out of the complaint, and since no one really wanted to dwell on their situation, or engage in an argument about whether it was right to kill folks, even if they were French dogs and rich with it, Charlie was allowed to retell an oft-repeated tale from his seemingly chained past.

He had been a sharp, the best working Covent Garden he claimed, able to spot a country flat lost in the London maze quicker than most could blink. Ben, Rufus and Abel listened, each one selecting what they chose to believe, noting any exaggeration, for the storyteller was prone to embellishment. Charlie took them from the moment when he spotted his mark, a stranger to the city, young, gormless, with more of substance in his purse than his head, to when he persuaded him to empty that purse on clothes, suppers, hands of cards and willing whores, all at the whim of his well-heeled, but momentarily embarrassed friend, Handsome Charlie Taverner.

'I say Chelsea,' said Ben Walker, bird-like eyes again fixed on the middle distance, as Charlie concluded his tale with his hurried flight from a sword-waving dupe who knew he had been dunned. 'This weather don't look set to ease yet, and without Abel gets us some unloading we won't even have the price of our four by four to sleep in. We'll end up having a lie-down on the Savoy Steps with the beggars.' Gloom clouded his features as he added, 'With this cold we might as well just chuck ourselves in the river.'

'We could sell our teeth,' opined Rufus, who tended to propose that course when things looked bad, for, Abel apart, they were still young enough to have molars of value.

'Cold means extra coal barges,' insisted Charlie.

'We ain't sunk that low,' Abel countered, for unloading coal was hard, poorly paid, and filthy work.

'Chelsea means a shilling for our mark,' Ben added, 'a hot meal and a bed right after.'

Charlie Taverner's smile disappeared, as he demanded, 'And what do you think there will be in droves within earshot of a trumpet sounding for recruitment?'

Walker tried to look questioning, but he knew as well as Charlie that every tipstaff from London and Westminster would have men there, waiting to take up the likes of those who normally feared to leave the Liberties of the Savoy, a sanctuary running by the side of the Thames, neither bound to Westminster or the City of London, where normal writ of debt and bondage did not run. Men of that ilk also patrolled the streets that enclosed this haven. Never mind Chelsea, just getting past them would require sharp wits.

'Charlie 'as the right of it, Ben,' said Abel. 'It won't be a bed in the barracks you'll get, or a chance to bayonet to death some Johnnie Crapaud, like as not as poor as you. A square foot of a cell in the Marshalsea is what you'll win, with the sound of the bailiff counting his fee for raking you in to send you to sleep.'

'Is that worse'n what we have now?' Ben demanded, his face red and his expression turning ugly. 'Stuck in half a dozen streets and alleys with a river at our back and ten men to fight for every job? No women barring whores, not a blade of green grass in sight and air fit to choke on. It might suffice for you lot, but I need to walk out of here, I do.'

'I say,' Charlie insisted again, holding out hand to calm his angry companion. 'Something will turn up.'

The low iron-studded door, set in the far wall, opened then and a tall fellow entered. Dressed in a black coat with wide severe lapels, a high collar and a tall hat with a large buckle on the front, he stood still for a moment. It was telling that the four near-destitute creatures could look at such a common occurrence, the arrival of a stranger, with hope.

The hot air hit John Pearce like a wall. Taking hold of the rusty metal latch, he shut the door behind him, thinking that he had run enough. He was tired and cold, and he knew that the vital spark that had kept him going since morning was ebbing away from exhaustion, hunger and thirst. Clouds of that cloying fug, the product of pipes and packed humanity, billowed out, dragged by the harsh east wind that whistled down the narrow, cobbled lane. It rose fast into the night air to curl round the swinging, creaking sign, painted with the huge-beaked bird that gave the place its name: the Pelican.

He prayed that the escaping smoke would disperse – if the men still pursuing him observed it they would guess where he had taken refuge. Eyes stinging, he peered through a murk pierced by lanterns fixed to the bare brick walls and the flickering blaze of a large fire, as well as the guttering tallow candles that glowed on the rough hewn tables.

What do they see? Pearce asked himself, as he stood for a moment on the landing by the door, his eyes ranging round the packed, low-ceilinged room. A felon on the run, or just some young fellow out for a revel?

He felt like a felon, and suspected he looked like one, unshaven and tired enough to feel an ache under his eyes. His clothes, too, were those of one who had slept rough these last few nights, and walked many miles on muddy roads. Yet it was hard to tell if the occupants of the Pelican saw anything at all, for if anyone had heeded his entrance, they did not seem to be looking at him now. Nevertheless he deemed it prudent to move quickly from the door, to avoid drawing attention to himself – for this was a place where the locals would be much practised in observing a stranger and discerning if he presented a risk, or possibly a bounty.

Pushing between the packed bench seats, looking into a mass of faces, he observed extremes that made flesh the satiric drawings of Hogarth and Rowlandson: outlandish dress, arch poses, jabbing fingers, open mouths, laughter, anger and despair, some who, even in a crowd, seemed to be alone, so intently did they stare at the table before them, while the odd creature, drunk or mad, would laugh for no reason at his passing. The chill that had seemed to reach his very marrow, part fear, part the cold of a windy February night, began to retreat in the face of a scene so ordinary, so familiar – one that as a boy he had observed in countless taverns throughout the length and breadth of England. As he wended his way to the rear, the odd pair of eyes lifted to catch his. But they did not linger, for this was not a place where souls were bared and friendship freely offered.

What he would not give now for a friend to whom he

could unburden himself, a sympathetic ear that might help him find a way through his difficulties, a voice that might do something to quell the ever-present sensation he harboured: that he was burdened with a task too great for his years and experience. Pearce felt a wave of loneliness begin to wash over him, and fought hard to control it, for such an emotion was the precursor to despair, and that he could not afford if he was to fulfil the undertaking he had come to England to perform. He forced himself back to the present, and the problem of where to sit.

The seats lining the walls were as crowded as the tables that filled the well of the tavern, but Pearce took time to pick his spot. If there was another exit, he might need it without being gifted time to find it. The Liberties might provide shelter for those on the run from the writ of a City or Westminster magistrate, but he reckoned himself pursued by the enforcers of a King's Bench warrant, and the men who served those, he knew from bitter memory, could collar their prey where they pleased.

A curtained arch by the serving hatch clearly led to the back of the tavern. Surely there must also be a door to the outside that did not oblige anyone from that part of the building to make their way through the main tap room. He pushed his way into a space between two groups of men, engrossed in their own talk, in a place that allowed him, back to the wall, to keep his eyes on the main door. Then, elbows employed to increase the available room, he rested his back against the wall, and some of the tension that had sustained him since early that morning drained away.

'Enough space you got there, friend?' His neighbour's expression was more arch than angry, for Pearce had forced him to move. 'Have a care with your jostling.'

Pearce sat up abruptly, tipping his hat, more to cover his face rather than as a mark of respect, and, after a mere five days in England during which he had been careful to avoid casual contact, avoided only by a whisker replying in French. What he did say in English sounded, to his ears, slightly foolish. 'My apologies, good sir.'

'Good sir!' the fellow cried. A large circular motion with his tankard made sure his companions attended to his response to this arcane mode of address. 'And a tip of that most singular billycock to go with the compliment. I'll have you know, friend, that I ain't so much knighted, as benighted.'

Laughter greeted the pun, that and repetition as two of the jester's companions tested the not very telling wit of the remark on their own tongues. Pearce wondered what this dim joker next to him would say if he found that his neighbour was the son of Adam Pearce, the radical orator and pamphleteer, a man had up in the past for inciting public disorder, who was once again under the proscription of the highest criminal court in the land charged with sedition, which in time of war equated very closely to treason. Would he cringe to be told that he was seated next to a fellow who had, for the last two years, lived in Paris, the crucible of the French Revolution? Would he care? What did any of these people in the Pelican, with their cheap gin, thin ale and tobacco know about universal suffrage, equality of the sexes, an end to the power of kings and the supremacy of the individual?

Four years before, in '89, such ideas had been all the rage – the news from Paris had been hailed by British society as a bright new dawn. It was very different now. The French Revolution was no longer a beacon for freedom. Paris and all of France lay under the shadow of officially sanctioned murder, a tyranny based on the use of the guillotine, not only for aristocrats, but also for anyone deemed to be an enemy of the people, which included many of those who had overthrown the monarchy in the first place.

Egged on by the likes of the Irish parliamentary firebrand Edmund Burke, the people of Britain damned the Revolution now, having watched it lurch into anarchy and war. When King Louis was beheaded for scheming against his fellow-countrymen, a nation that had lopped the head off King Charles Stuart in the previous century rose up in hypocritical disgust at such an act. Laws had been passed to render anyone who spoke out for equality in King George's dominions guilty of rebellion, and so cast as a criminal who must first be confined, then tried, and it was hoped by the more reactionary elements, executed. It was an irony too painful to contemplate that having left Paris under threat of incarceration, abandoning a father too sick to travel, John Pearce faced a similar threat in the country of his birth merely for being that man's son.

The feeling of irritation grew. Did his fellow drinkers care that, in the whole of the British Isles, the right of free assembly had been suspended, so that any group of more than four people gathered to talk could be deemed a combination inimical to the safety of the realm? He wondered if they even knew that William Pitt was their Prime Minister, for few here would be freeholders with the right to vote. They would know that Farmer George, tainted with madness, was their King, and that the enemy in the war just declared was France. But more than that, no; they were drunk on the illusion that they lived in a free country.

Sensing his neighbour, who had turned to grin at him,

recoil, Pearce removed the glare of suspicious hatred that such thoughts had brought to his face. He looked away to fix on the substantial female figure in a low cut dress who now approached, oblivious to the salacious catcalls of those trying to goose or pinch her behind. When she bobbed before him, Pearce was presented with an alarming depth of cleavage, surrounded by what seemed like an acre of pink, mottled flesh, then a pair of dark brown eyes that seemed, for a brief second, to examine some interest.

'What, sir, will you partake of?'

This was said in a lazy, drawling voice, one supposed to encourage the customer to spend money by holding out a promise of other delights. But the look did not match the seductive tone. This wench had hard eyes that had seen and endured too much to retain any amiability.

'Rosie,' cried the benighted one, leaning forward, leering down that cleavage. 'Never mind this fellow. When are you goin' to take care of me?'

Rosie had tired, corn-coloured hair, a full mouth, flushed cheeks and a smile that, like her eyes, denoted the boredom of one who was never free of such remarks. 'You ain't got the price, Charlie Taverner, an' I ain't got the time nor the puff.'

'Do you have spiced wine?' murmured Pearce, and when she nodded he added, 'With a dash of brandy.'

That made her squint hard at him, as if he was some kind of curiosity. 'You'll know the price of brandy, then?'

A foolish thing to ask for; brandy in England was now contraband and expensive. 'Any ardent spirit will do, and some bread and cheese.'

'Arrack?' Pearce nodded, as his neighbour leant forward, attempting to stick his hand down the front of Rosie's dress, which brought forth an angry cry of, 'Mr Taverner!'

'Mister,' the man exclaimed in his overly jocose way, half turning once more towards Pearce, ignoring an expression that denoted that he wanted no part of this raillery. 'She calls me mister, not good sir, as you do.' Then he turned his full attention back to the serving girl. 'Rosie, five minutes up those stairs, in the sweet privacy of your bedchamber, and I swear you would call me your loving Charlie.'

'Old Charlie, more like, an' since when did anyone your age last more'n two minutes?'

The girl's broad back retreated towards the serving hatch, followed by catcalls about Taverner's prowess and her patience. Pearce, smiling at the put-down, wondered at a life like hers, then shook his head to clear the thought. This was no time for causes, for reflections on the lot of the disadvantaged – the situation he had very seriously to worry about at this moment was his own.

'There's meat for man there, friend, wouldn't you say?'

Charlie Taverner was made to feel foolish because he was grinning, one hand raised and cupped to grip imaginary flesh, at a neighbour who was not responding. In fact the face before him, under that odd hat, seemed devoid of expression, even the eyes, grey and steady with dark circles underneath failed to flicker. Pearce knew he should relax – to stare at this stranger in such a cold way would not aid the obscurity he craved – but he could not. He did register the smiling face, note that this Taverner was of an age with him, and had, though thin, a pleasing countenance, with thick blond hair and bright blue eyes. He had an air that implied he thought himself handsome and gave the impression of a man whose main aim in life was pleasure. But smile he would not, for to do so would only expose him to more conversation. With a confused, 'Please yourself,' Taverner turned back to his companions, leaving his miserable neighbour with what he wanted most: peace.

The noise of the tavern faded to a buzz and the odd shout. Now fully warm, Pearce opened his coat, feeling the weight of his eyelids. Rosie came and went with his food and spiced wine, and took his money, extracted from a purse he took care to re-bury in a deep inside pocket. Pressing his nose to the top of the tankard, he breathed in the heady odours of cinnamon and arrack. Staring into the smoky room as he sipped the alcohol, he chewed his food and silently prayed that those who had pursued him throughout this long day had given up the chase, at least for tonight.

Four times Pearce closed his eyes, only to start back into consciousness for three. But he had not slept properly for two days, forty-eight hours in which he had travelled many miles, a fair proportion on foot, and with warmth and wine it was impossible to stay awake.

'Grim looking bugger that one,' remarked Able Scrivens, leaning forward to draw attention as Pearce's head fell to his chest and stayed there. 'Don't look to be from round here, do he?'

'Who in their right mind would want to claim that?' added Ben Walker, still sour.

'Hunted, I'd say,' said Taverner in a soft voice, 'and no knowledge of which way to jump.'

'Which makes him one of us, poor soul,' sighed Abel.

'He ain't poor, Abel,' said Charlie, his face breaking into a knowing look. 'And he might just be this night's salvation.'

Turning to glance at his sleeping neighbour, Charlie Taverner was at last free to examine him in repose, relaxed and less hostile, to look at the tall black hat with the square buckle mounted on the crown, that and the cut of his coat, just as singular, with its wide, severe lapels and high rear collar. There was no suspicion in the examination, just interest. Taverner reached out to place Pearce's tankard upright before what was left in the bottom spilt out. He ate the remains of the cheese, then put the plate on the floor.

When the clamour jerked him awake, Pearce experienced several seconds of panic until he realised where he was: not in the Paris which filled his dream, not sharing a tumbrel with his father, being spat at by a screaming rabble, or strapped face down beneath the sharp blade of a guillotine, but still leaning against that brick wall in the Pelican; though the panic was mixed with anger for the fact that he had fallen asleep in the first place. He could feel the sweat of those troubled dreams round his neck and a sip from the quarter-full tankard told him he had been under long enough to let the contents go cold.

Over the rim he saw what had caused the uproar – a massive, burly fellow was on his knees, a pine bench in his teeth, slowly lifting it from the floor, the tendons on his hefty neck distended. He was surrounded by fellow revellers, some cheering and others – those who had doubtless bet against the success of the feat – jeering. They began to groan as he got the bench high enough to tip back his head, which allowed him to get one foot on the floor and rise, slowly, until he was upright. The noise reached a climax. Removing the bench from his mouth, the huge fellow accepted a tankard from a grateful supporter, the first of several which he emptied quickly and with ease, while behind him bets were settled. Fascinated by the spectacle though he was, Pearce was aware that the tavern door had opened and he stiffened till he could pin an identity on the three men and a small boy who entered.

In soft waterman's caps, blue bum-freezer coats and bright striped petticoat trews, with their pigtails, greased and colourfully beribboned hanging at their backs, the adults were, by their garb, unmistakably sailors. The boy was in the uniform of a marine: red coat, white waistcoat and breeches under a black tricorn hat. They made their way through the throng, forcing themselves on to a near full table by the curtained doorway next to the serving hatch, where they engaged one of the serving girls to provide them with drink.

'You rested well, friend?' The voice made him turn to face Taverner. Having slept for however long it had been must have done something for his state of mind, because he smiled as his neighbour added, 'I have often observed that true fatigue produces the best sleep.'

'You may well be right, sir,' Pearce said.

His neighbour held up protesting hands. 'There you are terming me sir again. I shall introduce myself, for I am Charlie Taverner and I pride myself on my ease of manner. And you are?' Seeing the hesitation Taverner added quickly, 'You do not wish to say, I observe, which is very right and proper in such a place, for I daresay you are thinking that there are any number of thieves, low scullies and crimps in the Liberties.'

Pearce was still smiling. His lack of desire to answer must have been in his eyes, for he had indeed thought that such a tavern in such an area must harbour people it would be unwise to trust. He suppressed the callous thought that only dishonest creatures could reside here in this haven for debtors. Having once shared a prison with the unfortunate, a co-joined victim of his father's incarceration, he knew that men and women got into distress in King George's domains for any number of reasons. The main cause for those in debt might be fecklessness, but he knew enough of the world he lived in to be aware that society itself had an in-built malice against those given to slippage.

'You have a tendency, friend, to wear a thought on your face,' Taverner added, 'for you have begun to frown again.'

'My apologies.'

Taverner grinned and his face was so open and without guile that Pearce, being of a generally friendly disposition, was tempted to do likewise. But the feeling was overlaid by the sure knowledge that of the people he had met in his life, the most honest looking, the most overtly pious and eager to please, had often turned out to be the most villainous.

'I hope you will be satisfied if I tell you that my given name is John.'

'John will do, fellow, and it will allow me to introduce you to my friends.'

This Taverner did, noisily, quickly and indistinctly so that Pearce was left uncertain which one was Ben Walker, Abel Scrivens, or Rufus someone else he did not pick up. A hearty wave brought Rosie towards them, and Taverner had ordered ale for all before she was within ten feet. She did not turn to fetch it, but, hands on her ample hips, and a knowing look on her face, demanded how he was going to pay.

The fair-topped head with the tipped back hat jerked towards Pearce, eyes bright with mischief. 'Why my new friend here has the means, as I observed when he paid for his spiced wine and cheese. Deep in his coat there is a purse that has about it a decent weight. John is his name, and as a fine sort he will know that it is the custom to seal an introduction to the Pelican with a wet to the familiars.' Taverner turned to grin at Pearce, face and eyes alight with the kind of certainty that was the stock in trade of a trickster. 'Is that not so, John?'

Dunned, thought Pearce, catching himself in the act of nodding before he had even made up his mind to comply, for he did indeed have money in his purse, the remains of just over fifty guineas that he had changed from Louis d'or in Calais. This joker had had him over like the biggest country bumpkin and flat in creation.

'Now do not frown again, John,' said Taverner, his grin even wider now, 'for a man with much must, for all love, share what he has in the Liberties with those who have little. It is the custom.'

Pearce did smile, for in truth he was grateful for the companionship. 'I daresay it will not be the last custom I shall hear about.'

He bought the drink without fuss, and another after that, for they were an agreeable bunch – even if Taverner had about him a touch of the rascal – and company kept his mind from his anxieties. John Pearce was not one to judge his fellow men harshly; their reasons for living in the Savoy, eking out an existence from the bank of the river rather than returning to the world from which they had sprung, emerged in fragments, companions through chance rather than natural friendship, who had combined for reasons of economy. It was clear that they looked to the older man, Abel Scrivens for wisdom, and to jovial Charlie to brighten their stay.

What emerged was a compendium of familiar tales: Scrivens had worked for a lawyer who had run off with his client's funds, leaving his clerk to deal with the consequences. He recounted his tale without rancour, in a low steady voice, which, allied to his desiccated appearance, led Pearce to suspect it had happened a long time ago. The Rufus person, gauche, all ginger hair, bright blue eyes and a face that was a mass of freckles, whose surname turned out to be Dommet, hailed from Lichfield, which he pointed out with an artless air was the birthplace of Garrick the actor, as well as the sage and writer Doctor Samuel Johnson. Obviously a claim for distinction, his boast occasioned hoots of derision from his companions, who declared that Rufus was only fit to act the fool and could barely write his name. He had been bonded to a slave-driving employer in the leather trade, running rather than complete the apprenticeship. Pearce liked him for the way he accepted the drinks he had been bought – he took his tankards with becoming diffidence and a look that imparted a degree of shame for the ruse by which they had been extracted.

Charlie Taverner suffered no such mortification. With him it was debt, though he insisted the sum was a mere trifle, a common justification given by those who had got in deep. Reluctant to let on how he had lived, it was left to his companions to imply that Charlie had been a fly sort, making his living from occupations that stood on the very edge of legality. That fitted with his air of easy conversation. He was a man who could approach a stranger, just as he had Pearce, and find the words that would engage them. He was also, clearly, the sort who could weigh the contents of a purse by eye alone.

Walker was more of an enigma. Small and compact, and by his accent from the West Country, his bright, protruding eyes gave him an air of keen intelligence, underlined by the way he kept his counsel, being unwilling to tell a stranger, or it seemed those he shared his bed-space with, of his reasons for residing here.

'Ben is our man of mystery,' said Taverner, a remark that had Walker tapping the side of his nose with his finger. 'Might as well sound out a stone wall as ask anything of Ben.'

Whatever his story, it seemed to weigh on him, for he was the least likely to chortle at Charlie Taverner's attempts at a jest. Indeed, when not actively part of the talk, Ben was inclined to stare into his tankard, or into the middle distance, with a doleful expression.

Pearce fielded their enquiries with grins and platitudes, unable entirely to forget his own concerns – the task he had undertaken, to get the proscription on his father lifted so that he could come home, the worry that he now seemed to face arrest himself – which was annoying given that he did not want to dwell on them. He wanted to enjoy this interlude, for that was all it could ever be – he knew he would have to move on, though the offer from Abel Scrivens that they could squeeze him into their hutch for a night's sleep was one he accepted gratefully, at the cost, on the insistence of Charlie Taverner, of a third refill from Rosie's circulating pitcher of ale.

Yet that offer exposed him, as though information regarding himself was part of the price of a bed. To distract questions that were becoming increasingly personal, he pointed towards the bulky bench-lifter, who had now accepted the challenge to drink a yard of ale. Staggering around, clearly already very drunk, he appeared in no fit state for the task.

'Who is that fellow?'

'That's O'Hagan,' said Taverner, frowning, 'an idiot of an Irishman who earns decent coin by day and manages to return to poverty every night.'

'You do not care for him, I perceive?'

'I'm not fond of Paddy as a race,' Taverner replied, 'they flood our island and take work that should go to decent Englishmen, though,' he added, putting a finger to his lips, 'I would have a care to say so. O'Hagan is a man to avoid. That bulk you observe comes from an ability to dig trenches twice the height of his own head. He thinks he can drink like a camel, but in truth he has a very ordinary capacity for ale, and the hope is that he will fall down before his natural belligerence overtakes him.'

John Pearce looked through the smoke towards the table where the trio of sailors still sat, though the little marine was no longer with them. A glance round the room showed several knots of other sailors in two and threes, some with tarred hats rather than waterman's caps. One fact was obvious – they were neither talking to, nor looking at each other, a very strange way to behave for men who shared a profession. All the ease that Pearce had enjoyed was replaced with a return of deep suspicion. He had allowed his guard to drop, idly observed the opening and closing of that distant door to the outside street without really noting who came in as long as they were not the kind of men, in heavy coats and big hats, who were pursuing him.

'Those tars, Taverner, they look to be Navy.'

'Do they indeed?' Taverner replied, peering round the room himself. 'I daresay you are right, my friend, but never fear the Navy in the Liberties, for we are free from the fear of the Press here. Now, what do you say to standing your new friends another drink?'

Pearce was about to demur, to insist that his means would not stretch to it, when the low front door was thrown violently open, to be filled with more sailors, all streaming through with some kind of weapon. Those around the room, including the pair by the curtained doorway, had got to their feet and produced clubs and coshes of their own. The noise that ensued then, when the customers of the Pelican realised what was happening, was not any more of people enjoying themselves, but of panic as each sought somehow to find a way out.

CHAPTER TWO

'Sit still!' Pearce shouted, using one hand forcibly to restrain Charlie Taverner, and the power of a strong voice, which had the same effect on the others. An awkward stillness ensued, and Pearce had the uneasy feeling that, because of that commanding shout, this quartet of drinking companions were now looking to him for some kind of guidance. How did that affect the need he had to get out: would they stand a better chance as a body than he did on his own?

There was no way of telling, for having been party as a growing boy to many a riot, more than a few caused by the inflammatory radical statements his father had been hollering from the stump, combined with the brute reaction of those who fundamentally disagreed with him, John Pearce had had plenty experience of sudden disorder; that moment when unexpected violence erupts. Near both exits people were milling around, shouting and screaming, intent on saving themselves or avoiding hurt, but by their actions doing more to hinder any chance of escape than aid it. If he had learnt anything from previous bruising encounters it was that panic was inimical to safety. It was best to stay still, take a look – then react. Not that he was calm; he could feel the pounding of his own heart, and the tremor at the extremities of his body, a reaction to this sudden explosion of aggression and what he could conjure up in his imagination might be the outcome. But Pearce could also see and hear with a heightened clarity, and that helped him to spot a possible route of escape.

The main entrance was no use; near the front door, fists were flying, as those too close for a quick retreat fought with what was clearly a press-gang. But bare knuckles against clubs put the men there at a disadvantage, and the sailors had already got ropes round their first victims, lashing them tight and dragging them out into the night. Some bodies were slipping through the cordon of sailors unscathed, but they were the old, the fat and any females that sought escape. Others of the same shape, age and sex had retreated to the walls, hoping by inactivity to be spared, making considerably easier the work of singling out those this gang were after – the young males.

At the rear of the tavern, those closer to him were still in a state of panic, crowding the opening near the servery that would provide a route to the side street, a spot where the original party of sailors had taken a seat. They were not seated now; they were standing, thick, foot-long leather coshes raised, threatening to brain anyone who tried for that way out, determined to keep everyone in place until they had been sifted. There was a clear space in front of them that none of the potential escapees seemed prepared to cross, regardless of the pressure exerted on them from behind.

'They are forbidden to press here,' cried Charlie Taverner, suddenly finding voice, shouting so loud it was as if he expected the gang to hear him and desist. 'It is against the law.'

'They ain't going to listen to that, Charlie,' hollered Ben Walker, who stood, fists clenched, in front of old Abel and young Rufus, neither of whom seemed to have yet quite cottoned on to what was happening. 'And there ain't no law nowhere's around to make 'em.'

Coming off their seats had brought all five close to the swaying Irishman, O'Hagan, who was looking around him in a bewildered way, clearly unable to take in what was going on. As Pearce came into his eye line he swung a huge fist at him, a proper haymaker, easy to duck under and one that sent a man already unsteady even more off balance. Instead of avoiding him, Pearce went in close to grab him and yell in his ear.

'You've got to get out, friend. There's a press-gang after you.'

Inebriated, O'Hagan looked down at him, unfocused eyes reflecting his confused brain, doubt rendering him ineffectual. Pearce spun the Irishman round and propelled him towards the back of those standing off from the cosh-wielding sailors. Rufus lent his weight, which in truth was not much, to push him bodily into the back of the maul. The Irishman, fired up by indignity, wanted to fight regardless, and was less than fussy about who felt his blows. Roaring and advancing like a bull towards the crowd, he cleaved his way through, arms swinging wildly. Furious-faced and spitting, O'Hagan left behind him an avenue for Pearce, Rufus and the others to follow, though it took strong elbows to keep it open. Time was not on their side – behind them the tars had overwhelmed their quarry and were now dragging fools from under the tables where they had tried to hide. This lot would be next.

With the noise of yelling and screaming drowning out any

other sound, O'Hagan's progress surprised those at the front of the throng, propelling a pair into the arc of those coshes, which came down on their heads. Pearce stopped abruptly; he reckoned that once engaged those sailors could not hold a line – with such numbers they must leave a space to get to and through that curtain. He was aware that Charlie Taverner and his companions were with him, making no attempt to get past, obviously still content to let him to take the lead, which produced a sudden flash of annoyance.

It was O'Hagan who created the gap, momentum and drunken fearlessness carrying him on. One sailor missed him, his cosh taking him on the shoulder instead of the head. The unfortunate tar then found himself pinned back to the serving hatch, with the Irishman biting off his ear at the same time as he attempted to gouge out an eye. The panicked cry brought immediate assistance as his mates closed in behind and started to belabour O'Hagan without mercy. Strong he might be, with thick tight curls to protect his head and drink to dull any pain, but he could not withstand the punishment he was taking and started to sink to the floor.

Pearce followed on the Irishman's heels, throwing out blows of his own, some of which landed on female heads rather than those of men. But he had to clear a route, whatever it took, and the women were adding to the confusion for they had nothing to fear. The sailors weren't after women and pleasure; they were after young and fit men. O'Hagan was on his knees now, no longer a threat and the three who had subdued him turned to resume their defence of the archway, just in time to stop Pearce getting clear through. It was the rush of those following that saved him, for there were just too many heads to crown, and the man attacking him had taken his eye off his present target to look for the next, so the thick leather cosh swished past Pearce's ducking ear. But the sailor still blocked his way, until, that was, Pearce's fist came up hard into his groin, which doubled the man over and took him out of the fight.

Half-turning, Pearce saw Charlie Taverner go down to a cosh, now lifted for a follow-up blow. But Abel Scrivens grabbed hold of the weapon with both hands and, hanging on for dear life, saved Charlie from further punishment. Old and skinny Scrivens might be, but he had the strength of desperation. With his pointed features all scrunched up, flung left and right, he looked like an ugly mongrel dog contesting the end of a bone. The man tugging the other end left himself wide open to half a dozen fists, forcing him to relinquish his cosh just to defend himself. Scrivens turned it on the last of the trio of sailors, who dropped to his knees, forearms covering his head, and suddenly there was no bar to a general rush for the curtain.

Pearce was first through, vaguely aware of colder, clearer air, of long tables covered with dirty crockery, pewter pitchers and tankards, as well as the row of big beer barrels that lined one wall. Ahead of him lay the open door, beyond that the street and safety, but Pearce sensed that to rush through there constituted danger, so he slowed to let others pass. Pushed into the space between two of the barrels, his hand found the thick end of a wooden lever, which would be used to move the barrels when full.

This escape route was just too easy; no press-gang in creation would leave it uncovered. Those men had been by that curtain to slow things down, not to stop them, and so allow some of the sailors now free from the struggle at the front to come round and block the way. The truth of that was proved by Ben Walker, who, having been right on Pearce's heels, scurried past to be the first fellow through the door. Immediately he ran into a wall of sailors who suddenly filled the doorway, one throwing a rope around him, while two others wrestled him to the ground. That did not deter the crowd that had followed from still trying to escape; they knew what was behind them.

Pearce stayed still for a half a minute, fighting still going on at his back while individuals ran past him, his mind racing as he watched another develop out in the street. He could hear the cursing sounds of resistance as well as a loud, harsh voice of command, echoing off the walls outside, directing operations.

'Let that tub of lard go, he is of no use to us. That fellow there is, and he is trying to crawl clear. Rope him, Coyle! Damn you, Kemp, club the bastard if you must. Get that damned woman off Hale before she scratches his bloody eyes out. You two, look lively! Drag those fellows already roped down to the boats. Christ in heaven, will you get a move on, before we fall foul of the watch.'

A scuffing sound made Pearce turn. A squat sailor was coming up on his rear intent on roping him, with two others behind him carrying a trussed and groaning O'Hagan. Pearce's assailant got a boot on the shins for his trouble, and as he bent, Pearce laid a blow on his tarred hat that cracked it wide open. That lever, when he held it out, kept the other pair, who had now dropped O'Hagan, from getting close, as, with no alternative, Pearce backed towards the door.

'You might as well pack it in, mate,' one of the sailors said, with a slight and worrying grin. 'You ain't goin' no place whatever you do.'

'Give in easy,' the other one added. He was also smiling, and Pearce thought it strange that there was no malice in his look, no desire to inflict pain. 'That way you won't be so black and blue when you gets aboard ship.'

'There's another one getting away,' the commanding voice outside called. 'He's in his prime. I want that fellow caught.'

Still backing away towards that sound, Pearce emerged into a few feet of clear space, but there was still much wrestling going on at either end of what was no more than a wide alley, lit by the flaming torches of the sailors who closed off each end, allowing through only those that were of no use. Ben Walker was still struggling to free himself, his labouring breath a rasp, as the rope, intended to confine his body stopped at his neck and pulled tight, was almost choking him. Walker was done for – he would be taken up, dead or alive. Rufus, obvious by that flaming red hair, was under a clutch of sailors struggling feebly as they tied him up, while Scrivens had clearly taken a blow and was on his knees, a rope pinning his arms hard to his side, no terrier now, more of a sad old mutt.

Pearce knew if he stood still he was done for. Raising the wooden lever, he started to swing it over his head, running towards those coming to take him, to try and force a passage, heading slightly uphill and away from the river. The tars fell away on both sides, backs pressed to the wall, leaving what looked like a clear route to freedom, with only a torchbearer to stand in his way, a man who would have to be a fool to try and stop him.

What killed his hope of escape was no more than a flash of white below his eye line. Pearce fell headlong over the outstretched foot, hat flying free, landing and rolling on the hard cobbles, his thick coat saving him from injury, the lever spilling from the hand required to break his fall. Hampered by his topcoat Pearce came up to defend himself, fists ready, to find himself looking into the face of a child, the little red-coated marine who had arrived with the first party of sailors. Immature he might be, but this boy had a cosh to swing, so Pearce hit him with as much force as he would an adult. Connecting with bone, he felt the nose give way.

As the boy staggered back, holding his face, blood streaming from between his fingers, two of the sailors Pearce had scared off jumped on him and forced him to the ground, one ripping off the high, rear collar of his coat in the process. Pearce's response, a head butt, lost force from the prone position of delivery, but the second man received an elbow in his ribs that winded him. However, both had hit Pearce, one a clout that made his head reel. Trying to get to his feet, hard enough with his coattails, was made even more laborious by that blow. He knew before he was halfway up that they had got a rope on him. Pearce dropped down again immediately. He had to get that rope off – nothing else mattered as he rolled and scrabbled at the rough fibre, getting one arm free, thrusting it out to grab at a metal boot scraper, hoping to drag himself clear. The foot that came down hard on his forearm wore a polished shoe with a garish buckle, while the calves were clothed in white stockings. It was odd to pick out so clearly the pinchbeck quality of that shoe buckle, as well as the buttons that held tight the bottom of the breeches.

'Get that damned rope round him now!'

With four or five men on him, all cursing with the effort, Pearce was soon well trussed. The little marine slipped between them while he was still on the ground and fetched him a hefty kick to his cheek that brought the taste of blood to his mouth. The foot went back to land a second blow, but the harsh, authoritative voice stopped it.

'Belay that, I want these fellows whole. This one's a fighter, so get him properly secured. Mr Farmiloe, search the tavern, make sure we have not missed anyone.'

The ropes bit tighter as Pearce was hauled, first to his knees, then to his feet. Another rope was used to bind his hands behind him, with a tail that went to a second cord that hobbled his ankles. A torch was brought close and dazed, he looked up into the face of the man issuing orders, a purple-faced naval officer who managed a smile that had about it the look of a happy executioner.

'Your name?'

Pearce shook his head, which hurt. 'This is illegal.'

The thick, knotted rope, which the officer had in his hand, caught him painfully just behind the ear in a blow that half-stunned him. He would have fallen to his knees if the men holding the bindings had not kept him upright. 'Your first lesson of your new life, do not dare contradict an officer.'

His head numb, it was with some difficulty, and in a thick voice that Pearce replied. 'The law says you can only press those bred to the sea.'

The rope caught him again, and as his knees began to buckle the officer's face came right up to him to growl, 'From now on, for you, I am the law.'

Pearce was hurt, but he was still trying to think what to say. It was illegal to press in the Navy any man who was not a sailor by trade, but it was, notoriously, a law frequently ignored. Press-gangs would take up anyone they could lay their hands on and hope that once confined to a ship the victim would be in no position to do anything about it. Any person who missed the sufferer was unlikely to have enough influence either to find the poor soul or to get him free. Even then, a justice of the peace would have to be involved and, in Pearce's case, that was not the sort of official he could give his name to.

Those holding him spun him round and he could see, down the alley in the light of several lanterns, that the group with whom he had been drinking was reunited. They were trussed as he was, as were at least a dozen other souls, like chickens ready for the pot. All except Charlie Taverner, who, hatless now and bleeding from a head-wound, was bent over and clearly in no condition to run anywhere. O'Hagan, still shuffling and groggy, was dragged out through the door to join them, the man that Pearce had clobbered, hatless, staggering at the rear.

'Tavern's clear, sir,' said a light, youthful voice at Pearce's rear. 'Except for women and the useless.'

'Thank you, Mr Farmiloe, get these men into the boats and away from here.'

Flickering torches lit the way to the boats, three of which, sitting offshore, were hailed to come and collect their cargo. The officer and the youngster called Farmiloe got into the smallest and were immediately rowed away. One by one each of the trussed men was dragged through a few feet of Thames mud, to be thrown bodily over the side of the bigger boats, cuffed hard if they showed the slightest reluctance, before being told to lie down. The smell of stale seawater rose to greet Pearce as he was forced to his knees, then on to his side, where he and the others were bound by another rope, his lashing him to O'Hagan, who was mumbling incoherently. Pearce's head was still buzzing from the blows he had received, but he was, nevertheless, listening as hard as he could to the jocose talk of his captors, hoping, as they shipped oars noisily into the rowlocks, to glean from that some clue as to where he was being taken.

'Be a mite parky this night what with this 'er wind, Kemp, an' we've a fair way to go to the Nore.'

The Nore – the anchorage at the mouth of the Medway – Rochester, Chatham, Sheerness, naval and military towns that had never been sympathetic to any radical ideas. He tried hard to recall if his father had any friends there, which produced a blank even before he considered the impossibility of any form of communication with them.

'Tarpaulin capes, Molly, if Barclay gives us forty winks, other ways it will freeze your balls off.'

'I've got a big one if you wants to share it. Keep you right warm it will.'

The reply was tired, as if responding to an old joke. 'Sod off, mate.'

'You'll be rowing too hard, mate,' added a third voice, 'to ever feel cold, 'cause Barclay, I can tell you, is in a hellfire hurry.'

'He allas is, Coyle.'

Different accents, one sounding of the Midlands, the other, called Molly, of Norfolk, the last, the man named Coyle, unknown. But the name Barclay – which must be that of the officer – had been said loud and clear. How many different shades of English had Pearce heard in his travelling years, how many miles had he and his father coached, ridden or walked? How much stupidity had they seen in the glaucous looks of slack-jawed peasants, or in the ale-red faces of so-called squires? Were this lot dim enough to present him with a chance of escape?

The one called Coyle, clearly in charge, spoke again, loudly, to address those captured, standing to be visible to all. 'We will have silence now, d'ye hear. Not a word spoken, and especially not any cry for succour as we pass by the ships downstream, with their captains and crews sound abed.' A knotted rope was raised to swing shoulder high. 'This be the least you'll get if you break that commandment, and my mates, who will row this boat, can employ their oars, if need be, to ensure silence. It would be an error to think they might hold back for fear of knocking you to perdition.'

'Easy to enter a dead soul as a volunteer,' wheezed a pinched-faced sailor who stood beside Coyle. Pearce recognised his voice as the Midland one. 'Save the King a bounty, that would.'

'Belay that,' said Coyle, without much force, his eyes now fixed on Pearce, who was staring at him hard. 'But it would reward you to listen to Kemp there, given that him being a bosun's mate, and a real terror with the cat o' nine tails, he has maimed many a soul before.'

Pearce thought to make another protest, but decided it would be useless. If he could not persuade the officer called Barclay, then he had no chance with his inferiors, and the result would probably only be another blow to his already aching head. No protest came from the shore – there was no sign of any watchman or a rescue posse, those who had fled must have looked to their own skin and safety rather than showing any concern for the ones who had been caught. He could not see much from his prone position, but he could guess at the attitude of those with whom he shared this boat and his bonds – resigned at best, despairing at worst, frightened when they contemplated what might be about to befall them – for there were no end of tales to recall, stories of the harshness of life at sea. All the torches had been extinguished, leaving a single lantern hanging on a pole above the stern of the boat, to which Coyle moved, sitting down, hand on the tiller, next to the little marine.

He spun the boy's head to look at his swollen face. 'Well, young Martin, Dent by name and well dented by nature. You'll be even prettier when that nose is healed.'

Then, with a soft command to dip, the oars hit the water, the sailors either side leant forward, took the strain, and the boat began to move.

Rocking back and forth, aware that his backside now ached as much as his head, Pearce tried to sort out in his mind the consequences of what had happened and how he would get out of this. That was an absolute necessity, since so much depended on it. He had been sent back from Paris with the express task of facilitating his father's return – friends had to be mobilised, petitions had to be made to those in power to allow a sick man, now no more loved in Paris than he was in London, to come home to live out his remaining time in peace. A twinge of that guilt he had felt since leaving France surfaced then, the feeling that in acceding to his father's request to undertake this task his real concern had been to secure his own safety.

In a less than ordinary life, travelling from place to place with Adam Pearce, son John had experienced much upheaval – the early death of his mother, endless strange towns and cities, the smiles and kindness of those who shared his father's vision, the visceral hatred of those who did not, and finally the hell of prison life made worse by the calculated indifference of the warders in the Bridewell Gaol, who would do nothing; provide a decent cell, food and drink, or carry letters to those outside, friends who would help to alleviate their suffering without a bribe.

Eventually, after many months of effort, those same friends had secured them first a degree of comfort, then freedom. What followed was so very different from what had preceded their incarceration; the thrill of being close to a father whose time had come, for the French Revolution had rocked the established order. Now he walked alongside a man who gathered crowds by the thousand instead of the hundred, who was plagued by profit-seeking printers demanding pamphlets. For a whole year and more, life was exhilarating, but that euphoria faded, to be followed by confusion, as that seemingly massive support, frightened by events across the Channel, began to atrophy.

His writings had, by that time, made Adam Pearce a national figure – polemics railing against the wealth of the few and the poverty of the many, of exploitation and endemic corruption, views that had made him anathema to those who governed the land. Then finally, one radical pamphlet too many – too abusive to let pass, in which he had called for King George to be tried for treason – had given them the excuse to throw both him and the son who aided him back in gaol, this time with little prospect of quick release. Avoidance of that – and the men who would arrest them for a government bounty – entailed a hurried flight abroad.

Paris had made Adam Pearce welcome in the winter of 1790, for his fame and his ideas had crossed the Channel to a society dedicated to making them real. He was lauded as an honorary Frenchman, invited to address the National

Assembly and granted a pension; great thinkers had sought his views, radical newspapers had published his writings and the salons of the Revolutionary greats hung on his words. Not any more; that too had turned sour. His star had waned as French politics steadily became more deadly: men who had risen on the fury of the Paris mob to become the rulers of France could not tolerate dissent any more than the rulers of Great Britain.

Was his father still at liberty or had the Parisian tyrants carried out their threat to imprison him? How desperate was the situation here at home? He had been on his way, this very morning, to find out from an old family friend, one of those who had helped secure their release from the Bridewell. Only lucky chance had allowed him to see the men watching the house, and avoid the hand that had been within an inch of grabbing that prominent collar. How had they known he was back in England, for he had only landed on the Kent coast three days previously? Or were those men bounty-seekers, freelance narks just watching the house of a well-known radical politician in hope rather than anticipation?

Why did he have to run anyway? His sole crime was that he shared the blood of Adam Pearce, a man Billy Pitt and his minions saw as dangerous, a freethinker who expounded and wrote a message so perilous that his progeny must be likewise tainted. Such an accusation might not hold up in a court of fair judgement: but what court now, aware and in fear of the fervour across the Channel, and with war just declared, would acquit even the innocent?

There was a faint chance that some authority might intervene in the present situation, but as a hope it didn't rate very high; if the common gossip he had heard about press-gangs was true, and that had to be dredged from distant memory, this Barclay would take them straight aboard ship, well out of the reach of any law that could constrain him. He could swim but escape was very likely impossible, and almost certainly dangerous. Even assuming he could get free from the ropes that bound him, he was not sure they would not actually kill him rather than let him go. An oar on his head would mean he might drown, to become just one of the dozen dead bodies fished out of a river like the Thames every day.

It was not worth the chance. Best to get aboard ship, get free from his bonds, see the lie of things, and find some way of escaping or communicating with the shore. Could the latter be the most promising option? Adam Pearce had made some powerful friends, who if they did not share his father's views nevertheless did not agree that a man should be condemned and incarcerated for freely expressing them. These were people who had the power to get the proscription on both Pearces annulled – if they could work to get the King's Bench warrant lifted, they could likewise work to get him free from the Navy.

And perhaps, all that achieved, they could also help Pearce bring to bear on the offending officer, a man who had pressed illegally, the full majesty of the very same law that now threatened him. There was no doubt at all that Barclay had broken every statute in creation, so Pearce, in a pleasantly vindictive train of thought, and the all too painful memory of the blows he been forced to endure, comforted himself with the vision of that bastard, not him, in the dock of a court, as a red-cloaked judge passed sentence.

* * *

Cornelius Gherson stood with his back to the parapet of London Bridge, in the gloomy recess between two covered stalls, searching for the words that would get him out of the beating that was about to be administered. The man who would oversee it, though take no part, Alderman Denby Carruthers, stood well back behind the four bruisers he had hired to teach the young swine who had cuckolded him a lesson. The noise of the great artery that was London Bridge, of carriages, hawkers, and sedan chair lead-men yelling to clear a passage, was a low hum in the background. And in the spilt light that allowed Gherson to examine the faces before him, it was a world away.

It would do no good for him to plead an accident; that Denby's wife, Catherine and he had found themselves alone and overcome by passion. She was, after all, at thirty-three, a good fifteen years older than her lover. To say that, full of food and wine, nature had taken its course sounded very lame. Even worse would be to allude to love, first because it was untrue – if there was any devotion on Gherson's part it was to the love of conquest and access to her purse, and, secondly, it would not serve to calm the man whom he had offended. It was too late for promises of better behaviour and the look in the alderman's eyes did not encourage the idea that an apology would settle the matter. But given that it was the only thing Gherson could think of, he said, 'I am truly sorry, Alderman Carruthers.'

The four scarred faces between him and Denby Carruthers, the men who had trapped him in here, didn't move a muscle. But Gherson did note that there was no ill will in them, just indifference.

'I am here to ensure that you are sorry, Gherson,' said

Carruthers, in a voice that betrayed a great deal of suppressed emotion. 'Firstly, you will oblige me by handing over that fine topcoat you are wearing, and the silk one underneath. Also those fine silver-buckled shoes which, I think I am right in saying, my household monies paid for.'

Gherson obliged, trying to palm the purse he had into his breeches. But the villains before him were too practised to allow that, and swiftly had it off him.

'I know that in acting as I do,' Carruthers continued, 'I will be saving a substantial group of men the worry that they too might find themselves in my position. To think that I took you into the bosom of my family, and that you betrayed me so...'

'I...'

'Do not deny it,' Carruthers shouted, 'do not deny that you are a damned lecher and a rogue! I gave you employment when you were strapped, got you out of Newgate gaol as an act of Christian charity, only to find out later that I am not the first to fall for the lies you spill with such ease. God only knows how many people you have dunned, how many good women you have corrupted. You have left behind you a trail of broken hearts and damaged households. You, Gherson, are a menace to every decent man in the City of London.'

Gherson was thinking that there were few enough of those, and if they devoted their lives to the acquisition of wealth, and spent their evenings at the card tables or in the company of high-priced whores, it was hardly surprising that their neglected wives looked elsewhere for comfort or entertainment. But that too was not a thing to say out loud.

'I admit to a weakness, sir, one I have often fought to overcome.'

In just a shirt and breeches, with the cold stone of the bridge beginning to chill his shoeless feet he began to shiver, thinking it must look very like fear. Not that he wasn't frightened – there was no way of avoiding a beating – but Gherson wondered if it might be ameliorated, so he managed to get a bit of a sob into his voice.

'I realise that I have deeply offended you, and for that I can only curse myself.'

The tone became more woeful as Gherson berated himself for a wretch: swore that he would never transgress again; damned the God that had made him incapable of resisting temptation. Casting his head and body around in a theatrical manner, Gherson's eyes never ceased examining the faces before him, and he could not decide which was more alarming, the professional apathy of the alderman's hirelings, or the hateful look of the man himself.

'I deserve a beating, sir,' Gherson pleaded, 'and perhaps in your wisdom you will chastise me enough to change my nature. I swear that I shall go on my knees to God as soon as I can and beg to be relived of the burdens of my ardour.'

'He's a fellow,' said one of the hard men, finally speaking. 'He could do for a playhouse.'

'Girlish lookin', mind,' added another.

Gherson threw his arms in the air, knowing that his histrionics had made no impact whatsoever. It was with a last forlorn hope that he said, with what he thought was becoming bravado, 'Damn you all! Beat me if you must. Do your worst!'

'You think a beating sufficient, Gherson?' asked Carruthers, facetiously, adding himself, with a deeper timbre, the answer to his question. 'I don't, and I have in mind my responsibilities as a city alderman. The good citizens of London require to be protected. You speak of an ardour that requires to be cooled, and I feel that as a Christian soul it behoves me to oblige you with the means.' The voice changed to a low growl. 'Tip the bastard in the river, and let's see if the Thames chills him enough.'

'Sir,' Gherson shouted, before adding, 'help!'

He got no further. One of the ruffians slapped him hard to shut him up, then, with another they lifted him bodily on to the parapet of the bridge.

'Can you swim?' asked the man who had praised his acting, taking hold of a leg.

'No,' Gherson croaked, as a second ankle was grasped.

'Why that be a damn shame.'

Both heaved together, to send him tumbling over the edge, his body spinning in the air, a scream emanating from his lips, his mind a mass of whirling thoughts, of dozens of warm beds, endless tipped petticoats and pliant female flesh, of angry spouses and wives weeping with shame. The one thing he did not think of was cold water, but that changed as soon as he hit the black, freezing Thames, disgorging icy inland waters into the sea. The shock was near to heart-stopping, the mistake of that continued scream evident as soon as his mouth filled with liquid.

Gherson went under, into a dark void of nothingness, but his natural buoyancy brought him back to the surface, one hand raised, his flaying feet keeping him afloat long enough to let the water clear from his eyes. He could see the lights of London Bridge moving away from him; that is till he realised that it was he who was moving, being carried downstream on the riptide of creaming water that had come through the arches of the bridge.

The cry of 'God help me' was cut off by another mouthful of the Thames as Gherson went under once more, with his mind pursuing two opposing thoughts. One that he must stay afloat and survive, the other the certainty that it would be impossible and that he was about to die. Hands and feet lashing, he again resurfaced, feeling in an open palm a round piece of wood. He grasped it with all the desperation of a man in fear of death, pulling himself up until he got a second hand in place – which was just as well as his original grip had slipped due to the wet surface.

'God in blessed heaven!' cried Abraham Coyle, Master at Arms of HMS *Brilliant*, looking at the hands grasping an oar that, feathering, was only touching the water and acting as a brake.

'What have we got here?'

'Man in the water,' cried Kemp, in a voice that had Pearce trying to sit up to see what was happening, only to find his movement constrained by his being lashed to another, so that his view was cut off by the top strakes of the boat's planking.

'In the name of Christ get a hand on him,' Coyle cried.

That was easier said than done; having just shot through the central arch of London Bridge they were still caught in the disturbed and fast-flowing scud created by that narrowing of the waterway. Indeed, if Gherson had not been caught in the same current he would have been lost, but the tumbling cataract was carrying him downstream at almost the same pace as the boat. Dragged inboard, Gherson felt a hand grasp his wrist just as his grip was going for the second time. Then a rope was round his other hand and he was being hauled roughly over a rowlock, before he tumbled in a soaking heap amongst a pile of other bodies.

'Find out where he came from,' demanded Coyle, passing back the lantern. The question was put to Gherson by the sailor who had dragged him inboard, with Kemp holding the light close so that Coyle could see his face, an act which revealed his own rodent like features, and highlighted a drop of mucus that glistened on the end of his nose.

'The bridge,' gasped Gherson, 'London Bridge.'

Pearce had a view of him now, dripping water from a sodden shirt, slicked down, soaked hair and a youthful face that, even in the grip of a deep and justifiable fear, had a sweet and innocent quality – full lips, a slightly Levantine nose and pale unblemished skin. It was also instructive to look at the others who had taken an interest in this providential gift to the press-gang, Walker and Rufus among them. There was no sympathy for one who now shared their plight, more a look of abhorrence, as though this soaking specimen had somehow compounded the nature of their own situation.

'What will old Ralph Barclay say, young Martin,' Coyle hooted to the boy marine, 'when we tell him that hands are dropping out of the sky?'

Kemp lifted Gherson's head, none too gently by the hair, to glare into eyes that looked to be in the grip of the terror of death. 'Might be worth an extra tot of rum, Coyle, but with that sod it might also get you disrated.'

'Best rope the bugger.'

'No need,' replied Kemp, dropping Gherson's head. 'The only place this cove can go is back in the river, and looking at him, I don't reckon that is a way he would choose.'

CHAPTER THREE

Captain Ralph Barclay, ahead of Coyle in the pinnace, felt he could be content with his night's work, though he could not help but consider that his world had come to a sorry pass when a full Post Captain of twelve years seniority had personally to take to the task of recruiting. Nor was this night's effort likely to gift him many sailors, all he could hope for was a clutch of untrained landsmen, albeit ones who would find it hard to complain. But a body was a body: anyone would do to a desperate commander, as long as he had two legs and two arms. In twenty years at sea, Ralph Barclay had learnt that a bit of decent discipline could turn even the most dim-witted clod into a useful crew member. Given that he could be ordered to weigh at a moment's notice, he had no time to wait for those in authority to solve for him the problem of a lack of hands.

But underlying his muted satisfaction was a residue of worry. He knew well that he was not allowed to take a press-gang into the Liberties of the Savoy. Would there be a hue and cry? The majority of the people in the Pelican had escaped and they would have filled the streets with their noise. But in a city accustomed to riot, and it being late at night, he hoped that most of the inhabitants would keep their shutters and doors bolted. Nor could the majority of the customers, a bunch of debtors and felons, readily involve the law, which was available only outside the confines of where they themselves were safe. But it was a thought that nagged at him, given that the expense of redress, should he be arraigned for the offence, would be very high indeed. He ran over the faces he had looked into, mostly of creatures in distress. But there had also been one showing a defiance that called for a knotted rope's end, delivered hard and twice. That was a fellow, a mouthy sod, who might require further constraint. So be it, if it was necessary, then the captain of HMS *Brilliant* would provide it.

Try as he might to concentrate on such matters, thoughts of penury soon resurfaced to dominate Ralph Barclay's thoughts – it was eloquent testimony to the present state of his finances that he was leaving London, not even in a public coach, let alone a private one, but in a boat. With his frigate berthed at Sheerness, a visit to the capital should have been made overland. It would not have been comfortable, or speedy, but it would have been a damn sight more so than the pinnace in which he had set off in the cold predawn of that morning. He had lugged up the Thames Estuary on a biting wind with his longboat and cutter in company, masts stepped in favour of oars as soon as the river narrowed, because the amount of waterborne traffic precluded tacking and wearing under sail with any degree of safety.

Nor could he lay any claim to having had, of his three other appointments, a good day. His first port of call had been to the people he wished to appoint as his prize agents. The firm of Ommanney and Druce had impressive offices in the Strand: high-ceilinged rooms with elaborate cornices, heavy crystal chandeliers, excellent furniture, attentive and obsequious clerks and servants who never stinted on the Madeira. The partners themselves were rich men and the atmosphere of calm wealth that pervaded their premises, besides raising a degree of jealousy in their visitor's breast, stood as ample testimony to the many successful naval officers for whom they had acted. Portraits of some of those lined the walls, admirals, commodores and captains who had earned fortunes fighting England's enemies, including one by Joshua Reynolds of Ralph Barclay's late patron, Admiral Lord Rodney.

The partners had welcomed him as an old if not valued customer. Having commanded a frigate during the last stage of the American war, though without much in the way of distinction, he had put a modicum of money their way. Five years on the beach had frayed things and as men who knew to within an inch the value of a captain's reputation, as well as the nature of his present commission, they had judged Ralph Barclay to be worth ten minutes of their time. It was ten minutes of unstinting flattery because it was an axiom of the trade that you never knew who was going to be Midas – the most unlikely naval officer could capture a treasure ship and move from poverty to wealth in a blink, lining the pocket of his prize agent along the way.

Within those ten minutes it had been made plain that the firm of Ommanney and Druce was unwilling to advance him funds upon the expectation of future profit. Had he lined their pockets deep in the past, as had some of his fellow West Indian officers, it would have been seen as a credible risk, but he had not. He could exude as much confidence as he liked and claim that, with orders that would take him to the Mediterranean, the opportunity existed in a war so newly declared to snap up prizes in the Bay of Biscay. Both partners would know that he was short on his complement, they might even know that in the article of hands he had too high a ratio of landsmen to proper seamen, because such men saw it as their job to know everything. And they would know that Captain Ralph Barclay was neither famous enough, rich enough, aristocratic enough nor popular enough to man his ship with volunteers. He depended on the Impress Service and his own efforts, and that was no basis on which to advance large sums of money that might flounder due to the actions of a limited and inexperienced crew.

He was not a risk they were prepared to support. Let him go to a moneylender and pay his rates. If he had success he would be able to afford them, if he did not, he might end up being chucked into the Marshalsea, had up for debt, but that was no concern of theirs. They had seen him to the door that opened out on to the bustling Strand, an act of courtesy that cost them nothing, but one that should suffice to stop this rather undistinguished officer from taking his business elsewhere.

The day had not improved. He had to deal with a moneylender who was just as well informed as his prize agents, who knew the value of a year's sea pay for the captain of a sixth rate at eight shillings a day and that would only be settled by the Admiralty twelve months hence – taking no account of sums that might be wanting from the way Barclay ran his ship, or debts incurred by any number of extraneous factors. He was also a man who could calculate a risk to the point of obscurity, and Ralph Barclay left that office, grim-faced and irascible, with a purse much too light for his needs, and a debt to pay that should he fail to take a prize, would cripple him for years to come. His only comfort was that the queue of captains and lieutenants who filled the waiting room was testimony to the fact that he was not alone in being strapped.

If there was a naval officer who went to sea without the need to raise a loan he had never met him and he doubted he existed. Even admirals who had garnered riches in their careers could rarely raise the cash to fund the service they undertook in defence of their nation; they would, like him, pledge their plate and their credit then wait years, sometimes a decade, for the sums to be fully reimbursed by the penny-pinchers at the Admiralty and the Navy Board. As Barclay made his way to the Admiralty through the deep stench, streets full of horse dung and runnels of human waste, and the teeming crowds of London, he had reflected that if the whole Great Wen reeked of corruption, he was on his way to an establishment that in every respect outdid the city.

'Lord Hood will see you now, Captain Barclay.'

That request had broken Ralph Barclay's somnolent train of thought, the umpteenth rehearsal in his head of what he was going to say to the man who ran King George's Navy, a way to convey the parlous nature of his situation without in any way forfeiting the dignity that went with his rank. In his imaginings sweet words had flowed, convincing statements to sway even the most jaundiced soul – Hood would see his case as one requiring succour, and lift from his shoulders what he knew to be his major concern. But the sliver of confidence his reverie had engendered had been checked somewhat by the looks he had received from the other officers crowding the waiting room, one or two of envy, several of blatant fury that he was being favoured over them.

Hungry, it being well past his three o'clock dinnertime, Ralph Barclay had stood and nodded to the group, some of whom had been there when he arrived an hour and a half before. He had left behind numerous lieutenants and a pair of grey-haired captains desperate for a ship, a party for whom the fleet could not expand fast enough. Each would have, like he had in the past, bombarded Lord Hood with letters, backed up by pleas from anyone of influence they could muster: a senior officer with whom they had served who remembered them with warmth enough to put pen to paper, their sitting MP if they shared his politics, relatives and connections however distant and however light they stood in the counsels of government. Now they were on their last throw; the hope that a personal plea would gain them employment. They would sit here all day if necessary, and the following day as well, some fated never to gain entry.

Hood had not looked up as Ralph Barclay entered, which had done nothing for his mood, already unsettled from hunger and impatience. Instead he had riffled through a stack of letters, reading swiftly and briskly dictating to a secretary, each letter being added to a second pile as a decision was arrived at. With lamps lit due to the fading outside light, he had examined the admiral's face and demeanour. Having met Samuel Hood on quite a few occasions the reddish-cratered skin, the heavy brows over direct and intolerant eyes and the voice, full of sibilants from his ill-fitting teeth were familiar, though the bulbous nose was somewhat bigger than Ralph Barclay remembered.

Hood had been dressed in a blue coat edged with gold braid, with a puffy lace ruff at the neck, which had seemed a touch dandified for a man of his age and appearance.

'Regrets that I cannot oblige Captain Stoddart at present, but I am in anticipation that the expansion of the fleet will see his obvious merit rewarded, though a ship-of-the-line may be beyond my power to grant. This one to the Duke of Grafton. Your Grace has been practised upon. I fear the officer who sought your intervention has shown great economy in providing you with details of his career, which as a measure of character leaves much to be desired. I hope that I will not be brought to write to you again on this, but I assure you that should any officer of merit seek your assistance, I would be happy to have you plead in the future on his behalf.'

Hood had then looked up and said, 'Captain Barclay.'

'Milord,' Ralph Barclay replied, ready to continue, only to be rudely checked as Hood went back to another letter.

'This one to Mr Dundas. It has been my intention to provide for Lieutenant Macksay as soon as a suitable place can be found. I abjure you to be patient as I know him to be an excellent and competent officer worthy of your recommendation.'

Hood's tone was at odds with the words, but then Henry Dundas was a powerful man, head of a clutch of Scottish MPs and close to the Prime Minister, William Pitt; someone too puissant for a request that a man he favoured be denied. Lieutenant Macksay might be a donkey with two left feet, half blind, incompetent and a danger to any vessel in which he sailed. With a sponsor as powerful as Henry Dundas he would certainly get a place.

Ralph Barclay had then experienced a slight sinking feeling, for that thought had brought home to him his own paucity in that area. In the world in which he lived influence was everything, and that was a commodity of which he was very short. It galled him because he had realised that he must, in this room and in his situation, plead for help, and that was an act for which he was, by nature, unsuited. Nevertheless it must be so, and Barclay steeled himself to the task.

Samuel, Lord Hood, had sat back suddenly, waving away the secretary, in what Ralph Barclay had suspected to be a deliberate act of dramatisation – the message: I am seeing you because I feel I must, not because I would choose to do so.

'I am plagued by correspondence, Barclay. I swear most of my day is taken by it.'

'The burdens of rank, sir.' Ralph Barclay had meant that as a sympathetic remark, a platitude to soften Hood up, but his empty stomach had worked upon his natural irascibility to make his voice sound grating and unsympathetic.

'As you will find should you ever get your flag,' Hood had growled, before adding, 'but now that you have seen how occupied I am, perhaps you would do me the honour of coming to the point of why you have called, given that, unlike all the officers in this pile of correspondence, and that throng of ne'r do wells crowding my waiting room, you already have a ship.'

Ralph Barclay had fought to compose his features into something approaching empathy, difficult given that it went so much against the grain. He didn't like Samuel Hood and the man knew it, and it was a sentiment he suspected was heartily reciprocated. Barclay had been a client officer of Hood's one time superior George Rodney, and he was very partisan in support of the man Hood hated, and held to be the singly most corrupt officer he had ever had the misfortune to serve with. To Barclay Rodney had been a genius – if he was flawed, inclined to play ducks and drakes with official funds and a touch prone to promote undeserving officers – that was part of the estimable whole. Hood was a plodder, with none of the gifts of leadership that Rodney had displayed – the ability to inspire seamen to a superior order of courage in battle, to smell out his enemies and bring them to a fight.

With the sudden feeling that such thoughts might be reflected on his face, Barclay had blurted out, 'Hands, milord.'

'Hands, Barclay?' Hood had responded, voice grave and eyes enquiring under heavy grey eyebrows.

Ralph Barclay had finally found the tone he was seeking – of camaraderie – that of one serving naval officer sharing a worry with another. 'I am likely to be ordered to sea shortly, milord, to escort a convoy to Gibraltar.'

Those words, delivered with a wry smile, had done nothing to dent Hood's testiness; he had replied with an air of studied impatience that Barclay found infuriating. 'I have a vague recollection of your orders, Barclay, since it was I who signed them.'

Ralph Barclay had found it necessary to take a deep breath before replying. 'Well, milord, you may also be aware that I have scarce a dozen hands to send aloft on a topsail yard.'

'Do you want your orders changed, or is it that you wish to decline the duty?'

Hood, in his expression, had made no attempt to hide the fact that he would be pleased to see Barclay take the second route. He had appointed him to *Brilliant*, not through any appreciation for either his personality or his reputation, but merely because his claim to preferment, the accumulation of past service and the letters he had received reminding him of it, had been too strong to deny without facing accusations of bias against officers who had been attached to George Rodney. Powerful he might be, but in the tangled skein of present day politics he had a requirement to be careful. Not that he had over-indulged Barclay, who had sent in a list of subordinates he wished to take with him, a list Hood had taken some pleasure in refuting with the reply that HMS *Brilliant* 'would be provided a very decent set of officers' with which he was sure Captain Barclay 'would be most content'.

'I do most emphatically not want my orders changed, sir,' Barclay had replied, trying again for a comradely tone, 'but I'm short of my complement to such a degree that I fear it will render my ship ineffective should I come face to face with the enemy. Should fortune favour me with the opportunity, my natural inclinations would encourage me to be bold, to go yardarm to yardarm. It would be a great sadness to have to let an enemy sail by for want of the men with which to engage.'

Hood had frowned, heavy eyebrows coming down to cloud those direct blue eyes. 'Let an enemy sail by? That, sir, I find a startling statement to hear from the lips of a serving officer.'

'I have heard that the Impress Service is holding volunteers at the Tower of London.'

Hood had picked up another letter then, with the intention, Barclay reckoned, of avoiding looking him in the eye. 'Have you, by damn. I must say this is not something that anyone has seen fit to tell me.'

The word 'liar' had filled Ralph Barclay's head, but he was not fool enough to mouth it. Like most other officers short of men, he knew the truth. There were two fleets assembling, one for the Channel and one for the Mediterranean. Hood wanted the Channel Fleet, the premier naval command, which would keep him close to home and politics. Service in the Mediterranean would oblige him to relinquish all the perquisites of patronage that went with his office as the senior serving sailor on the Board of Admiralty – the ability to advance officers who were his followers.

But he had a rival for the Channel in the Irish peer, Admiral Lord Howe, known as Black Dick. Hood's superior officer on the admiral's list, Black Dick also happened to be a favourite of the King, who was a strong advocate of appointing him to the Channel, so the matter hung in the balance. Hence the men at the Tower, and Hood's reluctance to release them for duty; that he would do when he knew which fleet he was to command, and every volunteer would go to man his ships. Let the other lot go begging. It could be decided tomorrow, in a week, or it might take a month; all would be too late for Ralph Barclay.

'As for being short of hands, Barclay, I don't recall a time when I ever went to sea in any other state than short on my complement. Every other commander would doubtless say the same. Yet I think I can safely say I served country and my sovereign despite that constraint.'

Aware of the weak and wheedling note in his voice, and damned uncomfortable because of it, Barclay had replied, 'My deficit is in the nature of near thirty per cent, sir, and I am chronically bereft of trained seamen.'

'Seek volunteers, man.'

Barclay had glared at Hood then, any attempt at supplication evaporating, for that he had already done, sending recruiting parties out into the countryside, with posters promising wealth and adventure, and spending what little money he had been able to borrow to purchase drink and food as temptation, the only problem being he had to compete with parties sent out by dozens of other captains in the fleet. Every party seeking hands saw it as their duty to tear down each other's posters; to disrupt each other's gatherings and in extreme cases to pinch each other's recruits. Thus the lanes bordering England's coast this last month had resounded more from blows traded between competing crews than any other noise. His parties, after several bruising encounters with cudgels and cosh had gathered some volunteers, but nowhere near enough for him to both sail and fight his ship.

Hood had been just as unsympathetic to that explanation. 'You must, like all other officers, apply to the Impress Service without any excessive leverage from my office.'

Ralph Barclay had made pleas in abundance to the Impress Service, the official body responsible for naval recruitment, and they had fallen on deaf ears. As the agents of the Navy Board they were supposed to take in the men who volunteered, then parcel them out to the waiting ships by a process that was as mysterious as it was inefficient. They also sent out the official press gangs, made up of professional ruffians who would take up wandering sailors in the easiest place to find them, off the coast from incoming merchant vessels or in the ports that ringed the British shore. A bounty per head meant they were dead set against competition. Being both numerous and brutal enough to enforce their claim, it was a brave captain that tried to compete on their turf; he could well find himself losing hands rather than gaining any.

Whatever men were gathered – by fair means or foul – were sent aboard ships captained by those who knew how to return a favour, usually in coin. So the working officers of the Impress

Service, often men of low calibre, got a bribe to go with the cash bounty paid by the government. This was not an option for a man who had lived the five years since 1788 on half pay and had only recently got a ship, a man forced to pay usurious rates to a moneylender just to fund his first voyage. And all of that took no account of a selfish and ambitious admiral like the one before him who could keep the Press Tenders, hulks that should be full of sailors to man the fleet, empty. Indeed, keep hundreds of trained volunteers, prime seamen in the main, unoccupied at a place of his choosing, just so that he could man his own command.

Ralph Barclay had realised then that no amount of pleading would do him any good. Looking his superior right in the eye he had said, 'I have brought my boats upriver with me, sir, and if you could write an instruction to the officer in charge at the Tower to release the men I need...'

Hood had cut right across him, quite unfazed by Barclay's attempt to embarrass him. 'I never knew you to be hard of hearing, Captain Barclay. I have already told you I have no knowledge of this. If you take leave to doubt that I would be interested to hear you say so, and having said it I would then ask you to put it in writing.'

Which would be suicide, you over-braided bastard, Barclay had thought, as he reached into his coat pocket for a document which he hoped would protect from what he intended to do. 'All I wish to put in writing is in this letter, sir, which brings to the attention of the Admiralty my concerns, given the situation in which I find both myself and my ship.' Which was as good a way of saying to Hood, as he handed it to him, "Court martial me if you dare when I get into difficulties, of whatever nature, and a fair copy of this letter will be introduced as evidence to justify my actions".

Hood had proved a wily old fox, too well versed in naval politics actually to take the letter, knowing it for what it was, an attempt to blackmail him into releasing some hands. He also knew as well as Barclay that HMS *Brilliant* needed a complement of at least one hundred and forty men to both sail and fight; she was, if he was being told the truth, at present, forty short of that number. What did that matter, there were never enough men – the peacetime Navy had to expand ten times to accommodate the needs of war; the press-gangs had long since swept the country bare, and Sam Hood was not sitting with an officer he cared to indulge.

'You may leave it on my desk, though I doubt I shall have time to read it,' Hood had said, going back to his pile of letters, but his parting words had made Ralph Barclay wonder if he was a reader of minds. 'I daresay you will man your ship somehow, though I would remind you of the very necessary statutes that exist to ensure that, should you go pressing, you only take up men qualified for service at sea.'

Those very words were rattling round Ralph Barclay's mind as he came abreast of the Tower of London. He called to Midshipman Farmiloe, to draw his attention to pinpoints of light that dotted the bank and the green behind. 'See yonder, Farmiloe, those camp fires?'

'Sir.'

'I daresay you have no knowledge of who they warm?'

'None, sir.'

'Sailors, Mr Farmiloe, that's who. Prime seamen, every one a volunteer, come to the Tower as the place where the Impress Service is taking in recruits for the same Navy in which it is our honour to serve.'

Richard Farmiloe would have been wary of his captain whatever mood he was in – and that was not always easy to know. But the note of sarcasm in Ralph Barclay's voice rendered him doubly cautious. The man was capricious, and what seemed like the sharing of a witticism one second, could turn to unbridled wrath the next. So he took refuge in being obtuse.

'Why, that is amazing, sir.'

'It's a damned disgrace,' Barclay spat.

A voice barked in the darkness. 'Sheer off you fucking swab.'

'Damn you, Hale! Do you want to see us in the river?' Barclay shouted, at the sound of clashing oars.

This was aimed at his coxswain, Lemuel Hale, steering his boat. Distracted by the sight of those very same fires he had taken him so close to the wherry of a Thames waterman, leading to that shouted curse. Accustomed to such abuse, Hale merely made sure his eyes did not lock with those of his captain.

They were well past Tower Green and the sparkling camp-fires before Barclay returned to the subject. 'They are held there at the express orders of Lord Hood. What do you say to that?'

'Words fail me, sir,' replied Farmiloe.

'There's much that fails you, boy,' Barclay spat, 'not least that empty head of yours. Does it not occur to you to enquire why?'

'I would not presume, sir.'

'I doubt you know the true meaning of the word presumption.'

Ralph Barclay finally arrived at the decision that he would

be safer at sea than at anchor. None of the men at the Tower would be released until Hood had resolution of his dilemma. Even when the shackles were undone none of these men might be assigned to a ship bound for Mediterranean service. Even if they were, he did not stand high enough in the man's estimation to be at the head of the queue.

'I have done my duty, let others worry as to whether they have done theirs.'

His earlier concerns were not allayed – there would be hell to pay if he was caught with these pressed men, because not one of them was a sailor. Hood's parting shot was still fresh enough in his mind to induce a chill that had nothing to do with the winter weather. He reassured himself with the thought that the punishment for the offence he had committed that night tended to fade with time. Once he was at sea with that convoy it could be years before he touched the English shore again, years in which the pressed men would be either dead or inured to life at sea. If there was one aboard who could survive and had the wit to bring a complaint against him, he had, in mitigation, that letter he had left with Hood, which stated that Captain Ralph Barclay, in order to properly serve his King and Country, now found himself in a position where desperate measures might have to be employed to get his ship to sea.

For all his determination to see things in a positive light, nagging doubts existed. His orders could be suddenly changed, he had known it happen before; by the time he got back to Sheerness that convoy duty could have evaporated and he could be stuck at anchor waiting for a new assignment with some of those men aboard clamouring for release. Even if he weighed immediately, the sea was a capricious element. Ships had been known to run aground before they ever cleared the Thames and the Channel was one of the worst stretches of water in creation, a place where vicious cross-seas or thudding westerly tempests made the prospect of losing some vital spar or mast a distinct possibility. Vessels were often forced by such mishaps to run for one of the southern Channel havens to undertake repairs.

Ralph Barclay forced himself to concentrate on the more enticing scenario; a quick clean break from the shore, a voyage blessed with good fortune that would take him to the Mediterranean and opportunity. And if, as he hoped, his service were successful, say a fleet action or some single ship success, well, what he had done this night would count for nothing. No one would bring before a court a naval captain who had proved his worth against his nation's foes.

A tide going slack, a widening river and a cold east wind blowing up the estuary, slowed the progress of the longboat and cutter, so that the men on the oars were obliged to pull hard, though in a steady rhythm that belied the effort they were making. As the stars began to fade, the sky going from black to the palest shade of grey, Pearce looked at his fellow victims, heads lolling forward as his had done in the night, only to jerk upright at some shock. Then came incomprehension, as if they could not acknowledge their predicament; that followed by a look around the boat, as the truth became apparent once more in their bruised faces.

Naturally he picked out those he knew. Ginger Rufus looked like death, but that was in part due to the paleness of his complexion and the unformed nature of his features. Taverner's face he could not see – though he was hatless he was crouched over – most obvious was the black blood that stained his blond hair above the ear. Walker, at the very front of the boat, he noted was alert, those bird-like eyes never still, as though he was searching for means to escape. It took the movement of another before he got sight of Scrivens, who, not young on first acquaintance, looked even more aged now.

He had seen faces like that before, and much worse in the Bridewell. Recollection of that stinking pit of a prison sent a deep shudder though his already chilled frame. There was little room in this boat but that could not compare with the need to share a barred basement cell, thirty feet square, with over a hundred souls, and the stink of human effluvia that created. Old men and women, some of quality, others the dross of the streets, lay cheek by jowl with bow-legged, ragged and skeletal young boys and girls whose only crime had been to steal food in an attempt to ward off starvation. Some were those close to death when they arrived, and others he had watched as they struggled to survive in the cold, damp and disease ridden, rat infested hell-hole.

Worse were those wedded to crime, the dregs of humanity who made it necessary for he and his father to take turns in sleeping, if a half-comatose state on a filthy stone-flagged floor, with only a minimum of straw – home to a whole race of biting insects – could be called that. Of both sexes, they would rob whoever they could of whatever little they had, even down to the clothes on their back if they could be removed with enough guile. Set up supposedly to meet the needs of justice, the Bridewell was a true den of iniquity with the venal warders the top of the pile of human ordure, men who made sure that anything of value – a watch, a ring, a good shirt or handkerchief – went first to them as payment for some small act of partiality. He recalled how hard he had run that day, how his mind had worked to provide the right answers, ones that would keep him free from a return to that purgatory, only to find that fate in the end had played a cruel trick by delivering him into another.

Adverse luck had caused him to choose the Pelican, there was no point in looking for a deeper meaning, and there was some comfort in the fact that the men who had chased him all of the previous day would be hard put now to find him. But would anyone else in a world that seemed to have turned against him? As he ran through again and again the events of the last four years, of the highs and lows he had enjoyed, he had to ask himself again if anything his father had done in the time had been worthwhile.

'What does it matter now?' Pearce said out loud, in a voice so rasping that it told him he was in need of a drink of water.

'I would be after saying, friend, that talking to yourself would be the first sign of madness, if what we were about was not mad enough itself. What in Christ's name am I doing in a boat?'

The voice from the comatose body close to his, unmistakably Irish, was that of O'Hagan. And so was the face now that Pearce could look at it properly; big, round, coarse-skinned, with narrow eyes that could seem to be merry even in this dire situation, the whole topped with the black, tight and thick curly hair that had saved him from concussion. Gone was the belligerent drunk of the night before; this incarnation could even manage a smile in a situation that did not in the least deserve one.

'Where in the name of Holy Mary are we?'

Pearce managed a grim smile. 'In a boat, friend, as you say. We had the misfortune to run into a press-gang last night.'

It was clear by the confusion on O'Hagan's face that he could not remember. He pulled himself up with some difficulty as his hands, like Pearce's own, were tied, groaning as he did so, those bright eyes closing to pressed slits as he slowly shook his head. 'Jesus, Joseph and Mary, the drink has done for me again. Not that I had enough to fell me, they must have put gin in my yard of ale, the bastards.'

Pearce looked down the boat to see if Charlie Taverner had heard the statement, one with which he would certainly not agree, but he looked to be either sleeping or still out from the effect of the blow he had received. Out of the corner of his eye, Pearce also saw Coyle, the little marine asleep across his lap, looking at them. He was seeing him for the first time in daylight, and he observed that their chief captor had a face so red and fiery, and so round, that except for the lack of a smile it would not have disgraced a Toby Jug. He was glaring at them now, as if by merely communicating they were fomenting rebellion. Pearce jerked his head slightly in warning as the Irishman reopened his eyes, but it was ignored.

'O'Hagan, Michael, Patrick, Paul.' The bound hands came up as if to propose a shake, and Pearce was treated to another bit of evidence, in a pair of huge, heavy-knuckled fists, that he was with a man who would have been hard to take up sober. But with his own hands tied behind his back he was in no position to take up the invitation of contact.

'That's a lot of names.'

'It is in the Papist tradition, I suppose for fear that God or the saints might lose us.'

'Which one do you go by?'

'Michael.' He grinned. 'Or O'Hagan. Or "you damned bog trotter" if you prefer.'

'We met last night, Michael, and I recall that you tried to knock my head off my shoulders.'

Those merry eyes showed disbelief at first, then, with the addition of a slight headshake, acknowledgement. 'The drink, it is, for I am a lamb when not full of it. Your name?'

The reply 'John Pearce' came without thought, the next being that such openness was incautious. There had been a time, before he and his father fled to France, when the name of Adam Pearce had been on everyone's lips. Having been absent two years he had no idea if that notoriety had faded. Charlie Taverner had certainly stirred at the mention, or was that just apprehension?

'Ah! The simplicity of the English,' O'Hagan exclaimed. 'You never fear the deities will lose you.'

'My father is Scottish.'

'Of what faith?'

'None that I, or he, would admit to.'

'It is not possible to live without faith in Christ.'

Pearce smiled. 'It is. Michael, believe me it is.'

'Shut them up, Kemp,' growled Coyle.

Kemp made his way unsteadily up the boat, timing his move to miss the rower's actions, his decorated pigtail swinging behind him, causing groans and cries of muted anger as he stepped across the bodies that lay between him, Pearce and O'Hagan. When he reached them he leant over, his pointed rodent face as ugly as the whiff of his breath. As he leant forward the dewdrop of mucus, which seemed a permanent feature of what was a red-tipped and pinched nose, threatened to detach itself; but it did not – by some miracle it stayed affixed.

'You two ain't got the message, 'ave you?' Kemp said, raising a cosh and giving them each in turn a none too gentle tap on the crown of their heads. 'Coylie don't want you a'talking, so that means, my hearty lads, that you will shut your gobs.'

'That's a terrible thing to be asking of a son of Erin.'

'Don't get bold, mate.'

'Can I sing then?'

Pearce winced in sympathy as Kemp caught O'Hagan a heavier blow, one that caused an audible crack and made the Irishman duck away with his whole face screwed up. 'You'll sing enough when we get you aboard, Paddy, and to any tune we care to whistle. Now shut up, or else I'll be forced to stuff your mouth with this here cosh.'

O'Hagan looked up, his eyes full of defiance. But he met those of Pearce, and acknowledged the shake of the head.

'Sit down, Kemp,' said Coyle, who had been given clear orders from his captain not to allow the pressed men to be seen by anyone, with the added warning that should that happen he would not be alone in facing the law. 'We's passing Gravesend. There's Men o' War set there. Anyone on a ship about here sees you and that pigtail swinging a cosh they won't need much thinkin' to get what we's about. Remember this lot ain't rightly ours till they is sworn in. Be just the thing for some other crew of bilge-water buggers to get a boat in the water an' try and snaffle our goods.'

'Bollocks,' said Kemp, with a loud sniff and a deft use of the sleeve to clean the end of his nose, but the words were so soft only those next to him could hear it.

Pearce was one, and, looking up he could see the higher masts of half a dozen ships poking up into the morning sky. Gulls flew overhead, swooping down or swinging out of sight on the breeze, in a free manner that seemed to mock those confined in the boat.

'How long till we raise the barky?' asked Kemp.

'Few hours yet, mate. Tide's turned agin us,' said Coyle, 'an' this sodding wind don't aid us nowt.'

'Captn'll be well aboard before we, I reckon,' Kemp opined, 'which will not make him happy. Hope to Christ he didn't get back to a charge to weigh, for there was a rumour flyin' that the order was set to come from the Commodore to up anchor and make for Deal.'

'There's always a rumour on the wing, as you well know, mate, just as there's bugger all or little that'll make Ralph Barclay happy, 'cepting, happen, that pretty wife of his.'

'Now there,' said Kemp, with real feeling, 'is a flower it would be nice to pluck. I saw her in the Sheerness yard when she came down first to look out to the ship, pretty as a picture.'

'Happen you'll get the chance, mate. Old Barclay 'tends to take her to sea with him. He's even had a double cot shipped aboard for their comfort.'

'Not too sure I like that idea,' Kemp replied. 'Women aboard a barky brings bad luck.'

'It don't matter a dollop of shit what you like, nor any soul else for that matter.' The voice got harsh then as he growled at the crew of the boat, who were rowing but without much effort. 'Get your soddin' backs into them sticks.'

Coyle was not thinking about women at sea and bad luck. He was thinking that Kemp was right; that Barclay had missed his chance to weigh till at least tomorrow. And that was no way to be carrying on when your ship was berthed right under the Commodore's window if the order came to get cracking. There would be hell to pay and no pitch hot from that quarter, which would see Barclay properly hauled over. The captain was known to be a hard-horse commander – the type prepared to win the respect of his crew through fear if he had to – who cared little if he was loved or loathed, a man to pass that kind of raking on to another.

Someone would get it in the neck, for certain, and Coyle had no desire to be the one to bear the brunt of Ralph Barclay's anger.

CHAPTER FOUR

The captain of HMS *Brilliant* made Sheerness well ahead of his longboat and cutter, landing just as the guns boomed out to announce dawn, and being sensible of the fact that he had been off the station without permission, he went to the Commodore's office to cover his absence, only to find out from a clerk, and with a sinking heart, that an order had been posted the previous evening commanding him to weigh at first light, an instruction with which he was already too late to comply. His desire to depart immediately was quashed by the next comment that his superior, in need of some explanation as to why his orders had been ignored, wanted very much to see him. Gnawing on the forthcoming interview, he crossed a waiting room full of officers, here to demand stores, cordage and spars, or a plea to light a fire under the low thieving scullies that worked in the dockyard, taking station by the window that looked out over the anchorage, sparkling in the early morning light.

'Captain Barclay.' The high voice, with the burr of a Norfolk accent, made Ralph Barclay spin slowly round, and being sure he knew the speaker he dropped his head to return the greeting, looking into a pair of startlingly blue eyes and a youthful face, this under a hat worn athwart the head instead of fore and aft, a method of dress Barclay had always found affected.

'Captain Nelson.'

'Should I be surprised to see you here?' Nelson asked.

'I cannot think why.'

'I was talking to Davidge Gould,' Nelson responded, 'we met at the Assembly Rooms last night. He told me you and he were set to weigh this very morning.'

'That is so,' Barclay replied, nodding in the directions of the Commodore's office, 'but as you well know, sir, it is often easier to issue orders than to obey them.'

Nelson smiled, a natural reaction given his own reputation, which was one that could be said to hold a cavalier attitude to authority. 'Only too well, Captain Barclay, only too well.'

'But I shall weigh soon, never fear.' Barclay said that more in hope than anticipation, for at this moment he had no idea of the condition of his ship. He had departed yesterday from a vessel yet to complete her stores.

'Waste not a moment, eh?' said Nelson cheerfully.

'An admirable sentiment, sir,' Barclay replied, thinking that only someone like the man before him would employ such a worn and trite cliché.

'You chose not to attend the ball last night.'

Ralph Barclay wondered if Nelson knew he was in hot water, and was guying him. 'I was, Captain Nelson, otherwise engaged.'

'You missed an entertaining evening,' Nelson replied.

'Really?'

Nelson very obviously failed to pick up Ralph Barclay's

mordant tone, for the flat and featureless Isle of Sheppey, on which Sheerness stood, was a place reckoned by most naval officers to be damned dull. The inhabitants were a singular bunch, their view of the world formed by a flat, windswept, marshy landscape; fishermen, subsistence farmers who scratched at poor soil, prone to smuggling to make up for what they lacked in legal income. Excepting those that toiled in the dockyard, most were wary of a Navy that could press men and make sail in a wink, and damned reluctant to bow the knee to naval pretensions. They kept themselves aloof, obliging the Navy to make its own entertainment with regular gatherings at the Assembly Rooms and the occasional private house, all populated by the same familiar faces.

'But I daresay your wife will inform you of that,' Nelson added, 'for there can be no doubt that she enjoyed the occasion.' Ralph Barclay stiffened while Nelson burbled on in happy reminisce. 'I doubt there was one blank space on her dance card, sir, and pretty and vivacious as she is, Mrs Barclay lit up the whole affair. Davidge Gould was particularly attentive.' Nelson shook his head slowly, as if in wonderment. 'He certainly knows how to make the ladies laugh.'

'Since he is to be my junior on my allotted convoy duty, I have more interest in his ability to sail his ship.'

The tone of that response, and the far from pleasant look that accompanied it, penetrated both Nelson's naiveté as well as his good humour and he mumbled, in a slightly embarrassed fashion, 'You are bound for the Mediterranean, I believe?'

'We are.'

Back on safe ground, Nelson's bright blue eyes lit up again. 'Then we will serve together once more, as we did in the West Indies in '82, for I believe I am to be ordered to the Med also.' Nelson dropped his voice, as though what he had to impart was confidential. 'We may even, I am told, be under the same Commanding Officer.'

'Nothing is certain. I saw Lord Hood yesterday and he has not made up his mind.'

'If only it was his mind to make up, Captain Barclay. He aches for the Channel, but I for one hope that he is given the Mediterranean, because I know, and I am sure you agree with me, that he will be an active commander.'

Ralph Barclay looked at Nelson hard then, trying to discern once more if he was being practised upon. Hood had been the last Commander in Chief they had served under together, and it could hardly have been a secret that the relationship between the admiral and Ralph Barclay had not been warm. And Nelson, despite having a more friendly rapport with the man had, like him, spent the last five years on the beach, his pleas for employment made to that self-same Lord Hood ignored – good grounds for dislike, if not downright detestation.

But looking into the infernally trusting face of this short-arse before him, he had to conclude, on the experience of past acquaintance, that there was no nuance in the words, because it was something Horatio Nelson was incapable of. The man was an innocent, who had no idea how he was practised upon by those with more guile than he – which, on mulling it over, included just about everybody, not least a crew Ralph Barclay had seen talking to their captain on his quarterdeck as though he was a common seaman. The man had no notion of the difference in service before and abaft the mast, claiming to treat all, officers and hands, with equality. Of course, Nelson craved popularity, which was always a mistake. Come a desperate battle, men over-indulged would not fight as well as those who had been exposed to proper discipline.

'That service is not a time I recall with much pleasure, Captain Nelson.'

'Really?'

Left with Hood after Rodney had gone home, Ralph Barclay had not enjoyed anything in the way of a cruise that might bring in some money, and that in a sea teeming with privateers and American trading vessels trying to run the island blockade; that had gone to Hood's favourites, and was just another lump of grit in the relationship he had with the man who controlled the Navy. Mind, neither had Nelson been allowed to cruise, but that was because of the tub he commanded.

'It would surprise me if you did, given the vessel which you had under your hand.'

'Ah,' Nelson sighed, 'old *Albemarle*.'

'From what I recall, Captain Nelson,' Barclay replied, with deep irony, 'she was never new.'

Nelson looked pained. Barclay knew him to be one of those coves who hated to say a bad word about any ship he had captained. A lot of commanders were like that, superstitious that condemnation of a vessel's very obvious faults would bring ill fortune. Ralph Barclay was a man who could damn the planking beneath his feet in a hurricanno. Seeing the sudden sadness of Nelson's eyes, he had to look away in embarrassment, though he did not have to wonder what had brought that on, Nelson being notorious as a sentimental creature.

'I do not say she was perfect, *Albemarle*, but I cannot bring myself to condemn her.'

'Oh come, Captain Nelson, she was a complete dog.'

And she had been, a wallowing tub of a converted

merchantman, rated as a frigate, that missed stays with depressing regularity and was forever struggling to keep station on Hood's flagship, canvas of every description being employed in a bewildering set of changes to the sail plan that had provided a deep vein of amusement on what was otherwise the dull service of cruising in the hope of the arrival of another French fleet.

'Though I must add,' Barclay said hastily, as he saw that he had deeply wounded Nelson, 'that the crew must have been the best men aloft in the Caribbean.'

Nelson brightened at that; Barclay knew from their previous acquaintance that he was in the presence of a man who wore his heart on his sleeve. You could always get a smile from Horatio Nelson if you praised his crew. Personally, he would have flogged half of them for the liberties they took, and the state of a Nelson deck was not something to recall with fond memory. He wondered what it was about this man, whom he really didn't think he liked, that he bothered to care if he was happy or not?

'You would be amazed. Captain Barclay, how many of them have joined me aboard *Agamemnon*.'

So, Nelson, not far above him on the captain's list, had got HMS *Agamemnon*, a ship-of-the-line, albeit a small one of sixty-four guns, while he had been given one of the lesser frigates. There, in stark relief, was the way both men stood in the eyes of the man with the power to dispense commands. Perhaps Nelson was right to esteem Hood after all.

'Though you're still short on your complement I'll wager,' Barclay growled.

Nelson replied, with a cheerful grin. 'Never in life, Captain Barclay! I am happy to say that my muster book is near full, and the number of capital seamen who have come aboard is astonishing. A very high proportion, naturally, are Norfolk men from my own home county.'

Barclay was sure Nelson was exaggerating, that or boasting – the common view was that swanking was a trait of his. A sixty-four gunner required a crew of over four hundred men. 'You cannot have manned a ship the size of *Agamemnon* solely with personal volunteers?'

'Oh no. A hundred hands, prime seamen all, came only yesterday, shipped down from the Tower, I'm told, following a very obliging order from the Admiralty itself – I suspect the hand of Lord Hood. I must say he has done me proud, but the Impress Service officer did say that my own efforts were the cause, that it was a pleasure to provide men for a captain who could garner three-quarters of his crew without recourse to them.'

Barclay spun away then to hide his anger, and to keep Nelson from seeing the look of deep malevolence that filled his face. But there was a feeling of hurt too – of injustice that this pipsqueak should get so easily what he himself had been so roundly denied. Why? It could not be competence; when it came to ship management Ralph Barclay bowed the knee to no man, and even though he had never fought an action against a well-armed enemy he had no doubt that when the time came he would perform well. Did Hood hate him, or was it the memory of Admiral Rodney that plagued him?

He began to move away, lest his emotions become obvious, that action followed by an invitation from Nelson to 'join me for dinner at the Three Tuns in Sheerness, should the opportunity arise'.

It was fortuitous that the summons to see the Commodore followed right on that, because Ralph Barclay would not have been able to compose a polite reply.

The interview that followed was uncomfortable in the extreme; the kind of dressing down he had not had since he had ceased to be a lieutenant and achieved Post Rank. That he had succeeded in securing some hands, though he took care not to mention the source, counted for nothing in the face of what was seen as the gross insubordination of being not only out of his ship without permission, but actually off the station, and he was told that if he did not weigh with alacrity he might find himself once more on the beach.

If anything, his 'interview' with his wife could be rated as even more unpleasant, made more so from the haste with which it had to be conducted, for even in a hurry to get aboard ship it had been necessary, on the way to the rooms they had rented, to pay a visit to the Sheerness pawnbroker to retrieve goods he had pledged to fund the recruitment of volunteers – the silver buckles from his best shoes and some of the presents so recently gifted to them at their wedding. Emily was awake but not dressed, so he found himself trying to censure someone whose natural look of innocence was compounded by an appearance – tousled hair, night cap and gown, plus a pout on her face – that was almost childlike.

'You would surely not forbid me permission to go to a ball, Captain Barclay?'

'I admit I would not, but I cannot comprehend that you not only did so, but made an exhibition of yourself with my inferior officer.' The pout changed to a look of perplexity, as Ralph Barclay continued. 'Lieutenant Gould...'

'Is he not a captain?' Emily asked.

'He is a Master and Commander, the senior officer on his vessel, which gifts him the courtesy title of captain, but his substantive rank is lieutenant. Not that it matters. He is a bachelor who has a reputation with the ladies...'

Emily interrupted him a second time. 'He is also exceedingly kind, husband. It was he who found me at the Dockyard Commissioner's house yesterday afternoon – we were taking tea there – to tell me what orders had been posted for you, and to say that he had passed those on to your First Lieutenant, Mr Roscoe.'

'In that he did no more than his duty demanded.'

'I think he exceeded that, husband. For Lieutenant Roscoe informed him that your own personal stores were woefully inadequate. I spent most of the evening before attending the Assembly Rooms accompanied by Captain, I mean Lieutenant Gould, rectifying that.'

It was Ralph Barclay's turn to look perplexed, an expression that had Emily opening a drawer to produce a sheaf of bills, which she handed to her husband. As he, with increasing disbelief, read the long list of items she had pledged him to pay for, she kept talking, her voice a mixture of pride and humility, the former to cover her actions, the latter to admit to her need for assistance.

'Of course, I immediately admitted my ignorance to the ladies with whom I was taking tea, that included the Commodore's wife, and they were most obliging in giving me advice, though I can say the only item that all agreed on was the need for ample vinegar to maintain the sweet-smelling nature of your cabin.'

Indeed each naval wife had felt it her bounden duty to

forego their tea to ensure that Emily, whom they knew to be a novice in such matters, was aware of all the things absolutely necessary to a naval officer going on active service. Quill and paper was produced for the compilation of a list and the air was full of advice to ensure that food was plentiful, wine less so for men were weak creatures in the article of consumption. One lady was loud in praise of lemons, another insisting that tubs of purified goose fat be acquired for her husband's chest so that good Captain Barclay could ward off the chill without smelling like a common seaman, with the added advice that a bit of flannel next to the skin was efficacious in all weathers. There was tincture of this and extract of that – cheeses were compared for the taste and longevity, butter excoriated in favour of lard because it would go rancid – and all the while the list grew longer.

'I do so hope that you are pleased, husband,' Emily concluded, a wish that died as soon as he lifted his head from the handful of bills and she saw the look in his eyes, sad rather than angry, reeking of disappointment.

That was the only emotion he could muster, though inside he wanted to scream blue murder. Of all the people in the world, even furious, Ralph Barclay found it impossible to chastise his young wife in the manner he would another. In a world he saw as having been less than kind to him, a rough twenty years at sea climbing the slippery ladder of promotion, she was the one bright spot of good fortune. All the assaults he had received as a midshipman, all the tirades he had endured from idiotic captains as a lieutenant, and the desire he had to get vengeance on them and all those who had slighted him, faded within the orbit of Emily. He could still not believe that she had consented to marry him, a man seventeen years her senior, her second cousin, who had at the time, with no ship and no expectation of one, severely limited prospects. There was, of course, a family inheritance to protect, but Emily had never even alluded to that nor shown him anything other than happy acquiescence in the match.

'I fear you have been taken advantage of, my dear.'

'How so?' Emily replied, the pout returning to her face in response to the grave tone of his voice.

'These are the stores an admiral might take to sea, not a mere frigate captain.'

That was not strictly true – a frigate captain, if he had the means to buy on credit, might well include in his personal stores pipes of fine wine, quality hams both cured and dried, tubs of cheese that would mature and taste better the longer they were left, food salted as well as fresh and enough live animals, pigs, sheep and chickens to ensure good dinners for several months to come.

'I was led to believe,' she said, eyes now fixed on the floor, 'that you would wish to entertain both the officers on your ship, as well as those from other vessels, and that your standing amongst them would demand that you kept a good table.'

'I do think, Mrs Barclay, that when it comes to entertaining my fellow officers, I have the right to be consulted.'

'Of course.'

'And I do also advance the opinion,' he continued in a stern tone, 'that it is likely to make me uncomfortable to return to the station after an absence of only one day, only to be told by a fellow Post Captain that Gould, regardless of the rank by which he is termed, an officer with whom we are bound to have a high degree of contact in the coming weeks, was assiduous in his attentions towards you at an Assembly Room dance, an affair I doubt we would have even attended if I had been in Sheerness.'

That was wounding. Who was this other captain and what had he said to her husband? Whatever it was, it was not true. While Gould's attention had been persistent, it had not been excessive – he had not monopolised her attention and she had entered many other names on her dance card, not to still wagging tongues, but merely because she enjoyed dancing, something of which husband Ralph disapproved. The fact that he had gone to London had allowed her the chance to indulge herself in what might be her last dance for months.

'If I have embarrassed you in any way, I am most humbly sorry.'

'Please pack my sea chest, Mrs Barclay, and your own. I must hasten aboard and see how we stand in the matter of weighing anchor.'

His visit to the ship's chandler, which time certainly did not permit, in an effort to get him to take back the goods for which Emily had engaged, proved fruitless. She had, of course, been persuaded to buy from the most expensive and rapacious source in the port. He left the warehouse with the stinging rebuke in his ear, one that he had endured in the past and was only too pertinent now, to 'mind his credit, if he did not want to be had up for debt'.

Back in the pinnace, being rowed out to his ship, which was surrounded by hoys loading stores, Ralph Barclay calculated what he owned and what he owed, and came to a conclusion that was reflected in the face that came through the gangway, his mood not mollified by the line of waiting officers and midshipmen, the stamp of marine boots or the fluting of Bosun's pipes. He looked along the deck, glaring at the sight of his men toiling to get all they were due aboard, a task which should by now have been completed. Not one returned that look, or dared to observe their captains disposition too closely, reckoning that if by mischance they caught their commander's eye, given the mood he was plainly in, it would likely be seen as a challenge and bring down upon them a subsequent chastisement.

His crew respected him, and not just because he had the reputation as a man willing to employ the cat. More than half were long-in-the-tooth, deep-water sailors, and had served with hard-horse captains before; they had learnt either through their own experience or the misfortune of others what was punishable and what was not. And even if they had not shared a hull with him before they knew of Ralph Barclay's character – that he saw a direct stare as insolence, an untidily rolled hammock, a misplaced bucket or swab, even a rope not coiled neat as intolerable. He liked his deck planking snow white, his guns and the balls that lay behind them an even, rust-free black, and he had an eagle eye for anything that transgressed those high standards. And he had made it plain in his standing orders that, when it came to sailing, he wanted *Brilliant* to be a crack frigate, one that any Admiral would pick out by habit to perform the tasks that brought a naval officer wealth and glory.

Not that he had been gifted with subordinates who would make that easy. In the article of officers, who now stood in a line before him, HMS *Brilliant* was not a happy ship. Though careful to observe the proper forms, he disliked the First Lieutenant Hood had foisted on him, and had little regard for his second and third for the same reason. It was not vanity that made him want his own appointees around him. It was an axiom of the service that lieutenants should have a loyalty to their captain that transcended mere proximity of rank – indeed they should depend on him and be willing to sacrifice their own interests to his so that, in turn, he could repay such fidelity by making heartfelt recommendations for their advancement.

That was how he had stood in regard to his patron Admiral Rodney – the death of that man had put an obvious check on Ralph Barclay's career. There was nothing worse than being the client of a deceased flag officer. Years of allegiance that should have paid off with consideration went into the death casket with the cadaver. Had Rodney still been alive he would have had an active command, and being gifted that from the Admiralty would have presented them with a list of captains he wanted in his fleet – Ralph Barclay flattered himself that he would have been one of those. In turn he would have got a better ship, a bigger frigate or even a ship-of-the-line, with the ability to pick his own inferior officers, some of them lieutenants who had been with him as captains servants or midshipmen since before they were breeched. Like he had looked to Rodney, they had looked to him to get them a place, and Ralph Barclay had endured more than one painful interview in which, thanks to the intransigence of Sam Hood, he had been obliged to disappoint his followers.

The lesser officers he could do nothing about. No naval captain chose his Purser, Boatswain, Carpenter or Cook – they served on board a ship to which they were permanently attached by warrant. His crew he would come to know in time, and he expected they would fear to displease him, because he had and was proud of his reputation as a strict disciplinarian, something that would be known by any old Navy men. The rest, landsmen pressed or volunteers, would learn soon enough the boundaries of naval discipline as applied by their captain.

'Mr Roscoe.'

'Sir,' replied the First Lieutenant, stepping forward. Roscoe had a lopsided countenance, one half seeming, with a lazy eye and collapsed cheek, to have no muscles, and that affected his speaking voice. He also had a drooping lip, which often made a very ordinary look seem amused. Yet a person had only to glance at the sound half of his face to see that there was a man to whom humour appeared alien.

'I require an explanation as to why we have yet to complete our stores?'

'I plead the shortage of hands, sir, and the boats, barring one, were with you.'

'It did not occur to you to request hands and boats from another ship, a guard ship perhaps or one that has the luxury of time?'

What could Roscoe say? That Davidge Gould had got to the guard ships before him, and no commander of a fighting vessel in his right mind – the only option left – would lend men to someone like Ralph Barclay, captaining a ship short on its own complement and with orders to weigh. So he took refuge in saying nothing.

'Keep an eye out for our boats coming down river with the hands I have recruited.' Barclay paused, thinking he might actually have to weigh before they got here, then added, 'Some twenty in number, Mr Roscoe.'

'Sir.'

'I am surprised, sir, that you can take such a statement in

so calm a manner,' He looked to include the second lieutenant, a grey-haired, slow speaking Dorset man called Thrale, with the face of a kindly uncle, a nonentity; a touch deaf, timid and lacking in confidence. He thought of that Admiralty waiting room with the crowd of lieutenants begging for a ship. How had such a man so impressed Sam Hood as to get himself a place on this one? 'You too Mr Thrale, given your own failures in that department.'

It was these men he had sent ashore, when first commissioned to command this frigate, with his posters and his money, for which he had been forced to pawn his possessions, and the way they had let him down rankled every time he looked at them. Neither Roscoe nor Thrale responded. Nor did Roscoe add the obligatory, 'Aye, aye, sir.'

Ralph Barclay knew that his Premier had deliberately left out the acknowledgement that was his due, which made him growl as he looked at the mass of stores piled in various places, and the untidy ropes that littered the deck planking. A goat was wandering about as it pleased, and the lowing of the beef cattle in the waist grated as much as the clucking of the hens in the coop behind the wheel. His Standing Orders, detailed instructions for the running of the ship, written so that all his subordinates would have no doubt as to how he wished things done, had been very particular about that – no ship could ever be brought to a high standard of cleanliness if the most visible part of it was untidy.

'And this deck, Mr Roscoe! No doubt you will tell me it was holystoned this very morning but I cannot say it is evident.'

'If I may be allowed to go about my duties...'

'You had better, Mr Roscoe,' Barclay interrupted, 'for I shall be back on deck within the hour, and I expect to find it spotless and clear of obstructions. I will also then wish to know that I can, without excuse, weigh anchor according to my instructions.'

He heard Roscoe bark at Thrale as he walked away, the Premier exercising his right to pass abuse down the chain of command. He did not see the malevolent looks aimed at his back, from officers and men alike, who had been toiling like Trojans since before first light, and felt they had the right to see that acknowledged. Not that it would have affected him if he had; ship's captains required respect, not affection.

After what Ralph Barclay had endured that morning, the relief of making his own cabin was palpable. His steward, Shenton, was there to take his hat, as well as the redeemed silver buckles, which could now go back on his shoes to replace the pinchbeck he had been forced to substitute. His best uniform coat was exchanged for a workaday affair, no longer the deep blue of a twenty-guinea dress outfit, but faded by sun, wind and weather to a pale imitation of what it had once been; much stitched and with leather patches on the elbows where the material had been worn away. All the officers on deck, who had been obliged to put on their best uniforms for the ceremony of his coming aboard, would be doing likewise, getting back into working clothes to complete the tasks that lay ahead.

The ship's captain had work of his own – his desk was a mass of papers that could not wait. This was the lot of a commanding officer and it could not be gainsaid nor ignored. He had to write a report on the state of his ship, timbers, hull and masts, and the stores within her, as well as those coming aboard, of the quantity and grade of powder and the amount of shot in the lockers. Water, barrels of salted pork, beef and dried peas, what had been consumed and what was left, as well as the wood he needed to fire the cook's coppers so that his men could eat. There was rum to account for and the small beer the hands drank in lieu of fresh water. The amount of canvas he had in his sail locker and what gauge it was, as well as what he possessed in the way of spare yards. To this must be appended lists of everything from nails to turpentine, to cables and spare anchors. He also had to include a list of the numbers and ratings of his crew for the purposes of pay, and the whole thing would have to be sent in to the Commodore before the noon gun. His new volunteers would go on that list, rated as landsmen.

As he wrote some of the lists of stores he was aware that they related to what he had taken aboard in the month, including this day, and what he had used, and took no account of what might have been abused or stolen in the meantime, or eaten by the rats that infested the holds. At times it seemed as though every man aboard his ship was a thief – and that took no account of the dockyard scullies, villains to a man – so great was the discrepancy between what HMS *Brilliant* should possess and what could be hauled out and counted. And the corollary to that was that every merchant captain and fisherman in the reaches of the Thames was a willing purchaser of purloined naval stores, and not just his. He suspected the carpenter of selling timber and nails, the caulker of trading pitch, his boatswain of filching lengths of cable and his gunner of degrading the quality of his powder. That the purser was dishonest went without saying, Ralph Barclay having never met an honest one.

The marine sentry knocked and opened the door on his command to admit Midshipman Burns, a slip of a boy of thirteen who was a relation to his wife. Burns was wearing, over some working nankeen trousers, a uniform coat far too big for him, which made him look even smaller than his pint-sized three foot six inches. And he was plainly terrified. Though Barclay aimed a smile at the lad, it did nothing to stop him shaking, for Ralph Barclay was unaware how unnerving his smile could be.

'The Premier,' Burns piped in high, hymn-singing voice, 'has sent me to inform you that your lady wife has put off from the shore.'

'Thank you, Mr Burns.'

'Sir,' the boy replied, turning to leave, only to spin back again as his captain addressed him.

'I have not had a chance to ask you, Mr Burns, if you are settling into your new berth?'

Burns looked confused. 'Sir?'

'Well, boy, are you?'

'Yes, sir, I am sir,' he stammered.

'Good. Then be so good as to see a chair is prepared to hoist my wife and your cousin aboard, one with a stout pair of arms. I will not have her risk a soaking on a slippery gangway.'

'Aye aye, sir.'

'Carry on, Mr Burns.'

The boy positively shot out of the door, making Ralph Barclay think back to his own days as a midshipman, to the filth and the humiliations, the hunger, the rat-hunts, the fights, both those he had won, and the shame and pain of those he had lost. Hard as it was it had served to make a man of him, which is what it would do to little Burns. No doubt, in his first week aboard, he was suffering from bullying and all sorts of other tribulations, but that was part of growing up to be a King's officer. The family obligation required him to keep an eye on the boy, but it must of necessity be remote, for too keen an attention would single him out for ill-treatment – no midshipman endured more of that than one perceived as a captain's favourite.

'Shenton,' he called, 'my best coat and number one scraper.'

As the small wherry left the shelter of the projecting mole, Emily Barclay, still a bit flustered from the haste with which she had packed, noted that the water beyond was much more disturbed that that within and she pulled her hood around her head, suspecting that the wind would be stronger too. It made no difference that this was river water, disturbed only by that ruffling breeze – she feared that she would be seasick, knowing that if she were, it would disappoint her husband. After the words they had exchanged that morning Emily was determined not to succumb – or if she did, not to let it show. It would be a terrible thing to let him down twice in twenty-four hours. Thinking that, she put her hand to her mouth, a gesture that was mistaken by one of the women rowing the boat, an ugly brute with hefty forearms and a hairy face, who nevertheless spoke in a kindly, deep voice.

'Keep your eyes fixed on the ship, Miss, and that will help.'

'Missus, if you please. I am wife to Captain Barclay.'

The second woman rowing, if anything even less prepossessing, spoke through the unlit clay pipe that had been clamped in her mouth since they set off. 'You don't look near old enough for that estate, lass, and I know, given the number of sailor's wives I've ferried out for a bit of what cheers us sisters up. Not that all of them were wives mind.' Emily Barclay flushed deep red at the allusion, thankful that her hood hid the fact, and that it served to muffle the coarse laughter that followed that sally. 'Captain's wife eh? Must be right comfortable for a bit of rumpy, the cabin of a ship, tho' I confess to never having the pleasure of trying one.'

The confusion Emily felt then was also hidden by her hood. Though it was a private thought, never to be shared with anyone, she had found the consummation of her marriage both painful and uncomfortable. Nor had what had happened since led her to the pleasure some of her more worldly wise friends had promised. If conjugality was so disappointing on dry land, in a comfortable feather bed of proper dimension, what was it going to be like on board ship?

'It would oblige me if you would keep your innuendoes to yourself,' Emily said, with as much force as she could muster. 'I will have you know that I am to sail with my husband, for the very good reason that we cannot bear the thought of being apart.'

'What does innendo mean?' asked the woman with the clay pipe.

''Nother boat approaching, Rach, that might foul our prow.'

Emily looked ahead, to observe two crowded boats speeding purposefully towards HMS *Brilliant*. But she was too busy thanking the lords of the sea for no feelings of sickness to give it more than a passing glance.

'We got captain's spouse aboard, Patsy, lass,' she said, taking one hand off her oar to tap the brass-bound chest that filled the centre of the wherry, 'and all her goods and chattels, looks like. Happen that there cutter will have to haul off and wait.'

'Think she'll be piped aboard, Rach, proper, like a captain would be?'

Emily pulled her hood closer to hide her face. She knew it was no true question, more a set up for another lubricious jibe.

'Happen there'll be a pipe a'waiting, Patsy, and a right stiff 'un at that.'

'Smoke streaming out of the end I shouldn't wonder.'

CHAPTER FIVE

Coming back on to the deck of HMS *Brilliant*, Midshipman Toby Burns had to stop for a moment to try and recollect where it was he was now supposed to go. If he was unsure of that, he was certain of where he did not want to be and that was the midshipman's berth, his off-watch home during daylight hours. The last week had shattered any illusions he had about the romance of serving on a King's ship. The images he had of glorious combat and wonderful camaraderie with like-minded fellows who knew his worth had run foul of the truth – he was stuck in a filthy hovel too small for the half dozen occupants with the foulest people he had ever met in his life, longing to get back to the safety of his night-time berth in the gunner's quarters where he could, at least, sleep in peace.

'Mister Burns,' said Henry Digby, third lieutenant of the ship. 'What did the captain say?'

'Say, sir?'

Digby produced a half smile. 'I do believe Mr Roscoe sent you with a message?'

'Oh, yes!' Burns replied, for all the world as if he was

dredging up a distant memory. 'Captain Barclay has asked that a chair be prepared for his wife to hoist her aboard.'

'Then do you not think, young man, that it would politic to pass that message on?' The boy blinked and nodded. 'And might I suggest that having told the Premier of the captain's request, you immediately ask his permission to fetch an appropriate means of conveyance from the wardroom.'

It was hard not to chastise Burns for being so slow, but then Digby was not much given to that; he could recall his own first days aboard a ship with too much clarity. Not much bigger than this sprat before him, he had entered a world of dark and forbidding strangers, but he did have in his favour the fact that he was a scrapper, always ready to fight his corner. Looking at the pallid, plump face and flaccid eyes of this mid, he suspected Burns was not.

'I should shift on that task, Mr Burns, for if you look towards the dockyard you will observe that Mrs Barclay's boat has just come out from beyond the jetty.'

'Aye, aye, sir,' the boy replied, and shot forward to where Roscoe was supervising the slinging of a mainmast yard. The nod of approbation that Burns got for his suggestion, really Lieutenant Digby's, raised his spirits somewhat, it being the first he could remember, and he shot off to get the chair, as instructed. There was purpose in his step, for he was on a mission, as he barged into the wardroom.

'Hold up there, sir!'

Holbrook, the marine lieutenant, sitting cleaning a pair of long-barrelled pistols, looked extremely indignant, not difficult for a fellow of high colour and obvious conceit. Alone among the officers he had no duties to perform and he was enjoying the rare moment of peace that afforded him.

'I've come for a chair, sir.'

'A chair sir?' Holbrook puffed, 'I say you by your actions you have come for a barge. Charging in here without so much as a by your leave, sir. Where were you raised with such manners?'

'No, sir, not a barge, sir,' Burns insisted. 'A chair for the captain's wife, very like the one you are sat on.'

'Damn it if you don't want my seat?'

Burns hopped from foot to foot, aware that perhaps Holbrook was being jocular, practising upon him rather than being genuinely angry – but he could not be certain, and if anything plagued him it was that inability to tell a jest from a threat, and that mostly in the Mid's berth. The senior midshipman, forty if he was a day and crabbed as hell, was forever being scarifying, just like this blasted marine. Were the allusions to what might become of him one dark night when the ship was far from shore and female company just a common tease or was there some truth in it? Was the steady disappearance of the contents of his chest, so lovingly and expensively packed by his dear mother – the mention of each missing item met by his messmates with innocent incomprehension – true theft, or part of his initiation?

'Any seat will do, sir, provided it has arms.'

'Then sir, I shall give you a plain chair and my pistols, will that do?' Holbrook was looking at Burns, with his popped blue eyes wide open and his expression arch, but that did not last for it was obvious that his pun, rather a fine one he thought, had quite gone over this little idiot's head, so he yelled out, 'Steward, a captain's chair for Mr Burns, on deck at the double.'

'I will take it, since I was sent to fetch it, sir.'

'As I suspected,' Holbrook sniffed, shaking his head. 'Brought up in a sod-turf hovel. Well, here aboard ship we have servants, sir, and though you ain't got much in the way of dignity you are supposed to be a young gentleman.'

The marine searched for another witticism that combined arms and chairs, which imposed a pause in which he appeared quite vacant, but somehow 'cut to the chaise' did not seem to fit the bill and he had to cover the flatness of the remark with a cough.

'Servants serve, officers command, young man, which you must learn, and deuced quick! Return to the deck and your chair will be delivered to you.'

Back on deck Burns had the pleasure of saying to the First Lieutenant, 'I have ordered a chair brought from the wardroom sir,' which made him feel quite manly.

'You were damned slow about it, Mr Burns,' said Roscoe, deflating him.

'Our boats will reach the wherry carrying your wife, sir.'

Henry Digby stood by the bulwark, telescope to his eye, even though both boats were in plain view. Everything about him seemed somehow pristine; the young face that was not yet required to shave regularly, the unblemished skin of a not unprepossessing countenance, the newness of his hat, coat and breeches.

'Why was a boat not sent to fetch her?'

Digby stood erect to reply. 'With respect sir, all our boats are in use, and we were not told of a time to expect her.'

'Then tell Coyle to haul off and wait.'

'Speaking trumpet, Mr Burns?' said Digby. Pint-sized Burns hesitated, as though he had not heard the command. In fact he had, but had lost any notion of where the speaking trumpet might be. Digby chided him gently. 'By the binnacle, young sir!'

The trumpet in his hand, Henry Digby delivered his orders with a force that must have been noted on shore. Emily Barclay only half-heard him, still pleased that she had not been seasick. By the time she was being helped into the chair that had been slung from a whip on the yardarm, all her fears of that part, detailed to her by a husband trying and failing to reassure her, had evaporated. On a tidal river, she had nothing to fear from her method of coming aboard.

'Mrs Barclay,' said Ralph, coming forward to lift her out of the chair, and speaking in a voice, gentle and kindly, the like of which few aboard had heard him use.

'Captain Barclay,' Emily replied, taking his proffered hand, before turning to nod towards her husband's officers, all of whom she had previously met ashore.

'Shall I order Coyle to come alongside, sir?' said Digby.

'My wife's chest first, Mr Digby, then you may fetch our volunteers aboard. Mr Burns, be so good as to ask the surgeon…what's his name?'

'Mr Lutyens, sir.'

'Ask him to come on deck.'

'Mr Burns,' said Emily, 'you cannot go without greeting me, your own cousin, surely?'

Those who could see Ralph Barclay's face, as Burns smiled and moved to take his cousin's hand, froze in anticipation of the blast that was likely to follow. What they observed was a countenance in turmoil, as the captain's desire not to correct his wife in public fought with the sight of one of his midshipmen disobeying a direct order.

'You may greet your cousin, Mr Burns,' Barclay growled, 'then you will fetch the surgeon.'

Burns' handshake was perfunctory in the extreme, and he shot off the deck as though a pack of hounds were after him, narrowly avoiding being crowned by the chest of his female cousin that was being dropped towards the deck.

As they lay off the ship the crew moved amongst the men they had pressed, quietly releasing them from their bonds. Pearce had noticed as they rowed downriver, that whenever he caught the eye of one of the sailors and glared at them, he had been gifted with a look that he could only describe as disinterested, as though, having completed their brutal act they had put that behind them, behaving now with an attitude that was totally at odds with their previous violence. As to his fellow captives, some were looking around them with an air that had about it a hint of optimism, and it occurred to Pearce that if they were denizens of the Liberties, living on the edge of the abyss of destitution or arrest, there would be one or two in this boat who might welcome the change. They would certainly take it in preference to the other alternative to freedom – a debtor's gaol.

Rubbing his bloodless hands, Pearce sat up enough to see over the side of the boat, and with the prow pointing right towards a vessel, one of the dozens anchored within sight, he guessed it to be their destination. The ship lay low in the water, surrounded by boats of various sizes, all occupied in loading their cargoes onto the deck. Black from fresh paint, he calculated her as not much more than a hundred feet long, broad on the waterline, narrower at deck level. Three-masted, with a long blue pennant flying in the middle, the tall sticks were crossed with poles he knew to be called yards, and they had on them tightly rolled canvas and men working on ropes. He reflected on that bit of knowledge – the name of a yard was something a young man learnt early when his father talked often about the iniquity of hanging.

'What is it?' asked the dark-haired fellow who had been pulled out of the Thames the night before, shivering in a long linen shirt that was still very damp.

'Jesus, can you not see it's a ship,' said O'Hagan, a remark that earned him a glare that rendered that innocent looking face tetchy.

'I do believe they are known by their guns,' said Pearce, who had spent more time looking at the distance between boat and shore than at any of the anchored vessels. 'And I can count twelve ports on this side, which means the same on the other.'

'Small then,' added O'Hagan. 'I have heard they go as high as a hundred.'

'Matters not,' said the youth, with another shiver. 'I shan't be there long.'

'Want a wager on that, mate?' asked Kemp, who had heard every word.

There was petulance once more. 'You cannot just take up whosoever you choose.'

'Can't we now?' hooted Kemp. 'Lest you have a certificate in your breeches, Admiralty signed, which says plain, and has not been ruined and the ink run by your dip in the river, that you is exempt by trade or profession, then you be looking at your new home.'

The young jaw moved but no sound emerged, because

Cornelius Ghershon was thinking that, with the need to protest to someone with the power to get him released, he was somewhat short on candidates to provide the favour. The only people he could think of were friends to Alderman Denby Carruthers, the man who had set out to murder him by chucking him off London Bridge. If Carruthers ever found out that he had not drowned there was no certainty that he would not try again. Besides, he was bereft of clothes.

'I shall have words with the captain,' Ghershon said finally, though without much conviction.

'Shouldn't if I were you,' said a light, wafting voice. 'It would be a crying shame to have Barclay take the edge off such a pretty face.'

'Aye, aye,' crowed another sailor. 'Molly's picked him out already.'

'Goin' to show him golden bolt, Molly?' called a third, which was immediately followed by one of the boat crew breaking into song.

'Was in the aft hold where a sailor made bold, and showed me his ring a ding-ding.'

Half the crew took up the refrain. 'You can call me Nancy it's you that I fancy, and joy to you I will bring.'

'Stow it you lot,' yelled Coyle, 'This is no time for chanting.'

Pearce, Michael O'Hagan and Cornelius Ghershon exchanged a look, in which it was clear that two of them understood the meaning of the song, while Ghershon seemingly did not. There was no time to explain as Coyle, in response to hail from the ship, added another shout 'Bend to your oars,' he cried, and all three found themselves falling over as the crew sent the boat lunging towards the ship.

Pearce forgot about the sailor's joshing – he was too aware of the pain as the blood began to fill limbs that had been starved by the ropes that had so recently been removed. But it was nowhere near as hurtful as the words Coyle shouted as the boat came alongside.

'No need for bonds now, boys. You belong to King and Country as soon as you step on that there deck. So get off your arse and get up that there gangplank.'

'Mind your cursing, Coyle,' called Lieutenant Digby, who was leaning over the side. 'There is a lady on deck.'

'Aye aye, sir,' replied Coyle, touching his forelock, but Pearce noted that the respect in his voice was not mirrored on that bright red face.

Glancing at the others he had been taken up with, mostly bent and beaten in the very way they held themselves, Pearce determined he would not give Barclay, if the bastard was aboard, the satisfaction of seeing him in distress. Painful as it was, he used his hands to make less of a mess of his hair, retied the queue that had somehow survived the journey and employed his sleeve to wipe most of the accumulated grime off his face.

'Getting yourself up for a parade?' asked O'Hagan.

Kemp pushed both men on to the green, slippery, water-lashed platform at the base of the gangplank, admonishing them to 'step aboard right foot to the fore, to save cursing the barky.'

Emily, about to exit the deck, turned when the first of the 'volunteers' shuffled through the gangway, each one rubbing his hands and wrists, and clearly in pain, a few eyes lifting in wonder, as she had herself, at the height of those great masts, seen close up, a sort of collective murmur seeming to envelop them. The third one in the group did not look up, he looked aft to where she was standing, cloak half-open and hood now lowered in the lee of the poop, hair rustling in what breeze remained, and for no reason other than accident their eyes locked for a couple of seconds.

Pearce had a keen eye for a pretty woman, and the one he was looking at now was most certainly that, unblemished skin pink from the cold air, even features in a sweet oval face, clear green eyes, straight nose and a full-lipped mouth, slightly open, that was to him like an invitation to a kiss. For a moment it was as if the last twenty-four hours had not happened – he was free from pursuit or capture, back in a world where the sudden sight of a beautiful female brought forth the thrill of the chase. He was halfway to framing the words of an introduction when Barclay stepped forward.

'How dare you, scum, stare at my wife!' the captain cried, cuffing Pearce hard round the ear. The object of Barclay's anger just had time to register the shock on that lovely face before the force of the blow turned his head away.

The sight of that piece of casual brutality, and the way that the victim took it without vocal complaint, made Emily look at all the men shuffling aboard, not murmuring now but silent and fearful. She knew that her knowledge of ships and the sea was limited, really no more than common gossip mingled with what she had seen at tented raree-shows when a fairground was set up on the nearby common. But she was aware, for the very first time in her life, she was looking at men who had been press-ganged into the Navy.

Raised to deplore a thing of which she had only heard in whispers, Emily fought to compose her features, knowing that what sympathy she might have for the plight of such creatures was not to be shown. She was the wife of a naval captain and must behave like one.

'You are Mr Lutyens, the surgeon?'

The surgeon nodded, as Ralph Barclay tried to recall what little he knew of this fellow: short of stature, bright-eyed and pointy-nosed, with a startled expression, he was certainly singular. Very well connected apparently, of a sober disposition, and from a proper medical school, Lutyens was an unusual cove to find in a Navy more accustomed to men better at being barbers than mendicants – and quite often serious drunkards. So well qualified was this Lutyens that if he were to serve in the fleet at all, it should have been in some flagship with an admiral and a spacious sickbay. Apparently he had declined just such an offer, asking instead for a frigate, which made Ralph Barclay suspect there was something not right about him. It mattered little; here was another person he was not at liberty to choose – the Sick and Hurt Board provided his warrant and attested to his competence.

'Then let me welcome you aboard, sir, though I would appreciate more despatch when I ask that you attend the deck, especially in circumstances when we are obliged to weigh anchor with haste.'

'I was asked to clean and bandage a wound, I believe from a sailor who was with you last night.'

'It is customary, Mr Lutyens, to allow the captain of a King's ship the courtesy of sir.'

'Then, sir, far be it from me to contravene a custom.'

'I have acquired some volunteers,' Barclay added, ignoring a response that bordered on the facetious, though disconcerted by the way this fellow, with his protruding eyes, continued to stare at him, as if he was a needy patient. 'Naturally they must be passed fit for service.'

Lutyens turned towards the men lined up on the fore part of the quarterdeck, backs to the rail that surrounded the waist, a group of sorry looking specimens in damp clothing made to look more depressed by the evidence of the blows they had received. Behind them stood members of the crew, faces set firm, clearly there to stamp on any temptation to talk or protest.

'This fellow also needs his wound cleaned,' Lutyens said, as he stood in front of Charlie Taverner, the only one of the men who had bled copiously enough to stain his clothing, though there were bruises, scratches, black eyes and split lips in abundance.

'You may treat him as soon as he is entered on the ship's muster, Mr Lutyens. The King's Navy is not a charity foundation. What is vital is to ensure these fellows do not introduce any fevers to the ship. We will be at sea very shortly and who knows what ailments these creatures have been exposed to in the gutters from which they come.'

'Then if I am to be sure they are free of ailments, sir, they must strip off their clothing.'

Ralph Barclay reacted with a weary sigh. 'Mr Lutyens, be so good as to pass fit what men are fit. I have always observed others of your profession carried this out with a look at the eyes, an examination of the tongue and a quick check for venereals.'

That statement coincided with the moment Lutyens reached the end of the line of twenty souls, where he found himself looking into the eyes of one fellow who had a very defined spark of real defiance. Pearce was seething – even unbound he felt like a prisoner, and to be stood here like some exhibit in a travelling show was worse. That arbitrary cuff from Barclay as he had come aboard, so casual, dragging him from reverie back to reality, accepted by everyone around as within the captain's prerogative, just served to underline his situation, and he was not prepared to hide his mood to correspond to the benign look of the man before him.

'A proper examination requires the patient to strip.'

'They are not patients, Mr Lutyens,' Barclay sighed, 'they are hands. However you may request that they remove any outer garments and their shirts. The unbuttoning of their breeches will suffice for the rest.'

Seeing Barclay in daylight, Pearce was struck by the man's appearance. The uniform gave him a presence that commanded those around him – blue cutaway coat with twin gold epaulettes, the snow-white waistcoat and breeches and a face that perhaps had once been fetching. Now it had a puffy quality, and the veins on his cheeks were broken, either by exposure to the elements or a love of the bottle.

'If that is what you wish,' the surgeon replied testily, 'but they risk suffering from cold.'

Pearce thought this Lutyens an odd fish, pale complexion, popping eyes, a prow of a nose even if it was small, a high forehead topped by fine ginger-curled hair. The voice was strange too – it had a rolling quality on the consonants that seemed to imply it was not the surgeon's native tongue. And why was the bastard smiling at him, as though they shared a friendship?

'The men will get used to the elements soon enough, Mr Lutyens,' Barclay replied. 'Best they find out now that what the

Good Lord wills us in the way of weather has to be borne.'

'Coats off, you swabs,' barked Coyle, coming up on Pearce's left ear, 'as the good doctor wants, shirts an' all.' His voice dropped to a whisper as he spoke, for he, close to the 'volunteers', had seen the fury on the bruised face, which if anything had deepened at the command to strip. 'Now we can do this hard, mate, if'n that what you desire. But it will be done, so it best be done with a will.'

Glancing along the line Pearce saw that half the men, nudged and goaded by the crew members, had already begun to obey the command, though not without some vocal complaint. Within seconds those who had hesitated were forced to follow, each man obeying an injunction to place what he discarded at his feet. For him to rebel would be to single himself out, and that would have only one consequence. He knew enough about the Navy from hearsay and conversations with ex-sailors to be aware just how often the men who served were punished.

'I promise my examination will be brief, fellow,' said Lutyens, still with that smile which annoyed Pearce. 'Then you can get dressed again.'

Barclay's voice boomed out again. 'Mr Farmiloe, take possession of the volunteers' outer garments as they discard them, coats and the like, those they will no longer need. As they are sworn in I want them, as well as any possessions they may wish to place below, listed and then stored safely.'

That had Pearce doubly damning himself for his lack of foresight – he should have guessed that he and his money could be parted. Yet even as he cursed he knew that an opportunity to do anything about it was as lacking now as it had since he had been taken up and his hands bound – the last thing he needed to do was to draw public attention to what he possessed. Mind blank for a solution he unbuttoned the coat and slipped it off, followed by his waistcoat and his shirt. He felt the damp that had permeated his outer garments, and penetrated through to the linen, which made the wind doubly biting on his exposed skin.

'Any chance of getting off?' O'Hagan asked the ship's surgeon. Leaning close to Pearce's right ear, he added, 'I have a craving for a drop of ale to ease the ache in my head.'

If Lutyens heard the Irishman he did not respond. He lifted Pearce's arms, poked his chest, and prodded his belly, while Pearce looked along the line of semi-naked individuals shivering in the biting wind. Beyond that, the shoreline was visible, perhaps a quarter of a mile away, a row of low yellow-brick houses backing on to a flat featureless island, as well as, in between, a dozen anchored ships of war, some huge, with dozens of gunports, others tiny enough hardly to qualify for the title of ship. Looking over his shoulder he realised there was land even closer, a marsh by the look of, so flat as to be almost invisible, and between this ship and that shore, far fewer boats. In between was a river mouth leading to another clutch of huddled houses, wide, busy, and with a castle visible on the left hand shore.

Could he swim to the nearest land, and if so what would the men on those ships between him and the shore do? They would scarce let him float by, and even if they did, what would he find to aid him on land? Probably there was a whole raft of folk who would turn him in for a reward, and that after robbing him of anything he possessed. Turning back, he became aware that O'Hagan was looking at him hopefully, that the question he had posed was serious. Pearce slowly shook his head, at the same time wondering why the Irishman was seeking his opinion.

The surgeon barely looked at Pearce as he obliged with an outstretched tongue, nor when he undid he breeches, and as soon as he had satisfied himself regarding whatever it was he was looking for he simply said, 'Get dressed', and moved on to the next victim.

'Breeches, shirt and waistcoat, mate,' said Coyle, grabbing Pearce's coat from his hand as he tried to reclaim it. 'That's all you'll need. An' we'll be having your shoes and stockings as well.'

'There's something of value in that coat,' Pearce growled, not willing to say it was a purse or what it contained.

Coyle lifted the garment and felt the very obvious weight, nodding his head in recognition. 'Which be safe as houses, mate, you heard the captain, whatever it be. There ain't a man Jack aboard who don't have something of worth stowed in the holds, so you can rest easy, you ain't fallen among a bunch of thieves.'

'So taking a man's liberty is not thieving?' Pearce demanded, far from reassured.

Coyle came close again, his red face only an inch from Pearce's, his voice soft, almost supplicant. 'Take my advice, mate, an' accept what can't be altered. And don't go being the smart tongue 'board ship either, 'cause that will only get you trouble.'

'Cough.'

Lutyens command to O'Hagan cut off Pearce's response; besides Coyle had turned away. The Irishman cleared his throat of phlegm, as if he was going to spit. Coyle was ahead of him.

'Let fly with that in view of the captain, and you'll be the first to the grating on this commission.'

They all ended up much the same by the time the surgeon had finished his examination, shivering with cold, eager to end their semi-nakedness, aware that comments were being made about them by the crew working close by without being actually able to hear what was being said, only that it was belittling. By the time he reached the last man the surgeon had identified one case of the pox and pronounced one fellow as unfit for duty due to some ailment to do with his groin, but that was no recipe for release, since Barclay merely pointed out that in doing so Mr Lutyens had found himself a loblolly boy to assist in the sick bay. As to the pox Barclay reckoned there would be more than one fellow aboard who had that ailment, and since the surgeon earned a fee for treating the disease, he should be pleased.

'Right, Mr Roscoe,' called the captain, 'let's get them sworn in.'

That was a true farce, as, forced into a shuffling line, the required oath of allegiance to King George, his heirs and successors was read out to each man, any attempt to protest age or occupation as an excuse for release so quickly silenced that those bringing up the rear, the party who shared a boat with Pearce, declined to even try. Each man was told by Barclay, in a piece of hypocrisy even more staggering, that, in volunteering, he was entitled to a bounty of five pounds sterling, a sum which would be entered against his name to help pay for those things he would need throughout the voyage.

'I'd prefer any money owing to be given out to me,' said Abel Scrivens, when his turn came.

'Mark this man's name, Mr Roscoe,' said Barclay, disdaining to even look at Scrivens. 'Should he fail to show the respect due to an officer again I will see him gagged for a week.'

'Aye, aye, sir.'

Scrivens was grabbed and hustled to the back of the line.

Watching these proceedings gave Pearce plenty of time to think and observe. He noticed that the surgeon had taken up a position close by and was jotting in a small notebook as each man gave his name, which was worrying. What was the purpose of such scribbling? Whatever, it made him decide not to gift anyone his own. But he was damned if he was going to lie and refused to give any: this the Navy was clearly quite used to and was taken care of by the making up of a name to be entered into a ledger, in his case John Truculence, and the entering by that name of a cross.

Ralph Barclay stared hard at Pearce as he read him the oath. His look was returned in full measure, which made him wonder at the nature of the man. That cuff he had meted out for staring at his wife should have seen the fellow cowed, but he was far from that. He was well set, tall, with good broad shoulders and no fat at the waist. The legs were strong too, and the look in the eye denoted intelligence, in every sense the kind of physical specimen Ralph Barclay had set out to find. Yet he was possibly more – the fear of having inadvertently taken up someone well connected resurfaced, but this fellow, for all the glare of defiance, gave no name, made no protest nor demanded to be set on shore or taken before a Justice of the Peace.

Taken from the Liberties there was a distinct possibility of some criminality in his background, greater than mere indebtedness. No matter, whatever he was in life, he had ideas above his new station. That they would be knocked out of him – either painfully or by persuasion – was beyond doubt. If he had too sharp a tongue he could be gagged, too rebellious a personality, then he would find himself stapled to the deck for a day or more; and finally there was the lash, which would most certainly teach him his place. Nonetheless Ralph Barclay was reinforced in his opinion that he was perhaps one to keep a special eye on.

Barclay's ruminations on Pearce had to be put aside as Gherson, the last to be sworn, demanded that he should be sent ashore immediately: he was a person of means who had powerful friends who would miss his presence. This, because of his unconvincing delivery, the lack of any kind of name when challenged, and his present state of dress, bedraggled and shoeless, was treated as a general joke around the ship, which had the surgeon scribbling furiously in his little book, so furiously that he attracted the attention of the captain, which led Lutyens to cough and blush, and put his notebook in his pocket.

Once they had all been listed, Ralph Barclay produced papers and began to read. 'By the powers vested in me by the Lord Commissioners executing the office of Lord High Admiral of Great Britain, I hereby inform all who have volunteered to serve their King in this, his vessel, do so under the provisions of the Articles of War, which promulgated by said body, are as follows…'

The list was long, offence after offence, a worrying number ending with the admonition that the punishment for breaking that particular statute, cowardice in the face of the enemy, failure to obey an order, sleeping while on duty, striking a superior, sodomy, bestiality and mutiny, was death. All other punishments for gambling, drinking, insubordination, lese majesty, fighting, slacking, poor seamanship, sitting on the deck and ten dozen other offences were punishable at the captain's discretion.

When he said those words, 'the captain's discretion', Barclay looked up from his reading, giving them all a look in turn so that they would know what it meant; that he was the sole judge and jury in these matters; his word was law. Barclay met the look of irritation that the man entered as John Truculence threw him and held it for a moment before discounting it; he would learn soon enough that to display such obvious belligerence was unadvisable. Barclay finished with the words, 'anyone disobeying the aforesaid does so at their peril'.

That ceremony concluded, the whole party was finally led below, with the voice of Barclay following them down the companionway. 'We have had enough larking about for one day, Mr Roscoe, and enough of a show. Get the hands back to a proper rate of work. Then, when I am ready, you can join me in my cabin to sort out the watches.'

'Aye aye, sir.'

'Some King's bounty,' Abel Scrivens complained, 'given with one hand and damn well taken away with the other.'

'Happen you should go back up and tell him, Abel,' said Ben Walker.

'I've a damn good mind to do just that, Ben,' Scrivens grunted. 'There's no fair dealing when coin is offered and then taken back.'

The remark brought forth a chorus of agreement from the whole assembly, a steady growl that obviously emboldened Abel Scrivens because, in a piqued voice, he began a litany of complaints about being cold, being near naked, starving hungry and thirsty, that took the accompanying noise from a collective rumble to the beginnings of a collective wail. Pearce was paying little attention – he was looking along the deck, at the wooden tables in between the guns, each bearing a variety of objects, bits of clothing, quids of tobacco, knives, baulks of wood and the like – things that could be used as weapons. More enticing still, in front of those guns the ports were open, leaving a possible route of escape.

Escape to what – the river or the boats lying off the ship's side? Either would do if he could get away, though the thought did nag him that the loss of his purse was, for obvious reasons, a real hindrance. Both to the front and rear men were working, paying the newly pressed men no heed, helping to lower articles through the hatches to some point further down in the ship, so Pearce began to ease himself forward, heading for the nearest gunport, unnoticed by the men listening to Scrivens. The beams on this deck were too low for him to walk upright, and here he had his first whiff of a smell that pervaded everything aboard ship, one he recalled from two crossings of the English Channel, the rotten egg stink of bilge water mixed with the odour of damp wood, topped by the reek of animals and unwashed humanity.

'Belay that damned noise,' barked a new voice, which shut up Scrivens and his audience as if they were a bunch of errant children. 'And you,' he demanded of Pearce, 'where the hell do you think you're goin'? Get back with the rest.'

With no choice but to oblige, Pearce did so, glaring at the speaker, a bear of a fellow with a barrel chest, huge shoulders, little neck and a round, large, crop-haired head which rendered small what were decent-sized features. 'I am Robert Sykes, Bosun of His Majesty's twenty-eight gun frigate, HMS *Brilliant*. Just to prove we ain't true bastards, the captain has agreed to feed you, even though the hour for breakfast is long passed.'

Charlie Taverner responded with a slight jab at Pearce's shoulder, one that implied a friendship they truly did not share. 'Thank Christ for that, I ain't had a bite since I nicked a bit of your cheese last night, John Pearce.'

The fierce look that earned him was enough to make Taverner flush, for he had been close enough to hear Pearce refuse to volunteer his name to the officer swearing them in. He must have indeed overheard him when he gave it to O'Hagan. There was no doubt that the bosun had noted it now, because he gave a slight nod.

Kemp, who had come down as well, tapped off four of the group, Rufus among them, and ordered them to follow him, while Sykes told the rest to sit at some of the mess tables. As they did so the surgeon walked by, stopped, then stood several feet away, his eyes ranging over the whole group. He was followed by another officer, who stood before them with the air of a man about to make a speech, which he promptly did when Kemp and his quartet returned with lumps of bread and cheese.

'I am Lieutenant Digby, third of this ship, HMS *Brilliant*.' Digby paused to let that sink in, before adding, 'The method by which you have come to serve aboard this vessel is to none of you pleasant, but serve you must, for after taking the oath on deck you are subject to the Articles of War, and those articles do not allow for any insubordination. Do not, whatever you do, seek to fight the system of discipline aboard this ship, for I warn you that retribution will be swift and unpleasant. You will all be given a number and be assigned to a watch, of which there will be two once we weigh anchor, and you will be allotted duties to perform by Mr Sykes here, who as the bosun is responsible for training you up to your work. Without doubt this world you have entered will be strange, as will the tasks you will be asked to carry out, but in time you will learn enough to make you proper members of the crew.'

'Orders from Mr Roscoe, sir,' piped Burns, coming down the stairwell. 'He requires the new hands to be put to work immediately on the forward derrick.'

A deep frown creased the lieutenant's face – it was clearly an order he did not welcome.

'Wait here,' Digby said, making to go up past the little midshipman, before he was halted by the surgeon's voice.

'Lieutenant Digby,' said Lutyens. 'I do believe the Captain said I could attend to the man with the blood wound.'

'Of course.' Digby looked at Charlie Taverner, demanding his name. 'Go with Mr Lutyens.'

Roscoe was on the quarterdeck, in an old working coat, his lopsided face a picture of the kind of frustration that seemed to be the hallmark of a First Lieutenant. Though it was an office he coveted, Henry Digby was well aware that it was, in naval terms, and given the wrong type of commanding officer, the proverbial poisoned chalice. As Premier to a taut captain like Ralph Barclay you got scant praise and all the blame that was going if things went wrong. So the lack of a smiling countenance was hardly surprising.

'Sir,' Digby said, lifting his hat to a look of indifference. 'These new fellows have not even been shown the layout of the ship, I...'

Roscoe cut across him. 'Perhaps Mr Digby, with my permission, you can go to the captain and explain why the holds are not yet stowed. We are under orders to weigh, we still have stores coming aboard, and that does not allow for indulgence. Be so good as to obey the instruction you have been given. And might I suggest that someone who knows how to drive them, Kemp perhaps, be detailed to that duty, for they will not work with a will unless they are made to.'

'Sir,' Digby replied, because there was no other option.

Backside on a wooden chest, being attended to by the surgeon, Charlie Taverner was left to wonder how Lutyens had come by the title, for he had not received it for tenderness.

'This particular herbal curative is called Melissengeist, and is of German provenance, made by the nuns of a particular Rhineland abbey. The ingredients are secret, unlike the effect, which can be remarkable when used on a wound.'

If Lutyens had bothered to look into the face of Charlie Taverner, he might have had some notion of how ham-fisted he was being. Every time he jabbed at the wound on his patient's head, Charlie winced, though he kept himself from emitting any sound. On deck, the man Lutyens had already treated in a like manner, who also had broken skin on his crown, a quarter gunner by the name of Dysart, was warning his fellow crew members that their new surgeon, 'was as close to a sorcerer as he had ever seen, with his strange reeking foreign potions, as well as bein' a heavy handed bugger'.

'Charlie Taverner,' Lutyens said.

Though it was not a question, Taverner answered in the positive.

'You're not a seaman?' the surgeon asked.

'My you are the quick one, your honour,' Charlie responded, eyebrows raised, eyes twinkling, thinking that it was a daft question. 'You've gone and seen me for what I really am, a proper gent.' Lutyens just looked at Charlie, as he added, 'Hard as I tried to hide it.'

'You choose to be jocose?'

'I might if'n I knew what it meant.'

'What was your occupation?'

'How does grave robber sound? Bet you, being a medical cove, has bought a few corpses in your time.'

'I have, and I doubt they came from you, for robbing graves is hardly necessary when so many cadavers can be had from the streets or the river. So what was your true employment?'

'Let's just say this and that, your honour. Obliging Charlie Taverner they called me. You wanted something done, I was there to do it.'

'No trade then?'

'None that warrants the name.'

The surgeon was looking at him in an odd way, unblinkingly, like a cat would look at a caged bird, which served to remind Charlie of what he had temporarily forgotten – where he was and why.

'Are any of the others come aboard your friends?'

'One or two,' Charlie replied, more guardedly.

'Anyone in particular – that fellow who refused to give his true name perhaps?'

Charlie positively spat, 'No.'

Lutyens sighed, as if frustrated, seemed set to pose another question – then thought better of it. 'You are done. You may join your fellows on the upper deck.'

'Where would that be?'

It was pleasing to see the man hesitate for just a second – evidence that he was not himself certain. 'Just keep ascending the stepways, until you are in daylight.'

Charlie Taverner walked out, barging into a slip of a boy with two black eyes and a very swollen nose, waiting to be attended to. He recognised him as one of the party who had come first into the Pelican, and who, slipping out, had no doubt been the messenger to those outside to say that it was safe to raid. Clearly he had taken part in what followed and got clobbered for his trouble – now he had come to see the surgeon to have his nose repaired. Charlie, with a deft yet sharp use of the elbow, made sure it was bleeding again before the boy entered the sick bay, and he proceeded jauntily away from the stream of muffled curses that followed the blow.

The sight of the captain, with a woman clearly his lady on his arm, was enough to make him produce a show of haste.

Ralph Barclay had no time for this, showing his wife the layout of the ship – but it was a necessary courtesy. Heads bent under the low beams, he pointed out the various cabins, really tiny screened-off cubicles, occupied by the various petty officers, pleased as he pulled back each piece of canvas which served as a door to find them empty; that meant the occupant was busy, going about his duties.

'This is the home of the ship's surgeon, Mr Lutyens.'

That screen, pulled back, showed a boy sat on a chest with his head held back, while the surgeon sought to stem the copious flow of blood emanating from his nose.

'My dear,' said Barclay, seeking to shield his wife from the sight.

'I have seen blood before, husband. My brothers seem to be able to get into all sorts of scrapes. I would be blessed indeed if I had a guinea for every nosebleed or scraped knee I have attended to.'

'Mr Lutyens, allow me to introduce you to my wife.'

Lutyens shoved a piece of tow under Martin Dent's nose, then looked at his blood-covered mitts. 'Forgive me, Mrs Barclay, if I do not shake your hand.'

Emily smiled and nodded. 'I understand, sir, and acknowledge your consideration.' Then she looked at the boy on the chest. 'And you are?' Martin Dent responded with his name, but indistinctly, through blood and tow. 'And how did you come by this?'

'Won o' 'em biggers we took up lass night.'

Ralph Barclay cut in quickly. 'A blow taken in the line of duty, my dear, which I suggest would benefit from our leaving Mr Lutyens to attend to it.'

Lutyens gave a slight bow, but thanks to Barclay's hustling, it was to the female back. 'And now we come to the domain of the gunner, my dear.'

Emily tried to take in everything her husband said about the danger of gunpowder and explosions, of hanging magazines, fear nought screens that were wetted before a battle, men having to enter the magazine in felt slippers and no light to see by excepting that which came from a lantern shielded by glass, but it was all delivered at such a pace she was sure she only got the half of it.

'It is one of the most important keys I hold, my dear, and one of the most precious resources on the ship, for if the gunner does not properly carry out his duties, we would be helpless in a sea fight.' Another screen was pulled back, to reveal a plump middle-aged lady, sewing a piece of canvas by lantern-light. 'Ah, Mrs Railton, allow me to name my wife to you. My dear, this is the gunner's wife, the only other lady aboard the ship, who amongst other things, looks after the younger mids at night.'

The woman was up quickly, surprisingly so given her bulk, for on her feet she was as broad as she was high: that wasn't much; her head missed the beams by several inches.

'And I have duties to perform, my dear, which cannot wait,'

Barclay added, clearly eager to be off. Emily, having found a woman to talk to, was less keen.

'Am I at liberty to find my own way back to your cabin?'

Barclay, head already bent, came lower to kiss her hand. 'It is now our cabin, my dear, and of course you are at liberty to go anywhere you choose'. He added, as he departed, 'Though I would caution against going anywhere near the holds.'

'Mrs Railton,' said Emily, turning back to the gunner's wife, round red face, lowered so that she did not meet Emily's eye.

A curtsy, then a soft, 'Ma'am.'

Looking around the confined space, which could be no more than ten feet by four, Emily tried to imagine how this lady slept in it, never mind her husband and God knew how many others. Lost for a compliment, she said, 'Snug, very snug.'

'Ma'am.'

'How many boys do you care for?'

Finally their eyes met. 'Only one, ma'am. Mr Burns.'

Emily was about to say, 'Who is my nephew,' but Mrs Railton's guarded look stopped her. At ease herself in conversation with strangers, Emily was acutely aware when others were not, and what followed was an embarrassed silence.

'I daresay you have many duties awaiting your attention.'

'Ma'am.' Was the only reply she got, but the slight hunch of the shoulders spoke more of, 'leave me in peace'.

'Well, when I have found my feet we shall talk Mrs Railton, for all of this is very new to me, and I am sure I can trust a fellow member of my sex to advise me of the *do*s and *don't*s of life aboard ship.'

'Ma'am.'

'Captain Barclay's cabin is right back that way?' Emily said, pointing towards the stern. A sharp nod was the response.

CHAPTER SIX

Sauntering up to the deck, Charlie Taverner was cursed for being slow, then instructed to join his fellow Pelicans, employed to take on water. This was being pumped on board through a canvas hose from a square-shaped vessel alongside into barrels knocked up by the ship's coopers, the fluid acting to seal the wood as it expanded. Topped, they were hauled up high on a derrick then swung over a hatchway, to be lowered down at the command of the seaman overseeing the operation.

Down in the hold those barrels had to be stacked and wedged. Given the spillage of water from barrels as yet imperfectly sealed, as well as what leaked from the filling, they were allotted a spell at the pumps, then taken on to a windlass, hauling on bars to lift out of the bowels of the ship everything from sails to spars, nets full of shot, powder for the gunner and a barrel of salted pork for the cook. Ordered to the quarterdeck they were cursed for not having any notion of where that lay. But during that endless morning they learnt not only that station, but also the name of the other decks as well as the parts of the ship: the foredeck at the bows, the maindeck below which ran the length of the ship. The orlop deck lay below the main-deck, a dim place of small cabins, and further down yet were the dark, damp and smelly holds, where spells of work were curtailed due to the foulness of the air, and where the squeak of a rat was never far away, nor the scurrying run of a cockroach over bare feet. Sometimes a glint of a rodent eye would be reflected in the guttering lantern light by which they worked.

There was livestock to haul aboard; some more sheep and a pair of snorting pigs to add to the cattle, goat and chickens already on the ship. Soon their hands, with the exception of those who had laboured before, began to blister, for almost everything they were engaged in involved hauling work on a rope, the rough tarred strands of which worked on untried skin that went from red raw to a white swelling that eventually burst to reveal a running fluid and a tender pink layer that would eventually bleed. Those ordering them about were numerous, and as confusing in their titles as they were in their speech.

There were Carpenter's mates, Gunner's mates, Yeomen of this, that and the other, Midshipmen the likes of little Mr Burns who, short and young as he was, had the power to lord it over them. One or two termed midshipmen looked older than Rufus Dommet, while another, with a barking voice and a manner modelled on that of the captain, seemed of quite advanced years. There was a marine officer, his sergeant and corporal, and that was before they got to the purser, the master and his mates, the commissioned officers and the captain himself. As Michael O'Hagan observed, there were 'many around to issue instruction', and 'precious few to undertake the toil', which was 'much the same as digging a ship canal or a sewer'.

Pearce was more concerned by the constant presence of authority than anything he was ordered to do, which allowed him no time to probe – the slightest attempt to detach himself, to find a place to hide prior to a search for a way off the ship was thwarted by whoever had charge of them. He had to content himself with a study of the various personalities, given that knowledge of them might have a bearing on any future opportunity.

Sykes, the barrel-chested bosun, was one who stood out as a man respected and competent, for he had a voice to match his build and what seemed a need to be everywhere at once, chiding, goading, pointing, barking and occasionally cursing not just the newcomers, but the sluggishness of men who were clearly bred to the sea. But his strictures were taken without much in the way of resentment, so Pearce reckoned Sykes was a man for whom the crew had a degree of respect. Was he the type to turn a blind eye to a pressed man trying to run?

With Kemp, the rat-faced sod who had brought them downriver, there existed no doubt – nothing could be attempted while he was close, which was too often. Either by command or choice, Pearce knew not which, Kemp had decided that it was his task to cajole and discipline those he had helped take out of the Pelican, and his grating voice was a near-constant, as was the way he swung the rattan cane that seemed grafted to his right hand.

There was not much in the way of conversation, and not just because it was discouraged. Most of the twenty souls were as much strangers to each other as they were to the men who had been aboard when they arrived. Charlie Taverner made the odd joke, some disparaging aside on the men who ordered them about, but he was not the cheerful scallywag of the previous night – he was as watchful as Pearce, absorbing what lay around him with a view to exploiting what he learnt.

As the tide slackened Pearce noticed the exposed mud banks left behind on that low marshy island. Was that helpful, shortening the distance he would need to swim, or would cloying mud of an unknown depth be worse than water? There were those numerous supply boats that came towards the ship from all different directions. If he could get aboard one, and always assuming the assistance of those manning it – a very big leap of faith – it mattered what route they took back to their landing place. Directly and over water to the point where they picked up their stores was no good – what point was there setting foot ashore on a busy quay – he needed something that shaved a quiet strip of land close enough for him to wade ashore.

Two other things caught his eye; first, the little fish-faced surgeon was a nuisance. He seemed to be forever close to where he and his fellow Pelicans were working, trying to pretend indifference while surreptitiously jotting in his notebook when something took his interest. The other was the captain's wife, allowed for a brief period to walk on the deck just in front of the cabin, wrapped in the same cloak, the wind ruffling those strands of her auburn hair not contained by pins and bows. There was a hunger in the look Pearce gave her, not because she represented a means of escape, but more that she was a sign of normality, a symbol that there was a world beyond the confines of these wooden walls, one that he was certain he would return to. He longed to make contact with her, aware that it was as much her unavailability as her beauty that created so powerful a desire. What was her voice like: would she smile or frown to be approached and subjected to a show of gallantry? That she was another man's wife mattered not at all – in the world John Pearce had left behind in Paris that was a spur to dalliance, not a hindrance. That she was wife to the captain who had pressed him made her irresistible.

Michael O'Hagan spoke softly in his ear. 'I would look elsewhere, John-boy, if I were you, for you have had one clout on that account already. And if I can see the direction of your gaze so can others.'

It was good advice, so Pearce dragged his thinking from consideration of Barclay's wife to contemplation of those with whom he was working. Would escape be easier as a group than as an individual? It was a repeat of the situation that had faced them all in the Pelican. Could a situation arise where the same tactic could be employed, enough numbers to overwhelm those trying to stop them? Looking at them toiling, sizing up each one, he felt he had to disregard those he had not met, and concentrate on the men in whose company he had been taken up.

Rufus Dommet was a disappointment. As an apprentice, a letter to his old employer would release him from the ship, and he had the right to demand that contact be made. But the skinny ginger-haired youth had no wish to go back to either the tyrant or the trade to which he was bonded, and claimed to have always had, 'a half-sort of hankering for the sea'. His attitude was one of outright curiosity combined with a natural cack-handedness that made Pearce wonder how he had ever held down his apprenticeship, or been tolerated by those with whom he had made his living on the riverbank.

Ben Walker was actually whistling while he worked, which got him, in a brief moment when no one was in earshot to command silence, a barbed comment from Charlie Taverner.

'What the hell 'ave you got to be so cheerful about?'

'Happen you don't remember what I said about Chelsea Barracks, Charlie, even though I got scoffed at for my pains. Now I might prefer to be a soldier than a tar, but either is better than what we had, and ten steps ahead of what we might have looked forward to in those damned Liberties.'

Abel Scrivens was scathing in reply to that. 'Those damned Liberties served you well enough when you needed them. They kept the law off your back, an' since you ain't inclined to say what for I take leave to opine it were serious, so they might have saved your neck.'

'Well, as sure as hell is hot,' Ben growled, for once riled out of his habitual stoical composure, 'the law ain't coming to look for any of us here. 'Sides, it were never my intention to spend the rest of my days in the Liberties. This way, I might just get a chance to see something of the world.'

'Staying in the Liberties would have suited me,' whispered Charlie, indicating with a jerk of the head that they needed to be careful, for Kemp, briefly absent, was returning to hound them.

'And me,' added Scrivens, in a soft, wistful hiss.

Pearce, bent over to lift a bale of canvas, half-turning, saw Kemp closing on them, seeming to compose his face into a look that indicated a deep loathing, odd since as far as he could ascertain they had done nothing to rile him; nothing that is, except be forced to serve aboard this ship. Glancing askance at the screwed-up eyes, his sharp pointed nose with its permanent dewdrop of clear snot and the slash of a mouth, a face which would never have been comely even in repose, he reckoned he was looking at a fellow who took no pleasure from his own life, and was determined that no other should enjoy theirs – a man for whom the small amount of authority he enjoyed, not really much in the scheme of things, was everything. He had met too many of that type in the last year or so, given that the Revolution had allowed turds like Kemp to surface in abundance.

Although little was said when Kemp was close, it was possible to discern by observation and the odd spoken aside how the quartet he had met in the Pelican related to each other, easy to see that when it came to opinion a degree of deference was granted to Abel Scrivens, though he could be in no way counted as their leader, especially in their present circumstances. Would sounding out Scrivens act as a shortcut to anything approaching a collective attitude?

In the nature of their work it was not long before they found themselves together, hauling on a rope, behind the others, far enough from Kemp for an exchange.

'How do you fare?'

Scrivens half-turned and gave Pearce a look bordering on despair. It was obvious by his appearance that he was wilting more than his companions; lank thin hair in disarray, his face was lined with exhaustion as well as grime and when he spoke his voice sounded just as weary. 'I do not think I fare very well, friend, but I thank you for enquiring.'

Pearce was touched by the open admission of distress, as well as a civility that appeared to be innate, and whispered, 'Ease off. Let the others apply the effort.'

Half of a smile was all the older man could manage. 'Would that be right?'

'It would be wise.'

'I doubt that sod behind you would see it so.'

'With enough dumb show he will not see it at all.'

'Belay that gabbin',' snapped Kemp, who must have spotted moving lips. 'Save your puff to heave on that there fall.'

The oldest of the Pelican quartet would certainly do anything to be off this ship, but Pearce, looking at him, reckoned he would be a liability. Natural sympathy was quickly overborne by practicality, and his mind went back to Paris, to the way he had left his father, for the reasoning – uncomfortable as it was to recall – was not dissimilar. Scrivens would struggle to merely escape and in the event of a pursuit would as like as not end up having to be carried.

Michael O'Hagan, ahead of the old man and pulling with a will, would be game for anything Pearce suggested, as well as being strong enough to do the carrying should that become necessary. Should he sound him out – would a talk to Charlie Taverner help, perhaps even a notion of how to get away? Taverner was a fly sort, able quickly to spot and exploit an opening – had he seen something that Pearce had missed? Whatever, he knew it would have to wait – there were too many ears on deck to discuss anything now.

A gun boomed from the built-up shore, and everyone stopped pulling as all eyes turned towards the puff of smoke it created. To Pearce, looking aft, those on deck, officers and seamen alike, seemed for a second to be frozen in tableau. That did not last; Barclay appeared, hatless and looking to be in a foul mood, so the officers began to yell even louder at their various parties, as did Kemp. Abel Scrivens was slow to respond, and stood looking at the shore, which earned him a stinging blow across his shoulders.

'Will you get your back into it, they've made our number,' spat Kemp, his face furious. Having no idea what the bosun's mate was talking about, Scrivens failed to move at the required speed, and was forced to cower as he received another swipe, which had Pearce interposing his own frame between the bosun's mate and that of the older man to prevent a third.

Face to face with Kemp, he could see nothing but venom in his eyes, and total contempt in his expression, while at his back he heard the whimper of an old man who had been hurt, perhaps as much in his self-esteem as in the flesh. 'I think you have harmed him enough.'

'It'll be you that'll feel the pain if you don't step aside.'

'I can take pain,' Pearce hissed, sick to death of being on the receiving end of other people's malice, 'and be assured that there will come a time when I can also mete it out.'

The flicker of doubt that flashed through Kemp's eyes was enough to tell Pearce he had succeeded, planting in the man's mind some notion of future retribution. For a bully, that was enough to induce caution.

'Get back to work.'

'Mister Roscoe,' Pearce heard Barclay call, 'my cabin if you please.'

Ralph Barclay could not sort out the watch bills by himself. He might know the warrant and petty officers, but when it came to knowledge of the crew Roscoe, with his constant contact, knew more than he. The task was to balance the two elements that made up each watch so that they matched each other in skill and numbers – the right quantity of topmen per watch, including the older ship's boys who would deal with the highest yards; men to man the wheel and haul on the falls that controlled the sails, each group working four on four off while the others slept or idled below, with the caveat that should they go into battle over eighty percent of the crew must be able to work the guns or take station to fire from the tops.

'This will not be written in stone, Mr Roscoe,' he said. 'We have too many landsmen for that.'

'Sir.'

'The pilot?' Barclay asked.

'Already aboard, sir.'

Every minute of delay endangered the ship. The pilot had been in the wardroom for over an hour, with the Commodore's gun banging and HMS *Brilliant*'s number on his signal mast above the order to weigh immediately. The man who was supposed to take them safely downriver would, as like as not, be so drunk as to be incapable before the frigate finally complied with its orders. That was not unusual – pilots as a breed were addicted to the bottle and not shy of demanding that craving be satisfied.

'I need a time, Mr Roscoe?' demanded Barclay, as that infernal signal gun banged out yet again. Every other captain at anchor would be laughing up his sleeve at him, while secretly thanking God it was not himself on the receiving end of the Commodore's impatience.

'I would say as soon as the men have been fed, sir.'

This was imparted with some passion – Roscoe was clearly worried that Barclay would deny the crew that before they weighed, for they were, as the captain himself was well aware, disgruntled that dinner and the spirits they were entitled to before that, had been delayed.

'Then you have my permission to tell the cook to get his coppers lit,' Barclay said, before adding, 'I want that we come off river discipline on the first dogwatch. Come dawn, whatever our position, all hands are to stand to quarters as if we were at sea.'

That surprised Roscoe, and Barclay knew he might well be gilding it, for they could very well still be in the lower reaches of the Thames. But he wanted his ship to be an efficient weapon of war in record time, which meant working up the crew to sea duty as soon as it was humanly possible.

'I would point out, sir,' Roscoe protested, 'that many of the men have yet to be allotted any station for that. We could have mayhem.'

'We will not have that, Mr Roscoe, because you, along with the other officers, will ensure we do not. A certain muddle is inevitable – I do not expect everything to be just the thing. Dawn will not be for some three hours in this part of the year, ample time after the men are roused to get matters organised without anyone on any nearby ship observing the confusion.'

'Forgive me,' said Emily Barclay, emerging from a side cabin. 'Am I disturbing you?'

Roscoe had shot to his feet, careful to duck his bare head to avoid cracking it on the deck timbers, while Emily's husband had eased his backside a fraction off his chair. 'My dear, I think Mr Roscoe and I are done, are we not?'

'Aye aye, sir.'

Emily had only met Roscoe on two occasions, both ashore, and found him very stiff and formal. On the first her husband had made the introduction, which, having already been appraised of the nature of their relationship, accounted for his manner. But the second time had been the previous night at the Assembly Rooms and then he had been excessively reserved. Her sex and station made it impossible for her to encourage him to add his name to her dance card, and he had shown no inclination to place it there – indeed he had actively sought to avoid the sociable look in her eye.

She suspected that, regardless of his opinion of her husband, he did not approve of her presence aboard ship.

'I have been knitting, lieutenant, a comforter for my husband, to wear under his foul weather clothes when the weather is inclement.'

Roscoe's look made her feel foolish. Of course, with his lazy half face he had to work for any expression, but there was not a trace of a smile at yet another effort to be friendly.

'With your permission, sir,' Roscoe said, 'I will be about my duties.'

'Certainly,' Barclay replied, 'but be so good as to send my coxswain to me.'

'He does not like me, Captain Barclay,' Emily said, as the door closed behind him.

'Nonsense, my dear! He is shy of your sex, that is all. I doubt Roscoe has much experience of ladies outside the...' Barclay had to clear his throat then, as he had been about to say whorehouse, which was not a word to be used in polite company, let alone that of his wife. 'From the little I know his family is all males, brothers.'

'There must, in all conscience, husband,' replied Emily, with a twinkle in her eye, 'have been one lady in the house. It is a necessity of reproduction, I believe.'

The remark jarred, being almost too much like deck language, not blasphemous but outré, until Ralph Barclay recalled that Emily was almost of a different generation, one perhaps where liberties such as the one she had just taken might need to be forgiven.

'Of course, but I alluded to a lack of sisters, who are less inclined to indulge a son than a mother, who for the sake of nature is free with her partiality.'

132

Ralph Barclay had three sisters and Emily had watched the way they twittered around him, the head of the family, terming him their hero and flattering him for a wit that he could hardly be said to possess. They were, to her mind, mighty silly creatures, but of course she could not say so. She could only think that if she had possessed any reservations about coming to sea with her husband, the prospect of being left at home in Somerset with that trio had spurred her to bury them.

'Tell me, my dear, what do you think of your new home?'

'It is all very strange.'

'Naturally.'

With her husband looking at her expectantly, Emily was in a quandary. There were many unpleasant things about being aboard; it was cramped in the extreme, and in terms of creature comforts sadly lacking – no pictures adorned the walls and what furniture had come aboard was functional rather than eye-catching. Some of the smells she had experienced, especially on her short tour of the ship, had made her thankful that she had brought aboard a batch of herbs to make a nosegay, and there seemed to be no one for her to talk to. Poor Captain Barclay was buried under the pressure of his labours, the only other woman, the wife of the gunner, had shown a marked disinclination to share intimacies, no doubt due to Emily's rank, though there was hope that would alter with time. The officers and midshipmen were polite but silent, going no further than a raised hat, and connection to anyone below that was impossible, and very likely forbidden. Shenton, the steward, was not used to the needs of females, nor overburdened with what could be termed decent manners and had already barged into the side cabin after only the most perfunctory knock.

'I am sure,' she replied, walking round the desk to touch

her husband's shoulder, 'I will come to love it so much that I will scream when you try to put me ashore.'

Ralph Barclay laid his hand on hers, positively cooing. 'Take the word of an old salt, my dear, the day will come when you will scream to be ashore, for that is a state everyone reaches who goes to sea. But I would want you happy now.'

'When will we be able to invite your officers to dinner?' The sudden look in his eyes, a change from tender affection to a flash of annoyance had her adding, 'I would so like to feed up little Mr Burns – am I allowed to call him Toby? He looked so peeked when I came aboard.'

Ralph Barclay had softened his look, though inwardly he was still taut. Thanks to Emily he had the means to entertain his officers royally, and her question had reminded him of that. But it had also reminded him of the fact that his deck officers were not his choice. Sam Hood had foisted them on him, so the natural inclination to be social with them was lacking.

'You may call him Toby in private, my dear,' Barclay replied, hedging round the main question, 'but it would be a mistake to do so on deck, or even if he was our guest at dinner. As to entertaining the officers, let us get to sea, for I fear that you will observe me being stiff with all of them until the ship is properly worked up. I must also tell you that it is deuced difficult to be continually barking at a fellow one minute, which the nature of my duty demands, then hosting him to a meal the next.'

The knock at the door saved further explanation, as the shout of 'Enter' brought in Hale, her husband's coxswain, who immediately whipped off his tarred hat and knuckled his forehead, while at the same time shoving a quid of tobacco, which he had been chewing, into the side of his mouth.

'Mr Hale,' Emily said, noting the numerous scratches that covered the coxswain's face. 'I am very pleased to see you again.'

'Why that's right kind of you, Mrs Barclay,' Hale replied, his knobbly face creased with pleasure, the number of missing teeth rendered visible by a wide smile that showed, in a rather unpleasant way, the brown, tobacco-stained remainder.

Here was another person Emily thought she must get to know better, for Hale had served with her husband for many years, and had turned up to attend his captain at their wedding, walking all the way from Portsmouth to Frome, a distance of some seventy miles. He had brought a gift of a pair of embroidered linen handkerchiefs that must have cost much more than he could afford, which served to mark the depth of his respect and loyalty. The bond that lay between them was obvious in the way Hale had been greeted by her husband at the churchyard, with equal respect. Here was a man that Captain Ralph Barclay trusted absolutely. The thought struck Emily, that from Lemuel Hale she might learn more about her husband than she would ever glean from his own lips.

'I be right sorry, Mrs Barclay,' Hale said, twisting his stiff black hat in his gnarled hands, smile now gone, 'that you was forced to hire a pair of Medway brutes and their wherry to get yourself aboard the barky. Should have been me that fetched you, it bein' like my duty.'

'I am sure you had other duties more important to perform, Mr Hale.'

'Still, I made plain to Mr Roscoe that it weren't right, respectful like, but plain, but he would not spare me a boat and the men to crew it.'

Ralph Barclay shook his head slowly and tut-tutted at such

135

pettiness, but she could only nod, feeling a marked reluctance to enter into any discussion with the likes of Hale regarding any of the officers, and particularly Lieutenant Roscoe. At the very least it would be tactless, and quite possibly downright perilous, for Emily was already aware of some of the currents of friction that existed. Besides, it was a golden rule drummed into her by her own mother that one did not discuss one's peers with servants.

The fact that the two men obviously had some service matter to discuss saved her from any response and obliged her to move to the coach, the small side cabin which had been set aside for her as a place of ease, leaving her husband and Hale to their business.

As the morning wore on, a gun banged every half hour and each time they heard it those in command looked towards the shore with a troubled expression, before yelling at their parties to demand greater effort. During that time Pearce warmed more and more to Michael O'Hagan, for the Irishman, a prodigious worker, had a happy knack of getting under the skin of those put over him with seemingly innocent, softly delivered enquiries, questions that had Pearce struggling not to laugh out loud.

'Would you be after explaining to me now,' he enquired of some fellow in a blue coat, 'what it is you mean by stays, as any of those I ever saw were on a lady and never made of rope?' That answered, he had another, which earned him a swipe. 'Would them blessed stays you were telling me about, be like to hold in what you're after calling the waist?'

Michael got in another telling dig when Kemp showed them the heads, and the common sailors' place of easement, no more than an exposed wooden seat facing the prow with a hole that led to the filthy detritus-filled water that lapped against the side of the frigate. Kemp, eager that they should not mistake their station, pointed to another privy, one with a door. 'This here roundhouse, which be shut off from wind and weather, ain't for the likes of you. This be for those with the rank to go with the privilege.'

'Well, John-boy,' said Michael, with a look of wonder. 'There'll be a right rank stink emanating from that quarter. Happen we're better off in the fresh air.'

All the pressed men had felt a rattan cane on their backs at some time during the morning, but Michael seemed almost to go out of his way to encourage it, never once, to the further annoyance of those given charge of him, letting them know that he had even felt their blows. Abel Scrivens got his repeatedly for feeble inability and squealed like a stuck pig each time it happened, seemingly unaware that such a carrying sound tended to encourage a second blow. There were two others in the same mould, grey faced coves of the kind he had seen too much of in the Bridewell, who looked set to collapse, and for reasons he did not bother to explore, Pearce set himself to alleviate their suffering as he had Abel's, time and again getting his own body in between them and whoever was close enough to clout them. O'Hagan did likewise, and managed half their work as well, which went some way to getting the three of them through the hours of toil.

With Gherson, Pearce experienced the overwhelming temptation to borrow the rattan himself and give him a good hiding. When not grinning inanely at any passing sailor in the hope of eliciting some favour he moaned incessantly without ever seeming to consider that everyone else had suffered an equal loss of liberty. He refused to put any extra effort in where it might have aided another – indeed he was able to avoid labour while seeming to be extremely busy. He was lazy in a manner that was clearly endemic to his nature, yet he had the knack of never being near the means of an administered punishment when his ruses failed – that always seemed to devolve on to another back.

The pressed men had scant contact with the crew, most of whom would grunt at them as a form of communication rather than speak, though it was clear they were just as busy, and in many cases no less put upon. There was an occasional audible complaint that they were 'strapped' from not yet having had their dinner, which, with the coppers only just lit, was 'like to be held back in the face of all custom.' It was as if the newcomers were an alien species, though John Pearce noticed that in some cases the look in a man's eyes didn't always correspond to the grating tone of his voice. If it wasn't sympathy it was at least an understanding, the same kind of look he had had from that fellow who had sought to accost him in the back room of the Pelican just before he clouted him. It did nothing to soften his feelings for them – he despised them – and he made sure in his returned looks that they had a clear idea of how he felt.

Pearce had seen the fellow he'd clobbered several times, moving between the points at which he was working and the bows of the ship, had heard him called Dysart, and noted that he had a bit of Scotch about his accent when he replied. He wondered if he might seek retribution for a blow that had left him wearing a bandage under his hat. But there was no sign of animosity. Soon the deck was nearly clear of stores and the work began to slack off as the ship was tidied to the satisfaction of the Premier, who had finally left Digby in command.

There had been no sight of the little marine, though Pearce gave a smile when Charlie told him what he had done to make his nose bleed again. Normally Pearce would sympathise with the immature and vulnerable; was he already so corrupted by the harshness of the Navy as to take pleasure in pain being visited on one so young? A single hate-filled look from the boy, when he finally did espy him, disabused Pearce of any compassion. He watched young Martin make his way into the rigging and forgot about him, until a belaying pin landed no more than a foot from where his head would have been had he not been moving, and a glance aloft showed him the little bastard grimacing from above, furious with himself no doubt for having missed.

Work was easing, with men tying off ropes and clearing what remained of the detritus. Dysart, accompanied by another sailor, came then to give them an instruction, which was delivered in a benign tone, in sharp contrast to the grunts and cursing with which they had been treated up till now.

'One mair task, lads, afore ye get yer dinner.'

Dysart pointed to a couple of small bolts of canvas by the bulwarks, and ordered that they should open them out into squares. Then he bade them take a corner or an edge to stretch them out. The other sailor helped, explaining as he did so.

'At this time o' the day, wi' the topmen at their victuals, the seabirds like to drop what they have been scooping oot the water while we have been toiling. You might say it is their constitutional moment. You will see as the men are coming doon from the rigging how they are starting to rest on ony place they can lay their wee pink feet.'

Pearce was not alone in looking aloft, something he had

done often to check on the position of young Martin, and the truth of Dysart's words was obvious. Huge gulls that had been screeching and cawing all morning, flying about, floating on the water, never landing close to a human, were now filling the rigging as though it was their home.

'There's a duty tae perform, and being the newcomers it falls to you, to ensure that none of what emits from their dirty wee arses stains the deck of this here ship.'

He took hold of Charlie Taverner's arm and began to pull him in while others on the square of canvas followed. 'So, until the topmen go aloft again, when we know the buggers will fly off, just move around the deck so, eyes aloft to see what is falling and catch it in this canvas.' The voice became grave and serious, 'The Premier will inspect at the coming of the hour, and count what you have missed, and if it be many, and his deck be filthy, well God help you is aw I can say.'

They split into two groups and Dysart's silent companion led one to the foredeck, while John Pearce, Michael O'Hagan and Rufus Dommet were part of the group allotted the quarterdeck. Dysart said, eagerly, 'The best way is tae keep moving, and take it in turn to look aloft. When you see one o' those gulls shake their arse feathers, you will ken they are aboot to pass their packet. Then you just run underneath the wee sod and catch it, neat as you like.'

If he had not been so tired Pearce would have seen it for what it was, a way of guying the lubbers. But with a brain dulled by lack of sleep, too many insoluble thoughts and a lot of heavy toil, it was some time before he realised, time in which he and his companions staggered about the deck with scant coordination, tripping and falling as those who took the task seriously called for a move. It did not help that knowing left from right was not a unanimous ability. Every object on the deck was a trap on which to stumble and, worse, the ship's goat, excited by the movement, seemed determined to get under their feet.

The whole ship was involved in the jest, including the officer called Digby, who was standing by the wheel surrounded by every midshipman aboard, and behind and above him was the surgeon on the poop, scribbling away. Eventually the youngsters gave the game away, unable to contain their mirth. In an attempt to avoid exposure, they hid behind those with better control of their hilarity. The first loud guffaw from that quarter stopped the sport, as the ship erupted in gales of laughter. Men who had secreted themselves in hatches emerged from their hiding places to point at the fools who had fallen for Dysart's jest.

Pearce looked at his companions, some smiling in a way that tried to convey that they had all along been aware that they were being practised upon, a couple sheepish and actually blushing. Michael O'Hagan was red-faced and furious, for he clearly did not enjoy being the butt of another man's joshing. More worryingly, a pair who clearly could not comprehend what was going on were still glancing aloft as though the duty was a serious one.

'Some bastard's blood will spill for this,' growled O'Hagan.

'Take it for what it is, Michael,' Pearce advised, thinking, on the occasions he had attended a school, he had known much worse by way of initiation than this. Mirth was not painful, except to the vainglorious.

A grinning Dysart approached them, lifting his hat and tapping his bandage, looking at the man who had caused his wound. 'That, lads, is by way of being a welcome to the ship and a thank you for this. Now for the sake of Christ fold up those bolts and stow them, for if you do not, some of my shipmates will have a seizure.'

'Dysart!' It was the voice of Lieutenant Digby, who, like everyone else on deck was at least grinning. Some went further, staggering around in dumb show replicating what the lubbers had been about. 'You have had your jest, now take these men below and see that they are fed. And since you have had your pleasure I will allot to you the duty of making sure they are aware of the number of their mess and their rights in the article of food.'

As the rest trickled down the companionway, Pearce held back, drawn by the notion that the deck would be near deserted, the boats alongside possibly the same, his eyes ranging once more along the low-lying marshland. Those left behind on the quarterdeck, Digby and a couple of mids, were talking amongst themselves – would they spot him if he moved? He took a step, only to see one young head turn. So what – if he ran to the side and dived over was that fellow close enough to stop him? The alarm would be raised. Could he get into that tall marsh grass quick enough to evade recapture? Was it wise to even make such an attempt without clothing or money? Would another, better chance present itself?

'Will you move your arse, man,' said Dysart, in a peevish tone, his head popping up from below decks. 'I canna get my vittels till you lot have been served yours.'

The opportunity, if there had indeed ever been one, had gone. Pearce looked at the Scotsman, with his bandaged head, wondering if he had any notion of what thoughts he had disturbed.

'Does your head hurt?'

'It does that.'

'Good!'

Dysart just laughed. 'I canna say I blame ye, laddie. And a daresay ye'd gie me another belt in the same circumstance, if ye were tae get the chance.'

'I want to ask you a question?' Pearce said, as he followed him below.

'Ask away.'

'Where is my clothing stored?'

Dysart stopped and turned, his face quizzical. 'Now why would you be wantin' to ken that?'

'They said it was to be stored below. All I want to know is where below?'

Dysart carried on down, speaking over his shoulder. 'I'll tell ye, laddie. Not that it'll dae ye ony good. Yer stuff is in a storeroom hard by the bread room, tin-lined the same as that to keep oot the rats.'

'Thank you.'

'An I'll tell ye this an' aw. It's got a padlock on it the size of a cannonball, and the only wan that's got a key that's ony use tae you is Coyle.' The rest of the words were nearly lost in the babble of noise that greeted them at the bottom. 'Besides that, it's right close to the gunroom, where the officers hang oot, so you can forget whatever notion ye were gnawing on just noo.'

The maindeck was crowded, lined with lanterns casting a low light over numerous tables on either side of the deck. Pearce was directed to join his fellow Pelicans, who had been sat at a table that bore, in a metal plate nailed to it, the numeral twelve, which, Dysart informed them, was the number of their mess. In time, he told them, their mess could number eight souls – one addition would be a seaman, yet to be appointed, able to look after and train them.

'An' a hope tae Christ it's no me. So get stuck in.'

Rufus, who had been appointed to fetch their food, loaded what he had brought onto the table then sat himself down. They had small beer to drink, fresh bread fetched out from the shore that morning and salted beef in a stew that satisfied five of the party. For once Pearce found himself in agreement with Gherson in disliking the food and drink; the beef, bulked out with beans, was tasteless, tough and full of gristle, and the blanching and short cooking time had done nothing to kill off the excess of salt in which it had been preserved. The small beer was thin stuff and woody, having suffered from being too long in the cask. The cheese was the best; though hard, it was fresh and tasty.

Their mess table seemed like an island in a sea of noise. Conversation was quiet and contained, each member more concerned with making sense of his surroundings than any desire to talk. The seamen sitting at the other tables were a more garrulous bunch, exchanging endless ribbing, and sometimes a barbed insult in a babble of noise. If there was authority present Pearce could not see it, and though weary in both body and mind he could not help making observations. Most present were young, few much older than him, and they tended to be compact fellows rather than strapping, though there was the odd creature who could square shoulders and height to Michael O'Hagan.

Those just above the age of the ship's boys were the most raucous. They were slim, lithe fellows, not afraid of vanity or profanity, who moved easily and wore the most elaborate of the many pigtails on show, greased shiny and strewn with multi-coloured beads. Pearce had observed them working aloft, defying death on a second by second basis as they swung effortlessly about in the rigging as if determined to let everyone know of their superiority. Below decks as they added mischief to their catcalls and ribaldry, throwing bread at each other, as well as at other mess tables, earning frowns of either boredom or disapproval from the older members of the crew.

Such men were not older by much, but they seemed to have gained gravitas with the loss of their teenage years, as well as gnarled and scarred faces that testified to the rough life they led. At one table a huge fellow with an angry lived-in face was laying down the law to his silent companions. Pearce reckoned from their hunched posture that the listeners were either cowed, bored or both. But most other tables were lively, with conversations that had about them the air of good-natured argument, with pointed fingers, gestures of frustration or despair, laughter at another's plain foolishness and the odd thump of a mess table to emphasise some point that could not be gainsaid.

'Lively buggers, ain't they?' said Scrivens, yawning even as he was chewing, as a pair of the topmen began shadow boxing in the gap between the mess tables.

It was Ben Walker who replied. 'Not much different from folks ashore, Abel. We's mixed with worse than these on the riverbank.'

'Well, they are not the company to which I am accustomed,' sniffed Gherson, his eyes ranging around the deck with obvious distaste, an expression that stayed with him as he looked at his plate of food.

'And what kind of company would that be?' asked Charlie Taverner.

'I am used to a touch more refinement,' Gherson insisted, poking at a bone with his knife, leaving none of his messmates clear if he was talking about the food, them, or the whole crew of the ship.

'How come you landed in the river?'

It was Rufus who made the enquiry, all open-eyed and innocent, gauche enough to pose a question that everyone else sensed would be unwelcome, but one to which, judging by the way bodies eased forward, they all wanted an answer.

'It was a mistake, a foolish error.'

'I'll say,' scoffed Charlie. 'Dipping in the Thames is not a thing one does for a jest, and that in just a shirt and breeches of a winter's night.'

The ribbing tone riled Gherson, and he positively spat his reply. 'None of this is anyone's business but mine.'

'That be true,' Abel Scrivens cut in quietly, but with force enough to silence his companions. 'Happen you'll tell us if you want. Till then I, for one, am content to wait.'

So Abel Scrivens did have authority, or at least he was afforded respect from his peers, for they stopped staring at Gherson and concentrated on their food. Pearce welcomed the ensuing silence, which allowed him to get back to thinking about that which mattered most. Slowly chewing the tasteless food he tried to register every detail of the movement on the deck – the undercurrents of friendship or resentment that must exist with this many men cooped up in so confined a space. Every time some fellow went below the deed got special attention, not for the man himself, but for the fact that such an act seemed unimportant to everyone else.

Could he do the same, not now but some time later, to get

to his chest with his coat and his money, plus his shoes and stockings, which on land could be equally important. But not if he was going to swim; the coat and his shoes, worn, would make things difficult and would be even worse as a bundle. The money was the key; with that he could acquire whatever he needed. But how could he deal with a padlock?

'So, John boy,' asked Michael O'Hagan, nudging Pearce so that he turned round to face a mouth full of the plentiful bread and cheese, 'what is your plan?'

The Irishman was looking at Pearce as if he expected an answer. It was curious to Pearce, the different reactions the group had to him and Gherson, so different that he almost felt sorry for the other man – almost, because if Gherson had failed to win any friends it was his own idle and arrogant behaviour that was the cause. Pearce seemed to be accepted, as if merely having been taken from the Pelican conferred on him a sort of brotherhood, the same kinship that made the man who asked the question one of that select group.

Again it surfaced, that thought about a collective act of escape, and Pearce realised that if he decided a lone attempt, he might have to do as much to avoid these enforced messmates of his as he would to avoid any member of the crew.

'What makes you think, Michael, that I have a plan?'

O'Hagan responded with a grin. 'Sure, the look in your eye, which has not been still all this morning, and has been the same since we sat to eat. I swear if asked you could tell me the something about every soul on this deck, just as you could relate the number and size of every boat that came alongside. I would hazard also that you have a fair idea of the distance between ship and shore.'

O'Hagan's words had caught the attention of the rest, who

were all now looking at Pearce with an uncomfortable air of expectation. 'I have, Michael. It is too dangerous to swim at night and too crowded with ships to attempt by day.'

'Swim?' asked Ben Walker, a word that produced a distinctive shudder from Gherson. Ben leant back and rubbed his belly, adding a burp to let all know he was satisfied. 'Can you swim, John?'

Pearce nodded, looking keenly at the others. No one met his eye or wanted to tell him they shared that rare skill, one he had acquired almost at the same time as he had learnt to walk. 'I take it none of you can swim?'

'Why would anyone want to swim away from such plenty as this?' Ben asked, his West Country drawl even more pronounced because he was filling his belly.

'Best meal we've had in a month past,' added Rufus Dommet.

Cornelius Gherson managed to snort and sneer simultaneously. 'Then I do not envy you your table.'

The ginger-haired youth who had been, with Ben Walker, designated to collect their dinner was all enthusiasm. 'Do you know what we get?'

'Prison food,' said Scrivens, jabbing at a piece of bone, an act that made him wince as he jarred his bruised shoulder blades. 'That's what it is, prison food.'

'Not even Newgate Gaol would serve you this,' Gherson scoffed.

'How would you know?' asked Charlie Taverner, quickly.

'A guess,' Gherson spluttered, his face reddening to give lie to the words.

Pearce looked closely at Gherson then, to see if there was any trace of the effect of prison on his face. But, of course, there was none; his skin was flawless, and even streaked with the grime from his morning's work, absurdly handsome. If he had been in Newgate, by reputation even worse than the Bridewell, any marks would have faded, just like it had on his own. The scars of such confinement were in the mind.

'Chancy thing guessing,' Charlie added, 'might get us making up all kind of tales. Might be best if you was to tell us all about yourself. Confess like.'

'What makes you think I have something to confess to?' Gherson demanded.

That got a hoot from Charlie. 'If you ain't, mate, you're the only one at this board.'

'Leave him be, Charlie,' said Abel.

Charlie's bandage had not been very successfully applied. It had come loose and, dropping over one eye, made him appear piratical. But when he swept it back it was clear he had lost any trace of good humour, and he was not about to be put off. 'Happen there's more to you than you're letting on.' Gherson declined to answer, as Charlie looked hard at Ben and Rufus. 'You two may be content with this, but I am not, any more than Pearce.'

The use of his name again earned Charlie Taverner a glare, while those not sure of it looked happy to have it confirmed.

'Content?' They all lifted their heads to the voice, and saw a knobbly faced fellow with black eyes and a swarthy, scratched complexion, pigtailed under a shiny black-tarred hat. 'That be a lot to ask for in this life, to be content.'

No one replied, but that did not stop him from pushing on to the end of the bench.

'Take a seat,' said Michael, sarcastically.

'Hale.'

'Would that be a name or a salute?' asked Michael.

The look with which Hale responded to Michael's jest, and

Pearce's added chuckle, was humourless — more an expression of tolerance for an old joke than any ire at the affront. If he reacted at all it was only to chew slightly harder on the quid of tobacco in his mouth. Pearce hardly noticed; he was looking over Hale's shoulder, aware that their mess table was now under observation and that the level of babble had eased just a fraction. This fellow joining them had drawn attention. Why?

'You've been marked as the droll one, Paddy.'

Michael's face closed up. 'I am after being choosy who I allow to call me Paddy. Generally I grant the right to my friends, which is an estate you do not enjoy.'

Hale pulled the now-empty mess kid towards him, directed a stream of dark brown spittle into it, then replied calmly, clearly unfazed. 'Happen I'll tell them you're windy as well, given to speechifying.'

'You can tell them,' Michael added, raising a clenched fist, 'whoever them may be, that I dislike being practised upon, and that I am inclined to act upon such with this.'

Hale's sparse-toothed smile was slow and infuriating, though as he spoke he took a care to lean back slightly, which would take him out of the range of that ham fist. 'There's one or two aboard who will not shy away from that, Paddy.'

'You do.'

'Now, mate, on an open deck for all to see, and a bosun's cat and a disrating just waiting for the miscreants. Fighting begets punishment when it can be seen, but happen in a quiet corner you would find I would not shy off, for I am not one to measure a man by the size of himself or his fist.'

'O'Hagan has nothing to lose,' said Cornelius Gherson, with a snide air.

Hale grinned slowly. 'He has, and I reckon before this

commission is out he will find out what that is.'

'What is it you want, Hale?' asked Pearce, throwing a sharp look at Gherson to shut him up. He had a fair idea what Michael would lose: the skin off his back.

Hale executed a slow chew before replying. 'Why would I want something from the likes of you?'

'Mr Hale.' The compliment earned Pearce a nod. 'You were one of those who pressed us, were you not?' Another nod, slower to come this time, to confirm what had been a guess, because though Pearce thought he had heard Barclay shout the name, and allude to a scratching female, who could well be responsible for the very obvious marks on the man's face, he could not be sure.

One cheek appeared to swell as the tobacco was pushed sideways. 'It would be of interest to hear what you think of the likes of me.'

'It would not be pleasant to the ear,' said Charlie Taverner, 'but I am happy to try if you so wish it.'

'Like as not,' Hale replied, 'but what we was doing comes under the heading of necessity.' He could see half the table about to protest and held up a hand to stop them. 'I came here to do you a favour.'

'Like last night?' demanded O'Hagan.

'And to stop you from doing something daft, like trying to jump off the ship into a boat, or swim to Sheerness or the Isle of Grain. Thoughts like that be natural, but you has been told already under what laws you serve, and don't have a doubt they would be applied. You won't get clear of this ship so you'd best accept it. You'll be hauled in with a quick round turn and had up at the grating without doubt. It would do no good to claim you were pressed 'cause you are on the ship's muster as volunteers. Now I will grant that being had up like that is not agreeable, and

I know 'cause it was my way into the Navy just like you.'

'You were pressed?' asked Rufus, with his habitual innocent air.

Pearce was not surprised at Rufus's trusting response but he himself did not believe a word the man was saying. If sailors had a reputation for anything – apart from over enthusiastic carousing and whoring – it was for tale-telling that extended to downright falsehood. Hale had an air about him of that sort; the slight cock of the head, a lop-sided smirk, the earnest look in the eyes to imply sincerity that achieved the exact opposite.

'I was, lad, and younger than you, it being during the American War.'

'The American Revolution,' said Pearce, in a dogged tone of which his father would have approved.

'Call it what you will, mate, it was war and the fleet was short, and bein' a striplin' under the legal age of seventeen made no odds. I was taken just like you and I can recall to this day what I felt on my first night aboard ship. Lost, sitting in a huddle like you was, plotting an' a'plannin', cursing those who did the deed.' Hale's voice changed then, becoming eager and intense. 'But in time I came to see that I had fallen lucky. The work was hard, no error, but what toil ashore is any better? Life before the mast weren't half bad. I had food, clothes and money being paid that I could scarce spend.'

The black eyes, heavy browed, ranged round the table. 'Honest in your heart now, how many here have had more in their hand than would keep them sound for a week at most, eh?'

'I have,' insisted Gherson, looking to the others as if determined to make a point, underlining once more that he was not like them. The rest of his mess did not know him enough to concur, or esteem him enough to care, so that the added words, 'many times', sounded weak and unconvincing.

At the same time Hale's voice, and the look in his eager face, took on a fervent cast. 'And that be before we has a chance to take a prize. Why, I could tell you tales of fortunes made at sea, Spanish treasure ships so laden with gold they can barely float have been taken by the King's Navy, with money by the sack load for every man in the crew. Think of that! Look around this deck. Do you see heartbreak? Look at me. I ain't nobody now. I put myself to it, and I have an honourable station in this here Navy.'

'Mr Hale,' said Pearce, electing to speak for them all, including Cornelius Gherson, whose eye had lit up at the talk of gold. 'I thank you, even if your tales of prize money are romance.'

'Ain't romance, mate, it be the right sound truth.'

'So true,' Pearce replied, with cold precision, 'that you are still in your honourable station.'

The pair locked eyes, as if Hale thought that by doing so he could make Pearce back down. His adversary was tempted to let him know just how wise he was to such deceit. There was hardly a tavern in the land that did not have its ex-tar trying to keep his throat lubricated by exaggeration; sea monsters, deadly storms, compliant women, some of them two-headed, and most of all wealth, gold and sparkling jewels which by the most devilish ill-fortune had slipped through their fingers. Pearce had met them, listened to them and long ago learnt to see such storytelling for what it was; just that.

Hale broke the stare first, nodded, stood and said, 'Hark at what I said.'

'Which part, the truth or the fiction?'

That was received with a grunt, and the man turned. All eyes watched as Hale made his way to another mess table, to another huddle of pressed men from the Pelican. They would be talking the same talk, and Hale would no doubt deliver the same lecture, and hold out the same prospect. Who knows, thought Pearce, he may well find willing ears, for, as well as hearing the tall-tales, he had observed many a gawping soul who plainly believed every word.

'So, John boy, I ask again, what's the plan?' said Michael.

Faced with more looks of hope, and not wishing to say nothing, Pearce replied, 'Pen and paper, Michael.'

'Handy instruments if you can employ them,' the Irishman replied, holding up his hand again, this time with thick fingers spread. 'Jesus they're not much use to me.'

'And who would you be writing to?' asked Charlie Taverner.

'Anyone in authority that can get me off this ship.'

'Just you?'

Pearce locked eyes with Charlie then, but said nothing.

'I can write,' Gherson said, with a surprised look.

The notion seemed to trigger something in his mind, for he rose quickly from the table and walked away, to pass slowly each of the other mess tables set out at intervals along the deck. Even though Pearce could only observe his back, he guessed Gherson was employing that infuriating smile, ingratiatingly aimed at every member of the crew, some of whom were responding. At one table it was enough to allow Gherson to sit down.

'You must be able to write, Abel,' said Pearce.

'Happen I can,' the old man replied, his face and voice full of melancholy. The others, who knew him well, just looked away. 'But then what's the point when you ain't got no one to pen a letter to, 'cepting some sod that wants to chuck you in gaol.'

'Another visitor,' hissed Charlie Taverner, which forced Pearce to forget Gherson, and look instead at Kemp, who was heading for their table.

'They say,' Michael expounded, 'that the smell of corruption comes from what they term the bilges.' Kemp got a direct look then. 'But I take leave to doubt that's the true cause.'

'Your nose might be too close to your arse,' Kemp replied.

'While yours I would liken to a diseased prick, with the discharge you have hanging from its end.'

Kemp had been insulted too many times in his life to be fazed, but he did use his sleeve before he spoke again. 'Clear up around you, and the mess table, lest you want to be mother to your own tribe of rats.'

'We were promised clothes in which to work,' said Rufus Dommet, very obviously thrilled at the idea of being given anything.

'We have to weigh first,' Kemp replied.

'Would I be right to say that the purser advances goods against wages to come?' asked Pearce, too busy with his own thoughts to register what Kemp was saying.

'You would,' Kemp replied, ignoring a curse from Abel Scrivens; he added, 'an' he'll put it against your bounty if'n you ask him. So what is it you're after?'

Kemp's face showed a deep curiosity, an eagerness to know what this John whatever-his-real-name-is wanted to buy. Pearce had no intention of obliging him.

A whistle blew several notes, followed by a shouted command. 'All hands, stand by to weigh anchor.'

Kemp's rattan twitched. 'Time to shift.'

Pearce, holding the man's gaze, had felt his heart jump at the command to weigh, and cursed himself for missing what Kemp had said earlier. The frigate was about to depart the Nore anchorage; if he was going to go it had to be now, but standing, he found himself swept along with his own messmates as well as others, all heading for the capstan.

CHAPTER SEVEN

The Pelicans arrived to find most of the crew assembled round its bars, ready to bring the ship's boats on board. A rope ran forward along the deck, through a series of heavy blocks up to the deck above. At the command, the newcomers copied the action of the experienced seamen and took hold of the bars. On another command they began to heave, some fifty souls digging their feet into the planking and pushing with all their might to get the boats out of the water. Lanterns were lit as the boats were placed over booms that ran across the waist, for they blocked nearly all of the available light, dripping water on to the deck from bottoms that were green from time spent in the river.

Next the order came to 'Hove short,' followed by, 'Rig the messenger cable.'

That command saw the rope on the capstan cast off, to be replaced by one that was a huge continuous ring. Looped over and set in the capstan groove, the free end was taken forward to where a party of men and the ship's boys gathered by the thick cable that disappeared out of a hole in the side.

One sailor started singing, which was taken up by the others, a rhythmic chant designed to maximise the effort they were making.

'Who would be a sailor, I would me, go, go, go-Jack-Go.'

The last go had everyone applying pressure at once, and Pearce felt the first easy movement as the capstan responded, only to realise that all they had done was take up the slack on what the sailors called the messenger. The chant was repeated over and over again, but there was no quick speed gained, just tiny increments accompanied by the creaking of the rope that made it sound as if it were going to part. Ahead men were attaching cords both to the thick cable and the messenger that ran round the capstan.

'Why is not the damn thing moving?' said Michael, red-faced with pushing.

'The cable weight, pudding head,' gasped a sailor, 'without we raise it from the water and get it taut we'll be here all day.'

'Sure that would suit me fine, friend,' Michael replied. 'God alone knows why I am pushing this pole, since I have no desire to go anywhere, at all.'

'You'll push it,' called Kemp, moving towards him with his rattan raised, 'or you'll feel this.'

'I am thinking,' the Irishman said with a huge grin designed to infuriate Kemp, 'that such a thing as that would fit very neatly in your arse.'

'Well said, Paddy,' cried a voice, 'though I'll tell you he has the tightest arse on the ship.'

'Short arms and deep pockets, that's Kemp,' hailed another.

'God in heaven, these craturs are human,' Michael scoffed,

looking at Pearce with raised eyes. 'They speak, and here was me thinking they was dumb beasts of burden, not much above being donkeys.'

'Stow it, you cheeky sod.'

'Now who was that a'braying?'

'Happen you'll find out when we've won our anchor.'

Kemp jabbed at Michael's back with his cane. 'Meet Samuel Devenow, Paddy, who loves to bruise, and I wish you joy of the acquaintance.'

Pearce looked to where Kemp was pointing, into a scarred face going red with the effort of pushing, and a look in the eye, aimed at Michael O'Hagan, that was enough to kill on its own. He recognised it as the face he had observed haranguing a silent mess table as they had had their dinner, and decided it was even less prepossessing closer to than it had been before.

'What're you grinning at Paddy?' Devenow snarled.

'Sure, I have not had the honour to see such ugly features since last I looked to that grand and ancient church at Canterbury town.'

'Never met a Paddy yet that talked sense,' Devenow replied, a remark which was greeted by a degree of gasping assent.

Pearce, beside Michael on the capstan bar, could see the look in Michael's eye too, and for all the cast of amusement on his face, and the jocular tone of the voice, there was none in the gaze. For the first time since the Irishman had tried to clout him in the Pelican he saw something of the man that Charlie Taverner had identified as a bruiser.

'I suppose,' Michael continued, 'you're too much the heathen to go near a place of worship, even a blaspheme Protestant one. But I think the masons who built Canterbury were good Papists, and had the likes of you in mind when they fashioned their gargoyles. The ugliest one I reckon, demon-like and nasty, was an outlet for the privy, which suits, since what comes out of the hole of its mouth is not so very different to what issues from yours.'

That made a few of the men laugh, but a sharp bark from Devenow killed that, which underlined for Pearce what he had suspected before; they were in the presence of someone the crew treated with caution. As he pushed he was full of thoughts as to what that would mean – every shade of humanity would be on board the ship, and there would likely be a tyranny below decks to match or even surpass the one that existed abaft the mast. There was little doubt that Michael O'Hagan knew that too, and was prepared to challenge it.

They were moving now, not fast but at a very slow walk, and as they came round Pearce could see the thick cable coming in, covered in slime, dripping gallons of water on to the deck as it was fed through a hatch to be stored on the deck below. The boys detached the lengths of cord before the hawser disappeared, then ran back to the seaman who lashed them speedily onto the moving hawser. He could not help but examine the method, which was clever – the messenger was only that, a continuous rope that acted as means to get the much thicker hawser inboard. That itself was too thick to wrap round any kind of device, and clearly too heavy to be hauled aboard by humans.

'Anchor cable hove short, sir.' A voice called from above.

Roscoe's voice gave the response. 'Stand down half the men on the capstan.'

Another voice called then, 'All hands to make sail,' a cry that was repeated throughout the ship. Everyone bar the marines and the hawser party ran up to the deck, Kemp driving his charges before him to the quarterdeck, where they were ordered to 'clap on that there fall, and stand by to heave on command'.

Topmen were speeding aloft, spreading out along the yards and as soon as they were in position the order came to let fall the topsails. The pale brown canvas dropped, snapping like a wild animal, filling the air with noise as it rattled in the wind. As soon as the ropes attached to the lower ends were tied off, with much shouting as to how they should be eased or tightened, the sails boomed out with a life of their own, stretching taut, the frigate creaking as the pressure began to move the hull forward.

The whole exercise was accompanied by a huge amount of shouting, some to the men and boys aloft, more to those manning ropes, even more to a party they could see atop the buoy to which the frigate had been moored, men struggling with crowbars to free the other end of the hawser where it was looped around the great ring on the crown. As it came free it splashed into the water and disappeared – then the frigate took on a life independent of the shore. Barclay stood by the wheel alongside a fellow dressed in black, who looked to be hanging on to a spoke rather than applying pressure to it. All were looking aloft to see the billowing canvas against the now grey sky.

Pearce was impressed despite himself, aware that no one, least of all he, could watch such a majestic sight, the three great sails high on the masts, taut now, and not be moved by it. But more moving still was a sight of the shore, the increasing distance between it and the ship; for him the certain knowledge, and a sinking feeling to go with it, that getting free had just got more difficult.

* * *

HMS *Brilliant* won her anchor with ease, if not with elegance, thrilling the captain's wife, who had been allowed to take up a central position on the poop. From there she could look at the groups of sailors hauling on ropes, from the waist to the very deck on which she stood. The ultimate snap as the wind took the mainmast sail, it being so loud, made her laugh and cover her ears. Ralph Barclay knew that what appeared impressive to her would be seen as less so by those of his professional peers watching the frigate depart, for it had been a laboured performance. Like his fellow captains he had seen true crack ships weigh, seen the topmen aloft in seconds and the whole manoeuvre fulfilled in two minutes, a good twelve minutes less than his crew had managed. Once more he swore to himself that he would make this a ship to be proud of, and in his mind's eye he could see and feel the admiration that would come his way when it was.

Bleary eyed, looking left and right, the black-clad fellow muttered instructions to the two men on the wheel, watched by a very anxious master and an equally troubled ship's captain. Ralph Barclay had been in and out of the Little Nore anchorage dozens of times, and reckoned he knew it as well as this drunken buffoon who was hanging on to his wheel. There was plenty of water around them, but Barclay knew how narrow was the gap between the twin banks of the Sheerness Middle Sand and the Cheyney Spit, both now hidden by the height of the tide, but with not much more than a fathom of water to cover their mud. The deep-water channel was even narrower. Ships had gone aground here before, to be left high, dry and a laughing stock as the tide receded.

'Would you care for a leadsman in the chains?' he asked.

The pilot turned dark purple in the face, which was already

heavily cratered with the after effects of smallpox, and snorted. 'I daresay you knows your job, sir. Allow that I know mine.'

'Mr Roscoe,' said Collins, the master, 'I think a reef in the main and fore topsails would be prudent.'

'Sound, Mr Collins,' said the pilot, 'the wind demands it. I feel an increase.'

If the wind had strengthened, Ralph Barclay failed to notice it, and judging by the look on Roscoe's face neither had he. Looking more closely at Collins it was possible to see his glassy eyes, which meant that he too had been at the bottle, no doubt in the company of this rascal of a pilot. The comment about sails and wind was nothing but professional complicity, an attempt to tell the commissioned fellows on the deck that their blue coats and braid counted for nothing; that when it came to sailing a ship it would be best to leave it to those who thoroughly knew their business.

Convinced or not, Roscoe called out the orders. Aloft, the men bent over the yards and began to gather in the sail, hand over fist, reducing the overall area drawing on the wind, using long lines of ties stitched into the canvas to lash off what they had drawn up. Ralph Barclay hated this, the one time when he was not in command of his own vessel, and to stop himself from showing his frustration he went to join his wife on the poop. His master would set what sail was necessary – the pilot would con the ship – and Roscoe would convey his orders. He was not required.

'I have seen a ship at sea, Captain Barclay,' Emily cried, 'from a distance and looking enchanting, but nothing can compare with this.'

'You will observe better, my dear, when we get aloft a full suit of sails in anything of a blow.'

'Look husband, there is an officer there raising his hat to us.'

Ralph Barclay followed his wife's finger, towards the Great Nore anchorage, dotted with line-of-battle ships. The raised hat came from one of the smaller vessels of a mere sixty-four guns.

'That, my dear, is HMS *Agamemnon*, Agymoaner to the common seamen, and the fellow giving us the salute is Captain Horatio Nelson.'

Emily picked up the tone in her husband's voice – not dislike so much as disinclination – and looked at him with some curiosity. Then she saw him smile as he recalled that Nelson had once been grounded here in HMS *Boreas*, set on the sand so high and dry that crowds had come from all round the Medway to parade round the ship and jeer. The thought cheered Ralph Barclay immensely, a touch of comeuppance for a fellow over-full of himself.

'Did you not meet him last night at the Assembly Room dance? It was he who mentioned to me how much you enjoyed yourself. You may well come across him in the Mediterranean, my dear, for he has orders too for that station. Should you do so, beware, for I have sailed in his company before, and he is a terrible bore.'

And a proper tittle-tattle, thought Emily.

If the men looked for respite as they sailed down the north shore of the Isle of Sheppey, past all those settled and silent ships of the line, they were disappointed. Roscoe had laid out a list of tasks to be carried out and training to be undertaken, and that applied to the seamen as much as the landsmen and 'volunteers'. As soon as the pilot had set his course in the deep-water channel he set his plans in motion. Mess number twelve, being mere lubbers fit only to haul on lines, were being shown the use of a belying pin as a cleat. A line of pins sat in drilled holes, pushed down for a tight fit. If a rope was lashed to it with a double round turn it became a quick and secure knot, but by merely removing the pin the knot was released and with it the sail to which it was attached.

'Take the rope,' said Dysart, holding a spare line dropped for the purpose, 'fetch it under the pin, like so.' He then made a loop with the free end under the fixed end and lashed it to the pin, saying, 'Take a roond turn once, and loop that o'er the top, wi' another wan the same an' pull tight. It's a secure horse or a clove hitch. When ye've done that, always mak sure ye tidy what's left of the fall intae a neat coil, or the Premier will have yer guts.'

Dysart looked at faces of the party of which he had been given charge, seeing comprehension in the eyes of those who had understood, and mystification in that of the others. He had them try, noting that O'Hagan knew the knot and that the man who wanted to be called Truculence, along with Taverner, learnt it quick. Not the ginger bairn, though, and the other, much older one, Scrivens, looked as though he would never manage it.

'Right, and here's the beauty,' Dysart added eventually. 'The order comes tae let fly the sheets, which tae you would mean them sails we have set aloft. Nae time for untying knots, so ye just haul oot the pin and, there ye are, nae knot.'

There were parties all over the deck and aloft engaged in various tasks, mostly of an undemanding nature. But Ralph Barclay was not content to let matters rest at that – he had to get his crew to a sharp pitch of efficiency and he had no time spare for indulgence. He sent his wife back to their cabin, before calling in a loud voice, 'Mr Roscoe, there is a fire in the manger.'

'Watch on deck, fire engine forrard,' Roscoe roared, even though he knew the alarm to be false.

The cry taken up by the petty officers, which saw a group of sailors driven to the small engine that dealt with such an emergency, a wheeled pump with a hose attached to drop over the side into the river. No sooner had water begun to flow from the men's efforts, drenching the animals, which bleated and lowed in distress, than Barclay presented another task.

'There is a ship in the offing, Mr Roscoe,' he said, pointing to a merchantman on the same course as they, though in another channel. 'There, off our larboard quarter, which may be an enemy or a neutral. Pray launch a boat to investigate.'

'Permission to heave to, sir?'

Barclay allowed himself a smile then, for he was, while the pilot was aboard, only partly in charge of his ship. 'Denied.'

'Mr Burns, take charge of stowing the fire engine. Man the capstan. Mr Sykes, derricks over the side, and lash on the cutter. Mr Digby a party to man her.'

'Mr Farmiloe, gather a boarding party from the foc'sle,' yelled Digby. He added a call for the Master at Arms to issue weapons. 'A message to Mr Holbrook, and we require a file of marines.'

Mess number twelve, on deck to haul ropes when required, showed just how useless they were by the way they bumped into men who had what they did not, some idea of where they were going. Pearce, with Michael O'Hagan taking a lead from him, avoided the worse collisions by employing the same patient tactics he had used in the Pelican, letting matters clarify themselves before moving, which earned them both a stinging swipe from a rattan, a blow which landed simultaneously to the command to, 'Get a bloody move on'.

Pearce swung round, fists balled to retaliate. Dysart grabbed his shirt collar and hauled him backwards, then swore at an alarmed Kemp, which, as soon as the man saw he was safe, earned the Scotsman a rudely raised finger.

'Christ, laddie, you're well christened. Truculence by name an' truculence by nature.'

'If he swings that damn thing once more.'

Dysart just pushed him to where he was required. 'You'll gie him what he wants, if ye clout him, laddie. I've heard him boast what he's got in store for you, 'cause he kens yer temper. You at the grating and him wi' a cat in his hand. Now use yer heid and get toiling.'

On deck, the bosun was personally overseeing the clearing of the boats stacked above the waist of the ship, and men were rigging the sling that would be used to get the cutter over the side. Below, more than half the crew were being driven back to the capstan bars, which they grabbed from their racks around the base of the mainmast, for the cutter was heavy, and needed a lot of manpower. Above their heads, as the boat was raised from its booms, other men hauled on the rigged derrick that swung it over the ship's side. When they got level with the deck, the party that Farmiloe had gathered from the forecastlemen, the older and most experienced men on the ship, armed with cutlasses and axes distributed to them by the Master at Arms, leapt aboard, followed by four marines bearing muskets. As soon as the boat hit the water, the men fended off with their oars, and as those same oars dipped into the water to carry them to the imaginary ship, Barclay shouted.

'She's a neutral, Mr Roscoe, and has shown her colours. Pray get our boat in.'

The whole operation was put into reverse, but Barclay was not satisfied, for as soon as the cutter was inboard, dripping water once more onto the maindeck, he issued another set of orders. 'We will need topgallants in this light breeze, Mr Collins.'

The master jerked as his captain spoke – clearly he had been in some kind of reverie, or was still stupefied by drink. 'I had intended to set them when we came abreast of the Reculver Tower, sir.'

'I think now would be better,' Barclay insisted.

'Mr Sykes,' called Roscoe, 'topmen aloft and a party to fetch up the topgallants.'

'Now what in the name of Jaysus are they?' asked Michael O'Hagan, of a blue coat nearby. 'The best looking boyos on the ship, maybe?'

Whistles blew a different set of notes that sent the slim and agile topmen aloft once more. A set of ropes began to appear from the masthead, one end dropped down to the maindeck where these objects were apparently stored, another to the deck for the donkeys known as landsmen to haul on. They rose on the falls, long tubes of shaped timber with ends tapered to a point. Aloft, nimble topmen rigged them across the mast, seemingly suspended in thin air.

'Right, you lot below, to the sail locker,' called some strange fellow, and so inured were the volunteers now to taking orders that they followed without demur. As soon as they got to the orlop deck, Pearce, aware that the storeroom containing his possessions was on this deck made a crouching effort to try and slip away, only to be thwarted by Abel Scrivens and Rufus who tried to follow him.

'You three! Where in the name of Christ are you goin'?'

Glaring at the pair, Pearce knew in his heart that they had dogged his heels through ignorance, nothing else, but that did nothing to cheer him. Another sailor, bringing up the rear, prodded them to rejoin the rest at the barred door to the sail locker.

From inside that room they dragged heavy folded canvas, which had to be opened out, rolled and tied in a way that aided the topmen for lifting it aloft, where it was lashed through the deadeyes to the yard they had already put in place. Ralph Barclay had his watch out, determined to let no one doubt that the whole operation was taking too long. But when the sails were rigged, though not set, he said nothing in complaint, merely informing Lieutenant Roscoe that it was time to coil up ropes and sweep decks, called early because of the fading light.

Supper was a repeat of dinner in the quality of the food, as Mess Number Twelve contemplated a meal that varied very little from what they had had already, pork instead of beef. But if experience had made some of them fussy, toil had made them too hungry to care, and since the bread and cheese were still fresh it was not a wholly unpalatable meal, made more so by a tot of rum which, on an empty stomach, went straight to Rufus Dommet's young and tender head. As soon as they had finished they were ordered to call on the purser to collect their hammocks.

'You are entitled to what you have in your hands.' The fat little purser said, adding, with a cock of the head, an insincere smile, and a roll and a rub of his smooth pink hands. 'But I daresay you would aspire to a bit of decoration, like these bandanas I have.'

He pointed to a chest that lay near to the front of his deep storeroom, with bits of black silk inside. 'I am also prepared to advance you jackets and caps upon your mark, and of course, tobacco can be purchased against your bounty and your pay.'

In the dim lantern-light of the orlop deck, Pearce and his fellow 'volunteers', stood in a snaking line. He had been given and changed into duck trousers of the type he had seen the rest of the crew wear, wide at the bottom with ties to hold them at the waist, a checked shirt, a thick rough blanket that smelt slightly of mould and a rolled hammock in a small numbered sack that, he was told, would double as his night-time ditty bag.

'Should any of you wish to sell your shore clothes,' the purser continued, 'I will, provided they have a value, put a sum against your name for the purchase.'

'Not hard money?' asked Gherson, whose breeches and shirt, even after a dunk in the Thames and a day's work on deck, looked to be of good quality.

'Coin?' replied a startled purser, as though such a notion was outrageous. 'I fear you do not understand life in the Navy, man.'

'Then thank Christ for that,' snapped Charlie Taverner.

'We should have sold our teeth,' said Scrivens. 'Like Rufus said. The boy had the right of it for once.'

'I wouldn't be after selling my teeth to this spalpeen bastard,' said Michael O'Hagan, glaring at the purser, a remark that had no effect at all on a man so accustomed to verbal abuse, including that in the Irish vernacular.

'What will you give for these leather breeches?' asked Rufus.

Arched back to look at them, like a man being shown

the contents of a particularly rank night-soil pot, the purser replied, 'I doubt they would trouble my credit for more than a shilling.'

'This is prime leather, well tanned, that I made into breeks myself.'

The fat little fellow bent forward and made a good pretence of having a closer look. 'I fear you have been guyed by the man who supplied you with the material, for it looks to me as if the cow from which it was skinned was diseased. As for your skill with the needle I doubt the sail maker will be seeking you out. One shilling and three pence.'

Pearce spoke then, cutting across Rufus's response to robbery. 'I require a pen, ink, paper and wax.'

'I too,' said Gherson, racking his brain to think to whom he could write who would not have a connection to the man who had tried to kill him. Could he pen a plea to Carruthers' wife, Catherine?

'Certainly, and if you require the services of a scribe, I can supply that too.'

Pearce just glared at him, which had no effect on the fat, pompous little purser, who retired into the gloom to fetch what had been requested. Pearce then had to endorse each item in a ledger. Having just declined the services of a person to write for him, he could hardly make just a mark, so he took the proffered quill and signed John Truculence. The purser turned the book to look at it, and grinned.

'I am happy that you have chosen to record it thus, for that is, after all, the name under which you are entered.'

Gherson scribbled his name likewise, and the purser blew on the ink to dry it. They moved on to allow him to make the same distribution and pitch to those behind. Pearce realised immediately that they were unsupervised, but the same problem faced him as had done already – how to get away from his messmates. He had no choice but to speak, which he did quietly, and only to Michael O'Hagan, dropping his new hammock as he did so.

'Step in front of me Michael, you are broad enough to hide me.'

The Irishman went up hugely in Pearce's estimation then – he did not ask why, nor did he look at him – he merely squared his shoulders and half turned to cover Pearce, allowing him to slip away to the edge of the available light, then to the other side of the deck. He had to stop, for he had no idea where the bread room lay, or for that matter the storeroom containing his possessions. At his back he could hear the murmur of voices – ahead of him as he moved gingerly over the planking lay small pools of light and several screened-off cabins.

This deck, he had already learnt, was home to some of the lesser officers, as well as the surgeon if Charlie Taverner had the right of it. Dysart had said the gunroom, which was where the real officers lived. That had to be at the back of the ship, under the quarterdeck – behind him, so he had been moving in the wrong direction. Cursing, for he had little time, he retraced his steps. Adopting a normal gait, as though he had every right to be where he was, Pearce walked back the way he had come until he knew he was beyond the purser's store and the knot of pressed men outside.

The two storerooms were marked by their difference to all the others – not barred off spaces full of solid objects or screened off cells, but proper doors in a narrow alleyway with very obvious, and very sturdy locks. There was enough light to see the traces of flour on the deck, and enough of a smell to tell him which was the bread room. Pearce turned, bending down to examine, with a sinking feeling, the big padlock on a solid looking hasp that stood between him and his possessions – one that would take a blast of gunpowder to remove.

As he ran his fingers round the door edge, looking in vain for a point of leverage, he had no idea where it came from, the notion that he was being watched, just that it was present and it was powerful. He looked hard at the door to the rear of the after companionway, that must lead to the officer's quarters, but that was firmly shut. He also knew that even if it was merely in his imagination there was nothing he could do faced with such an obstacle as this padlock. He recalled Dysart's words about the tin lining designed to keep out the rats, creatures better equipped to gain entry than he; they could gnaw, he could not. With the fanciful notion that it was a clan of those watching him and hoping to gain entry, Pearce stood up and made his way back to join his fellows, just as Dysart returned to take them back to the maindeck so they could sling their hammocks, trying to recall, in all the things he had seen that day, if there had been some kind of lever, of metal rather than wood, strong enough to prise off that lock.

He got a questioning look from Michael O'Hagan, no doubt eager to know what he had been about, one that he could only respond to with a shake of the head.

Trooping back on to the maindeck, they saw that some hammocks were already rigged far forward, close to the manger where the smell of animals obviously did not bother the occupants. Mostly though the crew was still at their mess tables, waiting to be entertained by what was about to happen.

Naturally, the place allotted to the newcomers was closest to the open waist, and thus the cold air.

'See here on the deck beams is a number, and that is on your hammock an' aw'. Now I will show you how to lash it up, and give you some advice of how you can get yersels into it, but if you don't get it quick, I will not spend the night in useless instruction, and you can sleep on the deck planking to be nibbled by the rats.'

Dysart slipped Pearce's hammock out of its bag and it lay there like a long white sausage with a coil of rope around it.

'Look you at that and recall it,' said Dysart, 'for that is the bound article and when it has to be stowed it must be lashed just so.'

Dysart dropped one end and shook it out as they all gathered round. He took the end rope and reached up to a ringbolt attached to the beams above. 'Take the rope and pass it through once, fetch it doon to near the strands, cross it o'er and hold with thumb and finger, like that, before crossing it again. Bring the end through the V you have made and pull, then lash it off with a knot. Do the same wi' the other end and you will sleep sound and safe.'

'Could you do that again?' asked Ben Walker. 'But slow like.'

'I could'na go much slower, laddie, I was hardly moving.' To prove the point Dysart, his fingerings a blur, retied the knot at his own pace. Then he grinned and proceeded to repeat the manoeuvre at half speed. 'Now you lot have a try.'

Many a seaman had moved to watch and be amused, the first to oblige being those who thought their knots secure, who, leaning on their tied hammock fell flat as their attempt unravelled. Even the men who succeeded in executing the required hitch then had to get in. Dysart showed them one method, which required a swift roll that got the body weight central and stable. Naturally not one of the pressed men could execute this and, to sound of much hilarity, they thudded into the deck.

Pearce might not be a sailor, but he had crossed the English Channel twice, and since that was a passage that could take one day or ten, depending on wind and weather, he had been shown how to sling a hammock, as well as the best way to get into an arc of canvas that would never stay still. The knot suffered only from lack of practice and he had it after a couple of attempts. Then he reached up to the rough-hewn wood of the deck beam above, placing one hand either side and feeling for the indentation he guessed to be there between support beam and planking. Having found it, he took his weight and heaved himself in, if not with ease, then at least without taking a tumble.

'Now where, laddie,' said Dysart, who had stood back to watch the fun, 'did ye learn to dae that?'

Pearce ignored him, but he rolled out of the hammock quickly because Michael, who had the next space to his, was struggling. He had managed knots of a sort, though they were not the proper article, but his attempts to get in were farcical, and being as big as he was, and thus very obvious in his ineptitude, the Irishman, though not alone in his difficulties, was attracting much of the taunting, for being an ignorant bog-trotting turnip-eating bugger. With his height he assumed that the task would be easy, only to find that height did not favour him at all – he could not find the centre of the thing, and fell out continually. His anger only made his situation worse, fuelling the catcalls and jokes, which could only result in Michael stepping away from his tangled hammock and belting one of his tormentors.

'Here, Michael, let me help you?'

'This thing was not made for man,' the Irishman gasped, when he finally got in and lay backwards, stiff, a suspicious look on his face as though the hammock had a life of its own, and would toss him out if he relaxed. 'Lest to make them look fools.'

Pearce saw Scrivens standing several yards away, the drooped hammock in his hands, looking at it with utter incomprehension. Weariness was as much to blame as confusion, and since his friends were too pre-occupied with disentangling their own efforts, there was no one to aid him. If anything damned the press-gangs, and they were damned anyway, this was it – the taking up of souls totally unsuited to the life into which they were entered. Yet there was humanity on board as well as cruelty and ribaldry, for as Pearce moved to help he was beaten to it: one of the young sailors come to laugh at their efforts, seeing Scrivens, thin, weary and unmoving, came to his aid, and with quiet gentility, showed him how to rig his bed.

'Now I should have a go at taking them down for stowing,' said Dysart, when they had all got them rigged, 'then putting the buggers up again.'

It was freezing outside and the heads, on a winter night with a wind blowing over the gently pitching bows, was no place to linger with your brand new ducks around your ankles. So Charlie Taverner's desire to engage Pearce in quiet conversation, while he went about his occasions, was not entirely welcome.

'Can we get off the ship, that's what I want to know?'

Pearce stared out at the inky black of the night, listening to the sound of the water as it slid by the prow. He was sure he could smell the tang of the sea, but that was all he knew about where they were. The odd winking light from the shore gave no idea of distance – it could be a candle in a lantern no more than a hundred yards away or a substantial oil-lamp several miles distant.

'I have no more idea than you, Charlie, of how that is to be achieved.'

'I didn't think you had, unlike our friend O'Hagan.'

'Hardly your friend, given that I recall what you said about him.'

'I curse him less now than I did in the Pelican, for I have seen how he has come to the aid of others, especially old Abel.' Taverner followed that with a deep intake of breath, then added, 'I'm sorry for letting slip your name.'

'Can't be helped,' Pearce replied, with something less than complete candour, for what Taverner had done had annoyed him intensely. But even on such a short acquaintance Pearce knew this fellow was prone to talk more than was strictly necessary, and Taverner had no idea how much his gabbing endangered him.

'Why can you not call down the law on Barclay's head?'

The invitation to confide was obvious. Pearce was tempted to respond that if he couldn't trust Taverner with his name, he was damned if he was going to confide in him any details of his predicament. Instead, having seen to his needs, he stood, pulled his ducks back on, and said, 'How would you get back to the Liberties, even if you could get onto dry land?'

'I doubt I'd have much of a problem in the country. I'm not some famous felon. The Liberties would have to wait for a Sunday, when the writs cannot be served and the tipstaffs take a day off.'

'What would you face apprehended?'

Taverner sighed, stood himself and hauled up his new ducks. 'Six inches square of a debtor's gaol, John, in a cell with a hundred others and all the diseases they carry. No means to pay for food or decent bedding, dependent on charity, with little hope of ever clearing the burden that got me had up in the first place.'

That was something with which Pearce could wholeheartedly sympathise. 'Abel the same?'

'Aye, only the debt he carries is huge, so huge he would die in there if malice did not see him strung up or transported for that which he stood as dupe. God knows it makes little difference, for life at sea may do for him anyway.'

'Not if we help him.'

'We will all try to do that, for God knows he has helped us often enough.'

'The others?' Pearce asked.

'Rufus would suffer nothing more than a return to his family, for I think if they had the means to buy him an apprentice bond in the first place, they could very likely raise what is necessary to buy him out of it.'

'No point in asking about Ben is there?'

'None,' Taverner replied, as they made their way back to the foredeck. 'I suppose what I was asking, John, is this. If you find a way to get off this ship and clear of pursuit, we would be obliged to be included.'

'All of you?'

Pearce had said that because of his surprise. Charlie misunderstood. 'I think maybe just Abel and me. But there again, perhaps not. Ben is his own man, and would need to be coaxed, but Rufus will follow where I go.'

Pearce was tempted to point out how difficult a mass escape

would be. But just damning such a proposition was unwise; he might as well say he would make any attempt on his own and that could only increase the amount of scrutiny he was under from Charlie, the most watchful of the four.

'Should I sound them out?' Charlie asked.

'It can do no harm,' Pearce replied, not sure if that was a truth or a falsehood.

Sat once more at the mess table, Pearce pulled out his paper, pen, ink and the stub of sealing wax, thinking that, in terms of getting him quickly off the ship, letter-writing was tenuous in the extreme; no more than a pious hope. But it would serve, he hoped, to allay the suspicions of anyone watching him, which included his own messmates.

The paper had absorbed and been stained by some of the sweat from his body, and it was a thought that amused him – to reflect that the man to whom he was writing, the elderly Radical politician John Wilkes, would see those stains as proof of a deep distress. He took much care in his composition, as he had deciding on the recipient – the requirement for circumspection limited the choice. The message had to be brief, concise and coded in a way that was not obscure.

'That podreen-faced sod with the tarred hat who calls himself Hale has his eye upon you,' whispered Michael, 'and that little surgeon fellow, who thinks no man can see him lurking.'

'Can't be helped,' Pearce replied, pretending to sign with a flourish. He could not say to Michael that his being so public was deliberate, so he said, 'If I don't do this now, there might not be another chance.'

Pearce folded the letter quickly, wrote the address, then opening the lantern above his head, stuck the sealing wax into the stuttering flame. Once it started to drip he applied it to the join, watching as it solidified, wishing that he had about him a proper seal that would indent the wax with a design to prevent tampering. That done he slipped it back into his shirt, feeling the last of the warmth from the wax as it touched his bare skin.

He was now faced with the task of getting the letter into the hands of someone who could deliver it. If mail was to be taken off the ship, could it go in that? He doubted it. There must be some form of examination and a letter without the name of the sender appended would arouse suspicion. It occurred to him that his indifference to the crew of the *Brilliant*, his cold stares and unfriendly attitude, would work against him in this. The only person with whom he had shared an even half decent exchange was Dysart. He looked across the maindeck to where the Scotsman sat, easy to spot with that bandage, the sight of which militated against reposing such a crucial trust in that quarter. A man having suffered so much to take him up was not likely to have much heart for letting him go. But his train of thought did remind him that there was one of their mess who had made a point of sucking-up to the crew, the only other one who had asked the purser for pen and paper.

'You've been having words with some of the crew, Gherson,' Pearce said, sliding along the bench seat to whisper to him. 'What is about to happen?'

That earned Pearce a quizzical look. Once Charlie had found out his full moniker, he had taken to calling Gherson 'Corny', a tag adopted by everyone for the very simple reason that he obviously hated it, and he was such an annoying bastard that any chance to upset him was welcome. That Pearce had not done so was significant.

'Do I perceive that you are about to ask me for something?'

Pearce knew he couldn't trust him, but he also knew that Gherson had asked for the means to write, which could mean that he had also pondered a way to get a letter off the ship.

'I think in writing letters we share a purpose, and I was wondering if you have the means to fulfil yours?'

He might be irritating, but Gherson was no fool – Pearce had spotted that quicker than the others. There was a sharp if selfish intelligence at work behind that handsome, sensual countenance. No evil looks from Gherson greeted any member of the crew who was passing – instead they were gifted with a smile designed to win them to him, and Pearce had observed that in one or two cases he had succeeded, just as he had succeeded in getting a seat at other mess tables. He was not about to tell Gherson that he might have cause to regret his behaviour, for in his innocence he seemed blissfully unaware that he got his benevolent responses from sailors who had motives that transcended mere kindness.

Gherson was wondering if Pearce could be an asset or a threat. He had persuaded one of the forecastlemen, the one they called Molly, to take a letter from him – if he could get it written – and pass it over the side to one of the panders who would, he was informed, bring out the whores to any departing warship.

'Perhaps if you were to confide in me, who it is you are writing to and what the connection is, I might be able to help.'

'I would be prepared to say that he has a voice loud enough to start a hue and cry that might get us out of this.'

That was not an expression that was welcome to Cornelius Gherson. A hue and cry was an uncontrollable beast. 'Us?'

'Every man who came aboard yesterday,' Pearce insisted.

Gherson was truly surprised. 'Why worry about them?'

Pearce was about to suggest common humanity, but it was obviously a concept alien to the other man. 'Revenge,' Pearce hissed, forced to add in the face of clear disbelief, 'I want to see that sod Barclay up before a beak. Taking us up was illegal. It would be nice to see him pay the price for what is a crime.'

'We are bound for Deal on the East Kent shore,' Gherson whispered, 'the anchorage called the Downs where there is a convoy waiting. I have been told the crew will be paid there, and a number of boats will come out to trade with them. I have engaged one fellow, who says that no letter of a newly pressed man would be allowed ashore through the normal method, to pass mine to one of those traders.'

'He could pass two.'

Having overheard Pearce tell the purser he had money, Gherson's response was as quick as a flash. 'I have promised my fellow payment.'

'I will meet what is necessary,' Pearce said, observing Gherson's eyes flicker at the words. It was almost naked greed he saw there.

'You have deep pockets then?'

'Not bottomless.'

Gherson had no money at all, that had gone along with his coat, and since the service he was being offered was coming to him free, this was a chance to get some for when he got himself on shore. 'Still, a sum in guineas?'

Pearce had no intention of answering that. 'Name a price.'

'Five guineas?' said Gherson, who feared to pitch it too high, because that would mean he would get nothing.

'I can run to three,' Pearce replied.

'I cannot guarantee what you ask for less than four, and I

ask you to recall I will be requesting a favour for future, not present payment.'

'Done. Payment as our feet touch *terra firma*.'

Gherson nodded, but he was thinking that Pearce was at risk of giving himself away by showing off, using Latin where plain English would do.

'Give me your letter,' Gherson insisted. Pearce took it out of his shirt and handed it over and Gherson darted quickly to the table where Molly sat. The sailor moved to let him sit down, and, watching, Pearce wondered how it was that Gherson alone could not see the nudges such an association produced. Then he had to consider that Gherson could see as well as the next man and, as he put his head within an inch of Molly's, that he didn't care.

'Another letter?' Molly asked, with a worried look.

'Does that make any difference?' Gherson said, slipping Pearce's missive into an unwilling hand. 'I would have thought the risk was the same.'

'Two letters,' said Molly, thinking quickly, 'be best to look for two different carriers, rather than the one.'

'You are so clever,' cooed Gherson. 'Why did I not think of that?'

Molly tapped his head. 'You need a tar's head for such matters, and one a mite older than that you bear on your shoulders, boy. You leave it with me, and let's hope by the time we's due to weigh that there's a writ to be served that will get you back on shore.'

'I will always be grateful, I hope you know that.'

Molly put a hand on Gherson's knee and squeezed. 'Why lad, what decent soul would not aid a brother?'

CHAPTER EIGHT

Emily Barclay sat by the slightly open door, embroidery ring on her lap, listening with only half an ear to her husband's coxswain reporting back to him. Hale had been sent off to look over the men he called volunteers, and was now imparting to his captain, in his rolling Hampshire accent, what he had learnt. Emily felt a tinge of guilt at listening in to a conversation that was supposedly private, but then it was almost impossible not to eavesdrop in such a confined area, with only thin wooden panels separating the two cabins. Besides, if she was going to learn anything about shipboard life this appeared to be the only way, since her husband seemed disinclined or too busy to educate her.

'Dim is the word I would use for the most of them, your honour,' Hale said. 'They will rail for a while, but I reckon them to settle once they have seen there is now't else for it.'

'But not all?'

'No. There's the odd touch of sense, that mouthy fellow Gherson has a brain, and seems a dab hand at suckin' up to certain members of the crew.' Hale gave his captain a knowing look then, which was all the explanation Ralph Barclay required. "Sides that there are one or two it would be an idea to keep an eye on.'

'Names.'

'The big Paddy will like as not fight for his place, but I reckon there's enough aboard to put him down. Devenow for one, for the talk is they's already had words and Sam is lookin' to sort him out.'

That made Ralph Barclay frown. Devenow was a volunteer who had served with him in the Caribbean, and, no doubt strapped for a living ashore, had hurried aboard HMS *Brilliant* as soon as he heard his old captain had a ship. The presence was not one that Barclay was entirely keen on – the man was a mixed blessing, a hardcase who ruled the lower deck with his fists, handy in a scrap but a damned nuisance when he got drunk and unruly, which he did at every opportunity. Devenow saved his own grog and either bullied or bought others out of theirs, then downed the whole lot after Divine Service on a Sunday. Someone in authority would, inevitably, find him comatose, which meant a round dozen at the grating on a Monday morning. At least the man was honest in his dealings, taking his punishment without murmur as the price he had to pay for his liquid pleasures.

'Make sure if it happens that there is someone to restrain Devenow, for he will kill if he is free to, and God forbid we should have to hang him.'

That was a curious thing to say, thought Emily, almost as if her husband was prepared to condone violence as long as it suited his ends.

'The one listed as John Truculence,' Hale added, 'I heard

him called John Pearce by another. The Bosun reckons he heard the same so it is likely true.'

Barclay wheezed a slight laugh, the habitual one his wife found trying. 'At least we had the right of it on the first name.' Barclay was not about to admit that he had singled out Truculence himself, nor did he make the obvious comment that a man who refused to give his real name must have a reason. He merely enquired, 'Why him?'

'He's trouble on his own I reckon, your honour. But more'n that he is a man to dominate his mess, an' maybe a mite beyond the confines of that. He had a look about him that bodes nuisance. When I last saw him he was busy writing a letter.'

Ralph Barclay did not pose any more questions, which Emily again found curious, for Hale seemed to be warning her husband against a potential troublemaker. She could not know that when it came to below decks, Ralph Barclay had great confidence in his own ability to command men. He trusted Lemuel Hale, who had served with him for years: not only to spot trouble, but either to nip it in the bud himself or sound the alert to a higher authority. But at root he trusted his own judgement more.

She heard the coxswain depart, and Shenton tell her husband that their supper was served. When she entered the front half of the cabin it was to find a table set with the best of the presents they had received at their wedding, the centrepiece an eight-branch silver candelabra from Garrards that had, until very recently, been in pawn. The flames threw a warm and flickering light over the panelled walls, making even the great guns, black and menacing, bowsed to the ship's side, so ugly in daylight, look benign. There was a basket of wine bottles on the floor and a steaming tureen of soup on the table, and as well as Shenton, a couple of seamen in their best clothes standing by to serve them.

'Our first proper meal aboard, my dear,' said Ralph Barclay, handing her to a chair, with a smile and an exaggerated bow. 'The first of many.'

Emily bobbed a response. 'You are too kind, my dear.'

'Our dinner was such a perfunctory affair, I felt supper should be special.'

Emily had been grateful for the fact that getting the ship to sea had taken priority over food, for dinner at three in the afternoon, a good two hours before the accustomed time ashore, was something she was going to have to struggle to get used to.

'I cannot say they will all be as elegant as this,' Ralph Barclay added, 'but while we are in calm water, let us indulge ourselves. Let us see this as yet another celebration of our union.'

The undertone of that remark, and the look with which it was delivered, a direct stare under lowered eyebrows, was designed to tell Emily Barclay that he wished the first test of the double cot to be tonight. Not wishing to dwell on such a thought, she snapped open her napkin and said, 'You must, my dear, tell me about your day.'

His first thought was, I'm damned if I'll tell you I was ripped off a strip by the Commodore. Instead he answered her question with one of his own. 'What is there to tell you that you have not already witnessed?'

That imposed an uncomfortable silence, for the first thing she had observed had been her husband cuffing a man for merely looking at her. Temporary refuge was found in a spoonful of soup. 'There are so many things I do not know, husband, that I fear to speak lest I reveal my ignorance. And I readily admit to leading a sheltered life compared to that of a sailor.'

'They are, I grant you, very different,' Ralph Barclay replied, 'and I am glad you have alluded to it, my dear, for I must tell you that sea service is harsh, for both officers and men.' He dropped his voice then, to a more intimate tone. 'Though it will, by every effort of those aboard, be made as comfortable for you as possible.'

'I would not ask for partiality.'

'My dear,' Ralph Barclay positively crooned, 'your beauty and our station demand nothing less, but,' the voice changed, becoming more businesslike, 'there is a requirement aboard ship for order that can hardly be said to exist elsewhere, so you may witness things for which your refined upbringing leaves you ill prepared.'

The tone in his voice was that of a father talking to a dim child, which lent a certain piquancy to her reply. 'I think I have already observed a degree of difference.'

'Quite.'

'Yet who could doubt the charm of this,' Emily replied brightly, for her husband, she knew, could become morose, and that she did not want.

Her wish was not granted. If not morose, there was a touch of gloom in his response. 'Do not be deceived by the comfort we now enjoy, of a good dinner with the best of our wedding gifts illuminating the table, for once out of the Thames Estuary that would be too risky an item to set out.' Seeing a look which he interpreted as regret, he added hastily, with as jocular a tone as he could muster, 'It would never do to set light to the ship. I fear their lordships would not forgive me for that.'

'Then it will be all the better,' Emily insisted, 'when we can lay it out, for imparting a sense of occasion.'

Ralph Barclay, she knew, was a serious man, more obviously so now than at the time of their betrothal or even after their wedding. He seemed to be caught, as he often was, between wishing to make her happy, and desiring her to have some knowledge of the obverse side of life's coin.

'There will be, my dear, many a day when we will want for any kind of hot food. Every sailor prays for a calm voyage, well aware as he wins his anchor that such a thing is hardly to be expected.'

'How will your latest recruits fare?'

Emily knew it was a maladroit question long before the frown creased her husband's face, yet it was the one she had been dying to ask.

'You mean my volunteers?'

There was a moment's hesitation, a split second when she contemplated challenging him by saying, 'Were they not pressed?' The boy with the bleeding nose had all but confirmed that impression. But that was certain to fracture the mood completely. 'As you say, the volunteers.'

'Some will suffer, it is not unknown for one or two even to succumb.'

'Succumb?'

Ralph Barclay wanted to tell her the truth unvarnished. That men pressed to service brought aboard with them the diseases of their life ashore, fevers and the like that could prove fatal when combined with seasickness. He wanted also to say that during training, which of necessity must be swift, there was no guarantee that a man sent aloft for the first time could cope with the height and the motion of the ship, which in foul weather could be dramatic. Nor could any captain be sure that a new recruit would have the sense always to keep his feet, his body and his hands in a position that would render him safe. If trained hands could fall from the rigging, anyone could and only the good fortune of a heavy heel on the ship would allow a falling man to miss the deck. But that same heel usually meant foul weather, so it was a mute point which was worse; instant oblivion or a slow death from drowning in a sea that precluded the launching of a rescue boat. Unwilling to discuss loss of life in any form, when his mind was more on the possibility of procreation, Barclay took refuge in a platitude.

'We are all God's creatures, my dear, and no one, from the highest to the lowest on this ship, knows when they will be called.' He then added quickly, 'We must write to my dear sisters tonight, to ensure that they know how happy we are.'

Somerset dominated the rest of the meal – family, friends, local politics in the form of dastardly Tories, for Ralph Barclay was a confirmed Whig, the gossip of the county. It was a conversation which, for all the world, they could have had in their own house in Frome. If Emily still felt disquiet about shipboard matters she fought to hide it, and while not encouraging her husband too much, let him know that she was ready to grant him those favours that came to him by right. She would have been less happy to hear the words of the men who had served at table once they returned to the lower deck.

'A double bowline in your hammock knots tonight, lads, for old Barclay will be a'rutting.'

'Like a dog round a bitch's arse he was,' cooed another,

stripping off his best shirt, 'and her musk weren't too secret either. Strikes me as a hot one.'

Shenton had cleared the table, and was busy drinking a bottle of his captain's claret, sure that a man in his state would be too busy remembering his pleasure to recall how many corks had been pulled at dinner. The laughter was loud enough to penetrate the thin bulkheads, which made the steward smile, he being as aware as the others regarding what was taking place.

'So John Pearce,' asked Michael O'Hagan, softly, 'just who are you?' Seeing the hesitation the Irishman added, 'It is very hard to be close to a man who will not trust you.'

'Trust,' Pearce responded, to gain time to think, and time to look around to ensure that for once they were not under observation or close enough to anyone to be overheard. He and Michael were sitting at the mess table, the first moment since coming aboard when they had time on their hands. The others had gone to watch the dancing, which was taking place to the sound of a scraping fiddle.

'You should not be here.'

'None of us should be here!'

'That I will grant you, but you more than most. I am a labourer, no more, you are something very different.'

'Am I so different?'

'Your speech and your manner make me think so. And I am curious to know why you will not give them your true name, though I fear it is no secret now.'

'I was unwise to blurt it out to you; I did so without thought. Charlie Taverner heard it and let his tongue run away with him.'

'For which I think he was sorry.'

'He has said as much himself.'

'They reckon a Paddy to be slow in the head.'

That got a grin and a shake of the head, for Michael O'Hagan was far from that; in fact Pearce reckoned he was a classic example of what his father despaired over, a fellow that was only barred from fulfilment by a society that denied him an education. More worryingly, given the look with which he was favouring his fellow victim of Barclay's press he was also a fellow who was not going to be content to be fobbed off.

'I do not reckon you or your race to be that, Michael, and there are enough Irishmen of repute as proof, the playwright Sheridan and Edmund Burke to name but two.'

O'Hagan looked perplexed. 'These men I do not know.'

Without saying so, the Irishman had told Pearce that as well as being unable to write, he had no ability to read either, for the two names he had mentioned were often in the newspapers. He had to stop himself from enlightening O'Hagan, telling him of men like Sheridan who satirised the society Adam Pearce despised, and of Burke, the brilliant orator who used politics and a savage wit to uphold it.

'What would you gain from knowing that which I wish kept hidden, Michael?'

'I say again, you are not like me.' O'Hagan gestured towards the rest of the Pelicans, ten feet away, backs to the table, eyes concentrated forward as a cocky topman twirled a complex hornpipe, mere spectators, not part of what was going on. 'Nor,' Michael added, 'are you like those others.'

Pearce smiled. 'Not even Gherson, who claims to be a bit of a nabob?'

'Sure, above all, not him.'

'What do you make of Corny?'

'He's lazy and untrustworthy, a man who would betray you, me or anyone else without conscience.'

Pearce thought about the letter, and his promise of money to pay for delivery. 'The rest on our table?' he asked.

'Charlie Taverner I could tolerate, though I think if I were drunk he would live off my purse and be gone when I sobered. Ben Walker is deeper than you if that is possible. Rufus is too young to be anything other than foolish, Scrivens I have concern for, I reckon him doubly ill-suited to this life.' O'Hagan crossed himself swiftly, as he added, 'As we are all, and may God in all his guises get us out of it. But Scrivens is of little interest to me.'

'And I am?'

O'Hagan shrugged. 'I admit to prying. If you do not wish me to do that, sure, just say so plain, for a man has a right to his own tale. But in my life I have moved many times, to work on the shovel in different places with sundry gangs, and not all Irish. I have toiled all over England, sometimes spending a day in one place, at others more than a season, when the job was the digging of a canal.' O'Hagan held up a hand, massive and gnarled. 'But always with these. Now it stands to reason for such a life a man needs a sound body. But he must also have a quick eye to see those on who he can turn his back, and those who he must always face. If I was to say I would not fear turn my back on you, unless it was to aid you?'

'Ah yes,' Pearce replied, responding as Michael reminded him of the help he had rendered, to let Pearce slip away from crowd outside the purser's store.

The pause that followed the acknowledgement annoyed

the Irishman. 'You do not see fit to tell me what you were about?'

'I went to look for the storeroom where my coat and shoes are stored.' Faced with silence, Pearce was forced to add, 'Yours also. What I found was a padlock big enough to keep safe the Crown of England.'

'This ship will have its share of thieves, like any other.'

'Would that I was one of them, Michael, with the ability to pick a lock.'

'And having picked it, what then?'

'Which part of Ireland are you from?' asked Pearce, prevaricating.

'The West, Mayo,' O'Hagan replied, his voice a touch wistful. 'It is the poorest part of the green isle, which makes us good at digging, for the soil we have to work is thin and unforgiving. But that is of no consequence to the moment.'

'What is?'

'Let us say that for all the soil is poor I would rather be there than here. Where you would care to be I do not know.' Michael favoured Pearce with a wide grin. 'Not here I do know, and I confess here's me hoping that if you have some scheme to leave this ship you would not be thinking of going off alone.'

Pearce, aware from the beginning it was leading up to this, was at a loss to know what to say – that he wanted the freedom, should an opportunity present itself, to act alone or in tandem, to use the combined muscle of all of the Pelicans or none. He was not responsible for any of them, as much as they might wish such a thing upon him. Just as they seemed to think he had some kind of plan, when what he only had was a desire to escape and an acute eye for the chance to fulfil that desire, for which he had made a point of keeping his own counsel.

Of them all, he felt in his bones that he could trust Michael O'Hagan, but that did not mean he could easily open up to him, for he was guarded by nature – his vagabond upbringing had made him so. Every few weeks Pearce's father would move to a new town, to a new audience not tired of paying to hear him speak. That left his son, who carried round the collecting hat, little time for friendships – more for fights with local boys who smelt and disliked a stranger. There were better times, though few, when Adam Pearce found a patron willing to house and feed him, and support his work. That meant schooling and new companions for John, but still he was the outsider, which meant more fights to make his mark. Yet there had been friendships too. Faces swam before Pearce's eyes of boys he had loved. But he also remembered those he had allowed himself to trust who had been less than truly faithful. He was sure of only one thing, when it came to such an emotion certainty was not possible.

Getting off the ship would not be easy and Michael must know that. If what he had overheard was correct about the ship's orders, now that they had weighed from Sheerness, then a short stay at Deal would be the only chance, and that had to be a slim one. The Navy was well versed in keeping what it had taken, and just being on dry land was no guarantee of safety. Stories abounded of crimps who did nothing else in wartime than hunt deserters for a bounty. There was much to be said for being alone in any bid for freedom – the security that comes from relying only on yourself. But what if a great deal of muscle was required? If it was, here was the very man. Pearce felt a sudden tinge of guilt at cutting the others out of his thinking; the men who had judged him distressed in the Pelican and had the charity to offer him a bed. Logic might see them as an encumbrance, but that was a poor justification.

Such thoughts were pointless anyway. Right now he did not even know if he would be gifted a chance. If he was, he would have to move swiftly, and if that move needed the help of Michael's muscle then he would, at that point, have to trust him. Would Michael respond as he had previously, asking no questions? The thought that he might not weighed a great deal, but asked, he would never have been able to say why he decided to trust the Irishman now – it was instinct, no more, and perhaps, like other men, he sometimes felt the need to unburden himself was too great to bear.

'I must request that what I tell you goes no further.'

Michael frowned. 'Would a man not have to accept that before saying a word?'

He would, of course, and Pearce knew it well. Looking right into those green, unblinking Irish eyes he observed no guile or treachery and the way Michael held his gaze was reassuring.

'If you would like me to swear on the Holy Father or the Blessed Virgin I will do so.'

Pearce shook his head, smiled, and laid a hand on the other man's shoulder. 'I have known men, Michael, claiming piety, who could lie with their hand on a piece of the True Cross.'

'I have known men like that too, John-boy.'

'Yet I think you're not one of them.' That comment was answered with a nod so emphatic that Pearce found himself speaking almost without realising it. 'Have you ever heard Michael, of a man called Adam Pearce?' Michael shook his head. 'There was a time his name seemed to be on the lips of everyone in the two kingdoms.'

Pearce smiled as he recalled the nickname Old Adam hated, but one by which he might be more easily recognised. 'He is my father, who is also known to some as the Edinburgh Ranter.'

That meant nothing either. 'And what would this man, your Da, be ranting about?'

'At its simplest, Michael, this: if you dug a ship canal from an inland town to the coast, then you should be part owner of what you have created. Every time a vessel sailed that water, you should be paid. If you dug a sewer, the same.'

'A notion that appeals,' Michael replied, grinning broadly, 'though I will pass on what revenues I might get from a sewer.'

'Three years ago my father wrote some pamphlets, that brought on his head a charge of seditious libel.' It was clear Michael didn't understand what that meant, so John added; 'Billy Pitt and his government fear my father's ideas so much that he faces arrest if he sets foot in Britain.'

Pearce described the life he and his father had led – the time before the turmoil in France when life had been rough for what often seemed a lone voice crying in the wilderness: food scarce, barns to sleep in not rooms, occasionally the need to work to pay for a bed. He skipped over the hell of their stay in prison; to describe that too deeply would serve no purpose. Instead he went on to how life had changed following that incarceration, as Correspondence Clubs and Debating Societies sprung up all over the land on news of the Revolution. Adam Pearce went from being a pariah, a nuisance and a felon to a sought-after luminary, a hopeful beacon for the downtrodden of England. But he had also been dogged by government agents – men who wanted nothing more than to put him back behind bars. Every word he spoke was noted and reported, every disturbance caused by his inflammatory remarks held against his name. He had written much before, and it was moot if the pamphlet that brought forth a second King's Bench warrant was any more provocative than any that had preceded it. But the ground had shifted, disenchantment was rife regarding affairs in France and a government that had, up till then, been too frightened to act, took advantage of that.

'He had to flee the country – it was that or a return to the Bridewell – first to Holland and then to Paris. That's where he is now, Michael. Old, unwell, in danger of arrest there too, and for much the same cause – those in power do not like his views and he will not be silent. Indeed, he may well be in a French gaol now for speaking out about the excesses taking place, and I must tell you he lacks the strength to withstand it. I came back in the hope of getting that warrant lifted, for he has friends who might achieve such a thing, so he can come home.'

Pearce could not avoid putting his head in his hands then, assailed once more by the feeling that he had selfishly abandoned Old Adam for fear of what might happen to him, mixed with the deeper fear that his father might not be in prison, but dead.

'And you?'

'I fear I risk arrest too, just for being his son, or for aiding and abetting his writing or his escape from England, I know not which. The men who would arrest him tried to do the same to me yesterday. In running from them I chose the Pelican as a refuge.'

That produced a wry smile from the Irishman. 'And that is why you will not give your name.'

'I have no notion of how potent that name now is,' said Pearce, looking at the deck beams above his head, 'nor how public is the desire to apprehend him. All I know is I cannot help him from a prison cell, though this ship can hardly be said to be better.'

'You are sure you would go to prison?'

'No, but I could not risk it. What if my father and I are seen as one?' Pearce sighed, and produced a sad smile, wondering what had happened to that blind faith he had carried until only a few years ago, the certainty that everything his father believed in was right.

'One question for you, Michael.'

'Which is?'

'Can you swim?'

The Irishman responded with a rueful smile. 'I cannot, so if you get a chance John-boy, to jump overboard and make the shore, think nothing of Michael O'Hagan. Just do it, and if I can come between you and those who would try to stop you, I will.'

'Thank you for that,' Pearce said, again laying a hand on Michael's shoulder, adding, more from wishful thinking than any sense of anticipation, 'So let's hope for a boat.'

The Bosun's whistle blew again, and that was translated for the Pelicans as 'down hammocks'. Many had forgotten what they had learnt earlier about hammock-rigging and to avoid a repeat of the earlier hilarity, Pearce found himself helping several people, including Michael and Scrivens, to rig their hammocks. Once in he now found that Dysart's idea of being snug really meant a hammock slung so close to his neighbour either side that movement was barely possible. But he knew it to be comfortable.

'Ship's company, fire and lights out.'

The guttering candles that had illuminated the maindeck were extinguished, leaving only a glim from the lanterns left at the foot of the companionway and around the mess tables of those on watch. Pearce lay there, still thinking, still running over in his mind, and discarding, ideas for escape, trying and failing to convince his teeming brain that there was nothing he could do till morning and that sleep was now necessary. He heard Michael begin to snore beside him, but that was not singular, half the maindeck resounded to a veritable symphony of nasal notes – that, mingled with a stream of noisy farts. It was with the thought that he had slept in worse places than this, and the more troubling one that he might do so in the future, that mixed with the hope that the morrow and daylight might gift him the chance he needed, that the exhaustion of the last twenty-four hours overtook him.

The sense of falling was like part of a dream until his body crashed into the deck, shoulder first, sending a shaft of pain through his elbow that was quickly overborne as his head thudded into the same planking. The cry that came from another throat failed to penetrate at first, because he was momentarily stunned. But as he rolled his body to get up he saw, by the silhouette of those lanterns still lit, that Charlie Taverner was in similar distress, his hammock hanging down from one line, he in a heap cursing and swearing. Pearce was also sure that he saw a pair of legs scurrying away, belonging to a body that was small enough to slip under the slung hammocks.

He had to crawl over to Charlie Taverner, who had landed

head first, on the same spot that the surgeon had treated that day. He was hurt worse than Pearce, dazed and confused and touching his wound Pearce felt damp, which told him it had begun to bleed again. Pearce himself felt on his head the beginnings of a substantial lump and his elbow was painful. But having fallen in slumber he had been relaxed at the point of contact and reckoned the damage slight. He lifted the end of Charlie's hammock rope, holding it up the frayed end. Obviously it had been sliced through with a knife.

'What bastard…?' swore Charlie, in a thick voice, as Pearce tried to help him to his knees.

'The marine boy from the Pelican,' Pearce replied, as he set about trying to tie up Taverner's hammock with what little rope was left. 'The one they call Martin. I broke his nose last night, and this morning you gave it an elbow. I think he wants his revenge.'

Sleep was fitful after that – the level of snoring was stentorian, the lack of air, with so many bodies packed tight, was suffocating. Besides those constraints Pearce could not rule out a second attempt by the boy, and it was with relief that he heard the sound of Coyle moving through the packed hammocks shouting, 'Show a leg there', and 'Up or down', with the thud of a falling body for those who did not heed the last, as they found the lashing of their hammocks cut away.

A series of whistles blew, and the whole crew began to roll their hammocks. Lashing and stowing them, easy for the seamen, was another farce for the newcomers as none of their attempts at bundle would pass through the hoop help by a swarthy bosun's mate who had, even for a sailor, a rare line in foul abuse. But this time the crew were willing to assist and show them the way – Charlie Taverner found the attitude was not caused by kindness, but by the fact that any delay was likely to interfere with the crew getting their breakfast. Once lashed the hammocks were taken on deck to be stowed in nettings along the side of the ship, or in a rack of similar design at the front of the quarterdeck.

'For the sake o' Christ, dinna lose sight of where you have put it,' warned Dysart.

It was still dark, and cold, so that to be put to work was less of a hardship than standing still, that was until they touched a rope and felt on their raw hands a return of the previous day's pain.

'Mr Sykes,' called Lieutenant Digby, observing how gingerly they took hold of the fibres, 'may I suggest the latest volunteers would be best employed in cleaning below decks. If their hands remain raw they will scarce be any use if we need muscle in a blow.'

'Aye aye, sir,' the bosun replied, before turning to a lanky sailor with a spotted bandana tied above protruding eyes, a prominent nose and a jutting jaw. 'Ridley, you heard what Mr Digby said?'

'I did Mr Sykes.'

The sailor called Ridley took them down to the maindeck, admonishing them to dip their mitts in a tub that stood forward near the manger.

'Piss,' said Ben Walker lifting the lid. 'It's a bucket of piss.'

Ridley's large nose seemed to twitch in response. 'Chamberlye, mate, an' now't to be afeard of, for it is all your get at sea to clean your ducks till it rains. But it will aid your hands also, for there is something in piss that helps to harden the skin.'

'An astringent created by nature,' said the ship's surgeon, Lutyens, who had moved up behind them without being observed.

'Is he Creeping Jesus or what?' whispered Charlie Taverner.

If Ridley heard Charlie he did not respond, replying directly to the surgeon. 'Whatever it be, your honour, it does the trick, even with the poxed sons of bitches we has aboard this barky.'

'Forgive me,' Lutyens enquired, 'I do not know your name or station?'

'Ridley, your honour, bosun's mate.'

'A volunteer?'

'Course,' Ridley replied, surprised enough to double the size of those already popping eyes. 'Hardly have my rating if'n I weren't.'

'Forgive me,' Lutyens insisted, pulling out his little notebook, 'for I am as new as these fellows you command. The ranks and stations of a warship are exceedingly confusing. Would you permit me to write that down?'

Ridley smiled, nodded, and replied in a kindly voice, as though he was the superior person, not Lutyens. 'It'll come to you in time, your honour, just as it will come to this lot.'

Asked, Pearce would have admitted himself to be as baffled as the surgeon regarding who was who aboard ship. Officers in their blue uniform coats were easy, but there was little to determine many of the ranks, for everyone, though not dressed entirely alike, was at least clothed in a similar manner. That was less important than the way they behaved – for instance this Ridley seemed to share the same rating as the rattan-wielding Kemp, yet even on only a minute's acquaintance it was obvious he was very different. He didn't bark and scowl as Kemp continually did, but spoke softly with a benign expression. More than that his hands were empty – there was no cane.

'Now who's going to be first?' Ridley asked, pointing to the tub.

Abel Scrivens proved to be the least squeamish about the chamberlye, and had his hands dipped quickly, his eyes closing tight. Pearce followed suit, wincing as the caustic in the urine hit his raw skin.

'Do likewise when you attend the heads,' Lutyens added, 'for I suspect that the fresher the brew the more efficacious it is. You may also find that slush from the cook will help too. Grease entering into the skin has a soothing effect. There are other unguents…'

'If you don't mind, your honour,' Ridley interrupted, in a slightly exasperated tone. 'We has work to do, and the captain wants us to stand to quarters when it gets light, Christ alone knows why, 'cause if there be a French ship in the offing here, while we are no more'n a cable's length from the Kent shore, we's lost the bloody war without a month yet gone.'

'Of course,' the surgeon replied, in a tone of voice that Pearce sensed was disappointed, an impression that was enhanced by the hunched cast of his shoulders as he moved away and left them to their tasks.

'Now that is an odd bugger,' whispered Ridley. 'Has you seen him creeping round the barky, staring at all and sundry?' No one replied, and it was now Ridley who looked disappointed, and his voice turned gruff as he said, 'Well, you're a chatty crew an' no error. Let's get a'daubing.'

He passed out the materials the men needed, ragged cloth and mops, while a pair were set to filling buckets through an open gunport, not easy with a cannon in the way. 'We wants not to get the bloody deck or the scantlings too wet, so there will be no chucking water about like billyo! It's damp tow and a wipe an' no more, 'cause the bugger won't dry out in this weather, and there's not a one of you that won't be coughing near fit to bring on a rupture if it stays damp a'tween decks.'

Pearce was looking at the open gunport, which had been left that way even after the bucket had been filled, wondering if, with Ridley's back turned he could get through it. How long was a cable's length? Could he swim the distance, whatever it was? The blowing wind, a cold one that whistled round his bare feet made him disinclined even to try. The water would be freezing and besides it was still dark. But logic dictated that the only way to dry 'tween decks was to leave the gunports open to the breeze, and that might well last till dawn. He eased over, while vigorously rubbing the planking on the ship's side, as he tried to have a look at the possible route of escape.

'Now, mate,' said Ridley, who suddenly appeared by his side. 'You don't want to be a'rubbing those scantlings so they wear do you?' Pearce looked at him and said nothing, but there was clear comprehension in Ridley's look, even if there was no antagonism. 'And if you was thinkin' of taking a dive through that there open port I should tell you that there are, as often as not, marines on the deck with loaded muskets, and they will put a ball in you as soon as blink.'

'Would that not be murder?'

Ridley shook his head slowly, thumb and forefinger pulling at his nose. 'Shooting a deserter, mate. It wouldn't get no further than the captain's log, with as like as not a pat on the back from their lordships for doin' things proper when it's examined. Now for my peace of mind, since I don't like to think on anybody floating dead in the water or hauled bleeding into our eight-oared cutter, take up a mop and stay amidships.'

It made sense to comply, for this was not the time. But when the sun came up he would head for one of those open ports, and he would also know, before he made his exit, what was meant by a cable's length.

Ralph Barclay came on deck at four bells in the morning watch, when it was still dark, his face illuminated by the light from the binnacle locker set forward of the ship's wheel, unaware of the nudges from all and sundry as they looked to see if his night of carnality had had any effect on him. Looking at the slate, and calculating course and distance, he reckoned that the frigate was about to clear the North Foreland off Ramsgate. The Thames pilot had departed during the night, and he could thank God that his ship was briefly back under his control – briefly because he would need a Deal pilot to get him through the Brake Channel, which cut from the north-east between the East Kent shore and that ship's graveyard called the Goodwin Sands.

'Mr Collins, at what time do you anticipate a change of course?'

'Five bells, sir,' the master replied.

Half an hour, Barclay thought. That could be delayed because he would have to stand to off Pegwell Bay until a pilot came to him – it would be full daylight, probably the forenoon watch before that happened. Yet if he stuck to ship routine and gave the men their breakfast at the appointed hour of seven fifteen he would have to drag them from their mess tables when he beat to quarters, which was not a good idea. Better a late breakfast than a disturbed one.

'Mr Digby,' he said, to the officer of the watch, 'I am surprised to see that the decks have not yet been cleaned.'

'I had intended to wait until daylight, sir, so that the men could properly see what they were about.'

'Mr Digby, my standing orders for this ship do not allow you the liberty of such a decision.'

'Sir.'

Barclay's standing orders were, to Digby's mind, too inflexible. Be that as it may, all captains issued them and he was obliged to obey them.

'Note it, sir,' Barclay added. 'I will say nothing on this occasion, but should it occur again, I will feel obliged to put my displeasure in writing.'

'Aye, aye, sir.'

'Now, Mr Digby, oblige me by beating to quarters, and running out the maindeck guns.'

Whistles blew, a drum began to beat, and a hail of shouting ensued as the crew who knew their stations rushed to the cannon that lined the sides and cast off the guns, hauling them away from the side, to poke out of the open gunports, while others tied off the mess tables to the deck beams above and moved all the loose items like benches, barrels and bread sacks to the centre of the deck where they were out of the way. Ridley, shepherding his charges back up on to the upper deck was passed by a couple of midshipmen and Lieutenant Digby, as they descended from the upper deck and took position amidships between the guns, which had been run out as if they were about to engage in battle.

On deck Ralph Barclay, with Roscoe now at his side and

four men on the wheel, stood watching a sky turning from black to pale grey, as the shoreline changed, very slowly, from nothingness to a distinct line, beginning to colour until the buildings of Ramsgate began to take shape. Behind Barclay, his drummer, young Martin, back in his red coat and tricorn hat was rat-tat-tatting away, setting up a noise that echoed from white chalk cliffs. When that noise ceased and no perceivable threat could be seen on the horizon, that Barclay could 'see a grey goose at a quarter mile', all aboard knew that it was now officially dawn.

'Mister Collins, lay the ship on a course to put us off the Brake Channel.'

The increasing light brought little joy to Pearce, for although he could see land with full daylight, he could also see as they came on a parallel course just how much seawater now lay between ship and shore. With nothing against which to judge the actual distance he could not be sure, but if it could hardly be less than half a mile, and disturbed enough to throw up a light spume which, carried on the wind brought the taste of salt to his lips. There were fishing smacks about, with a crowd of gulls screeching around their rigging, but they were as far off as the coast, and no more enticing.

'Mr Roscoe, you may house the gun. Bosun, once that is completed you can pipe the hands to breakfast.'

Sent below again, the Pelicans were surrounded by barked orders that saw the guns bowsed up again so that their muzzles touched the wood of the now closed ports. Heavy rope breechings tied to great ring bolts fastened to the ship's side held them secure. Within a minute mess tables were being lowered from the deck head where they had been triced up, to nestle once more between the cannon, and benches made up of casks and planks to sit on were taken from amidships and put back in place.

Within minutes the deck had gone from a fighting platform back to what it had been before – the place where the crew took their ease and ate their food. Small artefacts that made each mess table a trifle different – tins, carved ornaments of wood and bone – were replaced and Pearce watched the scene as if it was a play, only performed in the open instead of in a theatre. It was only when the activity tailed off that he realised that he and his mess had stood watching instead of doing the same.

'Come on, you lubbers on twelve,' Dysart called, 'get your table unlashed and doon, then get them kids off tae the galley or you'll no get ony breakfast.'

'When we drops anchor at Deal,' said Molly, 'you won't be able to see the side of the ship for bumboats. But we won't rest long, 'cause I hear the convoy is ready to weigh and waiting for us. That's when I will get your notes into the hands of men who will do the deed.'

'For which we thank you.'

'Happen, I'll need a favour myself, lad,' the old sailor said, 'an' you'll be able to oblige.'

'You only have to ask,' Gherson replied.

'Who knows, if we are delayed by a foul wind, you might get yourself ashore before we weigh.'

'Then I pray for it.'

Molly put a hand on his shoulder and said, 'You'll not mind a bit if I don't share that. A sailor going deep would be a fool to pray for a foul wind.'

Pearce, watching from his own mess table, wondered once

more if Gherson knew what he was getting himself into, and as he returned to the table he had a terrible temptation to ask him. Back on the table Gherson had just left, a member of Molly's mess was joshing him. 'He's a pretty number, that one, mate.'

'He's nowt but a tease, friend,' Molly replied, aiming a smile at Gherson who had turned to look back at him. 'Who thinks by flashing me that smirk of his, and waving them long dark eyelashes, he can have me eating out of his hand.'

'Then why bother with him?'

'Bit of fun, just a bit of fun. But I won't go trusting him, 'cause I smell a wrong un' there.'

Gherson's letter, and Pearce's along with it, had gone into the hands of Lemuel Hale. The coxswain would take them to the captain, who would know he owed the source a favour. For someone like Molly that was precious – a favour in the bank with someone like Ralph Barclay was to be prized.

CHAPTER NINE

'John Wilkes,' exclaimed Ralph Barclay, as he looked at the superscription on Pearce's letter. He had already read Gherson's letter, a straightforward plea to a woman to rescue the man whose heart she had so completely won, with an aside to keep her husband in the dark regarding both their love and his situation.

'John Wilkes,' Barclay repeated, 'is that old rogue still alive?'

'Captain Barclay?' Emily enquired, looking up from an embroidery ring on which she was sewing HMS *Brilliant*, for she was not sure if her husband was addressing her, or just talking out loud.

'This letter, from one of my volunteers, the one who entered himself as Truculence, is addressed to John Wilkes at Grosvenor Square.' The look of incomprehension on his wife's face invited him to add, 'He was a famous, or should I say infamous, radical politician. Libelled half the government when he was a Member of Parliament, and claimed privilege to save himself. Did it once too often though and found himself in gaol for his sins. Must be eighty if he is a day. Before your time, my dear – dammit, what am I saying, it's before my time.' Forced to give a look of apology for that lapse in language, Ralph Barclay took refuge in breaking the seal.

'You intend to read it?' Emily asked.

'It is my duty, Mrs Barclay.' Looking down to read he did not see Emily frown – in the world in which she had been raised you did not read other people's correspondence. She watched him as he scanned the lines, his brow alternately furrowing and clearing.

'Fellow has a good hand, and damn me, begging your pardon, if he don't write in French, which I can only make out one word in ten. Would you oblige me, my dear, I know your French to be much better than mine.'

'I'm not sure, husband…'

Her husband's response was quite sharp. 'Mrs Barclay, I cannot believe you would hesitate to help me.'

'You are sure such inquisitiveness is necessary?'

'Inquisitiveness? What a strange word to employ. I have told you it is my duty. Hale has already alerted me to this fellow, and I have marked him myself. Do you not recall his insolence yesterday when coming aboard? He is the one I had to chastise for daring to stare at you.'

'Him?'

'Yes, and he could be dangerous, this could be dangerous.' Seeing her still hesitate as he brandished the letter, he added, 'I believe young Farmiloe has decent French.'

Emily remembered better than her husband knew that very brief exchange of a look that had ended up with the poor fellow being punished. Unsure of her motives, mentally reassuring herself that she might as well do as she was asked because if she did not, Farmiloe would, Emily held out her hand, took the letter and began to read, Ralph's eyes on her and him fidgeting impatiently.

After a full two minutes, during which he was certain his wife had perused it more than once, he demanded, 'Well?'

'It is not in any way a normal letter,' she replied, 'indeed, apart from the date and the name of the ship, it almost seems to be written in some kind of code.'

'Read it to me.'

'It addresses your Mr Wilkes and has some kind words to say regarding his reputation.' Ralph Barclay snorted derisively at that. 'And refers to a man and a youth that he met in the company of James Boswell in June 1790 at a certain house in Arlington Street, Piccadilly.'

That made Ralph Barclay's heart jump; Boswell was the biographer of Dr Samuel Johnson and quite a well-known Scot. 'This fellow has, it seems, connections.'

'Then it goes on, "Having yourself been at the mercy of an unforgiving and malevolent law, you realise more than most that flight from proscription is not the answer. You will know for certain to whom this refers when I tell you he resides in the Quartier de Saint Généviere, in the rue Saint Etienne de Gres, Paris, an address from which he has written to you on several occasions."'

'I do believe that Wilkes fled to Paris to avoid arrest,' Barclay mused, 'but Lord in Heaven I was scarcely breeched when that happened.'

'This place of seeming refuge has become too dangerous for one who in some sickness needs friends to see his proscription lifted in the land of his birth. I, the younger of the two you met with Mr Boswell, came to effect that, but now I find myself in the same condition as Doctor Johnson's black servant, and in need of the same office that you performed for him.' Emily looked up and added. 'As you know, there is no signature.'

'Wilkes,' Ralph Barclay said, shaking his head.

'I am forced, husband, since you say this all happened so long ago, to ask how you know so much of this historical creature.'

'My father, your Great Uncle once removed, tried to arrest him on a magistrate's warrant, and was had up for trespass because of Wilkes' parliamentary immunity. He has, therefore, been a person of some consequence in my life, but not one with any happy associations.'

'Doctor Johnson's black servant?' Emily asked.

'Means nothing,' Barclay lied, taking back the letter, for he knew very well that the man in question had been taken up by a press-gang and thanks to the intervention of John Wilkes had been released on the instructions of the Admiralty, a service that this Pearce fellow clearly sought for himself from a man who, old and infirm as he was, still had some influence. At the same time he was mulling on the surname Pearce, for there was a nagging thought at the back his mind, one that he could not pin down, that it meant something.

Emily wanted to beard her husband and nail his lie, to ask why a man like the writer of the letter in her hand would volunteer for service at sea. He was clearly educated, and he could write, in excellent if idiomatic French, which implied that he also spoke the language with some fluency.

Ralph Barclay was thinking once more of the dangers inherent in pressing men like this – those who could write and had contacts with people who could plead at the highest level on their behalf. But this man had not pleaded those connections to him, which would have seen him immediately released, and, in addressing his complaint, he had not made it directly to the Admiralty but to an intermediary he hoped would act for him.

'This fellow,' Ralph Barclay said, 'has something to hide.'

'I think the nature of his letter implies that certainly,' Emily replied, without adding the obvious concomitant that the man her husband called Truculence, and she knew, thanks to her eavesdropping, to be named Pearce, also very obviously wanted to be free from this ship.

'Then far be it from me to challenge his wish. The Navy between decks has been home to many a scoundrel before. One more will make little odds. Let him hide on my maindeck. If he does not wish to do so, let him speak up.'

Ralph Barclay folded Pearce's letter and placed both it, and Cornelius Gherson's, in his desk drawer. But at the back of his mind he lacked the certainty he was determined to display for the benefit of his wife. HMS *Brilliant* would, within an few hours, anchor off Deal, hours in which he would think on this, and the option of putting the fellow, who might well be trouble, ashore.

Cleaning the decks followed breakfast; wetted from head-pumps rigged over the side, they were then coated with a thin dash of sand. The Pelicans were in the line that worked on that, trousers rolled above their knees to stop them getting wet, using great blocks of stone called holystones, which they rubbed over the planking to remove the stains and indentations that had been left by the previous day's loading. Behind them came the sweepers, the men who removed both sand and sawdust, leaving the swabbers, to mop the now scarified deck.

Lastly came a team with long cloths, they flogging the deck in a futile attempt, in such a cold and damp climate, to get it dry. At least, with all the activity going on around them, it was possible to talk as they worked.

'Take it easy, old fellow,' said Pearce, who had got himself on one side of Abel Scrivens, while Michael O'Hagan had taken the other.

'Less of the old,' Abel replied, panting through the smile, even though he could scarce be said to be toiling hard. 'Were we on land I might show you a clean pair of heels.'

'The only clean heels I ever saw,' said Michael, his small holystone, called a bible because of its size and shape, rasping on the sand, 'were resting on a poor man's neck.'

'Amen to that,' Abel sighed. He raised his back to straighten it, a hand going to his spine, obviously in some discomfort from his position, until a voice from behind ordered him to get labouring and a toe was jabbed into his backside.

On the far side of O'Hagan, Charlie Taverner was guying young Rufus, heavy breathing punctuating his words. 'Bet you're glad you ran from...that bond of yours, Rufus...Just think, a few years of this...and you'll be a full-qualified drudge...I can just see the sign above your tradesman door... raw mitts holding a ragged mop.'

'Bugger off, Charlie,' Rufus replied testily, and with a similar shortage of breath.

'Well, tan my hide...not that you would be able.'

'Half of London...was up for that job, Charlie...if only you'd stood still...long enough.'

'It's a mistake...to stand still...Rufus... Dogs piss on your leg.'

'Sure,' said Michael O'Hagan, hardly puffing, 'are we not being pissed on now.'

'We are that, O'Hagan.'

'Oh for a pitcher of the Pelican's best ale.'

'Talk about piss,' Charlie wheezed. 'Must be handy...selling beer...and having a tavern...right by the Thames.'

'Handy for more'n thinning ale, and this we're doing is the proof enough.'

'What in God's name...brought you into the Liberties... every night, O'Hagan?' asked Charlie Taverner. 'You never had...a writ out on you...did you?'

'If it were not you I was talking to I would be tempted to say I came for the company.'

Charlie scowled for a brief second, until he realised that O'Hagan was ribbing him. 'Well...few in the Pelican sought yours...I can tell you.'

Michael grinned. 'Rosie was quite partial, I seem to recall.'

'She had rotten taste...I recall!'

The snappy way Charlie Taverner said that told Pearce a great deal: that his dislike of Michael was not merely to do with drunken brutality, it had just as much to do with jealousy. He recalled the blowsy serving maid with her broad hips and huge bosom, and could not help but smile as he conjured up a picture of Michael and her in a sweaty embrace.

'But then, of course,' Charlie added, in a sour voice, 'you had the means...to pay for your pleasure.'

Michael elbowed Taverner. 'Which comes from having led such a virtuous life. There's a lot to be said for being an honest fool instead of a thieving one.'

'All hands to wear ship.'

That loud call cut off any chance of a response from Charlie, and they were hustled back on to the ropes as HMS

Brilliant changed course, and the wind that had come at them from near dead astern now came in over the starboard quarter, making the frigate heel slightly so that the deck was now canted. They were also in a swell that gently dropped then lifted the bows, so that many a face was turning green with the motion.

'Mr Sykes,' said Lieutenant Roscoe, 'I think it is time we saw which of our new fellows can get aloft.'

'Aye, aye, sir,' the Bosun replied.

'These are called the shrouds,' said Sykes, pointing to the wide squares of rope that ran from the side of the ship, narrowing to a point a third of the way up the mast where a constricted hole led to a platform, which the bosun termed the cap. 'And just so you know, we are sailing easy with just topsails set, and the wind coming in nicely over our starboard quarter, with hardly a heel on the barky, so we ain't got nothing to worry about.'

Sykes, rolling easily, indicated both sails and wind direction, knowing that these men would be unfamiliar with the sea. The pity was, he thought, looking at some of the vacant faces, they would still be that way even if they circumnavigated the globe. Every head of those taken from the Pelican was craned upwards, looking at the yards, none showing any degree of happy anticipation, for having watched the topmen at their labours all knew what was about to be asked of them. One or two, either through indifference or stupidity, were more interested in the sword fighting lessons taking place of the forecastle, which under the direction of old and deaf Mr Thrale involved most of the seamen on the ship as well as the midshipmen.

'They are like a ladder,' Sykes added, 'pay attention there – and as safe as that if you clap on proper. And just so you know that what I say be true, I have fetched a couple of my mates to show you.'

Pearce recognised Ridley, who had supervised them at their t'ween decks cleaning that morning, and just as then he had a kindly look about him. The other bosun's mate was a swarthy sailor with un-English features and a jet-black pigtail who answered to the name Costello. He was actually grinning, though whether in friendliness or in anticipation of the fun to be had from their inexperience it was too early to tell. Behind this Costello stood Kemp, rattan in hand, glaring at the group in his habitual way as if by doing so he would scare them into paying attention.

Called first, Costello came forward and jumped nimbly on to the side of the ship and began to climb slowly, as Sykes talked. 'You will observe that Costello has gone up on the weather side, so that the breeze, for what it is, is at his back, pressing him on, just as it will create a heel on the ship which aids the climber by making the ascent less steep. It is not much now, but in a strong gale going up the wrong side means a vertical ascent and the risk of being blown off into the sea. Note that he always has one hand and one foot engaged.'

Sykes added as Costello disappeared, 'He has gone through what we call the lubber's hole on to the mainmast cap, but that is not the route you will take in time. Aloft Ridley.'

The second bosun's mate sprung up to the ropes and ascended much more in the fashion that Pearce had observed of the fancy topmen, quick hands and feet, almost racing until he reached that hole. But, like them, he didn't go through it, he transferred his body to another set of shrouds that lay near vertical, and scrambled on to the outer edge of the cap with little difficulty to join Costello.

'I sense Mr Sykes has done this many times before,' said Lutyens, as both Costello and Ridley returned to the deck, hand over hand and with ease, by way of a backstay. 'He is easy in his manner of instruction.'

Emily Barclay gave a slight start when Lutyens spoke for she had not heard him move to join her at the poop rail, where she too was watching the training proceed with a degree of absorption, not least because the author of the letter she had read to her husband was part of it, very obviously so because, with one exception, he was the tallest of the group. Having read his words she was intensely curious to observe the source. Part of her reaction to Lutyens was induced by the guilty knowledge that such an interest was unwise.

'I hazard he could instruct all he likes, sir,' she replied, to cover her confusion. 'Nothing would induce me to climb to such a height.'

'I confess a similar reluctance,' Lutyens replied, 'while acknowledging that it must be safe, for the men who work aloft do it dozens of times daily.'

Emily frowned. 'How many of those men below us would share that sentiment?'

'Few, but it is to be hoped that familiarity will breed…'

'Not contempt?' Emily asked, mischievously interrupting.

Lutyens smiled. 'I was about to say competence.'

She looked at the surgeon's singular profile; high forehead and hairline, eyes that protruded enough to be obvious and a nose-shape that reminded her of a whippet puppy, and wondered what had brought him aboard HMS *Brilliant*. He was, according to her equally curious husband, the only son of the Pastor of the Lutheran Church in London, a place of worship frequented by Queen Charlotte, a native German, and sometimes by King George himself, who still had an attraction to the religion of his Hanoverian ancestors. Lutyens' father was a fair way to being the Queen's confessor, which made him an intimate of royalty and the court. With connections like that, the ship's surgeon could surely have had what he wanted in terms of employment. Emily Barclay might know little of the world outside her Somerset home, but she did know that it was singular for anyone to have influence and not employ it.

'How do you find life aboard, Mr Lutyens?' she asked. 'After all it must be very strange considering that to which you are accustomed.' He turned and smiled, which had a pleasant effect on his unusual features. But he did not speak. 'Forgive me,' Emily said quickly. 'It is unforgivable to make so direct an enquiry.'

'Not so, Mrs Barclay,' Lutyens replied. 'I am happy to admit it is strange, and to confess to my ignorance to the whole of my surroundings. I certainly find everything very unfamiliar, as, I hazard, do you, yet I also find it a matter of deep fascination.' Emily Barclay's enquiring look encouraged him to continue. 'Take the men you are now watching...'

'I came merely to take the air,' said Emily brusquely, at the same time giving Lutyens a searching stare to see if he had divined her true interest, relieved to see that he was not looking at her at all.

'Quite, and very efficacious it is. But for myself there is another motive.'

'Am I to be allowed to share it?'

'Why not? I confess to an interest in the human spirit in all its guises, the way it reacts to upheaval, sudden change

– dislocation, perhaps, being a better word. Those fellows, literally being shown the ropes, must be suffering from an extreme degree of that. Two days ago they led a very different existence and it is clear that they were not, as statute has it, bred to the sea, so they should not in truth be here. Do you not find their situation curious also?'

Emily, disconcerted by what the surgeon was saying, which only served to underline her own disquiet regarding her husband's actions, was spared a reply by sudden activity on the quarterdeck. It was almost palpable the way the officers below them stiffened as soon as the marine boot crashed on the wooden deck. Ralph Barclay appeared and stood arms akimbo, then moved to the windward side of the deck, which was immediately cleared, for this was by custom the captain's private space. Close to the weather gangway as he paced forward, he stopped to listen to Bosun Sykes explain, in detail, what was required to work aloft, thinking that in size and shape he had pulled together an unlikely bunch.

'Mr Sykes,' he called, 'I suggest that time is not on your side. We are about to take on board a Deal pilot and once he is on the deck I cannot delay. If you wish these men to experience climbing the shrouds before that happens you will need to be quick.'

'Aye, aye, sir,' replied Sykes, before looking at them with a smile. 'Now who is going to be first?'

'Mr Sykes, the man closest to the shrouds should be first, and I trust you know how to deal with any reluctance.'

Rufus Dommet, in his gauche way, had failed to notice that those who stood with him had inched back since Costello had first started to clamber up the shrouds, leaving him well to the fore. Thus it was he Sykes indicated should proceed, a request which made Rufus step back smartly. Sykes was at his side in a second, his voice low.

'Get up them shrouds now, boy, for I don't want to have to drive you to it. But drive you I will, if I must.'

'Is that disinclination, Mr Sykes?' called Barclay, in an encouraging voice. 'Let one man delay and they all will.'

Sykes called back, 'Just gifting him some advice, sir,' before he took Rufus's arm and hauled him to the bulwarks. 'Now you have been told, just clap on. As long as you have one arm and one foot working you need never fear.'

Rufus remained rooted to the spot, until both Ridley and Costello moved either side of him to propel him forward. Having got him to the side, they lifted him bodily on to the top of the bulwark, forcing him to reach for one of the ropes on the shrouds.

'Right, mate,' said Ridley, 'get a foot on there and start climbing, for if you don't that bastard Barclay will keelhaul you.'

'Ever seen a man keelhauled?' asked Costello, in a gravelly voice. 'Seen a man go under the ship and come up the other side with scarce an inch of unbloodied skin on him?'

'That there water looks cold,' Ridley added, 'and that is where you are going if you don't go aloft.'

The grisly thought of a keelhauling, and the threat of that freezing grey-green water, made Rufus put his foot where it was required, and slowly he began to climb. The next candidate was brought forward before he was a third of the way up, treated similarly, placed where he really had no choice. Michael O'Hagan stepped forward without demur, saying to Pearce, 'Sure, if you'd seen some of the scaffold I have had to work on, built by men of little sobriety, this would not cause you to fear.'

Pearce followed him, not with any confidence, because he had little knowledge of heights, but determined that if this was a test of nerve it was not one he was going to fail. He soon discovered it was nothing like any ladder he had ever climbed. The ropes in both his hands and beneath his feet had a life of their own, and the motion of others on the same set of shrouds made the whole apparatus live. Above him, one fellow slipped and was left hanging on by a hand, scrabbling with his foot, and Pearce had the sudden vision of him dropping and taking everyone below with him into the sea, but the fellow managed to get a foothold and began to climb again. Pearce didn't move, he looked over his shoulder, thinking that closer to shore, and in smoother, inshore water, to dive from here could put him well clear of the ship's side, with the chance to swim at some speed.

'This is too slow, Mr Sykes,' called Barclay, his tone less patient.

'Move you,' Sykes snapped at Pearce, before replying to the captain. 'It is my opinion that more haste makes for less speed, sir.'

'I think he means,' Lutyens whispered to Emily Barclay, 'that one falling man would make his task even harder.'

'Impossible, I should think,' Emily replied.

'I have noted that opinion Mr Sykes,' said Barclay, 'but you will oblige me by following what I now say to be a direct order.'

Pearce was well above the deck now, and, looking down at Ralph Barclay, he felt a wholly specious sense of superiority. Progress had slowed as each man gingerly negotiated the lubber's hole, affording him a chance to turn again and look at the view, which while not spectacular provided some interest, given the low lying nature of the nearest shore, the great bight of a sandy and muddy bay and the snow-white cliffs that edged it to the north. For the first time since being brought aboard he had a slight feeling of pleasure, for to be so high and be afforded such a view was agreeable.

It was now Ridley's turn to yell at him. 'You there! Truculence, move you arse,' forcing Pearce to look up and see that his route was now clear.

'Take that man's name, Mr Thrale,' yelled Barclay, to the officer of the watch. 'I will have no foul usage of language on deck with my wife aboard.'

'Women is ever trouble on a ship,' said Kemp, still hovering on the gangway just in case he and his rattan were required. Several heads on the foc'stle had turned, having heard what the captain said.

'What, like the gunner's wife?' asked a carpenter's mate, kneeling next to Kemp, busy repairing a broken cleat.

'She don't count, fat sow.'

'What about them two lovelies that's stowed in the cable tier?'

'They ain't women, they's whores,' snarled Kemp, flicking his cane to the poop, not sure if the carpenter was joshing him. It would be maddening if he was not – the idea that some of his shipmates had smuggled women aboard and he was ignorant, for he had long ago learnt that, being unpopular, such things were not vouchsafed to the likes of him. The thought gave extra venom to his next remark. 'I'm talking about a proper woman, like that stood up there wi' the surgeon, one with ears too gentle for a bit of a blaspheme.'

'It would perhaps be best if I went below,' said Emily, in an embarrassed whisper. 'I would not want my mere presence to be the cause of a man getting into trouble.'

'I would advise that,' said Lutyens, with an upward jerk of his head, 'for if we are here to indulge in a touch of observation we are not alone. Eyes are upon you.'

Emily looked to the mainmast cap, to where Pearce now stood, obviously looking directly at her. He had on his face the kind of half-amused stare that young men used in a crowded ballroom to let a girl know that she was the object of their interest, and not just the possessor of a dance card. The odd thought popped into her head that such an expression was utterly at odds with the man's station, that he had somehow managed to block out the present surroundings and take her back to a more familiar world. She could almost feel the power of his personality, and it was very disconcerting. Emily dropped her eyes quickly, and blushing, made for the steps that would take her back to the cabin, aware as she left of Lutyens' eyes following her. When the surgeon looked up again it was to find himself under scrutiny.

Pearce, for just a precious minute free to stand at stare, was wondering about this surgeon; was he as ubiquitous in the officer's part of the ship as he was before the mast, scribbling down anything that took his fancy? Was the captain's wife a subject of that study, and if so, what had Lutyens concluded? He had an overwhelming desire to know what they had been talking about, a craving that found no satisfaction in the face of the man he was staring at.

'Not Abel,' said Rufus Dommet in his ear, breaking that train of thought. 'He'll never get up here.'

Pearce looked down to see a solitary Abel Scrivens, the last of the group, trying to edge backwards, then lifted his eyes to observe the way Barclay was fixated by the scene before him, standing, feet spread to take the motion of the ship, hands behind his back, exuding impatience.

'Hates heights,' added Ben Walker, 'always has. He would never do any ladder work.'

'Then God help him,' Pearce replied.

'Name?' demanded Sykes, of a man who was shaking with fear, backing away, seemingly determined not to go aloft.

'Scrivens.'

'Move, Scrivens,' the bosun growled, 'or I will be obliged to fetch over Kemp, who I think you know, to get you to shift.'

Kemp had already moved from the gangway, drawn to a man who afforded him some gratification when struck, being as he was, a right noisy squealer. Sykes did not want to force Scrivens up the shrouds, for to his mind there was no point. Some men could not do it and there was an end to it, with no good coming of coercion, more likely something dire. Anyone aloft and uncertain threatened not only his own person but those with whom he worked, and no Yeoman of the Sheets, in charge on the ship's yards, would thank him for that. He had served with captains before to whom he could have appealed, and left the likes of Scrivens to haul on ropes for eternity, but he had also shared a deck with men like his present captain who would brook no dissent.

Ralph Barclay might not have bothered if he had not been so short-handed, especially in the article of trained hands. To get from his ship what he wanted every man who had a rating of able or below would have to be of use in every department, on the guns, aloft on the yards, or just hauling on a fall to position a yard.

'Mr Sykes,' Barclay called, his voice even, almost benevolent. 'I am aware that your warrant is a new one, and that perhaps you have not clearly understood my order.'

'I have, sir.'

'Then be so good, Mr Sykes, as to follow it to the letter.'

It was crude but effective. The bosun might have sympathy for a man like Scrivens, but Ralph Barclay had just humiliated him in front of everyone by referring to the fact of his recent promotion from bosun's mate to a full warrant as a standing officer. He could not remove him, promote or demote him, for his warrant came from a higher authority, but to a man who needed to keep the respect of the crew, what had been said should be sufficient to harden his heart.

'Right,' he said to his two assistants, 'get this bugger up them shrouds, and clout him if he freezes.' Then Sykes turned, upset at his own harshness, and saw that Kemp had come to assist. 'You can stow that rattan, Kemp. You're too free with it.'

Kemp had the cane raised ready to strike at Scrivens' back, but even though he opined that Captain Barclay wouldn't object, he declined to use it in the face of such strictures from a man who was his immediate superior. Scrivens was lifted between Ridley and Costello and they tried and failed to drag him to the side. Where the scrawny creature found the strength to dig in his heels surprised them, for he didn't budge.

'We'll chuck you in the bloody drink so help me, you skinny toad, if you don't get up them shrouds,' snarled Costello, no longer the grinning and jocular fellow he had been earlier.

What emerged was very close to a cat's meow. 'I can't.'

'You got to,' Ridley added, jumping up on to the bulwark and holding out a hand, 'for we ain't taking no grief for you being shy.'

Scrivens kept his hands firmly by his side, and Kemp stepped forward, this time without interference, and swiped him hard.

Costello ignored the screaming response and grabbed Scrivens' hand and lifted it to where Ridley could grab it, and with a heave Scrivens was pulled upwards, Costello pushing at his feet to get them on to something solid.

'Don't look down,' Ridley grunted, as Costello joined them on the bulwark and together they dragged the unwilling Scrivens to a point where they could place his hands on the ropes.

What followed was slow, painfully so, each hand and foot movement forced on Scrivens. Getting him through the lubber's hole looked to be impossible until first Pearce, and then O'Hagan took a wrist to haul him on to the platform, where his mates were quick to congratulate him and tell him there was nowt to fear. Standing there, forty feet in the air and as white as a sheet, free to look about him and down, swaying on a mast that was moving slowly back and forth through an arc of some ten feet, Scrivens was promptly sick.

'Enough of this farrago,' said Ralph Barclay. 'Get those damnable fellows down.'

It needed a competent pilot to get HMS *Brilliant* to a secure berth in the Downs but it was Barclay's misfortune to be saddled with an idiot who, it later transpired, had got his situation through his connections not his ability. He very nearly ran them aground before they went half a league and only a leadsman in the chains, alerting the quarterdeck to the rapidly shoaling water, allowed Ralph Barclay to haul off, obliging him to take charge himself.

An anchorage that stretched five miles from the bottom of Pegwell Bay to Walmer Castle, with a width of three between the treacherous Goodwin Sands and the shingle of the Kent shore, should have had ample room to accommodate a frigate and Davidge Gould's sloop, which was following in his wake. But with hundreds of merchant ships, the components of several convoys crowded in to that space, none of them showing any inclination towards regimentation in the way they anchored, it needed a strong nerve and a skilful crew to get a man-o'-war safely to the part of the waterfront reserved for the Royal Navy.

Barclay certainly displayed a strong nerve, even though inside he was terrified of public disgrace. His ship, however, did not have the skilful crew it needed, so progress was not only slow, but hazardous, with the frigate forced to back topsails half a dozen times to avoid a collision with either a vessel or the taut anchor cable that kept it secure. And all the time his consort, *Firefly*, looked set to run him aboard across his stern. Several times Davidge Gould's bowsprit came over *Brilliant*'s taffrail. Only exemplary seamanship from Gould in backing and filling, and good fortune for Barclay, saved both vessels from calamity.

It was a blessing that the wind stayed light, for in any sort of blow, Barclay would have been forced to luff up and drop his best bower wherever he could. As it was, after a scary two hours of manoeuvring, in which he and his officers became hoarse with shouting, and his crew disgruntled once more at the delay to their dinner, *Brilliant*, with HMS *Firefly* in attendance, dropped anchor opposite Deal Castle, just south of the Navy Yard, in that part of the anchorage reserved for King's ships, several of which, on the seaward side, rode at anchor nearby. No sooner had the metal fluke hit the water than the admiral commanding at the Downs sent up from his official residence an order for both captains to repair ashore immediately.

Pearce, hauling on ropes, running here, there and everywhere on the frigate's deck, had been praying for a collision as the sails were backed and reset, only to be backed again two minutes later. He saw all about him a chance to escape, for sometimes the frigate was a mere twenty feet from the side of another ship, and a hollering, angry and blasphemous voice telling them to sheer off. He was flabbergasted by the number of craft within view, from enormous vessels flying the flag of the Honourable East India Company that dwarfed the frigate, to craft that looked too small to brave the open sea.

The mass of smaller boats bobbing around, transporting supplies or people from ship to shore was just as staggering, and it was not Pearce alone who looked hungrily at those returning from some errand without goods or passengers. And there, no more than a hundred yards distant, and plain to the naked eye was the Deal seafront, rows of tall, salt-streaked houses perched on the edge of the steep shingle beach, split by a series of enticing narrow alleyways that promised to take a running man out of sight. What lay beyond that he did not know – more obstacles no doubt – but since there was no way of foreseeing those he tried to put it out of his mind. More important was the way the waves hit the beach, leaving a thin strip of darker pebbles; the tide was making and would help carry a swimming man inshore.

'Mr Roscoe,' called Barclay, 'muster book if you please, and my barge. Mr Sykes you will oblige me by getting the jolly boat in the water and squaring our yards. Also ensure that no other boat gets anywhere near my ship in the time I am ashore.'

'Which is where we all want to be,' hissed Charlie, 'you black-hearted bastard.'

He looked at Pearce then, a sort of hunger in his eyes that

made the recipient uncomfortable. 'This looks more promising than Sheerness, Charlie.'

'For you, maybe,' Taverner responded, with a look and an air that spoke volumes. For a man who could not swim the small boats slipping by, seemingly so close you could reach out and touch them, and that shingle beach, might as well have been a mile away.

'If Corny has the right of it there will be boats right alongside before long.'

Gherson glared at Pearce then, for the use of that nickname or for making public what he had only vouchsafed to him, Pearce couldn't say. But those words made him respond to the enquiring looks from the others. 'I have it on good authority.'

'I wonder how you paid for that?' said Charlie, smirking.

Stung by that, Gherson replied sharply. 'If I have the sense to seek help, and you do not, then that is your affair.'

'Tell them what you learnt,' said Pearce. Seeing the hesitation, he added, 'Or would you rather I did?'

Gherson obliged after the merest pause, becoming quite showy in the way he explained. 'The crew will be given what wages are owing to them before we sail, it is the custom. After that, Barclay must allow the men some liberty to spend what they have been paid, and every trader and procurer in Deal will come alongside to secure their share. I have been told not to credit this notion of a swift departure, that he has been in the Navy too long to place much store by such orders.'

Orders came to get on the capstan bars. Sidling closer to Pearce as they made their way down the companionway, he whispered, 'Why did you speak so?'

'It's only fair that we all have a chance,' Pearce lied. He wanted them looking at boats, not at him.

'We must not jeopardise the possibility our letters will present, which will most certainly happen if any of those fools try to get aboard a boat.'

As he pushed to lift the captain's barge, then the jolly boat for the bosun, Pearce reprised in his mind, now that they were off Deal, the inherent flaws in placing any hope in a letter. Gherson's, in plain English, could go straight to a local Justice who might choose to act with alacrity, but his could not. It was addressed to John Wilkes in London and would have to go by post with the man he hoped to help him having to pay for the delivery. Gherson might be right about the ship being delayed here, but surely not for the days it would need for his plea to arrive and be acted upon. The only thing it might achieve was to blacken Barclay's name, which would be some comfort.

'You're right, of course,' he said to Gherson, who was moaning on about what Pearce had done. 'Stupid of me. If any of them show an inclination to try, I must stop them. Best you keep an eye on them as well.'

'Right, boats in the water,' called a voice, as the rope leading from the capstan went slack. 'Strike the bars.'

As soon as the capstan bars were removed to their racks a bosun's mate piped 'up spirits'. Pearce watched as some of his mess, Gherson included, rushed off enthusiastically to get their ration of diluted rum. Pearce hung back, half torn for a second between the notion of trying to get off the ship now, or getting back to that store with something to break open the padlock.

'You don't seem in much of a rush, mate?'

Pearce turned towards the voice, and found himself looking up into a scarred and unpleasant face with a well-thumped nose. Close to the prominent bumpy forehead were small dark brown eyes, the whole not made any more becoming by the man's attempt at a smile.

'Devenow's the name, Sam to those I call friend.' Pearce just nodded. 'Best friends I have, and many. None be too partial to grog, so for a consideration they allows me to have what they don't require.'

With his mind so fixed on escape, the question to ask was obvious. 'What kind of consideration?'

'Different from one to another, mate,' Devenow replied, putting a large hand round Pearce's shoulder. The way he exerted pressure made it obvious this was no gesture of friendliness. 'Some gift it out of kindness, some for a favour, like sorting some grass combing bugger aboard who is giving them grief. They know they can rely on Sam Devenow to put matters straight.' The voice changed, becoming gruff, as the pressure on Pearce's shoulder increased, bringing Devenow's head closer, so close that Pearce caught a whiff of tobacco on his breath. 'Then there are those who would wish to avoid upsetting me, 'cause I have it in me to be a bad bastard at times.'

Pearce was aware that he was trembling slightly – his fists had clenched, and his shoulders had stiffened – for he had been threatened with physical violence many times in his life and he could smell it a mile off. Devenow was telling him that to surrender his rum ration would save him from a beating. Maybe it was those squaring shoulders, or the way that Pearce moved a foot to enhance his balance and give himself room to swing, that alerted Devenow to the fact that this newcomer was not about to be browbeaten – that he would fight if he had to. The thought produced a smile in Devenow, but it was not a humorous one.

'Happen you will have to wait, seeing as you're a gamecock. If I don't shift I won't get my own grog, let alone yours. But we shall talk again, and that might just include a bit of a lesson.'

Watching Devenow's crouched back, looking at the huge shoulders and the height that prevented him from walking upright under the deck beams, Pearce was looking at a man who had an inch or two on Michael O'Hagan. The feeling he had in his gut, as he contemplated having to fight that giant was not one to reassure him. Fight he assuredly would if he could not get off this ship, because it was not in his nature to back down, but just as assuredly he knew that with nothing but his fists he would lose to a bruiser who had the advantage in height, weight and experience.

Kemp's voice, coming from the companionway he had been about to climb, broke that depressing train of thought, and the smirk on his face was evidence that he had a good notion of what had just taken place. With that sod watching him, he had no choice but to trail in Devenow's wake.

The queue had formed before the purser, the Master at Arms and the small keg from which the rum was being dispensed. Pearce recalled the exchange the Irishman had had the day before when on the capstan, of the look on both their faces, thinking that it was only a matter of time before that pair squared up to each other.

Last in the queue, he saw that Devenow had got himself in behind Rufus Dommet, and was whispering in his ear, with not one of the sailors he had walked in front of protesting. He observed Rufus's ginger head half turn, and fancied he saw fear in the profile. Clearly the man who had tried to bully him was working on the youngest of the Pelicans. Abel Scrivens was behind Rufus, and he would no doubt be next to be told

'If you don't want a beating, give me your grog ration.'

'Rufus,' he called, 'come and join me. You too, Abel.'

Rufus Dommet positively shot back at Pearce's request. Scrivens was slower to react, but looking at Pearce, then following the direction of his gaze, which had him craning to look into the scarred face of Devenow, he soon did likewise.

'Happen you and I will have to have words soon, mate,' Devenow said, glaring at Pearce. 'Very soon.'

Every head between Devenow and the trio of Pelicans had turned to stare, with varying degrees of reaction – pity, a recognition of stupidity, the odd shake of the head, but more worrying the fact that by his action Devenow had made him an object of scrutiny just when he wished to be invisible. Last to be served with his grog, Pearce had little choice but to make his way towards his mess table, when an over his shoulder look from Charlie Taverner alerted him. Turning, expecting danger from Devenow, he was unprepared for Martin Dent skipping by, and a hand jammed under his jug that sent the contents flying all over the deck. His free hand just failed to catch the pest by the shirt as he doubled back towards the companionway and shot up to the upper deck.

'You should have broken his damned neck, Pearce,' said Charlie, who had left his seat too late to intervene, 'not his nose.'

The chance came suddenly, as Pearce had always suspected it would, an open gunport, no one in authority close by to intervene, with nearly all of the crew titivating themselves, shaving close, changing into clean clothes, greasing and re-doing pigtails, talking excitedly about the women they anticipated would soon be coming aboard and planning how to thwart the authority that would seek to stop them. Ducking down for a look showed him a clear run to the shore and a sea with waves of a height that would not hamper swimming. There was no time to think of money, coats, shoes or anyone else, only of the one person who was close to him.

'I need your back again, Michael.'

The Irishman asked nothing, even although he must have guessed what Pearce meant, for there was a look of longing on that broad ruddy face as he turned away. 'Then you have it, and may the blessing of Jesus and the saints be upon you.'

Pearce was halfway through the gunport, and had one leg over the lip before he spoke. 'I will do my best for you all.'

'For which I thank you.'

Those parting words registered as Pearce's head dipped below the level of the gunport. He hung there for a second, bent arms holding his weight, very aware of the rough planking through his shirt, looking up, relieved to see no head popping over the side, very aware of what he was risking. The drop to the water was the point at which he would be in the greatest danger – the noise of the splash would give him away. At that moment a gun boomed, and as its effect echoed around the anchorage Pearce straightened his arms and dropped, going under immediately then resurfacing to spit what felt like half a gallon of seawater out of his mouth.

It could be fatal to wait and see if the cannon boom had covered his departure; registering only the heart stopping cold that stung his skin and the horrible taste of salt in his mouth, he struck out, shaking his dripping head to try and catch a glimpse of the shore, for in the lee of the ship there were no waves to tell him which direction in which to swim. Sure at any second that he would hear a shout behind him; that the water would zip by his ears with musket balls trying to kill him, he fixed his gaze on the top of one of the onshore houses, noting as he moved so it did, across his vision – the tide was carrying him not only inshore but to a point up the beach to his right. It mattered not – the shore was the thing.

The feeling of intense cold eased as he stroked rhythmically through the water, lifted slightly every few seconds by a wave that helped propel him forward. Close enough to the shore to hear the swish of the waves rushing up the shingle beach he did not catch the sound of the oars behind him, nor the command to raise them as the jolly boat shot alongside and into his vision. The hand that grabbed his collar stopped him swimming – the oars dipped again were in front of him blocking his path, and the voice in his ear was as rough as the grip.

'Damn you!'

It was the bosun, Sykes, and Pearce tried to spin his body and use an arm to break the grip. A fist caught on his ear, stunning him slightly, as Sykes yelled at him.

'Belay that you fool, you can't get away now.'

Treading water, his body lifted out of the water by those muscular arms, Pearce could see very clearly just how close he was to the water breaking over the shore. He tried, by raising his arms, to drop out of his shirt, but a second hand caught his hair, and even wet managed to hang on to it, while at the same time, Sykes who grabbed the tail of his shirt and hauled it tight in a way that rendered his arms useless.

'Stop struggling you swab or I'll fetch you a clout with a spike.'

Pearce did not obey that command, he did not have to for he was done for, constrained by the material of his shirt as well as the hand holding his hair.

'Now,' Sykes growled, 'we's going to drag you inboard, and you'd best come easy. Ridley, give us a lift here. Costello, keep an eye on the ship and make sure nobody in a blue coat spots what we're about.'

'Still only that useless little bugger Burns on deck. There's a party at the foc'stle, but I reckon them to be Truculence's mates.'

'Which be lucky for you,' Sykes said, right in Pearce's ear, as he hauled him over the gunwale, the wood of the boat's side digging sharply into his stomach. It must have been Ridley who caught his legs and threw them over, for Pearce found himself in heap at the bottom of the boat, with a heavy foot firmly placed on his back, and Sykes saying, 'Now bloody well stay there.'

'Anyone paying notice, Costello?'

'Not a blind bit Mr Sykes, not a blind bit.'

'Well, our friend here is lucky as well as stupid. Row us back to the ship.' The voice became a growl as Sykes leant over to talk into Pearce's ear. ''Cause if they wasn't so busy aboard the barky, officers as well as hands, thinking of whores on their backs, you would have been spotted for certain.'

'I must get ashore,' Pearce said, his voice croaked as much through despair as the seawater he had swallowed.

'Must you now?' Sykes replied, his voice become more normal as he sat up. 'Well, it ain't going to be on this day. You stay low till we get alongside and set you back through a gunport. Thank your lucky stars that the captain ain't aboard, 'cause he can smell a man trying to run, an' his remedy is the lash. Bring us alongside, you two.'

Pearce heard the slight bump of wood on wood as the ship and the boat met. Once more it was a strong grip on his collar, hauling him upright, and he found himself looking into the screwed-up face of Sykes. 'Now me, I can see why a man might want to run, especial when he's been had up in the wrong way. But that's the way of things and it ain't for alteration. You best pass that message on to all your mates.'

'Please...'

'Don't even try to plead. Help him you two, while I hold the boat.'

Ridley and Costello took his lower legs and lifted him, and Pearce found himself handing his body off the ship's side as he was raised to look through a gunport at the face of Michael O'Hagan.

'Would this be in the order of a resurrection, John-boy?'

As the Irishman grabbed him, he heard Sykes call to the quarterdeck to say he was coming aboard. By the time that happened, Pearce was standing on the maindeck, dripping water on to the planking, looking into the disappointed faces of those with whom he shared a mess.

Are they disappointed in me, Pearce was thinking, or the fact that I failed?

CHAPTER TEN

Ralph Barclay came back on board a hour later with a fair quantity of the admiral's claret in his stomach, not drunk exactly, but certainly light-headed. Faithful Hale followed behind him as he made his way from his barge up the side of the ship, doing what a good coxswain should to ensure that if his captain missed his footing, or failed to clap on to the manropes, he would not get his shoes and stockings wet.

'We weigh an hour after the men receive their pay, Mr Roscoe,' said Barclay in a pleasant tone. 'We will take up station to cruise off Dover and ensure that when our charges weigh at first light no rascal from the French shore is tempted out to attack them.'

'The men will be paid when, sir?'

'This very afternoon, of course,' Barclay replied, 'but be warned, before any clerks arrive with their money I want the anchor hove short, and we will weigh as soon as possible after they depart. The longer we stay the worse matters will become. I have no intention of turning this ship into Paddy's Market for the benefit of the sharps and whores of Deal.'

Implementing what he wanted would not be easy – the very necessary act of paying the men before they sailed for the Mediterranean would bring out from the East Kent shore boats by the dozen selling everything from trinkets through sexual congress to spirituous liquor, even if, with the men new to the service, there was not much in the way of coin to be distributed.

'I will want the gangway up as soon as the clerics go,' Barclay continued, 'and marines posted to make sure that neither whores nor drink get aboard.'

He knew Roscoe reckoned him too strict in the article of women on board. The Premier had already loudly declared at a wardroom dinner that he had served in ships where they were so prevalent as to almost count as part of the crew, and under captains who saw nothing wrong in taking a goodly number to sea, and to hell with regulations. Even if the harpies fought amongst themselves, at least if the crew's animal passions were contained there was less fighting between the men. And they performed other useful tasks, even, if the ship was in extremis, hauling on ropes to get the vessel clear. What captain, he had demanded, granting the hands that privilege, could deny some license in the article of women to his officers? Overheard by the wardroom servants, the conversation had been relayed to Shenton and Barclay's steward took pleasure each morning as he shaved his master, in passing on such gossip.

'Did you hear what I said, Mr Roscoe?'

'I did, sir,' Roscoe replied quickly. 'No women.'

'Quite. The men may trade through designated gun ports only, all on the shore side and all with a marine guard. Any traders between us and the Goodwin Sands, well, you have my permission to take out the bottom of their boat with a dropped round shot.'

Barclay looked at Roscoe then, wondering if he would protest, knowing he was asking for the impossible. No Navy ship ever left for a deep-sea voyage in anything other than Barbary order – the men got their outstanding pay, and did whatever it took to spend it. It was not uncommon for a ship of the line to be held up for days before the vessel could be cleared of unofficial visitors and even then it was never a clean sweep. Ralph Barclay fully expected he would find himself discharging more than a couple of whores when they were at sea – which might occasion the despatch of a boat to get them ashore again. And if the imbibing got out of hand, because too much drink had come aboard, he would have to rig the grating before *Brilliant* cleared the South Foreland.

He might know every trick in the canon, as would Roscoe – they had, as midshipmen, employed every tactic that would be in use this day – but that did not mean they would see the line dropped over the side with a purse on the way down and a flagon on the way back up. Nor would they see the bribe or threat to one of the red-coated lobsters guarding the gun ports that would have it open just long enough for a strumpet, with leggings under her skirts full of liquor, to slip through. The purser might prowl in the hope of stopping the purchase of tobacco, which, because he was the shipboard supplier would eat into his profits, but he would do so in vain.

Having issued his orders, Barclay made his way none too steadily to his cabin. With his mouth beginning to taste like bilge his first request, after greeting his wife, was that Shenton break out some wine, which the steward was happy to do, seeing it as his duty to take a good taste before serving, to ensure that it was not corked.

'Admiral Wood was most obliging, my dear, but, I fear, in

a terrible rush to get us to sea, so my intention to have him dine aboard and perhaps take you ashore for a return of the compliment will not now be possible.'

Emily had seen him like this before, just as she had seen her own father. She reminded herself that she must be tolerant, for men were weak in the article of wine. 'That is a great pity, husband.'

'Only thing he would not do, damn him, begging your indulgence my dear, was loosen my orders a trifle, can't think why.'

'Did he not vouchsafe you his reasons?'

'Oh yes. He's not going to risk upsetting the Admiralty.' It was clear on his wife's face that she did not understand. 'Convoy duty is a bloody swine!'

The reply was firm, and made without prior thought. 'I fear your meeting with the admiral has rendered your language a trifle salty, Captain Barclay.'

That sent his eyebrows up, just as it sent her eyes down, for Emily had never, as far as he could recall, even come close to chastising him. But she had now, and in a circumstance that made it very difficult to object. Drink had caused him to blaspheme, and his wife had every right to remind him that it was unacceptable behaviour. That did not make it pleasant, so his admission, 'You are perfectly right, my dear,' was rather forced. 'I shall explain,' he grumbled.

'Please do,' Emily replied, giving him a look of deep interest that mollified him somewhat.

'I am obliged, by standing Admiralty orders, to avoid losing sight of the convoy of which I have charge, so I am tied by apron strings to a bunch of lubberly sods.' His hand was up quickly. 'I apologise again, my dear, but if you have ever seen the behaviour of merchant captains you too would have cause to cuss.'

Ralph Barclay rambled on, moaning about merchant captains – that they were a contrary lot who could never keep their station, always sailed with the minimum of crew so that they were laggardly, especially at night when they would shorten sail in spite of any order he gave not to; that those apron strings would preclude him chasing any potential prize, and that his request to Wood, Port Admiral at Deal, to write some orders allowing him a touch of leeway had been denied.

'Yes, Mr Burns,' he said, as the midshipman knocked and entered, eyes fixed rigidly ahead, avoiding both Emily's eyes and her welcoming smile.

'Mr Roscoe's compliments, and can he have the muster book back as the clerks from the Pay Office are about to come alongside.'

'Some of your uniform, Mr Burns,' said Emily, her eye on the coat and breeches, which were clearly too big for the boy, 'could do with a touch of adjustment.'

'Mama said I would grow into it,' Burns replied, in a hesitant voice and with a bit of a blush, eyes moving between his cousin and his captain, fearing that he might get a rebuke.

Emily's response was to stand up and place herself in front of him. 'I'm sure you will cousin, just as I am sure, like me, she would have you as smart as you can be.'

'Yes, ma'am.'

It was virtually impossible not to sigh at the formality, but Emily smiled nevertheless. 'If you have spare clothes, as I am sure you must have, bring them to me and I will do what I can to make them fit you a little better.'

Burns was about to say that if his cousin wanted his spare

clothes, she had better ask his fellow midshipmen where they had gone, but Ralph Barclay's impatient cough killed the notion, obliging Emily to stand aside so both he and Burns could leave.

'That boy is not happy,' she said, softly, to herself.

Barclay appeared on deck, book under his arm, and looked over the side, happy to see that his orders had been obeyed – that the bumboats full of the Deal contingent of whores, panders and gimcrack traders were standing off his ship. Once the men were paid he would allow an hour's indulgence – not one second more – then he would weigh, and sling off the ship anyone who should not be aboard.

'Mr Hale,' he called to his coxswain, whispering an order in his ear as he came close. Then he spoke to Roscoe. 'Line the men up.'

'Down to the orlop with you lot,' barked Hale. A dispirited Pearce, still damp, sat at the back and so excited no attention. 'Captain Barclay's express orders, an' you are to stay there till we weigh.'

'What about our pay?' asked Rufus, pointing to the men making their way to the upper deck.

Hale shifted his quid of baccy, tipped back his tarred hat, snorted like a hungry pig and pointed to the scantlings. 'You could turn and ask the plank of wood at your back and it'd have the answer, but plainly you are thicker than that in the article of brains. The Navy don't pay out on a day an' a bit, an' any bounty you had is now held on the purser's books. Now move. Or do I have to get a file of marines down here to force you?'

Pearce felt a wave of despair sweep over him. Barclay had made a shrewd move, alert, as Sykes had said he was, to any attempt that his pressed men might make to slip ashore in one of the boats being fended off the frigate's side. The Pelicans were shepherded down the companionway, to sit in the gloom of the orlop under the supervision of a less than pleased marine, their spirits of the same order, watching sights that in normal times would have amused, for the three hours between the crew being paid and weighing the anchor were pure mayhem, officers shouting, marines being sent hither and thither, sailors, clearly drunk on illicit rum being chased, while others searched for a corner, not necessarily a quiet one, in which to rut with some whore they had smuggled through a gunport.

Barclay could be heard all over the ship, cursing, swearing and damning individuals including his own inferior officers for their laxity, threatening the midshipmen, who, instead of impeding the crew, seemed more inclined to aid, abet and emulate them. They would, he promised, 'kiss the gunner's daughter before they saw the French coast'. That was when he was not ordering that some woman or trinket-trader be chucked over the side.

Put to the capstan to finally haul HMS *Brilliant* over her anchor, it seemed that the Pelicans were the only sober group on the ship. Aloft, top-men too inebriated to properly perform their duties made a poor fist of setting the topsails, so that the frigate departed the Downs in the fading daylight like a lubberly merchant vessel with a crew of cack-handed scrape jacks aboard. There was some consolation that Davidge Gould was having the same difficulties in HMS *Firefly*, but none at all from the jeering hoots which came from the deck of every other naval ship in the anchorage.

There was a tense moment as they shaved the shingle off Walmer Castle, watched by a whole regiment of redcoats who filled the beach with their fires, behind them a tented encampment that filled the surrounding fields, quite enough in numbers to render futile another attempt to swim ashore. A bleary-eyed Barclay was to be heard screaming a change of course to a helmsman who was, like the others, well under the influence. With the Pelicans now on deck hauling on ropes, under instructions from petty officers made extra crabbed by the effects of drink wearing off, they finally cleared the southern end of the Goodwin Sands. HMS *Brilliant* made deep water, where, cruising back and forth in the choppy Channel water, with a strengthening wind, a full half of the people aboard were sick.

The convoy emerged at first light; a long string of some fifty vessels stretched out over several miles that took hours to get into any form of order. The air was full of endless banging guns, as both frigate and sloop were obliged to sail hither and thither in steadily deteriorating conditions to deliver verbal instructions and threats to merchant skippers, each one of whom saw it as his bounden duty to annoy the captain of HMS *Brilliant* – not difficult as the mere presence of several hundred sailors he was absolutely forbidden to press, manning those ships, was enough to make him exceedingly irascible. That they took as long as they liked to comply with his orders, only added grist to that mill. An angry captain on the deck, and officers who took the brunt of his strictures with barely disguised hostility, combined with hangovers and endless orders, naturally meant little contentment t'ween decks, as the misery worked its way down to the lowest on the ship.

* * *

Martin Dent brought matters to a head, for like a thief who has stolen a couple of times and got away with his crime, he would not leave John Pearce in peace. The Pelicans were working in the holds, fetching out more supplies for the cook – water and casks of meat – in a sea that was far from calm. They were grateful to be below for there was now a wind blowing that was strong enough to sting the eyes. HMS *Brilliant* was pitching and rolling quite markedly, and although this might be less obvious below than on deck, they had to take extra care.

At the very bottom of the hold, the casks rested in the shingle ballast used to weight and keep steady the hull. Those on top nestled in the space between the two below and the entire weight pressed down to ensure no movement, with wedges malleted into any point where a barrel could come loose. Being at the beginning of a commission, the holds were full, and the confined space was difficult to work in, especially given the foul miasma created by bilge water, rotting wood, the gases given off by imperfectly sealed meat casks, and the general corruption of a dark airless compartment that never saw daylight and where rodents ruled rather than men.

There were seamen leading the party, who knew how to cradle each numbered cask in the sling, how to use pulleys to lift and move it without damage to a point where the main lifting tackle could hoist it right up through the hatch. Careful as they were, however, they were also forced to work at some pace, because to stay in the hold too long, with lanterns guttering and flickering from too little oxygen to burn, was to risk passing out from the lack of anything to breathe.

With water, there was no problem, any barrel would suffice, but the packed meat was numbered and dated with the time of its butchering, salting and sealing. In a perfect world, the casks would have come out of the hold in the exact reverse of the way they had gone in. But the ship had victualled in a hurry, and since the purser was adamant about which casks he wanted – those with the longest provenance, the ones most likely to be corrupted if left – a great deal of shifting and stacking was required.

After quarter of an hour in the hold, Pearce was feeling slightly nauseous as he laboured to transfer casks from one pile to another. Each one moved for temporary storage had to be secured by wedges and ropes, for the motion on the ship was such that they could easily begin to roll, and it had been made plain by the purser before they came below, and was now repeated like a chant from his position above the hatch, that any loss through smashed staves would be laid against the name and pay of the offender.

Given the weighty nature of the task, Michael O'Hagan was the greatest asset, for, although they were too heavy to lift, provided one cask rested against another he could hold the whole weight of one on his own. He, Pearce and Scrivens were working together, the former two making sure that impatient members of the crew did not bully Scrivens for his ineptitude, for added to his natural weaknesses he was still suffering from seasickness. Charlie Taverner, Rufus and Ben Walker, all three a bit green at the gills as well, formed another working trio, all six cursing Gherson who had managed to get himself a job easing the casks up on the main tackle, a position where he was required to do no lifting, merely tasked to manoeuvre lashed and weightless casks. And, being right under the open hatch, the bastard had proper air to breathe.

'Abel,' gasped Michael, arms outstretched to hold a moved cask. 'Two wedges under this bugger.'

Scrivens moved slowly, and his use of the mallet was so weak that the wedges were not driven home. In fact one dropped into the gap between the two barrels on which the men were standing. Michael went to a one-handed hold and moved Scrivens to where his other hand had been, coaching him with scant equanimity on how to hold the cask.

'Stand there and get both hands on the thing. Right, now stretch right out until your feet are wedged and your arms are straight. As long as you stay like that, it will not budge.'

Michael dropped to his knees to find the fallen wedge, not easy for no light penetrated down there, leaving Pearce and Scrivens restraining the cask. The sudden increase in weight was partly due to the dip of the frigate, but Pearce had experienced that more than once already, and he knew that provided they had enough pressure on the cask they were holding it would not move. This was different – as he and Scrivens pushed hard to hold their position it seemed that the cask had doubled in weight, and was actually pressing down to crush them. Pearce felt his bare feet slip on greasy wood – the barrel had moved and was continuing to do so. What faint light there was showed Abel Scrivens begin to bend, his thin and already aching back rising to take the rigidity out of his body, and Pearce knew that whatever was exerting pressure on the cask was rendering it too heavy to hold.

He yelled to the Irishman, who was on his hands and knees scrabbling about. 'Michael, get out!' There was no hesitation from a man who had worked on tunnelling and ditch digging – when a cry like that came you shifted without looking and he was clear on hands and knees within a second. 'You too, Scrivens, for we cannot hold it!'

His shouts brought men to try and aid them, but they

were too far away and Pearce, the veins in his neck feeling fit to burst, called to Scrivens, who was at the end farthest from safety, to save himself. He never knew whether the push Scrivens gave him was motivated by a desire to help or sheer blind panic. There was not much weight in the push, but Pearce, already under pressure, was sent flying out from under the barrel, the rear end of which had already begun to fall. It caught Scrivens, who was stationary, rolling on to his body in an action that seemed to last an age, yet only took a second. The scream that came from Scrivens' throat was cut off as the heavy wooden cask crushed the air he needed out of him. In the glim of the guttering candles in the lanterns – carried by the sailors too late to help, Scrivens' face looked like something from engravings Pearce had seen of a soul entering hell.

The silence lasted for another second; then the air was full of the cries of men trying to effect a rescue. The sling was there quick, a rope attached to it and flung under the end of the cask. Pearce was on his knees beside Michael, both cursing as they tried, in the gap created by Scrivens' crushed body, to get enough purchase to ease the weight.

'Bring more light, for Christ's sake,' one sailor called, while two more cursed endlessly as they tried to get a line under the cask. 'And the surgeon.'

A quick knot was tied to the sling and the order given to haul away easy. Slowly the cask began to lift, and there was enough light to see how badly hurt the poor sod was. The light picked up the blood streaming out from about three different parts of his body, his eyes were closed and he was beyond the point of feeling any pain.

'Hang on, Abel,' Pearce said uselessly, while Michael, who had crossed himself, was praying in a whisper. 'For Christ's sake hang on.' Looking up, as if to the heavens and a God in which he did not believe, Pearce looked into the faces of Abel Scrivens' friends. Charlie Taverner had his head in his hands, Rufus had tears in his eyes; Ben Walker was on his knees, face anxious, bird-like eyes fixed on the old man, calling down words of encouragement.

'Stand aside.'

Lutyens pushed Pearce and Michael out of the way and knelt down to touch Scrivens' neck, then lower to search for breath. 'There is life still. We need a sling to lift him out, for I cannot attend to him here.'

More shouts brought a hammock, and Pearce was vaguely aware of the men on the main hoist adding ropes to make a different kind of sling and the voice of Lieutenant Digby enquiring what had happened. Lifting Scrivens' body was not easy – for all that he was a featherweight, the position in which he lay was awkward, and all who had hands on him knew that they could damage him more than help him. Scrivens' body twitched several times as they moved him, evidence of the deep pain that was penetrating his unconscious state. Slowly, having been placed in the hammock, he was eased out and upwards, to the sound of raised voices.

'Get that party out of there,' said Digby.

'The cook needs those casks out for the men's dinner,' protested the purser.

'The men have been down there long enough, sir,' Digby insisted. 'Apply to Mr Roscoe for another party to complete the task.'

It was easy for Pearce to imagine the fat little purser puffing out his toad chest then. 'I think you exceed your authority, sir.'

Digby's response was icy. 'Since I have some, sir, and you have none, I think my opinion is the one that will count.'

'The captain will hear of this.'

Digby shouted then, his voice every bit as unforgiving as Barclay's. 'The captain might be too busy overseeing a burial to listen.'

Pearce and Michael climbed out to find the two faces close to each other, Digby, red faced and angry, towering over the purser, who was relenting. 'I am merely trying to do my duty, Lieutenant Digby. There is no need to adopt so high a tone.'

They were by the steps leading up to the orlop deck when Pearce looked back to the officer and the purser, who were now engaged in mutual apologies. He saw Martin Dent slip out through the hatchway, throwing an alarmed look at him, before scurrying away, leaving Pearce with the certain knowledge of where the extra weight on that cask had come from.

'I suggest,' said Michael O'Hagan, when Pearce told him, 'that you kill that boy before he kills you.'

Lutyens knew that he was going to lose his patient as soon as he got him on to the table in the sick bay. Probing fingers felt ribs so crushed that internal damage was inevitable, likewise the hips, while the heavy bleeding implied damage to the spleen. It was the loss of blood that took him, for Lutyens, try as he might could not stem it in time, because there was no obvious place to put either a ligature or a tourniquet. He was aware of the men behind him, the big Irishman and the one entered as Truculence, and he saw the flash of hate in those eyes when he indicated, by a shake of the head and a request for one of them to fetch Lieutenant Digby, that his patient was slipping away.

Scrivens died before Digby made his appearance, the life going from his inert body without even a last gasp of air. Barclay was informed, and ordered that the body be prepared for burial. Then he consulted his Bible for an appropriate lesson to read out at what would be the first, but certainly not the last burial service of this commission.

'I think it would reassure the men to see me attend, Captain Barclay,' Emily said, firmly. 'I would not want them to think me heartless.'

'As I say, my dear, the choice is yours. No funeral is pleasant, even that of some low creature without much hope of salvation in his life.'

That angered Emily, for whoever this Scrivens was he was the possessor of a soul. 'Did you not say, husband, we are all God's creatures, when you advised me that some of your volunteers may succumb.' The emphasis on the word volunteers was unmistakable.

'I did, my dear,' Barclay replied, guardedly.

'Then I think that makes us all equal in his eyes, does it not? The poor man is as welcome in heaven as the prince.'

Ralph Barclay responded in a hurt tone, well aware that if anyone else had chosen to speak to him in such a manner he would have bitten their head off. 'I cannot help but feel Mrs Barclay that there is a tone of chastisement in your voice.'

'Not chastisement, husband, but pity that you seem to see the man just deceased as somehow unworthy. However,' she added quickly, to the shocked look on his face, 'I am sure I have misunderstood you, and that it is only the experience of so much death in your profession that makes you sound callous.'

'Callous?'

'Perhaps inured is a better word.'

The men gathered in their divisions, officers in dress uniform, under a grey sky, to bury a man few of them knew, and less than half a dozen had cared about when he was alive. But they were solemn, all of them, for in a profession where the risk of death was a commonplace, it was tempting providence to show anything other than respect. Sown in canvas, lying on a hatch cover, with a piece of roundshot to weight down his shroud, Scrivens was not visible to the burial party, so all could imagine him as somehow a better specimen, a bigger and fitter man, perhaps even a younger one, than he had in fact been.

'He was good,' sniffled Rufus, 'even if he did get on at me, it was well meant.'

'Never would have survived on the Thames bank without him,' added Charlie Taverner.

'Amen to that,' added Ben.

'Silence there,' said Lieutenant Digby, a command that was soft enough to respect their grief.

Barclay read the burial service, watched by his wife, in a sonorous voice, and Emily was pleased at the mood he struck, mournful but also hopeful, the certainty that the man being buried was going to a better place. She searched the faces of the crew, pleased to see that in the main, by the expressions of piety they wore, they seemed to agree with their captain; that man was born into nothing and left this earth with nothing, that an all-seeing God would be there to greet him at the gates of eternity to count his virtues and his failings. This poor creature, obviously unsuited to a life at sea judging by his behaviour in climbing the shrouds, would go to a better place.

She could not help but look for John Pearce, for he was an educated man in the midst of a high degree of ignorance, stood between the big curly haired fellow, who had his head bowed in prayer, a man who crossed himself frequently in the Papist manner, and a handsome youth who looked to be crying from the way he dabbed at his eyes. Pearce was doing neither – he was staring straight ahead at her husband and the bible in his hand, with a look that could only be described as malevolent. There was no piety in that countenance and the thought that surfaced then was unwelcome.

Her husband had pressed these men – his so-called volunteers – they were here against their will. Was there a woman somewhere, a mother, sister or sweetheart who would mourn the man's passing? Would they ever know how he died, or where he died? Abel Scrivens should not have been aboard this ship, and if he had not been he would still be alive. Instinctively, Emily Barclay knew what Pearce was thinking – that Captain Ralph Barclay had as good as murdered Scrivens, and the real problem she had was that she could not disagree with such a thought.

'And so, we commit the body of…' There was a pause then, as Ralph Barclay had to look at the flyleaf of his Bible, where he had noted in pencil the name of the deceased '…Abel Scrivens to the deep.' The hatch cover had been picked up, taken to the side, and one end laid on the bulwark. As Ralph Barclay intoned the final words of the burial service, the cover was lifted and with a hiss followed by a splash, the shroud slid into the sea.

'And may God have mercy on his soul.'

Emily Barclay had her eyes tight shut, as she sought to submerge the words that filled her brain. 'And yours, husband, and yours.'

Pearce had no intention of killing Martin Dent, yet he knew the boy had to be stopped. But how? An appeal to bury the hatchet would be more likely to be taken as an invitation to stick an axe in his head. Would a word to Lieutenant Digby work, or even, God forbid, Barclay? He didn't know, and he sought out the only person he thought he could ask.

'We aw' know wee Martin,' said Dysart, grinning. 'A right tyke he is, though liked by the crew, for he will as like as no, provide a laugh as much as mischief.'

'He's trying to kill me.'

'Och! Away man,' Dysart cried. 'Has yer imagination got the better of ye?'

Pearce decided an appeal to a national commonality was necessary, even if he risked imparting information in the process. 'You doubt the word of a fellow Scot?'

'You, a Scot?' Dysart said dismissively. 'Ye dinna sound like wan tae me.'

'I spent most of my formative years south of the border in England.'

'Well, it's no done much for yer wits.'

Martin Dent was intent on avoiding Pearce and Charlie Taverner, staying out of their way until he had another chance to impose trouble. He knew the ship better than his adversaries, the places to hide, and those where to accost him would be public. Every mention of the name underlined what Dysart had said – he was popular, more so than the other ship's boys. It was pointless for Pearce to speculate on the nature of this popularity, though difficult to avoid doing so. He had to stand outside himself and examine the problem objectively, something the Abbé Morlant, his French tutor, had taught him always to do.

How distant Morlant seemed now, and those comfortable days in Paris – the calm of proper study with his soft voiced Abbé mingled with the excitement of an upheaval that truly seemed to make people free. He remembered citizens smiling at each other in the streets, or engaging in fearless and open debate; the common bonds of humanity that culminated in the great Festival of the Revolution, when it seemed that everyone in the city had come to the same place with the same purpose – to express their happiness at the present state of their country and their lives. In that great expanse of the Champs de Mars – a huge open field where once soldiers drilled and cannon fired salutes to Kings, now filled with flowers, food, flaring torches, dancing, laughing, kissing and embracing commoners – it had been truly possible to believe that the world had changed.

'That sounds like shite to me,' said Michael, when Pearce advanced the proposition that there was good in everyone and that the boy would have been chastened by the death of Scrivens, that he would give up his grudge from mortification at the result of his actions. Michael took a mouthful of grog before adding, 'The little sod will not stop till he has killed you and you cannot, for your own sake, think he will.'

'Well, Michael,' Pearce replied, with just a trace of exasperation, 'if you have any ideas on what to do, I would be grateful.'

'Simple,' said Charlie Taverner, who felt equally under threat. 'Collar him, gag him, and drop him overboard on a dark and windy night.'

'That sounds about right,' added Ben Walker, with a gleam in his eyes and a tone in his voice that made Pearce reckon him easily capable of killing a fellow human being.

'Murder?' said a shocked Rufus Dommet.

'Preservation,' Michael insisted. 'Charlie and Ben are right, for if I have learnt one thing in my life, it is best to collapse a ditch on a man who is your enemy before he collapses one on you.'

'And you believe in God?' said Pearce.

'I do,' O'Hagan insisted, 'but I have no yearning to meet him before my given time.'

'We're all at risk,' said Ben, slapping the table with a flat hand. 'You do know that Pearce?' The silence that followed allowed Ben to look at each of them in turn, and for the first time Pearce saw, in that serious troubled face, a degree of determination that underlined how much he was his own man. 'Abel did the boy no harm, yet he died as a plain result of his actions. If any of us come between Pearce and Dent...'

'And me,' Charlie interrupted, 'don't forget me.'

'...we will suffer the same fate as Abel.'

Silence greeted that sobering thought, as Ben again looked from one to the other, until all four had nodded to acknowledge the truth of what he was saying. 'Then it stands to reason that we all have to have eyes for each other's back. We goes no place alone, an' we stay close to each other at all times.'

Rufus shuddered. 'Christ, Ben, that be scary.'

'Not scary, Rufus, deadly more like if'n you don't harken.'

'I think I will try talking to him,' said Pearce.

'Try that, Pearce,' growled Charlie, emptying his jug, 'but I reckon Ben has the right of it. And when you have failed, then help me to chuck him overboard, for that is what I will do if I get the chance.'

Silence fell as Gherson approached. It was understood between them – without anything ever being said – that they should not trust him.

Martin got Charlie Taverner with the boiling water at an unguarded moment, just as he and Rufus were collecting from the cook their chosen piece of meat, as well as their rations to make a pudding called duff. Aiming for Charlie's head, his lack of height allied to haste meant he got him on the legs, and although it hurt like the devil when the water penetrated Taverner's ducks, it did not scald him as it was supposed to. Martin was gone before Charlie got out his first cursing screech, the mess kid with the dinner inside dropped to roll on the deck, the boy emerging from behind the cook's coppers grinning like a monkey. That grin faded as Martin saw Pearce and O'Hagan standing in front of him, Ben Walker just behind them.

He dodged well left, to get outside Pearce, who had to dive across the planking to grab his ankle. Once he got a grip on that he hauled the boy in, fending off the scrabbling, scratching hands that Martin used in an attempt to get free. Holding him close, he just avoided a bite that would have removed his nose, and with his free hand he began to slap the boy on the face, side to side, not too hard, but enough to stop him struggling.

'I want to talk to you,' Pearce said.

'Fuck off,' Martin spat.

'Belay that.'

The bark was from Sam Devenow; Pearce knew that before he looked. 'Take your hands off young Martin, you green-livered swab.'

'Young Dent tried to kill me, Devenow,' said Pearce, wondering how something so true could sound so feeble.

Devenow snorted, then started to move towards Pearce. 'Then the pity is he ain't succeeded!'

From the look in his eye Pearce knew that he was going to have to fight. Was it about grog or was it about Martin Dent? It didn't matter now – all he could be sure of was that slight tremble shaking his body that always came when danger threatened.

'It was him that caused that burial this morning,' called Charlie Taverner, emerging from the galley, to stand close to

Pearce, with Rufus, looking very fearful, just behind him. 'And he has just this second tried to maim me.'

Devenow stopped and glared at Charlie. 'Who asked you to butt your nose in?'

'It's my business, too,' called Ben.

'Then I'll deal with you,' Devenow growled, looking past Pearce, 'once I have dealt with this bugger here.'

Pearce knew that to wait would be fatal – he reckoned he had no chance anyway, but that would be ten times worse if he did not get in the first blow. He threw Martin Dent at Devenow's feet, which took the sailor's eye off him for a second, grabbed the second mess kid out of Rufus's hand and slung it at Devenow's head. The man was too quick or too wise, he ducked under and it flew past, the contents, flour, suet and raisins, going everywhere.

'You just shot your bolt, mate,' he said, rolling up his shirtsleeves to expose thick matted forearms.

'Kill him, Sam,' said Martin Dent, with a look of hate quite startling in its intensity.

Devenow grinned. 'I might just do that, young Martin. Happen there'll be another bit of canvas dropped overboard on the morrow, and a lesson learnt by all and sundry of these pressed bastards. That it don't do to be flighty with Samuel Devenow.'

'Back away, Pearce,' said Charlie, who then looked confused at once more letting slip the name.

'I can't, Charlie.'

He was aware of the gathering crowd, and of men who had made their way to the companionways without bidding, their task to keep a lookout for anyone in authority. Gherson had come from the table, but sensing what was happening he stood well to the rear of Ben Walker, who had his fists bunched, and a dogged expression on his face, one that said he was willing to take on all comers and had moved to the edge of the throng. The cook had emerged from behind his galley stove, and his bulk cut off the view from aft. Pearce felt the knot in his stomach, fear mixed with the notion that there was not a soul on this ship who would intervene, and that Devenow might be right. With a sword he could take him, for all his lessons in Paris had not been on logic and philosophy, but he might as well whistle for a seizure as that. Any weapons were locked and chained in racks that could only be undone by the Master at Arms.

'Would the word I'd be looking for be belay?' asked Michael O'Hagan, a quizzical expression on his face, as he stepped forward to stand in front of Pearce.

'What?' asked Devenow, confused.

'Well, now, you stupid sods have this tongue that no Christian can grasp. I want to tell you to lay off, but I know if I speak plain English you'll be too dim to understand it.'

'Michael,' said Pearce.

O'Hagan half turned his head. 'I think what I should say to you, John-boy, is stow it.'

'This is my fight.'

Pearce was still trembling slightly, and he felt it was in his voice too. But he knew from the past that once he started to fight, the trembling disappeared, only to recur more violently once matters were settled.

O'Hagan gave him a very gentle backwards push. 'And it will be your hurt for sure, an' maybe a maiming.'

'Step aside, Paddy,' growled Devenow.

'Hold your wind, Devenow,' Michael replied, without turning, and it was evidence of the respect his size and weight afforded him that the t'ween decks bully stood stock-still.

'Be that as it must,' said Pearce. 'I cannot let another fight in my place.'

'Yet you can put yourself between that bastard Kemp's rattan and a weaker man's back?'

'That is different.'

'I did not have you down for a fool, John-boy. Sure, I am going to have to have words with this ugly bastard at some time, and it would not, to me, make sense to wait until he had beaten you senseless.' The Irishman grinned. 'I had a mind to get you to teach me to read and write, for I am taken with this notion of yours that if I dig a canal I should own it.'

'Still,' Pearce protested, aware in both heart and head that it sounded weak.

'What would you suggest then, John-boy, that I wait till all taken from the Pelican bow the knee to this sod. Not just you, but Rufus, Ben and Charlie, for he will oppress them all unless he is stopped. Think on this, it is not just for you, it is for all of us, for if I cannot get respect here then not one of us will be safe. And I think if we are to get respect anywhere else on this damned ship, or to ever get off it, you will be the one to bring it about, for which we need you whole.'

'I don't follow,' insisted Pearce, though he knew in his heart what Michael was driving at. It made no difference whether he wanted the role or not, the men of mess number twelve, with the exception of Gherson, saw him as some kind of leader. He was educated, they were not; he had seen a larger world and they looked to his knowledge to somehow rescue them from the hand fate had played. Dammit he could even swim.

'You have the head, and I have the muscle, so, as I said, John-boy, stow it.'

'Are you pair going to natter much longer?' asked Devenow.

O'Hagan turned back to stare the man down, cutting off Pearce's last feeble protest. 'Now I have a mind to do this right, shirts off, a mark on the deck to go toe to toe.'

'Suits me,' said Devenow.

'With no one having the right to step in.'

It was the one-legged cook who answered then, producing from under his apron a huge meat cleaver. 'I say aye to that, and I will take the arm of any man who interferes, Paddy.'

'Jesus, Mary and Joseph,' said Michael, his voice lilting and wonderfully sarcastic, 'and here's me thinking that Sam here was universally loved.'

As they took their shirts off, the proceedings took on a natural formality; a square was formed, a piece of line laid across the deck for the fighters to step up to, and hushed bets were placed. There was no noise, nothing to alert authority to what was none of their business. Pearce looked at the assembled crewmen, at their eyes, trying to see what they thought, hoping that in their hearts they wanted Michael to win, to see a bully humbled, thinking that if they used their heads they would back the man they knew. The Pelicans were hopeful, and keen to let Michael know it, all except Cornelius Gherson, who took care to avoid any notion that he might be involved, showing no desire to exchange a glance with Pearce. He suspected that if asked, Gherson would have backed Devenow.

There must be others who would pick up on what was happening, the likes of Sykes the Bosun, or Coyle, the red-faced ex-soldier who had brought them downriver, but a look around produced no evidence of their presence. They might be close, but they would stay out of this, as he had seen men of authority do many times in his life with an account that could not be settled any other way. Perhaps the officers likewise would turn a blind eye. Kemp he could see in the crowd, forearming his dripping nose, his rat-like face alight and eager for bloodshed. Ridley the other bosun's mate was there too, his face showing, if anything, a hint of worry. Hale, the captain's coxswain, elbowed himself to a place near the cook, and whispered something in his ear, which made the fat, sweating, one-legged fellow wave his cleaver and nod. Then a movement caught Pearce's eye, and behind a stanchion he was sure he saw the popping pale-blue eyes of the surgeon.

'Right,' said Costello, the dark-skinned bosun's mate, who had stepped forward to take charge. 'You know the rules. As long as your toe is to the line you are fighting. You may step back to change your toe at any time, but not to delay or rest, for that will mean a forfeit. The first man to fail to stand up to the line for a count of three is the loser.'

'Michael,' said Pearce again, for, stripped off, Devenow was even more formidable, a mass of rippling muscles covered with tattoos: anchors, female names, a mermaid and on his hairy chest a flaming cannon. 'I ask again.'

'I have been to fairs, John-boy,' Michael replied loudly, jabbing a finger at the tattoos, 'where they have painted ladies like this one here. They are nought to be a'feart of.'

'Where you are going, Paddy,' said Devenow, 'you will see more pictures than this.'

'Step up,' said Costello.

With his dark complexion, flashing Latin eyes and good looks, Costello had the air about him of a showman. Obviously he had selected himself as the adjudicator, and no one seemed to want to challenge him for that role, which Pearce surmised meant that the crew, who were split in their support, trusted him. Very well, if they did, so could he, and any doubts that Michael would get a fair fight – his last worry – were eased.

Both men obliged. Costello stood, hand raised between them, checking the position of their feet. Then, standing well back, for he had no desire to be caught between the first blows, Costello counted, 'One, two three,' then dropped his arm.

There was no rush of blows – more parrying, easing back, ducking and weaving as each man felt the other out. Pearce had got himself a good spot, in the front row, from where he could look, by moving left and right, at the fighter's eyes. Neither man's gaze left the other's face. Whatever body movements they made they stayed locked on, looking for the first real attempt at a punch, which would come soon. The whole thing was carried out in silence – there was not even whispered encouragement, and Pearce was forced to admire the self-discipline of these sailors, who knew that even quiet goading would make too much noise.

It was Michael who threw the first punch, making to move back from a jab then suddenly coming forward to parry the blow with one hand while he thumped Devenow on his flaming cannon tattoo with the other. The man didn't move, even though it was a well-delivered knock, and Pearce looked at Michael to see what effect this would have on him. All he saw was a grin, which had nothing to do with being pleased, more to do with riling his opponent.

Devenow was too long in the tooth to fall for that, but the punch had changed his expression from one of watchfulness to one of determination, his brows closing down over his eyes as he settled himself for what must come, a trading of blows, for there was little science in this, it was pugilism of the most basic kind. When it developed it was almost rhythmic, made more so by the soft encouragement from a crew who were fighting themselves – to contain their excitement – the sound of landing fists was louder.

Michael cut first, above the cheekbone, and that brought a satisfied grunt from Devenow, who made the mistake of trying to follow it up as the Irishman did a rapid change of feet which left the sailor exposed on his own left side. The shock, as Michael hit him left-handed, with a blow that was every bit as telling as his right, registered on Devenow's face, as did the blood that spurted from his gashed eyebrow. Michael hit him with his right before he had time to recover and forced his opponent to step back for a count of one.

Devenow was toe to the line again in a second, his shoulders now more hunched as he sought to get all his weight behind his punches. With not much chance for guile, Michael's next attempt at a foot change worked more against than for him, proof that Devenow had, when it came to fighting, natural cunning, for he caught Michael on the upper jaw with a punch that sent him reeling away, then scrabbling back into position with his head shaking.

Pearce knew that his friend was on the defensive, parrying blows and ducking away rather than delivering, and he had an eye on the one-legged cook with a view to snatching that cleaver and going after Devenow, for he was well aware that if Michael were beaten he would be next. The notion that it was not fair did not enter into his head – growing up he had learnt the absolute necessity of winning, and sometimes when the odds were too heavy the wisdom of running. To lose a fight was to suffer not only ignominy but pain, and to risk much worse. If he used whatever came to hand to gain a victory, a length of wood, a heavy stone, John Pearce could always reassure himself with the knowledge that all he required was enough submission for his own safety; that, just as he had never abandoned a friend in distress, he had never continued to beat a man who was down.

The steady thud of exchanged blows continued for a long time. Michael was weakening; the blows he was giving seemed to have less weight than those he was receiving. Those sailors who had bet on Devenow were trying to increase their stakes; those few who had backed Michael were attempting to cover what looked certain to be a loss. Devenow seemed confident now, his punches reaching further, nearly overbalancing him as he sought to beat Michael back off the line. That was when Michael did another two-step move, and caught the off-balance Devenow with a haymaker to the left of his head. He got in a second one before changing feet again, this time catching his opponent out because Devenow had changed his own feet to parry the danger from Michael's left hand.

'Come on, Michael.'

Charlie Taverner got many a sharp look that said shut up. It wasn't much of one because they were enthralled by the contest, now much more even as a recovered O'Hagan put as many blows into Devenow as he received. The tattooed sailor was now forced to take a two-count break, and several deep breaths before coming back to the line. Michael gave him no respite but hit him on arrival with a straight jab that caught Devenow right under the heart. Aimed to go through his body and come out the back, it was a huge punch that stopped the other man's breath, most of which came hissing out of his lungs, forcing Devenow off the line for another second.

But he was back trading with Michael in a series of exchanges that seemed to last for an age. It was clear that both men were tiring, their labouring breath mixing with the steam rising off the sweat on their bodies; their faces a mass of cuts and swellings, their lips sliced open in more than one spot. Devenow could hardly see, so gross had those heavy brows become, and with so much blood running into his eyes.

Michael was in no better state, but it seemed that his stamina was just that much greater. He might take an age to get his arm up but it came up all the way, while Devenow's seemed only able to reach chest height, not the shoulder height he needed. All the tattoos on his body were smeared with blood now, and it glistened in his thick matted body hair, as Michael leant into his assault, throwing punches that were a tenth of the strength he had started with but had a relentless pressure that drove Devenow off the line half a dozen times. But he came back, until Michael, nearly over-reaching himself, summoned up the strength for a killer punch, that took the hunched Devenow right under the point of his chin. The cheekbone seemed to pop out to the side as the jawbone went, and Devenow staggered back. He was game, he tried to make the line, but his toe got there just as Costello called the count of three, and declared the contest over.

There was a pause of a few seconds, looks of disbelief on many a face, and Michael O'Hagan sunk to his knees, fists out before him.

'Charlie, Rufus, hot water,' said Pearce as he knelt beside his champion.

'Now do me a favour, John-boy,' said Michael, thickly, through heavily swollen lips. 'Get hold of that little shite Dent, and throw him overboard.'

CHAPTER ELEVEN

The howl of the wind in Pearce's ears, which for hours had doubled the discomfort of his unquiet, empty stomach, died the instant he dropped down the companionway, replaced by the sound of timbers groaning so loud that it was easy to imagine the ship tearing itself apart. That he had heard it before every time his watch was called on deck, and that the frigate was still afloat, did little to reassure him that he was not about to drown. There was no respite from the motion either so that he had to clap on to the deck timbers with still-blistered hands, just to get to the bottom, his bare feet slipping on the dripping wooden steps. Soaked to the skin, he already knew that he had ahead of him four hours of deep discomfort in which sheer exhaustion would, if he were lucky, bring the sleep he craved.

It had been like this for four days now, the weather steadily worsening as the whole convoy struggled to make some headway down the English Channel in what was heard to be, 'a right true bastard of a sou-westerly'. If the meaning of tacking and wearing had been obscure to Pearce at first it was not so now, as the bowsprit of HMS *Brilliant* drove left and right then left again into the teeth of the wind. Roused at four in the morning, still wet from the watch they had worked until midnight, Pearce and his messmates had gone on deck in the pitch darkness, the only visible light a reflected glow that lit the faces of the trio of heavily garbed sailors on the wheel. They had come up on to a heaving deck swept by stinging salt spray, and endless toil. Occasional relief came from equally hard graft on the capstan, lifting some heavy object into or out of the night sky, or a spell at the pumps to keep the water in the well from rising to a point where it would threaten the frigate's stability.

Above their heads, in pitch darkness, the topmen of the larboard watch worked on the sails, jerked endlessly forward, back and sideways by the motions of the hull. On the deck, constantly screamed at by those who had charge of them, Pearce and his fellow landsmen, the lowest of the low, hauled on the ropes that controlled the angle of the yards. Beneath their feet the starboard watch had swung in their hammocks, with water dripping on them through the working of the deck planking, trying to get their four hours of allotted sleep. Now, roused out, they came back on duty to continue their labours in the cold light of dawn.

The experienced hands on Pearce's watch were nowhere to be seen. They had shot below with the speed of men who knew what they were about, to get out of their soaking outer garments and do what they had done the evening before; take up most of the space around the back of the galley fire, which had warmth enough to dry their ducks, heat their limbs and provide a light for pipes in the only space on the ship where they could smoke.

Behind Pearce, framed against the grey sky, Charlie Taverner had collapsed the moment they made the relative quiet of t'ween decks, only to be kicked by Kemp as he followed him down, each strike accompanied by a swearword, as well as a flick from his rattan. Cornelius Gherson had to be prised off the newel post at the base of the stairs so that Pearce could get by, while Rufus Dommet was leaning over at the other side, retching from a stomach that contained nothing with which to be sick, next to Ben Walker, who, head on his chest was also in some distress. Ahead, in the gloom, Pearce could just make out Michael O'Hagan, legs and hands spread, bent under a too-low deck head, as he tried to stay upright, and in front of the Irishman the easily swaying figure, in dripping oilskins and a foul weather hat, of Lieutenant Digby. Behind him, looking like a wet rag doll and less assured in his stance stood the diminutive figure of Midshipman Burns.

'Belay that, Kemp,' Digby shouted, bending a knee to ride the action of the frigate as it crested another wave. 'There is little use in the beating of tired men.'

'With respect, sir,' Kemp shouted back, 'the Premier wants that the new men should know their duty, an' in that I am following his express orders to drive them hard.'

'These men are in my division, Mr Kemp, and when they are off the deck, I will decide how they are to be driven. Now I suggest that you have other duties, and I would be much obliged if you would return to them.'

'Mr Roscoe…'

'I will speak with Mr Roscoe, Kemp, and unless he issues orders to the contrary mine will stand.'

Kemp had to obey, but the look on his crooked face and the forced 'Aye, aye, sir,' with which he acknowledged the order left no one in any doubt of his sentiments.

'Don't tell me we're shot of the bastard, Michael,' hissed Pearce.

'Silence,' said Digby. 'Those of you who can, help your shipmates to a mess table. Two men who have the duty to fetch something hot to eat, the rest of you get out of your clothes, for they will not dry on your backs.'

'Nor will there be space by the galley fire,' said Pearce, 'for there was none yesterday.' He remembered just in time to add 'sir.'

'There will be, Pearce.'

The use of his real name, instead of Truculence, the first time anyone in authority had employed it, made Pearce look hard at Lieutenant Digby, who met his gaze with words that were soft, but firm. 'You must not lock eyes with me so, man. It is insubordinate.'

Pearce continued to do so – a problem the lieutenant solved by issuing orders, for it seemed that the mess carriers were too far gone for the task. 'You and O'Hagan are the least affected. Go to the cook, whom I have already had words with. He will provide you with a couple of kids of soup.' As they departed Digby added. 'The rest of you get your outer garments off. Use your blanket to keep out the chill. And for God's sake don't seat yourself under a leaking stretch of planking. Once you have something inside you, make your way to the galley, where Mr Burns here will ensure you get a fair share of the available warmth and a chance to dry your clothes.'

'I need sleep,' groaned Gherson, a remark that brought a growl of agreement from most of the others.

'You need food,' barked Digby. He then softened his voice. 'Believe me, lads, you must do as I say. It's better to have food and three hours sleep than four hours abed and a four hour watch with an empty belly. Taverner, help Dommet there, and make sure he takes in some victuals.'

Lieutenant Roscoe, as officer of the watch, had taken station by the wheel, behind the men conning the ship, using their bodies to shield himself from the worst of wind, though not from the spray, which came in as heartily over the ship's windward quarter as it did the bows. Above his head grey clouds scudded along in the early morning sky, and indistinct in the blowing spume he could just make out a dozen of the convoy ships. Fifty more vessels were out there somewhere, including the second escort, which would become increasingly visible to the lookouts as the light increased. He ordered them to search the horizon astern for an East Indiaman, old, and much smaller than her more recently built consorts, that had hauled its wind at the last of the light the day before; his captain, mad at the time, forced to put the needs of the majority against the requirements of one ship, would want to know if she had rejoined.

To one side he could see Collins, the master, shut up in his little day cabin, poring over his charts in the hope of finding some clue as to their position. Observation had been difficult with neither a clear sky in daylight nor any sign of a star at night, so all Collins had to go on was dead reckoning, taking the frigate's last certain position when they had lost sight of land off the high Sussex promontory of Fairlight, hard by Hastings, and by calculating from the ship's constantly changing course and speed where they were now. In the hands of a competent navigator the result of such a calculation was uncertain. In the hands of a man like Collins, it could be fatal.

The man should be here on deck with him, keeping an eye on the sails and making adjustments to ease the way on the ship, a task that Roscoe was performing because, if he did not, danger beckoned, as it always did at sea. Midshipman Farmiloe was huddled by the poop steps, looking and feeling miserable, while an oilskin-cloaked marine stood guard over the door to Captain Barclay's quarters.

Around him the ship pitched, rolled and groaned, while the wind set up a constant whistle as it howled through the mass of rigging. Just faintly Roscoe could hear the clanking of the pumps as the men below laboured to rid the frigate of the water she was taking in, water that came through working seams in the scantlings and the decks, or poured in gallons down hatchways and between the boats boomed on the waist. Ahead of him on the quarterdeck, other parties were working on the rigging, it being too rough to clean the decks. Mentally he was checking off the mass of tasks with which he could occupy both them and the watch off duty, throughout the coming day, for bad weather or no, training had to continue.

It was nearly imperceptible, but Roscoe sensed by a changed note in the rigging that the wind had eased just a fraction. The possibility presented itself to spread more canvas, which would, in speeding the frigate through the water, ease her passage. Perhaps he would be able to holystone the decks after all, even if it was pointless, because he was sure if he did not do so Barclay would not only comment on his failure of duty, but would enter the fact in his log. Moving out from the scant protection of the poop, he was in the process of lifting his speaking trumpet to issue orders when a voice called from the tops.

'Deck there. *Firefly* signalling.'

'Mr Farmiloe!' snapped Roscoe. 'The signal book and a glass.'

Lanky Farmiloe uncoiled himself too slowly for an impatient Premier, and had to scurry when Roscoe barked at him to 'double up'. The light was poor, grey skies full of scudding dark clouds and the spume set up a fine, all-encompassing mist which, with a group of merchant ships pitching and rolling in the waters between the two warships, made reading Davidge Gould's message difficult.

'Get aloft, Mr Farmiloe,' shouted Roscoe, telescope to his eye, straining to see the triangular flags that stood out stiff from *Firefly*'s mainmast, 'and take the book with you.' Then he shouted too for someone to man the frigate's halyards and acknowledge Gould's signals as they were deciphered.

Stuffing the book under his foul weather hat, that being the only place from which it would not disappear, and with telescope slung by a strap over his shoulder, Farmiloe headed for the rigging on the weather side, fighting to cross a deck pitched at an angle of fifteen degrees. Being tall and gangly made it easy for him to get up on the bulwark and as he began to climb the rigging he felt the security of that wind on his back, pressing him into the ropes. Nevertheless the climb was laborious and clearly too laggardly for the officer of the watch. He could hear Roscoe belabouring him with the epithets of 'damned lubber' and 'useless bugger', this because he had chosen, with the foul conditions, to get to the safety of the mainmast cap through the lubber's hole.

From that secure platform Farmiloe had a better view, and with the bulk of the mast to kill the wind he could risk taking out the signal book from under his dripping hat. Telescope pressed to his eye, he read the still indistinct flags on Davidge

Gould's sloop. Flicking through the book he hesitated to call out what he thought they said, and because he was fresh to the task of signal midshipman, took another look to make sure, which earned him another shouted rebuke from Roscoe.

Finally, Farmiloe called down to the deck. '*Firefly* signalling, sir, enemy in sight.'

'Acknowledge,' shouted Roscoe, before turning to the marine sentry. 'Rouse out the captain.'

By the base of the mainmast two sailors struggled with the signal halyards, to get aloft the flags that would tell Gould his message had been read and understood. This would allow him to send the second part of the signal, the bearing on which this enemy lay as well as some indication of the size of the threat. By the time that had been done, Ralph Barclay was on deck aware that the enemy was a single ship bearing south-south-east and that Davidge Gould was asking for permission to engage. Assessing the situation, Barclay stood, silently, for a full two minutes before he issued his orders.

'All hands, Mr Roscoe and a signal to Captain Gould to hold his position.' There was no immediate threat; if there had been Gould would have engaged without waiting for orders. 'Mr Collins, I need to know our position.'

The reply was hesitant. 'I would put us at – about – let us say – Latitude forty-nine degrees North, Longitude some three and a half degrees East.'

Ralph Barclay conjured up a mental picture of the long neck of the English Channel as it trended west between the south coast and France to that point where he could turn southwards once he had weathered the great Atlantic headland of Ushant. Collins' calculations placed the convoy past the Channel Islands and somewhere between the Brittany shore and Devon to the north, closer to the French side than England, not much distance covered for four days sailing. That was, of course, only true if Collins had the right of it, which looking into the man's worried countenance was far from certain. Right at this moment it mattered little, as long as he had plenty of water under his keel.

'I need you to shape me a course to get to the south-east of our convoy.'

Pearce and Michael O'Hagan approached the galley from the rear. The small space was crowded with a shuffling mass of half-clad sailors standing in a cloud of blue pipe smoke and steam, none of whom showed the slightest inclination to move. Behind the pair, a high-pitched voice, without the least trace of authority or confidence, piped, 'Stand aside there.'

'By Christ, there's a future admiral come among us,' said a jester from the throng, a remark that was greeted with general laughter. 'Hard horse ain't in it.'

But they did move enough to let little Burns through, which was nowhere near enough space for the pair following. O'Hagan bunched his fists, but John's voice in his ear stopped him throwing a punch that, given the bruising those hands bore, was like to hurt him more than any victim. Michael's face was less swollen than it had been after the fight, each bruise now black with a yellow surround. The stitching above his badly cut eye was a mess, evidence that Surgeon Lutyens was no master of that particular art.

Having beaten Devenow, who was on light duties now with his broken jaw, the Irishman was acknowledged as the hard man of the ship – but the men of this crew had soon worked out that he was nothing like his late opponent. O'Hagan might be a pest when drunk, but sober he had to have a reason to fight, and hated to be thought of as a bully. Devenow had beaten up others for pleasure, when he was not doing so to steal their grog.

'We'd be obliged if you would make way, lads,' Pearce said to a sea of bland faces.

'Hear that, boys, Truculence has spoken.'

'Don't you mean the dolphin?' said a voice from the rear. 'I hear tell he swims like one.'

'Damn near pierced my ears, Truculence did,' called one wag, making very obvious that, hardly surprisingly, his true name was common knowledge. Not that it mattered; they were too far from the English shore now.

'Sounds like a bleedin' officer,' said another voice, before adding a mordant, 'beggin' your pardon, Mr Burns.'

'Sure as God made trees grow that little bugger don't sound like one.'

'Sounds like a rat, looks like a runt,' called the jester from the back.

Voices came from both sides, the owners hidden by their mates, as Pearce pushed into the mass of bodies, to be greeted by a steady stream of coy, salacious remarks, and a hand that, in the press of swaying bodies, goosed his backside. He could hear O'Hagan behind him growling at his tormentors, who knew just how far to take the joshing before backing off. On the other side of the crowd they were faced with the cook, red as usual from the heat of the fire underneath his coppers. Burns was eagerly supping from one of the wooden mess kids they had come to collect. He blushed, as Pearce looked at him hard.

'For the men, I think, Mr Burns.'

'Carry on,' Burns slurped, making it obvious that he had no intention of returning with them, preferring to stay with the heat and the prospect of more food. Pearce took the rope handle of one of the small wooden buckets, passed the other to O'Hagan, and they turned to retrace their steps. Michael O'Hagan stopped before the throng that barred their passage. He passed his kid of steaming soup back to Pearce.

'Right mates,' he said, 'if I swing for it, I'll belt the first bastard to lay a hand on those there kids. My mates are beyond, freezing, cold and wet and in need of food, and so help me I don't care a tinker's curse what anyone says.'

The crowd parted like the Red Sea in the time of Moses.

'All hands on deck, at the double.'

The men responded to that command with a speed that surprised Pearce and O'Hagan. Within seconds all the lines that had held damp clothes were empty. What was less obvious was what they were to do themselves, which was not helped by Burns skipping by, and knocking half the contents of one kid onto the deck.

'Get on deck, you pair of slow arses,' called Coyle, who was coming along the maindeck repeating the command for 'all hands'. He tried to grab the full kid from John, who pulled it out of his reach. 'Don't you know an order when you hears one? Put those bloody mess kids down and get on deck.'

'Lieutenant Digby told us to fetch these.'

The red face went a deeper shade. 'Christ Almighty, if I had a starter now you'd feel it.'

The cook intervened, stomping over to push Coyle on his way and get about his duties, before he turned his sweating face to Pearce. 'All hands, you stupid half-brick means what it says. Everyone on deck, at the double, 'cause the captain apprehends danger. Do yourself a favour and fill your mouths, but if you don't want the cat skinnin' your backs, move your arse.'

'We'll take them with us,' said Pearce.

'You ain't even half a brick,' shouted the cook at their retreating backs.

They were the last on deck, and they found the others already hauling on the falls to the leeward side of the quarterdeck. Rising and falling twenty feet on each wave, bare feet slipping on the planking, they were seeking to bring the yards round to take more wind, which earned them many a curse from their shipmates. All was confusion, and, taking advantage of that, Pearce, followed by O'Hagan, walked along the line of heaving men and lifted the heavy wooden kid to each pair of lips.

'A good idea, Pearce,' shouted Digby from the rear. 'Make sure every man has something and if they refuse force it down their throats.'

He made his way down the line, feeding Taverner and Ben Walker in turn. Gherson tried to refuse, and got a slap round the head from Pearce, who was in no mood to accept a refusal. Rufus Dommet, his hair dark red from spray, his face gaunt from four days of being sick, needed O'Hagan to hold his head to obey. And in truth by the time they got to him the soup was getting cold and had within it a goodly dose of salt water. It was only when they had finished that both the providers realised that they had left nothing for themselves.

'Mr Digby,' shouted Barclay, from beside the wheel, 'would you oblige me with some notion of what you are about. I am informed that you are feeding the hands on deck.'

'So that they will fight better, sir,' Digby shouted back, then in a quieter voice, 'Get rid of those kids, damn you.'

'British sailors, Mr Digby,' replied Barclay, as the small wooden buckets disappeared over the side, 'will fight on an empty belly if needs must.'

'Aye, aye, sir.'

Finally accepting that the yards on the course and topsails could be hauled round no more, Barclay ordered them to be sheeted home. As the falls were securely lashed off to a belaying pin the men who had been hauling on them relaxed, some just to lean, others to collapse – that was until a quiet word from their divisional officer reminded them that they must stand up, especially here close to the quarterdeck, within plain view of the captain.

If Pearce had learnt anything this last awful week it was the division that the mainmast provided. Astern of that great round timber, the height of two men in diameter, was the preserve of the officers, termed the quarterdeck for no reason that he could discern. He was allowed to cross the divide to carry out any task allotted – scrubbing the decks, hauling on the falls – but he was not permitted to linger or address anyone unbidden, and that was a stricture that applied to the whole crew of seamen, regardless of their rating.

No social division pointed out to him on land by his father – and there had been plenty – had ever been so clearly defined. It was like an invisible wall that separated officers from men; those who held or, like midshipmen, anticipated commissions, from those whose task it was to carry out whatever orders such people dealt out. Whether they made sense or not, were issued with kindness or malice, the most depressing aspect about the system was the way the men on the ship accepted this divide and respected it. Sovereign of the quarterdeck was the captain – that was where he was deferred to most, his rank acknowledged in endless lifting of hats, barks of 'aye, aye, sir' and obsequious looks meant to convey to him just what a puissant personage he was. Each time he thought on it, or witnessed the sight of what to him appeared mere grovelling, Pearce felt himself sickened.

Ralph Barclay, unaware of the stare of malevolence aimed in his direction, was running a mass of facts through his mind – the accumulation of his own years at sea and the teachings of those who had preceded him. Was the wind easing, and with it the swell? The sky was certainly clearing, the heavy cloud cover lifting. How was *Brilliant* handling, had her holds been stowed right; were her masts taking the strain or labouring; how much sail could she carry on this heading, into the wind but twenty points free, on a course that he hoped would put him between the Frenchman and his home shore?

'Topgallants, Mr Roscoe.'

'Aye, aye, sir.'

Half an hour later Ralph Barclay was wondering if he should clear for action, knocking out the bulkheads and striking below everything not required, but that was a disruption to the ship that was best avoided. Against that, it was an exercise the crew had not yet had time to practise, so it was likely to be a slow and laborious affair if he had to order it done. And what would happen if they saw action? With the lack of time and foul weather he had not been able to get in some exercise on the great guns, or even a bit of practice with small arms.

With all these worries to contend with, there was some satisfaction to be gained from the knowledge that the crew, despite failing to act as the unit it would one day become, would already have carried out certain tasks. Mess tables would have been lashed off to the deckbeams, all extraneous articles secured, and the gun crews, even if the order had not come, would be close to their weapons. Behind him, the marines were lined up on the poop, muskets at the ready, prepared to act wherever he sent them, and the topgallants were being rigged, if not at pace, with efficiency.

'Deck there. Chase in sight.'

'Mr Roscoe, orders to the gunner. Please ensure that we have enough cartridges for a prolonged action. And send someone to alert my steward to get the cabin furniture below. I require that my wife be moved also to a place of safety.'

'Aye, aye, sir,' Roscoe replied, managing, even with only half a face, to look exasperated.

'And, since the hands have had no breakfast, I suggest that the Master at Arms be sent to the purser to request an extra ration of grog to keep their spirits up.'

Information was shared with the whole ship as each new fact was called down to the deck. The chase was a two-masted barque of seven guns a side, flush decked and wearing a tricolour at the main, facts which made sense to most of the crew, but remained a mystery to the pressed men of the afterguard. The fact that she was likely to be 'nippy' in stays meant even less to the Pelicans than the speculation that she would be fast on a bowline. But that she would be a 'right fine prize' and 'sure to be bought in if taken' was enough to raise the spirits of Gherson, who understood quicker than the others that every member of the crew had a money share in any reward for a capture.

'Mr Digby,' called Barclay, 'I require you to cast off a pair of the quarterdeck guns, and teach some of these new fellows how to handle them. We cannot go into a fight short of men to man our armaments.'

'Will the maindeck guns not suffice, sir?'

To Digby, that made perfect sense. The ship they might fight, being only a flush-decked barque and lightly armed, could not match the calibre of *Brilliant*'s main armament. To man every gun, especially in this sea, was gilding the lily.

'It was customary,' Barclay replied, with deep irony, 'in the Navy in which I was raised, for lieutenants to obey an order from their captain.'

'Sir.'

What Barclay was asking for was plain daft. To teach totally inexperienced men how to handle an eighteen-pounder cannon required a calm sea, a flat deck, and time. A pitching deck was more dangerous to the trainee gunners than the gun could ever be to the enemy.

'I would request the aid of two experienced gun captains, sir.'

'Mr Burns, double below and ask Mr Thrale for the loan of two of his best gunners.'

'And we require flintlocks,' Digby added, responding to Barclay's raised eyebrow with, 'for verisimilitude, sir.'

As Burns disappeared, Digby was tallying off two groups of six men, while admonishing the rest to listen and observe. Then he tapped the black painted barrel of a cannon bowsed tight up against a gun port.

'Be warned, this is near two tons of metal and wood with a mind of its own. There are lines to control her and you must never let go of them. Once she is cast loose, those on the breechings and levers have to act together, for if you do not, a man could lose his leg, if not his life.'

285

Then he picked up a ball from one of the rope-garlands that kept it from rolling around the canting deck.

'This ball is eighteen pounds in weight, hence the gun is an eighteen-pounder. From what we know of our quarry she will be light in her scantlings, that is her side timbers, so any well-aimed shot will go through and make mincemeat of any flesh it finds on deck. This is not the case with a ship of our own size or greater, so when aiming, the gun captain will lever the muzzle of the weapon up with that quoin under the barrel and fire into the rigging, hoping to hit a mast or dislodge a yard.'

Whether what he was telling the two crews detailed to man the pair of guns was making sense was hard for Digby to know. The blank wet faces that greeted his instructions seemed indifferent or too tired to take it in. After flintlocks had been fitted by a gunner's mate, he was glad to see two experienced gun captains arrive, for he had no desire to be too close himself the first time these men tried to control that weight. It was obvious from the faces of the two newcomers that they shared his opinion of the exercise – they both looked as though someone had pinched their extra grog.

Assigned to a gun, Michael O'Hagan and Charlie Taverner were allotted to the ropes on one side that ran through blocks lashed to the bulwarks, while Rufus Dommet and John Pearce took those on the other. Being compact and looking nimble, Ben Walker was given the swab, while a volunteer landsman whose name they did not know was allotted the rammer. Digby sent for two buckets of water and these were placed between the guns. One, he explained, for the swabber to wash the sheepskin head on his pole, the other had a ladle out of which the men could drink, for, manning a gun was 'damned warm work'.

'First you must cast off the breechings.' This they did, and the cannon rolled back on the swell, Digby shouting at the rope men to 'hold her steady, and ease her back until the lines were taut'. While the gun port was opened, the two front men, O'Hagan and Pearce, were ordered to take up the levers and jam them under the front wheels of the carriage. The reason was obvious – as the angle of the deck altered, the levers acted as brakes. This allowed the gun captain to bring forward the cartridge and the wad, and behind him Ben Walker had the black painted balls, none of which, since this was all to be in dumb show, were actually placed in the barrel. Digby had both swab and rammer employed as though the gun had been fired, then on the gun captain's command, all six men hauled on the breechings to pull the weapon up to its firing position, which put the muzzle well beyond the side of the ship. Still in pretence, the gun captain pulled the flintlock and created the spark that, in real life, would fire the powder pricked onto the touchhole, which in turn would explode the cartridge rammed into the barrel, sending the ball towards its target.

'Now this, lads, is when a gun is at its most dangerous. For when it fires it shoots back damned quick on what we call the recoil, and is out of control, with some of the wheels jumping the deck. So the men with the levers must be ready to get them under those wheels, for if they do not, the gun will roll forward again and crush the men waiting to swab, load and ram.'

Digby smiled. For all his misgivings the first attempt on both guns had gone smoothly. 'Now, let us try the whole procedure again.'

In the great cabin, Emily Barclay was aware and grateful for the fact that the weather seemed to be improving, for she had

had an uncomfortable time. Her husband's predictions of days without proper hot food or comfort had been truly borne out and she had learnt that in stormy weather the simplest task went from molehill to mountain. Merely to move from one side of the cabin to another required forethought and calculation, not least to time the movement to avoid the large amount of filthy seawater swilling about on the floor.

Even sitting down it was impossible to do anything – sewing was a series of endless skin punctures leading to abandonment, reading by salt streaked cabin windows or by a constantly swaying lantern, with one hand fixed to some object for security, feet raised to keep them dry, was unedifying in the extreme. Husband Ralph, when he wasn't on deck, showed her great concern, obviously worried that she might be seasick, equally showing pride that she did not succumb. Worst was the fact that because of the weather and the amount of work needed to keep the ship operable, the deck was barred to her, which meant no fresh air. Indeed the cabin had become rank from closed casements and constant human occupation, a situation not aided by the leavings of the hen-coop being washed astern. The only place of comfort was their matrimonial cot, slung so that while the ship moved it remained still, with the caveat that a moving room was like to make her stomach churn, even though all it contained was ship's biscuit and soup.

And now, not only had the ship's motion eased, there was the prospect of action – there had been alarm and commotion, a change of course, the beating of a drum instead of the wail of pipes. A French privateer had been sighted, and she was stuck in this place.

'Shenton!' The steward took his time in replying, hanging on to the jamb of the door, exaggerating, Emily thought, the difficulty of keeping his balance. 'Are we about to have a battle?'

'We might, ma'am, but it'll be a right while yet.'

'My cloak, and please take a request to my husband.'

Vaguely aware of the training going on to windward, Ralph Barclay was thinking that his ship was not sailing at anything like her best. Looking at the sail plan he had the notion that there was too great a press aloft on the main and mizzen, and that the weight of the wind on that excess canvas was forcing the ship's leeward head into the water.

'Sir,' said Barclay's steward, who had come up to whisper in his ear. 'Your wife wonders if she might be allowed to come on deck, since she has been informed that there is as yet no danger.'

Barclay nodded, for Emily was right. At the present rate of sailing it would be an hour before they could engage, and that would only be if the Frenchman held his course, 'Which he will not do my dear,' Barclay explained, 'for he would be a fool to engage a frigate.'

'Yet you tell me he sails on?' Emily asked. 'He has not turned to run from us?'

'To see what mischief he can create, my dear. I have told Gould to hold his position to draw him on.' He led her over to the mizzen ratlines on the windward side. 'Now, if you take station here and use a rope to steady yourself, you will be able to observe all that happens, and' – the smile was paternal, indulgent – 'not be in the way.' Then he called to no one in particular, 'A piece of tow for Mrs Barclay's hand. I would not wish my wife's palm to be covered in tar.'

'Aye, aye, sir,' came the response, as every midshipman rushed to obey.

'Mr Collins,' he called to the master, as he resumed his position by the wheel, half-aware that he was showing off to Emily, and enjoying the fact that he was doing so. 'I require that a reef be let out on the forecourse and that the maincourse be goose-winged to allow the wind some play on it.'

Collins had a remarkably vacuous countenance at the best of times, all puffed cheeks and sloth eyes, and hesitation did nothing to aid his appearance. It seemed an age before he responded and gave the orders that Barclay suggested. The topmen, too slow for the captain's liking, let out the forecourse one reef. Meanwhile those on the mainmast lifted one corner of the maincourse to windward so no longer blocked the wind from the sail in front. The effect was immediate and satisfying; the way on the ship smoothed and Barclay was certain they had achieved a discernible increase in speed.

'Aloft there,' Barclay called. 'Does the Frenchman show any sign of changing course?'

'No, sir.'

'Mr Collins, return the sails to their previous configuration. But I want the men standing by to reverse the procedure again, but this time with some alacrity.' He continued in a voice loud enough to ensure that his wife heard, saying words that, had she not been present he would have kept to himself. 'Let the fellow come on, judging our speed by what he has already seen. Then we shall give him a fright.'

Half an hour went by with the pressed men of the afterguard toiling away at the cannon, till they had got the action smooth enough to satisfy Lieutenant Digby. Once that had been achieved and he had discerned that Captain Barclay's attention lay elsewhere, he had them secure the weapon, then sent them off the quarterdeck to await orders on the leeward gangway. The volunteer who had worked with them on their gun moved away to join his own mates, clearly not wishing to associate with pressed men.

'God, my hands,' said Gherson, looking at his red and raw palms, his young face creased with torment. 'Is there nothing aboard a ship that does not require a rope?'

'You're just soft, Corny,' said O'Hagan.

'Don't call me by that name!'

'I can think of one or two others you deserve,' hooted Charlie.

That produced the pout with which they were all familiar. Gherson was outside the group – it was in his face and the way he held his body. And it was also plain that he liked it that way, below decks happier in the company of sailors than mess number twelve.

It was Pearce who gave the opinion that they were all soft, because he, in his life had been no more of a worker than bumptious Cornelius Gherson. Reading books, practising rhetoric, expounding philosophical texts, intermingled with occasional practice with an épée, and sometimes riding a horse was scant grounding for this. As for the others, the life of the Liberties, the odd job loading and unloading boats had not prepared them for such endless, heavy toil.

'You feeling any better, Rufus?' he asked quietly.

Although he nodded, it was hard for Rufus Dommet, with his pale freckled skin, to look anything but unhealthy. But the underlying pallor brought on by seasickness seemed to have finally abated, and since the breeze had eased and the new course of the frigate had put her less at the mercy of the cross-sea, he was in a fair way to be wind dried as well. Looking at his messmates, Pearce felt a tinge of amiability, for they had

291

ceased to be strangers. Friends, no, though he would be happy to afford that title to Michael O'Hagan. But Gherson aside, they had begun to act collectively, a melding created by Martin Dent that had carried over into their everyday existence. He also thought that, though they looked rough, they also looked better than they had for days.

'Who was the fool that suggested we linger in the Pelican?' murmured Charlie Taverner.

'Why, I recall,' crowed Ben Walker, producing a bitter-free laugh for the first time in days, 'that it was you, wagering that you could get a drink out of John Pearce here.'

'And did I not get it?' Charlie insisted, then smiling at Pearce he added. 'You was easy meat, John.'

Pearce, who suspected Charlie might be right, smiled back. But he also signalled that they should keep their voices down – even if Kemp was no longer shadowing them there were more like him aboard who would take as much pleasure as he did in checking them.

'So it's your fault,' said Rufus, softly, looking at Pearce with a wan grin to cover his temerity, in not only having such a thought, but expressing it.

'Odd,' Charlie added, 'when you came in I said to Abel you was hunted-looking. You were running, John, were you not, though you've yet to confide what from?'

'Does it matter now?' Pearce replied, glancing at O'Hagan, who responded by looking skywards. 'I don't recall Ben there telling why he was taking refuge in the Savoy.'

'That I'll keep close yet, if you don't mind,' Walker whispered, but Pearce's words clearly reminded him of the cause, for a look of pain crossed his features.

'By Jesus, it matters not to me,' said O'Hagan, scowling,

'for either of you. We're here now, and all that is past is past. What we got to do is find a way to make this life more easy.'

'What about getting free?' demanded Gherson, querulously.

Charlie Taverner answered that with a jeer. 'Such a thing, Corny, needs dry land, and I doubt you, or any of your chancy mates, could see any of that even from the tops.'

Pearce looked at his messmates again, but this time with a sense of objectivity. If he was stuck aboard this ship he was also stuck with them; who he liked and disliked made no odds. Michael had his Irish ways; Charlie Taverner, who looked more weak and foolish now than the rascal he had first thought him to be. At least he could always be counted on to conjure up a jest, and that was something. Rufus had quite gone off the notion of life as a seaman, unlike Ben Walker. He had suffered as much as anyone but managed to bear up as soon as a chance to relax had been gifted to him. Gherson was pouting because of the way Charlie had put him down as a pest, but by Christ he was a handsome one. The general opinion, voiced when he wasn't around, was that he was deep in some kind of ordure, and it was no wonder to all that his bumptious nature had got him into trouble.

Freedom? Easy to talk about, damned hard to find in this service and this place. He pointed out to the others how the malignance of the crew, especially after Michael's bout with Devenow, was already easing into acceptance, and if there were a way of escape, then these men bred to the sea would know of it. The smug look on Gherson's face stopped him from going further on that tack.

'Until then,' Pearce hissed, 'we are stuck on this damn ship, for as long as it takes to get a sight of land and a chance to get ourselves ashore, and I say being useless will not aid that. We should look, listen and learn, which is what I shall do.'

Looking back at the quarterdeck, he observed Barclay, swaying easily with the motion of the ship, hands behind his back like a caricature. Pearce had listened to him giving orders and had found himself interested in both the way they were issued and the result. Was Barclay a competent sailor and a doughty fighter? The fact that he wanted him to be neither, wanted him to be a coward he could despise, would not make the man so, any more than wishing he were ashore would put him on dry land.

'What I am saying is that I agree with Michael here,' Pearce added, ignoring the frown on Charlie Taverner's face. 'We have to make a fist of what we've got, for as sure as the devil resides in hell, if we don't we will go under.'

'Don't say that,' moaned Cornelius Gherson.

'Mr Roscoe,' said Ralph Barclay, loudly enough to be heard all along the deck. 'I think we may clear for action.'

Number Twelve Mess was set to work again, as labourers, watching as more experienced men knocked out the wedges that held the bulkhead walls of the wardroom in place, before being detailed to take away the small individual panels and the frame that held the door. Going below, they were joined by those carrying the interior walls to the captain's cabin, and followed by others bearing furniture; wine cooler, leaved dining table, chairs and chests, a mirror glass wrapped in canvas, the double cot, brass wall lamps that lit the cabins, all carefully stacked by a petty officer in a way that protected each object from damage.

They returned to a maindeck already sanded so that bare

feet would not slip, bare from stem to stern and with the guns run out through open ports. The men who had been with them moved swiftly to their allotted positions, while a harrying voice to the rear ordered them aloft, back to the weapon on which they had been practising, to a deck and sea view in which not much seemed to have changed. Captain Ralph Barclay was still standing swaying amidships, hands clasped behind him, surrounded by his fawning officers and midshipmen. Mrs Barclay was still by the weather ratlines, looking in the same direction as everyone else, towards the French barque that was still holding the same course. The number of marines on the poop had thinned, and, looking around and up, Pearce saw that some of them had clambered up to the main and foremast caps. Kemp had moved close again and was glaring at any pressed man or volunteer landsman who caught his eye.

'Mr Digby.'

The shout made Pearce look round, only to see that the puce-faced captain was pointing right at him. Although alarmed, Pearce registered that the captain's wife had turned also, to follow that accusing finger, and he could not help but look at her face, pink from the crisp air, eyes staring at him with what he thought was curiosity, as though she was truly wondering, as he was himself, how he had got here.

'Start that man. He is not here to stare over the rail, he is here to work the guns.'

'Sir,' Digby responded, before insisting quietly. 'Move, man, before you earn the rattan.'

Kemp managed to get round Digby and give Pearce a swipe, followed by a defiant look at the lieutenant and another at Pearce that was virtually an invitation to retaliate. He had to fight the temptation to oblige.

'I will not have passengers, Mr Digby,' Barclay added, a comment that endorsed the action of the snivelling bosun's mate, and cut off whatever it was Digby had intended to say to him.

Mess Number Twelve were round the gun again, and although it had only been a half an hour since they had been practising, it was clear that most of the party, with tired minds as well as exhausted bodies, had forgotten where to stand. Pearce, his back still smarting from the blow Kemp had given him, and aware that he was close enough to administer more, ordered his messmates into place, as he overheard Lieutenant Digby, in a stiff voice, acknowledge the captain's words.

'Michael, with me on this side, Rufus, you and Corny on the other.' Ben Walker, seeing where the others were going, realised his own station, and picked up the swab, and the volunteer who had joined them, though he had yet to exchange a word with them, took up the rammer. A young boy of about ten years presented himself, carrying half a dozen square cloth bundles, roughly sewn, and looked around the faces, clearly seeking someone to whom they should be given.

'Cartridges,' he piped, only to be greeted by a sea of uninterested faces. 'Which one of you buggers is the gun captain?'

'Sure that is the one thing missing, John-boy,' said O'Hagan, nudging Pearce.

'Happen you should take that on, Pearce,' added Gherson in an arch voice. 'You seem comfortable giving out orders.'

'Someone's got to take them,' said the boy. 'I'll get my arse whipped if I ain't back at the gunner's window in half a shake.'

'Mr Hale,' barked Digby, realising the dilemma, and calling to the coxswain who had just come on to the quarterdeck, armed and bearing his captain's sword and pistols, 'double to the maindeck. Get me two gunners standing by, experienced enough to act as captains. We won't get the real thing this time. I want them on deck as soon as we engage.'

'You're asking for the moon on this barky,' Hale griped, his objection clearly more to being given the task in the first place than the requirement it placed upon him, 'there is hardly a soul aboard who knows stem from stern.'

'You, boy,' Digby added, 'lay those cartridges along the back of the shot garland. The rest of you, for the sake of the Lord do not cast off until you are ordered to do so. This is your station but because we are short of hands there will be other tasks to perform. Go to those tasks, then return here when they are complete, and don't, at your peril, stare at the captain. Keep your eyes firmly the other way and no slouching.'

'Mr Collins,' said Barclay, just as Digby finished. 'I believe it is nearly time to show our Frenchman the nature of his mistake.'

'Sir?'

So close, Pearce could see in the way that Collins responded, that he posed very much a question, instead of what Barclay clearly expected, which was an acknowledgement.

'Damn you, man,' the captain hissed.

Ralph Barclay's blood was up, and even if he was happy that it was so he had no time to indulge the idiots with whom he had been saddled. Right now he would have given his eye-teeth for the men who had sailed with him on his last commission, officers and a master who knew his ways and anticipated his orders, who trusted him and never ever returned him a questioning look when given a command.

'Stand by to adjust the sails as we did before, sir! Are you not aware that at any moment now that Frenchman is going to luff up and run? Do you know nothing, sir, or guess less?'

CHAPTER TWELVE

Not one of the tyro gun crew, Pearce least of all, was obeying the last injunction of Lieutenant Digby to look away, all were intent on watching what was happening on the quarterdeck. There, the two men on the wheel were stony-faced and staring straight ahead; the flustered Master, face creased with worry, was trying to compose in his mind the order of words he would need to obey the Captain; Farmiloe, the lanky midshipman, fiddled with the leaves of a thick, oilskin-covered book. Plump little Burns in his oversized coat stood by and Lieutenant Roscoe, the fallen side of his face hidden from them, glared at his captain's back as Barclay moved over to talk to his wife.

'You must go below now, my dear. The deck will be no place for you once the balls begin to fly.'

'Will there be wounded, Captain Barclay?' Emily asked, glancing to where Lutyens had taken station. Her husband's eyes followed hers.

'Mr Lutyens,' he called, 'I suggest you would be better placed below decks. That is where your duty requires you to be.' A rather abashed surgeon obeyed, as Ralph Barclay turned back to say quietly to his wife, 'It is very possible, nothing is certain in a fight at sea, though I hope the injured are French dogs rather than any of my own men.'

'Then with your permission, I will go to Mr Lutyens and offer my services.'

Barclay had to think about that. Was it proper for his wife to help there? She had never seen a cockpit after a sea fight. Was she up to the amount of blood and gore that could be generated, the lopping off of limbs from frightened men, their screaming mingling with that of the wounded awaiting their fate at the hands of a man who could be more butcher than surgeon? Lutyens with the knife and saw was an unknown quantity.

'Do you have any idea, my dear, of what an unpleasant place that can be?'

'I cannot be useless, Captain Barclay, and I hope and pray that you would not want me to be.'

Barclay had to draw in his breath then, struck, as he had been many times since their betrothal, by the sheer beauty of Emily when she took on her features that look of determination. He wanted to refuse her request, partly in order to spare her, but more from a fear that, faced with the reality of a bloody cockpit, she might embarrass him by fleeing. But those green eyes fixed on him were death to any resolve, and he found himself nodding.

'But, my dear,' Ralph Barclay added, without conviction, 'if you become distressed, you must leave immediately.'

He got another direct look, and words that made him wonder if this young wife of his could read his mind. 'I would not dare to do that, for it would disgrace your name, our name.'

'Mr Burns,' Barclay called, without turning, for he was still held by those eyes. 'My wife will not be going to the cable tier. I require you to escort Mrs Barclay, once she has changed her clothing, to the cockpit.'

Then he did turn, to look around the ship, the expression on his face seeming to desire that all aboard should match that spirit. The triumphant ocular tour brought him right round to the gun, and the staring faces of Mess Number Twelve.

'Mr Roscoe, are you aware of those men and what they are about?'

Roscoe, who had been looking in the direction of the chase, was startled, and his body seemed to jerk as he threw himself towards them, snarling in what was an excessive reaction. 'I have you marked, you bloody swine, and I'll see you damned.'

'Language, sir,' Barclay admonished him, 'my wife is still in earshot.'

'Mr Farmiloe, take the names of these men,' Roscoe added.

'I have your name, sir,' Barclay continued, glaring at Roscoe, who was forced to turn and face him. The man had been daydreaming, which at a time like this was unforgivable. 'I have it in my head, and by God I shall soon enter it in the log, and I assure you it will not be as a paean to your competence.'

'Now there, by Jesus,' whispered Michael O'Hagan, his body halfway across the gun, his heavily bruised face bemused, 'is a man prone to the making of enemies.'

'Silence, there,' said Midshipman Farmiloe, who had come to take their names.

'All hands to change sail,' the master yelled.

For the first time since being dragged aboard, Twelve Mess shot to the place where they were required without either orders or the use of a rattan, leaving the lanky mid looking very foolish. Sore hands or not they stood ready to haul on the ropes that controlled the great mainsail. A line appeared out of the sky, as it had on the previous occasion, but this time, without being ordered to do so, Rufus Dommet caught it and hauled it to the belaying pin that held the corner of the sail taut, while Ben Walker, again unbidden, began to undo the binding. The other members of the mess took hold of the rope attached to the corner of the sail, to hold it so that it would not fly off on the wind and leave the sail flapping uselessly.

Someone, somewhere, showed a degree of competence, perhaps the master, for two experienced sailors arrived to tie the knot that would splice the two ropes together, then to supervise the way it was paid out so that the corner of the maincourse could be raised to form a triangle with the apex lashed to the yard very close to the mainmast, all the time without once allowing the pressure of the wind to carry it away.

'Bugger me, mate,' said one of the experienced hands, with a look of surprise. 'Happen you're learnin'.'

'What's that called?' asked Pearce. 'That manoeuvre?'

'It be called a goose wing,' said one of the sailors. 'Capt'n reckons the forecourse'll draw better that way 'cause by lifting the corner of the mainsail the wind can get at it.'

'Thank you, friend,' replied Pearce. 'Much obliged.'

They were moving away, back to wherever they had come from, when one sailor said to the other, 'Much obliged. Happen there's somethin' to be said for having a gent aboard, Smithy.'

'Well, we're short of the commodity on the quarterdeck, mate,' the other replied, 'an' that's no error.'

'Do we go back to the gun now?' asked Charlie Taverner.

The question was addressed to Pearce, underlining how he, without wishing for or seeking it, and with Gherson objecting, was being deferred to. His affirmative nod had them all moving.

'Look out for that midshipman that was set to take our names,' hissed Rufus.

'That sailor was right,' said Pearce, 'we are learning.'

It was a silent group that shuffled back to the gun and when they got there they kept their eyes firmly away from the knot of officers on the quarterdeck, though they could hear clearly enough whatever was being said.

'There he goes, sir,' called Digby, 'he has let fly and ported his helm.'

Barclay responded boastfully. 'But we have stolen half a cable's length on the son of a bitch.'

Lieutenant Roscoe snorted with what could only be termed derision. 'Hardly that, sir.'

Pearce had to sneak a look, guessing that if he had deliberately set out to rile his commanding officer, Roscoe could not have chosen a better way. He saw Barclay swell up. 'I take leave to surmise you would not have done anything. I admonish you to learn from this, sir, for it is to the pity of the Navy that you may one day command your own vessel.'

'Sir, you cannot address me so,' Roscoe protested.

Barclay's reply was icy. 'Sir, I am the captain of this ship. I can address you howsoever I like.'

'That, sir,' Roscoe responded, 'will, I think, be decided by those in higher authority when I demand a court martial.'

'Demand away, sir. I look forward to a public exposure of your conduct. Now you will oblige me by being silent. We have, in case you have forgotten, an enemy to fight.'

'On deck there! *Firefly* signalling.'

Farmiloe was glad to be back in his signal book. He was able to see clearly the flags, and was no longer obliged to stare straight ahead and listen to the bitter, embarrassing exchanges of his Captain and First Lieutenant.

'Captain Gould is asking again for permission to pursue the chase, sir.'

Pearce saw Ralph Barclay lose his temper completely then, yelling in a voice that could be heard all over the deck. 'Am I to be plagued? Is there an officer in the service that understands an order when it is given?' His voice dropped, but not much. 'Mr Farmiloe, repeat the signal to *Firefly* to hold his position.'

'I feel I must speak, sir,' said Roscoe. 'My duty demands it.'

'What?'

'Captain Gould is surely a match for the chase.'

'So?'

'It flies in the face of all reason not to let *Firefly* pursue, and I can only assume that another reason, not a tactical one, intrudes on your thinking.'

'Mr Roscoe...'

'Please, sir,' Roscoe interrupted, 'make sure that those remarks are noted in the log along with anything you may choose to enter.'

'I will note that you have undertaken to exceed your position. Now oblige me by remembering your rank.'

Ralph Barclay had to turn away then, because his Premier

had stung him into examining what he was doing – and Roscoe had the right of it. Davidge Gould did command a vessel that could sail closer to the wind, and his sloop was well enough armed to fight the Frenchman. But Gould did not need what he needed, which was something that could be set against his name to elevate it. Gould had influence and a seeming rapport with those in authority. The captain of HMS *Brilliant* enjoyed none of these advantages; indeed he was sure in his own mind that amongst those who mattered at the Admiralty there was a conspiracy to do him down.

'I will respond to you, Mr Roscoe, so that when we meet in court, in front of officers who comprehend the matter more clearly, the thing is clear. I agree that *Firefly* is a match for our Frenchmen, but she is no more than that. Thus, in an engagement, when nothing is certain, she may suffer either in casualties or shipboard damage. That is something, which as joint escorts, who are not yet clear of the Channel, we can ill afford. Who knows what force we might meet at this, the beginning of a war. And, sir, I would remind you that we are bound for the Mediterranean and it is incumbent upon us to arrive whole and of some use. We, on the other hand, risk nothing against such an enemy. If we cannot catch him we will at least drive him off.'

Roscoe snorted again. Pearce reckoned he could not say the captain was a liar, not openly anyway, but wished to make it clear he thought him so.

'I cannot comprehend this,' said Pearce softly to his mates. He was wondering how, when these men had a ship to command and a possible battle to fight, in which the sailors under their command could be wounded or die, they could indulge themselves in a personal quarrel.

'It's simple, Pearce,' said Ben Walker, in his measured West Country drawl. 'They're both bastards, but one is a bigger bastard than the other.'

The Frenchman could not have been unaware of the approach of HMS *Brilliant*, because quite apart from her course, the signal gun was in almost constant use to alert merchant captains to get out of the way. Barclay was crowding on sail, topgallants and fore and outer jib, and ploughing through the water looked set to ram any sod that got in his way. Not everyone reacted with the required speed, and the frigate captain showed his impatience by putting a roundshot over the bows of one merchant ship that was a tad laggardly in backing its top hamper to let him through.

The captain of the French barque had done what Barclay had supposed he would – put up his helm and headed for his home shore over the eastern horizon. Barclay's intention was to cut an angle that would bring the fellow to battle before he could get clear. It would be touch and go, he could see that, but he was slightly strung in the amount of canvas he could bear aloft. The overnight gale had abated somewhat but he still had to contend with a blustery west wind that was far from constant, so that what appeared a sound sail plan one minute looked excessive the next, as the frigate heeled over in a gust and the lee rail came close to the water.

'Holy Mother of Christ,' groaned Michael O'Hagan, as the pea-green sea, flecked with foam, rose up to meet him. The others, particularly Gherson could not look. Pearce was far from sanguine, though he had seen the Dover to Calais packet in the same state and recalled that, alarmed as he had certainly been, the vessel had always righted itself.

Just as Barclay was about to ease something to take the pressure off his sails the wind would decrease, leaving him with the conundrum of knowing that very likely he would face the same dilemma in a few moments. The chase was not idle; sailing large, with the wind coming in over her stern, the enemy ship had also crowded on canvas to escape. Barclay realised that with such a wind on such a bearing the barque could trend away southwards whenever she liked, increasing the distance at which he would cross the T of her course.

'Mr Collins, I require a little more southing,' said Barclay.

'Then we must take in some sail, sir, or ease the braces. With the yards so far round the wind will be coming in over our beam.'

'Let us see how she fares. She is a good sea boat I think, and will serve us well.' It was a gamble, because Barclay was risking carrying away something major. *Brilliant* would not be thrown on her beam-ends but one of his tightly lodged and stiff masts might go by the board with so much pressure on them. 'Mr Roscoe, a party standing by to ease the wedges on the mainmast.'

'Chase is altering course to the south, sir,' said Collins.

Even given the time it was taking to close there was added tension on the ship. Pearce had the feeling that not everyone was happy. Collins, from what he could see was incapable of the emotion and Roscoe was miserable, convinced that what his captain was about was wrong. But it was the crew that interested him most, or those he could see. All were looking forward one minute, then at a mast when it, and the rigging that held it, groaned with the strain. It looked to be a strange combination of exhilaration and fear.

'A bow chaser, Mr Roscoe,' Barclay ordered, never once

taking his eye off the prize. 'Only the windward port can be opened with any safety I think. Get it manned and run out if you please. Let's try the range as soon as it is loaded.'

Burns was sent with the message and the bow chaser was fired within minutes, sending a great spiral of black smoke billowing out and across the front of the ship before it was carried away on the wind. Craning, Pearce tried to see the fall of the shot, but at the height of the deck and in a choppy sea that was impossible. The information came from the masthead, where they could see.

'A whole cable length shy of the target, your honour.'

'Very well,' said Barclay. If he was disappointed it did not show.

Every ten minutes the guns fired, it being noted that although the range was closing it was not yet true. Ralph Barclay knew that he could have the fellow, because at some time soon, when they were in range, he could change course to bring more guns to bear.

'Chase has altered course again, your honour,' called the lookout.

'Heading due west by my reckoning,' said Collins.

'The man's a fool,' hooted Barclay, 'though I cannot say his stupidity displeases me.'

'He's bending on more sail, stun sails and kites by the look of it.'

Moving forward Ralph Barclay raised his telescope to his eye, and an enemy ship that was in plain view anyway swam into focus. He could see the crew on the deck, numerous, as befitted a privateer vessel, as they struggled to get aloft a mass of canvas. It was ten minutes before they succeeded, during which Ralph Barclay felt he was holding his breath, for what his adversary was about made little sense. With a frigate on his quarter he should have kept his previous course, maintaining as much distance as he could so that when the gap between the two ships closed, *Brilliant* would still be at maximum range. By his present actions he was exposing himself to a broadside at a distance where it could do serious damage in the very first salvo, damage that would make escape impossible.

Being disabused of the notions he was considering was a moment of deep discomfort for Ralph Barclay. Almost as soon as the Frenchman had sheeted home his extra sails the barque leapt forward. Fresh from port she had a clean bottom, and her lines were such that she had always looked swift. Now she showed just how good she was, leaving the captain of HMS *Brilliant* in no doubt that, if he did not react, he would be lucky if she ever came in range.

'Alter course to the south, Mr Collins.'

'Sir,' said the Master, 'we are carrying too much canvas.'

'Get those wedges knocked out on the mainmast now,' growled Barclay, 'and Mr Collins, do as I bid.' Then he shouted in a stentorian voice, 'Bow chaser, maximum elevation. Try the range again.'

As *Brilliant* turned, the wind took her over until the boom end of her maincourse yard was nearly in the water. Everywhere on the steeply canted deck people were hanging on for dear life. But that did not last long, for the forecourse ripped right across its length from the pressure of the wind and the decrease in force began to right the ship. But without that sail the pressure on the rest would increase and it was only a matter of time before a mast went by the board or another stretch of canvas ripped itself asunder.

'Mr Collins, ease the braces then bring me round onto a

parallel course to the chase. Mr Roscoe, a new forecourse from the sail locker immediately, and all hands to bend it on.'

The command to ease echoed down the ship – one loop being taken off the belaying pins by men who knew they had to leave the second one be, to keep a grip on the falls. The great sails began to flap, cracking like angry gods as they lost the pressure of the wind. As the rudder was hauled round and the bows trended eastwards, on one side of the deck they were pulling hard, while on the other Mess Number Twelve was easing out the ropes while maintaining control with a single loop. Ralph Barclay was pleased by the way the manoeuvre was carried out, because his ship never lost steerage way and once the head was round the command to sheet home was given and the yards were tied off.

'Jesus,' said Michael, 'did we do that right or what?'

'Nobody cursed us,' said Ben Walker, 'and that has to be a first.'

'Now, Mr Roscoe,' said Barclay, with grim determination, 'we will see what our ship can do.'

'*Firefly* signalling again, sir,' called Farmiloe. 'Do you require assistance?'

'Negative.'

Ralph Barclay's mind was teeming. He was on a course now that would suit his ship, with the wind coming in over his starboard quarter, probably her best point of sailing. He could get aloft as much sail as his ship could bear, but he would not discern for an age if he had the legs of the chase – although he knew she was a bit of a flyer. Against that he had a standing order to stay in sight of the convoy.

'A signal to Captain Gould, Mr Farmiloe, to take station to the east of our charges.'

Firefly's masthead would be the convoy as far as he was concerned, and he hoped that Gould would smoke his intention and put himself as far eastwards as he dare. This would allow him to extend the range to which he could chase a quarry running before him.

'Now, Mr Collins, I require to be shown what my ship will bear aloft.'

By the time the men had been released to have their dinner, Ralph Barclay knew that with the wind now steady in the west, blowing stiff but not hard, he could catch the Frenchman, but what was worrying, as the afternoon wore on, was the season. There was not much daylight left. It was gratifying to observe that his crew was eager – few stayed snug below for long, though it was cold on deck, for what they were after represented a cash bounty to every man aboard. His dinner had been a hurried affair, taken in full view of those on the maindeck, for his cabin walls were still in the holds, and Emily, who had craved to do so, was allowed to join him on deck. There he pointed out to her the various sails he had aloft, near a full suit, rising through courses, topsails, topgallants to kites.

'While those, my dear, on the weather side, that being where the wind is coming from, are called studdingsails. Look behind us and you will see how the mizzen gaff is braced right round to take the wind, and forward we have everything twixt foremast and jib boom she will carry, spirit sails included. We are, at present, maintaining a steady nine knots.'

Pearce, back at his station on the larboard side where the gangway joined the quarterdeck, watched Barclay as he patiently explained matters to his wife. The wind, still strong but now of a more even temper, coming over the other side of the stern, carried the captain's words to him, not all distinct but enough for him to follow what the captain was alluding to. Pearce was impressed, as much by the rate of progress through the water as by the beauty of the huge quantity of taut sails.

The ship they were pursuing, drawing gradually closer, but at an imperceptible rate, had a beauty of her own, showing a clean white wake astern. The air, now that the wind was not coming in over the bows, was not wet, but it had about it a tang of cleanliness the like of which he had rarely experienced. Hate his situation he might, but he felt it would be churlish not to take pleasure from what he could, though the prospect of what was coming to the Frenchman was not something he could be happy about.

'First,' Dysart had told him and his fellows, 'we will gie the bugger what for wi' the bow chasers. Maybe knock away a spar or two. Then we will range alongside and if he disna strike his colours damn quick we will give him a what for of a broadside, aimed high, mind, so that the hull will no be damaged.'

'Then?' asked Charlie Taverner.

'Well, if he's an eejit, we will board.'

'Idiot,' Pearce had translated, which earned him a raised eyebrow from Dysart, as if he was saying, maybe you're a Scot after all.

'But like as not he will strike, and then we can do a wee calculation and see how much everybody has made.'

'Do you have any notion now?' asked Gherson, long lashes fluttering in a way that made Dysart frown.

'Two eighths of the whole is what we get.'

'That is a quarter,' Gherson added pedantically.

'Is that a fact?' Dysart replied, without much certainty.

There was general air of excitement, but that soon faded as reality intruded, despite the best efforts of Dysart to fabricate a better case. Pearce wondered, as the Scotsman explained, at a system of rewards so heavily weighted in favour of officers. Up to three eighths for the captain, two if he had to give one to an admiral; one for the superior officers, one for the warrants, one for the petty officers and just two for the men who did the actual fighting, who naturally, being the largest numerical group, had a portion sliced exceedingly thin. It was the kind of arrangement against which his father had railed half his life – those who had the most, got the most, while the needy were given what would, when it was split with so many, be a pittance. It was good to discern that the crew of the ship, as they discussed the matter, were as unimpressed as he and they had made it plain that, while any payment was welcome, the way monies were split was a bone of contention throughout the entire fleet.

'Masthead,' Barclay called, 'do you still have sight of HMS *Firefly*?'

'She's hull down now, your honour, but I can still see the main jack yard as she rises on the swell, and her pennant is plain regardless.'

'Mr Roscoe. What was the name of that missing East Indiaman, the one that hauled his wind last evening?'

'She was the *Lady Harrington* out of London, sir.'

Barclay stared right at Roscoe then, as if challenging him. 'Tell our lookouts to keep an eye out for her.'

He got a stare back, then the beginnings of comprehension. Barclay could leave sight of the bulk of his convoy in only one instance; to look for and chivvy stragglers. That would be entered in the ship's log, to cover the captain against chastisement.

'Mr Roscoe,' Barclay added, 'I think we must try the bow chasers again, both cannon this time. The hour demands it.'

Pearce had to stand aside as Ralph Barclay took his wife forward, so that she could witness the firing of the guns from beneath her feet, and, Barclay hoped, see the spouts of water created by the shot, though it was a forlorn hope that she would see a ball strike the chase. Emily Barclay smiled at Pearce. Here before her was that writer of the coded letter, and with that in her mind she said, softly, *Pardonnez-moi.*

The object of the apology had returned her look until she spoke, grey eyes steady, then he nodded his head and executed one twentieth of a bow to accept her greeting, wondering why she had spoken to him in French. Ralph Barclay was curious regarding two things; why his wife had addressed him at all, for he had only heard the sound not the words, and what this low-life was doing reacting like a gentleman in a fashionable salon.

'Mr Digby,' he called. 'This fellow on the gangway does not know his manners. Please be so good at to show him how to salute a captain and his lady.'

The face was close enough to see each broken vein. Pearce was thinking, don't respond, his fists clenched and his whole body as tight as a drum – that damned trembling afflicting him again. Fortunately Barclay and his wife moved on, Burns in tow like a footman, as Lieutenant Digby came to obey his captain's instructions.

'Officers, Pearce, lift their hats,' Digby said gently: then he made a loose fist, and touched the knuckle to his forehead. 'You salute in this manner.'

'And,' Pearce responded, staring straight at the officer, his voice even and his body beginning to relax, 'if I do not choose to make such a demeaning gesture?'

'Not to do so is a punishable offence.'

'So, in order to avoid punishment I must show my knuckle to a man I despise.'

Digby tried very hard to look furious, his face succeeding while his voice failed. 'I could have you at the grating for that.'

'Then you must do so, Lieutenant Digby, for nothing on this earth will get me to salute Captain Barclay.'

'Then stay out of his damned way, and his eye line.'

The booming cannon allowed Digby to turn away from a look he was at a loss to cope with. He knew it to be one of his failings as an officer, his inability to impose discipline by any other method than persuasion. Up till now, in the main, it had worked for him but as he moved away from Pearce he had very serious doubts if it would work with the man who had just challenged him. Suddenly, he spun round.

'Be assured Pearce, I will have you at the grating if need be. That I will take no pleasure in doing so will not stop me.'

Slowly, with just a trace of a smile on his face, Pearce raised a fist, and knuckled his forehead. 'Sir.'

'I hope you believe me,' Digby insisted, as a pair of cannon boomed out behind him.

'I believe you would take no pleasure in it, sir.'

'Short by the length of the chase, your honour.'

There was no need for the masthead report. Ralph Barclay had seen how short the balls had fallen, and if his wife was excited by the waterspouts that shot fifty feet in the air he was not, for it took no great genius to calculate that the rate that they were overhauling the chase would mean that he would sail not only into darkness, but out of sight of the convoy. He looked at the sky, which was nothing like the lowering clouds of the morning. As the day had gone on the cloud-base had lifted, but it was still overall grey, which meant that when darkness came there would be no moon or stars. Also the wind had moderated, although that applied to both him and the chase, yet there was no sense that it might fall away completely – this was the bight of Brittany. A calm here in March was as likely as a snowstorm in June.

Yet he so nearly had the fellow, another two or three hours and he would pour so much shot into him that he would be forced to strike. Where was he headed?

'Mr Burns, fetch me a glass.'

The telescope, on the rise, showed him he was pursuing the *Mercedes* out of the port of St Malo. To the south lay the wild shore of Brittany, a place no man in his right mind would head for in darkness. Quite apart from the hazards of rocks both submerged and above water, the tidal rise and fall was huge. The Frenchman could turn north, but with a wind fair for his home-port why bother, and if he did so he risked at dawn finding HMS *Brilliant* between him and safety.

The notion that he was hunting a straggler of an East Indiaman would not pass muster under malign scrutiny, but Ralph Barclay knew that if he had a capture the examining eyes would look more kindly.

'Mr Burns, please tell Mr Roscoe that the hands are to be piped to supper.'

Emily looked at her husband then with admiration, and he, returning that look thought of what success would bring for her. That she was a lady was not in doubt; neither was the fact that she would grace his rank to whatever heights he rose. In his mind he imagined the benefits she would enjoy from being wife to a successful sailor, a taker of numerous prizes: carriages, a beautiful home, servants, and children so well found in wealth and position that if they ever did decide to go to sea, they would do so with none of the constraints which had dogged his career.

'And Mr Burns, please ask Mr Roscoe to prepare to darken ship. We are going to continue the chase once the light goes, but I have no notion to let the fellow know it.'

It was ghostly sailing along in the dark. A tarpaulin had been rigged before the binnacle locker so that no light showed forward. Below decks only enough lanterns were lit to allow a man to pass from one place to the next without injury, and screens had been rigged to ensure that nothing showed aloft. HMS *Brilliant* ploughed on in stygian darkness that, with solid cloud cover, allowed for no phosphorescence, either from the crest wave, the frigates bow, or even the wake of the chase. Men were forward, one out on the bowsprit, eyes peeled for a glimmer of inadvertent light – for the chase had darkened likewise – or for some clink of sound as someone moved around the deck, able to report back to Ralph Barclay, sat in his cabin, that the odd noise could be heard as, 'those lubberly French dogs moved around.'

'Orders to Mr Roscoe,' Barclay replied. 'Men to sleep by watches, two hours each. Any man making a sound I will flog to oblivion.'

That such reports of noises ceased as the night wore on did not bother Ralph Barclay over-much. He assumed that with everything set and braced, on a breeze that was holding steady, his adversary had sent most of his crew to their hammocks. He started to doze in his chair, unaware that his wife, worried about him, was having difficulty sleeping at all in the restored and screened off cot.

* * *

'Pearce, wake up!'

Dragged from a lubricious dream that largely featured the captain's wife – naked as well as willing – and life on land and comfort, Pearce was slow to respond to the shake, reluctant to leave such an agreeable fantasy. When he did awake it was to the immediate knowledge, through sound and smell, that he was still aboard ship. Such interruption was doubly unwelcome given that sleeping two hours on and two off exacerbated the exhaustion of the normal four-hour regime. Eyes open, he had to think hard to recognise the voice that was urgently repeating his name, for there was no light at all on the maindeck of the darkened ship.

'Rufus,' he guessed.

Dommet answered with an urgent whisper. 'Corny's in trouble.'

'Good,' Pearce murmured.

'It's serious.'

Pearce yawned before he responded. 'Even better.'

Rufus shook him hard again. 'It's no jest. I mean it. I was on my way to the heads when I heard the clack of dice coming from one of the boats.'

Still reluctant to be awake, wishing to return to the agreeable reverie of his dream, Pearce growled at Rufus. He, like some of the others, had spotted, since coming aboard, that there were any number of surreptitious activities taking place with the crew off watch; sailors slipping away from the maindeck with backward looks that could only be described as furtive. He had reckoned gambling or secret drinking, without wanting to think about anything else certain members of the crew might be getting up to in the dark corners of the lower deck.

'Then I heard that boy Dent. He were whispering but I'm sure it were him.'

That name brought Pearce fully awake. 'Dent.'

'He was talkin' murder, John.'

Pearce growled, 'Wake Charlie and Ben!' Swiftly he rolled out of his hammock, jostling O'Hagan to rouse him, pressing his mouth close to the Irishman's ear and using Dent's name to cut through any confusion.

Michael O'Hagan was on his feet in no time at all because he, like all the other members of the mess, was under no illusion that, just because he had beaten Devenow in a fight, Martin Dent had ceased his vendetta against Pearce and Charlie Taverner, as well as all those associated with them. Ben was up in a flash, like a man who lived in the fear of a hand on his collar. It took longer to get Charlie Taverner stirring, but within a minute all five men were huddled under their hammocks as Rufus told what he had heard.

'It was when I were coming back that I heard a bit of commotion, double quiet like, but much like a bit of a scuffle, so I stops to have me a listen. Then I heard Corny's squeak. You know how he wheedles.'

Pearce could not see the heads nod in the dark, but he could almost feel their reaction; the other three knew and disliked, just as much as he did, the tone Gherson used when he was after something.

'Anyway, I got a bit closer. Then I heard Dent saying that a pressed man was not to be trusted, that he might start a'gabbin' and the safest way to be secure was to chuck the bastard overboard.'

'No need to enquire who the bastard is,' hissed O'Hagan.

'We've got to look,' said Pearce.

'Why?' demanded Charlie Taverner in a soft, but bitter voice. 'That sod would see us swing as soon as look at us.'

'You don't know that for sure, Charlie,' whispered Ben Walker, 'and he's one of our mess, for better or worse.'

'If you don't move quick,' Rufus insisted, in what for him was a rare show of determination, 'he won't be. We'll be down to five instead of the seven we started with, and that little sod Dent will be huntin' for another victim.'

Pearce nudged Rufus to lead the way, tapping the others to follow, thinking, as they complied, they were motivated more by apprehension at what a slip of a boy might get up to next rather than any desire to save Gherson. The need to be quiet was paramount for the ship was still after that Frenchman – even the marines doing sentry duty on the quarterdeck and outside the magazine had been told to discard their shoes, lest a clicking heel carry to the enemy, and no petty officers were touring the decks as was normal on watch.

Barefoot, they made no noise at all as they slipped up the companionway steps and, feeling the cold of the night air, scurried on to the gangway, crawling forward, ears straining for a sound, until Rufus, stopping, forced the others to do likewise.

Pearce heard what had stopped him, muffled voices, but disputatious, coming from under the canvas that covered what he thought would be the cutter, a good place to gamble, being out of sight and a spot from which, under a thick tarpaulin, no light would escape. It did just then, for the briefest second, before an angry voice commanded someone to shade it, leaving Pearce to wonder at men so obsessed with their compulsion that they would take a risk on such a night as this, when Barclay would certainly flog to oblivion any man he caught alerting his quarry to his position.

A grunt brought forth another command to 'silence that bugger and get him over to the bulwark'.

'Stop right there, mate,' said Pearce, in a voice he feared was loud enough to carry to the quarterdeck, praying that the sound of the wind and the creaking of the masts and rigging would muffle it.

The response was a hiss. 'Who's that?'

'Twelve Mess, mate, and I reckon you have one of our number.'

'You're wrong, friend.' A short low moan followed, then a slight thud. Pearce knew the first had come from Gherson and the second from whoever had hold of him. 'And you be takin' a right risk raising your voice so.'

'Dicing is a risk on its own, friend.'

'Who's to say what we was about?'

'I don't care about that,' Pearce growled, 'and neither does the man you are holding.'

'You ain't listening, are you?'

Michael had eased up beside Pearce and it was he who replied. 'For sure, it is you that is not using your ears.'

'It's the big Paddy,' said another voice

The fellow who was the leader hissed then, 'Will you cap that bloody noise!'

'There's more than the big Paddy, brother,' Michael added. 'There's enough here to take you on, and sod the noise.'

'You lot would suffer along with us.'

'Be that as it may,' Pearce whispered, 'it is what will come to pass. Best just let our man go.'

'He's like to squeal.'

'If I guessed gambling was going on aboard, so can those in authority.'

The pause before the speaker replied worried Pearce, but eventually the fellow said, 'It be the sure way for quiet.'

'Only Martin Dent would say that, and you should be sure his aim is the same as your own.'

The sudden sound of scampering feet alerted Pearce to the boy's presence. It also told him that Martin was not going to hang around.

'Martin who?' the sailor responded.

'I am going to count,' murmured O'Hagan, 'quiet like and not past three. If our man is not set free then I will come into that boat and start swinging.'

'Get those bonds off him,' the voice said, after another pause.

'Leave them on,' said Pearce suddenly, and too loudly for safety, for he was fearful that Gherson, free to take off his gag and yell blue murder, would do just that and damn the consequences. 'Just help him out and we will take him below.'

'If he talks...'

'He won't,' Pearce insisted, 'you have my word on that.'

'I know who you are, mate, with that gent's manner of yours, and if that word is broken it will be you I come after.'

Once released, Gherson started to mumble through the gag, until Michael threatened to throw him overboard. They hustled him down to the maindeck, eyes fixed towards the invisible quarterdeck, sure that every sound they were making must carry to whichever officer was on watch. But nothing stirred from that area, and soon, by feel and with a writhing Gherson, they got back to the spot under their own empty hammocks, not without grunts from those whose slumber they had disturbed.

'Un-gag him,' said Pearce. 'But leave his hands.'

'I...'

'Shut up,' hissed Pearce, 'or that gag goes back on. You get into your hammock, you close your eyes, and you say nothing, do you understand?'

The reply took several seconds to emerge, and Pearce could easily imagine Gherson trying to calculate which was the best for him. The needs of the men who had just saved his life would probably not count.

'Yes,' he whispered eventually.

'Undo his hands. Then let's try and get some sleep.'

Michael O'Hagan had the last word, speaking from his cot to a wide-awake Pearce.

'Why did we bother, John-boy?'

But not the last sound. That was of sobbing coming from Gherson's hammock.

CHAPTER THIRTEEN

The time was marked without bells, each turn of the half-hour sandglass merely scored on the slate. But Barclay had left his orders, and he was on deck well before the first hint of light, whispering admonishment to the men proceeding to their battle stations to be quiet. He even went down to the maindeck to talk to the bow chaser gunners, aware as he passed each loaded cannon that not every one was manned, for he needed his topmen aloft to take in sail damned quick. With so much set he risked a great deal if anything important was shot away by his quarry's stern chasers.

The first hint of grey produced no silhouette. That was not a worry, both ships would have made subtle alterations to their course throughout the night, and indeed *Brilliant* might have head-reached the chase and been forced to come about to engage. The slow March dawn was agonising, taking as it did almost an hour from the first tinge on the horizon until there was enough daylight to see a patch of seawater. As the light increased it revealed an ocean bereft of ships. Ralph Barclay waited until he could see the proverbial grey goose at a quarter of a mile, till he knew that he was alone on the water, before issuing any orders.

'Stand the men down, Mr Roscoe, and resume normal duties once the ship has been put back to rights. Mr Collins, we need to come about and make a rendezvous with the convoy. Pray be so good as to shape us a course.'

Everything that had been struck below was brought up again and put back in place. The guns were housed, cartridges returned to the gunners, rammers, swabs and crowbars stowed over the replaced mess tables and the makeshift benches. The only thing that was not the same as before was the mood of the ship, which ranged from quiet disappointment to spoken disenchantment.

Ever since waking, and thinking about what had occurred the previous night, Pearce had felt a nagging doubt. Contemplating murder was a somewhat extreme way to cover up an activity such as gambling. At his station beside the quarterdeck cannon he had tried to examine Gherson's face for some clue to another reason – without enlightenment, for the subject of his scrutiny would not look any of his messmates in the eye, and especially not John Pearce, confining any communication to an occasional grunt, one of which was a less than fulsome thanks. The near-silence lasted through the morning rituals of cleaning and eating breakfast, and it was not until they began to carry out deck work, greasing blocks and pulleys, that Pearce could get Gherson far enough away from the others to pose some questions.

'I was not snooping,' Gherson insisted, his face taking on the habitual look of a thwarted child.

'It's natural to be curious,' Pearce replied, soothingly, 'and

I myself wondered what some of the crew were up to creeping about, and I daresay the others have too.'

'Who? Idiots like Taverner or Dommet. That I doubt.'

Pearce was about to say that it was unwise to underestimate Charlie, but thought better of it. 'It was Rufus who told us you were in danger. Odd that you have not asked how we came to your rescue?'

'I am grateful. I have already said that.'

Pearce thought if he was he did not look it. 'What was it those fellows were up to?'

'Gambling, of course.'

'What else?'

Gherson's reply was, to Pearce's ears, too emphatic. 'There was nothing else.'

'So why were you there?'

'I admit to a weakness for dicing. I was looking for a way of making that known, when I was set upon and dragged under the canvas.'

'Silently?' Pearce asked. 'You made no noise.'

'I had no chance to,' Gherson replied with a direct stare that challenged Pearce to disagree. That was followed by a look over his shoulder and the warning word, 'Kemp!' Pearce was left none the wiser. But he was still curious, and listened with care as the others asked very similar questions to his own, and ribbed Gherson for his less than convincing replies.

The sight of a pair of fishing boats, inshore of the frigate, caused Ralph Barclay to change course and close with them, ostensibly to buy fish but in reality to ask if they had seen his quarry. Pearce and his mates were on the foredeck, with

Dysart, picking shakings out of old ropes that they had been told were too far gone for use, so when HMS *Brilliant* came alongside they could hear the exchange of words, though only Pearce could comprehend them. Young Farmiloe was fetched forward by the captain to interpret, and made a good fist of his task, his questions about the privateer subtly interspersed with haggling over the price of the fish, which was eventually brought aboard in a basket.

'You know what they are about, don't you?' asked Michael. 'As you would, having lived among them.'

Pearce had been listening with obvious intent, ears cocked, wondering if he could drop overboard unseen and stay out of sight until the Frenchmen could pick him up. He might manage the former, but the latter was too risky – unable to shout because that would alert the frigate, he might find himself left to drown.

'I know that if those fishermen have any information about that ship we were chasing they are not saying.'

'What are they saying?'

Pearce smiled. 'They're damning the Revolution, Michael, for it has made it harder for them to get a decent price for their fish, let's say making music for an Englishman's ears.'

'Is that right?' asked Dysart. Neither Pearce nor Michael had seen the Scotsman move closer to them. In answer to their look of alarm, he winked. 'Dina worry yersel. Ah'll no tell onyone ye speak their heathen tongue.'

Pearce and the Scotsman exchanged a look, a half smile met by a nod from the sailor, then noticing that Dysart no longer wore his bandage he asked, 'How's the head?'

'Dinna go pretending yer concerned, laddie,' Dysart replied, but without rancour, lifting his hat to reveal a patch of shaved head and an ugly red scar. 'Dae ye want tae see yer handiwork, and that right though ma bluddy hat?'

'The surgeon's done a good job.'

'Like hell! I'd have been better off goin' tae the gunner's wife, cack-handed bugger that she is. At least she can use a bluddy needle, for as sure as God made little apples he ca'nae.'

Pearce, smilingly, could only agree. Dysart would bear that scar for life, even if it was hidden by his re-grown hair. 'I promise not to do it again.'

Pearce got a gentle elbow in the gut. 'You'll no get the chance, laddie. I'll shoot you first.'

Behind them the transaction was completed – Barclay and the wardroom had their dinner, freshly caught fish, some still writhing in the basket, and HMS *Brilliant* parted company, resuming its previous course.

In the last hour of their watch Pearce and his mates were ordered aloft. First they were required to climb and re-climb the shrouds, then when HMS *Brilliant* was on the starboard tack, the yards braced round so that they ran their whole length above the planking of the deck, they were being instructed on how to make their way on to the maincourse yard. They had come, if not to like, at least to accept climbing the main shrouds to the point where they joined with what was called the futtock shrouds, with the wind on their backs. Pearce felt reasonably secure clapped on to those ropes, even if the ship did sometimes heave over so that he was leaning backwards. Now he was required to move out into what seemed like thin air, with only a rope under bare feet to rest on, and that bordered on the suicidal. He looked at the looped lines that hung from the yard to hold that footrope, heard them called stirrups, and reckoned the whole assembly too flimsy for security.

'Look at that, lily-livers,' said Costello, as Michael O'Hagan, without a blink or a backward glance, put his foot on the rope and, arms and half his upper body over the yard, eased himself out. The ropes bent alarmingly, but they did support him. 'Now if a heifer like Paddy can trust his weight to the footropes, so can any other man here.'

His words earned him a glare from Michael, who was confident enough to free one hand to point a finger. 'Don't call me Paddy, and if I am a heifer beware of my hoof.'

Costello responded with his habitual grin, white teeth flashing, and ignored him, instead addressing Pearce, the next candidate. 'Well, Pearce, are you going to let this bog-trotter shame an Englishman, or is it only swimming you can manage?'

Pearce declined to challenge the nationality, and had no desire to acknowledge the other. He took a deep breath, and put out one foot.

'Call "Step on,"' said Costello, 'let the man already on the rope know you are coming, so that he will be aware of his own footing on the ropes, which will sag with your weight. If he is not properly set he will take a tumble.'

Pearce obliged, and that was followed by a command to, 'Clap on to that preventer stay,' Costello adding, in response to a look of utter incomprehension, 'that bloody great up and down rope right in front of you. Haul yourself on, then do what our Irish friend did and hang your body over the yard. Right, now move on out so that the rest can follow.'

Pearce, breathing deeply, hung as he was told without any feeling of security, the rope biting into the still-soft soles of his feet. That was when he heard the first faint sound of gunfire, a dull boom that reverberated across the water and was more obvious to those aloft than on deck.

'Jesus Christ,' said Costello, looking forward.

'What can I do for you?' asked Michael, with a mischievous look.

'Get down now,' the bosun's mate yelled, 'and stuff your jokes.'

Another dull boom came floating through the grey morning air as Ralph Barclay, hatless and coatless, came on deck, his eyes straining forward. 'Masthead, what do you see?'

'Nothing, your honour.'

'God damn the eyes of those fishermen! Mr Roscoe, all hands, get the best lookouts on the ship aloft and for God's sake someone get me more sail.'

What followed was a repeat of the previous day, for although the wind had shifted slightly to the north it was still not a breeze to favour the course they were steering. *Brilliant* was labouring into both a wind and an incoming Atlantic swell. And all the time the dull booming sound of the guns grew louder until finally what Ralph Barclay feared most was confirmed. The ship he had been chasing all night was attacking what looked like the East Indiaman that had become detached from the convoy.

Crowding on sail took no account of potential damage to the top hamper. Twice topsails blew out of their deadeyes and had to be reset. Ralph Barclay became frantic when the firing stopped, incandescent and railing at the course the Indiaman must have been sailing, which was nothing like that of the convoy. He was angry – even more so and unfairly – when he was told that *Firefly* was nowhere to be seen. He fell silent when informed that the *Mercedes* was hoisting sail, and that a French ensign flew over the East India Company pennant, declaring that she had just captured the valuable prize.

But despite that, he knew, as he cleared for action, he had a chance to redeem matters. He was between his quarry and St Malo. If the Frenchman headed for his home port he would have to get both barque and prize past the frigate; at the very least he would have to abandon the East Indiaman. At best *Brilliant* would take her back and board and take her captor as well.

'He is setting his course south, your honour,' called the lookout.

'Damn the man,' Barclay cried, almost wailing in frustration, casting his eyes towards the rugged North Brittany shore, just a faint grey line on the southern horizon.

'Mr Collins, look to your charts and any profiles you have of the shoreline. Tell me where he might be headed.'

Within seconds he was pacing up and down the deck, more concerned with the consequences of failure than the prospect of success, for he would find it hard to justify searching for a vessel that not only had he failed to find, but that he had allowed to be captured. Suddenly Ralph Barclay was aware of the impression he was creating, improperly dressed and very obviously agitated. He shot into his cabin, to come face to face with his wife.

'There is something amiss, Captain Barclay?' she said.

Given his mood, the reply was sharper than necessary. 'It is nothing with which you should concern yourself. My coat and hat, Shenton,' he said, breathing heavily.

It was an awkward silence that followed, one in which he could not bring himself to tell her he had been humbugged, one in which she waited in vain for him to express regret at being so brusque. That he did not do so, merely donning the called-for clothing before departing, made Emily cross.

'Shenton, my cloak if you please.'

The steward looked at her questioningly, but in the face of her own direct and uncompromising glare he had no choice but to oblige. She emerged on to the deck of a ship in the act of coming about, lines of men running this way and that as they adjusted and realigned the sails. Now aware of the safest place to be, she took up a position between two of the quarterdeck cannon, watching a husband too busy with Collins and his charts and shoreline drawings to notice her presence. She was still there when, with HMS *Brilliant* settled on her new course, the gun crew returned to their station.

Pearce ignored the dig he got from Michael O'Hagan for staring at the captain's wife, now only a few feet away. He also ignored the cursed injunction to stand still as he took a step to close that gap, too busy forming some words he could use to establish contact. Unaware of the man's proximity Emily Barclay started as if she had seen a ghost when she half turned and he came into her eye line.

'Pearce, you omhadhaun,' hissed Michael. 'Look away.'

'Madam, you addressed me in French yesterday. Might I be allowed to ask why?'

'Did I?' Emily replied, flustered, feeling the warm blood began to fill her face as she blushed. That inadvertent use of French had been foolish in the extreme. She might as well have said to this man, "I have read your letter."

'An affectation of mine, I do assure you,' she lied, which made her blush even more.

Pearce was enchanted by the beauty of that reddening face, putting the blush down to a becoming shyness, rather than duplicity. Smiling, he was just about to acknowledge the acceptance of her statement when her husband's voice roared from across the other side of the deck.

'You!'

'Holy Christ, you are truly a fool, in English as well as the Erse.' said Michael, as Pearce turned to look at Barclay, now advancing, his fist raised to strike. A sailor talking to Emily was bad enough – this one, a bloody landsman whom he'd already had occasion to clout, was tantamount to mutiny.

'You dare to address my wife on my quarterdeck!'

Pearce felt his limbs begin to tremble and shaped to defend himself, mentally damming the consequences, sure that if Barclay laid a finger on him he was going to retaliate. His own bunched fists were ready, when the captain's lady intervened.

'It was I who spoke to him, husband.' That stopped Ralph Barclay dead, as much the firm tone in her voice as the words themselves. 'And I fail to see that a mere exchange of pleasantries should occasion such a reaction.'

He was still staring at Pearce when he said, 'Mrs Barclay, you will oblige me by leaving the deck forthwith.'

'I...'

'This second, madam!'

'I would plead that this man is innocent, husband.'

Barclay had to restrain himself from shouting at the top of his voice, but the tone of voice he employed was obvious enough. 'Leave now!'

Emily did so, with a backward and sympathetic glance at Pearce, which enraged her husband even more. The two men were left staring at each other, the captain aware that if he struck this man, he would get a blow in return. The temptation to bring that on was high, for to strike a captain would see this bugger swing. Yet here he was, with an enemy in the offing, one he was once more pursuing. His dignity did not permit of a bout of fisticuffs.

'Master at Arms, I want this man in irons.'

The whole ship had been watching, some fearing what might happen – others anticipating it with pleasure. Coyle, one of the latter and the man called to react, was alongside Pearce in a second, with a very willing Kemp to aid him in securing the prisoner. 'You're for it now, mate, an' if the powers that be are kind, I'll be the one swinging the cat,' he snuffled happily.

Taken below, chained and locked in the cable tier, Pearce was not witness to the way the privateer, along with his capture, evaded Barclay and HMS *Brilliant*. Both ships were plain to see, the sleek barque and the Indiaman with her damaged bulwarks, smashed stern rail and the jeering men lining it, the Frenchman who had taken possession of her. The pursuit took the frigate in dangerously close to the rock-strewn shore of Brittany, to an inlet that his quarry knew well and Barclay did not. Eddies of water showed the location of the submerged rocks, while great rolling waves broke over those that were visible. By noon, on a high tide, both the chase and the Indiaman had entered a long inlet, forcing Barclay to haul off. The risk of going in further was too great, with uncharted rocks everywhere around that could rip out his bottom and sink him.

'Mr Collins, have you yet managed to discern what is this place?'

The master replied with some certainty, 'I believe it is the estuary of the River Trieux, Captain Barclay, and my charts tell me there is a small port about a half a mile inland called Lézardrieux.'

'With deep water at low tide?'

'I fear so.'

'Mr Roscoe, Mr Collins and I will require the cutter to be launched. Once we are aboard her I wish you to take our ship out into deep water and out of sight of land. Please arrange a rendezvous with Mr Collins before we depart.'

A tiny mid-stream, uninhabited island allowed Ralph Barclay to enter the estuary without being observed from upriver, and provided, when he climbed to the top of the scrub-covered rock, a good view of what he faced, which avoided the need to take the cutter in close and reveal that he was reconnoitring the area. The two ships were anchored out in deep water, prows facing seawards. Lézardrieux lay on the western shore, a run of low buildings interspersed with the odd two- or three-storey edifice – really no more than a fishing village, dominated by a hillside church. A dilapidated bastion lay at the northern edge – a stone-fronted gun emplacement that had been allowed to fall into disrepair, though he could see cannon muzzles poking out and a certain amount of activity around the embrasures. Most of the local boats, small fishing smacks, were tied up in the lee of that.

Thick woods ran from the surrounding hills on both sides of the narrowing estuary down to slender strands of sandy beach. There was no sign of any occupancy – no farm or manor houses, though there was a good chance that such things existed inland, hidden from view by the tall trees. There would be few roads into a place like this. It was very likely a village that depended on the river for contact with the interior – a good place for a privateer to lay up without in any way drawing attention to itself.

The *Lady Harrington* was anchored upriver of its captor and Ralph Barclay could see boats plying to and fro disgorging men on to the shore. But of more interest was the fact that no cargo was being moved, which underlined his supposition that the *Mercedes* had run for this place to avoid him, and that as soon as *Brilliant* departed she would make for a bigger port in all likelihood St Malo, a place where her crew could get a good price both for the cargo and find a willing buyer for such a valuable hull.

Could he get his ship in here and alongside the sod? If he could he knew that he could take the privateer with ease and at the same time subdue any fire from that rundown bastion. But there was the rub; he would need a favourable wind, which he did not have, and he would need to be quick, which ruled out towing *Brilliant* in with boats, for a slow approach would allow his enemies to mount a defence by warping both ships across the channel alongside the land-based cannon, thus presenting him with an array of fully manned guns he would find it hard to match. And his approach would be fraught with danger, bow on to broadsides. The damage they could inflict before he could swing round to bring his own guns to bear might be terminal, and that took no account of underwater hazards like submerged rocks or sandbars.

'Mr Collins, your opinion on the risks of bringing HMS *Brilliant* into this estuary?'

The master, who had been busy sketching what they could see, so that his captain would have a record of their observations, actually shuddered at such a notion. 'It would need a week of soundings afore I would even think of giving you an answer, sir.'

'We do not have a week, Mr Collins.'

'Then, sir, I must most emphatically advise against it.'

If a man as timorous as Collins was wont to make such a clear-cut statement, then most certainly the risk was too great. But Ralph Barclay was conscious of one very pertinent fact; that he had to find a way to try and get that Indiaman back – his whole future could depend on it.

'Mr Collins, I require you to remain here overnight, and I will detail some men to stay with you. I will take with me what you have already drawn, and wish you to make what observations you can before darkness falls. But more pertinent is what you can see at first light when the tide is lower. No fires, even on the seaward side of the island, so I fear you will be cold, for flames and smoke will alert anyone looking from those hills above the woods, or even from the port itself to your presence. I will send a boat in to pick you up before the tide peaks tomorrow.'

It was dark before the cutter rejoined the ship, even though Roscoe had brought HMS *Brilliant* inshore to the pre-arranged rendezvous as soon as the light of the day began to fade. In a long, uncomfortable and wet journey, in an open boat with only his foul weather cloak to protect him, Ralph Barclay had found many things to worry about, and he was also, after a long and dispiriting day, wet through and very tired. An argument with his wife about naval discipline the moment he made his cabin he did not need, and had no desire to engage in. But Emily would not be fobbed off.

'I find it utterly barbaric, Captain Barclay, that you can even consider punishing a man for merely talking to me.'

'It is not you, my dear, but what you represent.'

'I do not represent anything.'

'You do,' Barclay insisted. 'Me!'

The mutual stare was short but telling, with both parties thinking along the same lines; had it been a wise decision for Emily to come on board ship? Ralph Barclay was deliberating that if Emily could not comprehend the absolute requirement for discipline then he was in for a difficult time. She was thinking that the proximity imposed by the cramped accommodation, in which each party saw too much of the other, never mind actions of which she thoroughly disapproved, was inimical to harmonious relations.

At the base of Emily's concern was the knowledge that she had been foolish; she should never have addressed this Pearce fellow at all, even out of politeness, and certainly not in French. Ralph Barclay had a nagging thought at the back of his own mind; wondering if she had, as she had said, spoken first, and if so what had been the content of her conversation, for he could not forget her reluctance to translate that letter.

'I am asking, husband, as a favour to me, that no punishment is given to that sailor, for I swear he is innocent of any crime. Any transgression was mine, and I must bear any reprimand you choose to issue.'

It was tempting to give way to such a supplicant look and the very obvious manner, which denoted a future full of submission; a mere allusion to this moment would be enough to quell these burgeoning signs of wifely determination. Against that he had been publicly insulted, by a pressed seaman on his own quarterdeck. To allow that to pass, with the officers he had aboard and his crew yet to take his full measure, could lead to all sorts of problems. Ralph Barclay had seen it before – one act of leniency seen as weakness, which allowed the whole system of naval discipline to collapse. He was contemplating battle, one which he would trust no other to lead, and the sooner the entire ship's company, including his wife, understood he would brook no dissent, the better.

'Shenton,' he called, saying slowly and deliberately as his servant appeared. 'A message to Mr Roscoe, that I require the sentence of punishment for the man in irons to be carried out at first light, before the decks are cleaned. I will decide what that is to be dependent upon his attitude, but it will most certainly require a grating to be rigged and the bosun to make up a cat.'

Then, looking into the still-pleading eyes of his wife, he added. 'You do not understand, my dear.'

The sudden light sent the rats, which had been scrabbling around the cable tier eager to investigate a warm living body, scurrying for cover. The lantern also lit up Pearce, who was sitting on a slimy cable, chains round his wrist, and the face of Lieutenant Digby, who held it out before him.

'The captain has decided to institute the punishment in the morning.' Seeing Pearce's look of incomprehension, he added, 'It is customary for such a thing to be carried out on the following day.'

'And what is the punishment to be?' asked Pearce.

'If you plead for leniency, perhaps it will be nothing more than a verbal reprimand.'

'Do you believe that, Mr Digby?'

'No.'

'Am I to be flogged?'

Digby nodded, and Pearce fought to prevent a very natural shudder as the lieutenant added, 'But I do know that a plea has a chance of reducing the number of lashes you may receive, to perhaps as little as half a dozen.'

'That requires that I plead to Barclay, does it not?'

'Captain Barclay,' Digby insisted. 'And it is I who will do the pleading, you are merely required to look contrite.'

Pearce was aware that, possibly, he was being foolish – any plea Digby made would not be believed by anyone who heard it anyway, least of all the man who wished to chastise him. So was it a meaningless gesture to decline such alleviation? His father's voice was in his ear then, telling him, as he had all his life, that most of men's folly was brought about by pride, and it was that which he could not swallow.

'That, I am afraid, I will not do.'

'All hands aft to witness punishment, Mr Roscoe,' said Ralph Barclay, looking south to an empty sea, grey as it reflected the colour of the sky, devoid even of the fishing boats he had expected to see, the very same vessels he had observed tied up by that bastion at Lézardrieux.

HMS *Brilliant* had hauled off from the Brittany shore once more and it was no longer in view. He had already formulated most of a plan to cut out both ships that very night; when the master rejoined that would finalised, but he had no intention of alerting his opponents by beating to and fro in full view throughout the day. Let them think he had gone back to his convoy. That way he would gain the most telling advantage: surprise.

The bosun's mates had rigged the grating to the poop rail and the marines, fully dressed and armed, were lined up behind that, overseeing the deck on which the crew would congregate, the captain's protection against protest. All the officers and midshipmen were in full dress, best blue coats, number one scrapers on their heads, swords at their waist, held by one white-gloved hand, and they moved to head their divisions as the men took their place. Barclay was at the windward side of the quarterdeck, staring idly out to sea, the picture of unconcern. But he was no fool, he knew what he was about would be unpopular, not because this fellow Pearce was a favourite amongst the crew – he was after all a landsman – but because they would be aware he was being punished to discourage any others who might be tempted to be over-free with his wife.

Roscoe called out as soon as the assembly was complete, 'Master at Arms, bring forth the prisoner.'

Pearce, standing by the companionway, was aware that the trembling he always experienced before a fight was wholly absent. And yet he was very afraid – afraid of the pain that was coming, as well as the mutilation to his skin. But the greater fear was of personal disgrace; that he might not bear himself as he thought he should – take the punishment, make not a sound, make no gift to Barclay of a pleading or supplicant look. He might break down and scream for mercy and that image, as Coyle edged him up the companionway steps, induced the greatest degree of dread.

The whispered words as he passed from a crew that was, in the main, still strange, had a profound effect. 'Head up, mate' hissed one, that amongst many a 'Good luck' and 'It ain't right.' Even Devenow, as he passed him, gave him a slow nod, an unsmiling one for sure given his jaw was yet to heal, but nevertheless an acknowledgement that he did not approve of what Barclay was doing. His fellow Pelicans, when he saw them standing in their ranks, all had an attitude, which ranged from Michael O'Hagan's barely suppressed fury, to Rufus's inability to look at what he knew was going to be gory.

Then he was in an open space, a square formed by the rise of the poop and the assembled men, able to see clearly the grating to which he would be lashed, to see little Martin Dent in his red coat and hat, trying not to grin, ready with his black-covered side drum and sticks to provide the muffled rat-a-tat-tat that would cover the flogging of the man who had broken his still swollen nose. He was every bit as gleeful, Pearce reckoned, as those brute women, like Madame Defarge, who sat knitting at the bottom of the guillotine steps.

How different to Paris and the scene around that instrument. This was ordered and silent; a revolutionary beheading was strident and smelly, a dense crowd packed tight in a cobbled square eager to ensure that each prisoner brought to the block knew that they thought him a traitor. The stink of packed, unwashed humanity mingled with the very relevant smell of voided bowels as those about to die first clapped eyes on the instrument by which they would be dispatched. On this deck the air was clean, there was a breeze that would carry away any smell should he fail to control his own muscles. And he was not about to die – instead of a guillotine he was threatened by the contents of a red baize bag held by Sykes, the Bosun. He would be humiliated, he would be bloodied, but he would live.

Emily Barclay came on deck, which set up a murmur that rippled through the entire assembly, quickly suppressed by the divisional officers. Her husband's body actually quivered with the effort not to show his shock at her presence: there was no sham indifference now – the desire to tell her to get back to his cabin was very evident in his contorted features. Pearce, too, was surprised. He jerked his head to curtail the natural desire to look at her again. Overborne by cries of 'Silence there', Emily Barclay merely nodded to her husband and, wordlessly, ascended the steps to a point on the poop from which she could observe proceedings.

'Mr Digby,' croaked Barclay, 'this man is in your division, and has been arraigned here on the charge of disobedience to a direct order.' There was a pause, the point at which Barclay should have read out the specific charge, but it passed in silence from a captain who exercised his right to disoblige. 'Do you wish to plead for him?'

Digby stepped forward smartly and raised his hat. 'He has expressly requested that I do not, sir.'

That set up a soft murmur all along the deck that had every voice of authority calling for silence.

'Has he by damn!' Barclay's eyes were wide open with surprise, Pearce's closed as if he was again wondering at his own folly. 'I have scarce heard of such arrogance.'

'It is not, sir,' Digby added, in a measured tone, 'a sentiment that I am familiar with. But I am bound to respect, perhaps even admire, any man who espouses such a plea.'

Digby might as well have slapped his captain with those words. Did Barclay see the nods, slight but visible, from the crew, the eyes of his officers raised a fraction higher to denote dissension, the look of unhappiness on Roscoe's face and the drooping shoulders of Sykes? Emily Barclay's head dropped in a gesture of sadness, as though she was seeing a champion humiliated.

Barclay snarled his response. 'You may respect such a person Mr Digby, you may even extend to admiration, I do not! To my mind it comes under the heading of the same degree of arrogance that sees him here in the first place. But I am man enough to respect the request. We will see if he is so haughty after two dozen of the cat. Bosun, seize him up.'

Coyle struck off the chains that bound Pearce's hands, as Ridley and Costello, the two bosun's mates who had acted as his tutors, approached. At least, thought Pearce, sensing no malice in them, it was not that rat-faced bastard Kemp who so relished the thought of inflicting pain.

'Your shirt, mate,' said Ridley, in a kindly voice, while Costello added, white teeth flashing, 'No good gifting the purser extra profit.'

Pearce was confused. The image he had of a flogging, the common tale recounted by everyone he had met who had witnessed such a thing, was of a calculated brutality designed to humiliate the offender and discourage others from transgression. These men were supposed to handle him in a rough manner, bind him tight to that grating then rip his shirt off his back, not help him pull it over his head, roll it up and hand it to Charlie Taverner for safekeeping. They led him without compulsion to the grating and tied him in such a manner that he was secure enough not to fall, yet not so tightly bound as to deny blood to his outstretched hands. A strip of hard leather was produced, well chewed by the look of it, and a gentle hand was placed on Pearce's shoulder, as Ridley said, 'Bite hard on this, mate.'

Beyond Ridley, Pearce could see Sykes. Standing next to Barclay, he opened the red baize bag, reached into it and pulled out a cat o' nine tails, that black, menacing and iniquitous whip. He shook it so that each of the nine lines hung loose, then swung it quickly to create a swish that promised much pain, which brought from his commanding officer a nod of approval. Costello came back into view, to take off the bosun the instrument of punishment, likewise swinging it in test, as he moved to stand behind his victim. Finally Barclay spoke, loud and clear, so that he could be heard in the forepeak.

'Bosun, carry out the punishment.'

As he tensed himself, Pearce had a sudden thought that this was inevitable; the sure knowledge that he could never have so knuckled down to the nature of naval discipline to avoid a flogging. Not that he could accept the right of anyone to inflict it on him – that flew in the face of everything he believed. And what was it about the men witnessing this that they could watch in silence and not act to prevent it? What was it that made such people accept the disciplinary right of a man to beat them to a pulp merely because he wore a blue coat and couple of epaulettes, and carried in his pocket a piece of paper from an even bigger set of rogues allocating to him a wholly specious authority?

Why were there so few men like his father who were prepared not only to speak out against injustice, but to do so despite personal risk – to say to those who wished to protect their wealth and property that any fight they created was not one in which those who were dispossessed wished to be part, for it was they who were maimed or killed. But they did. Pearce had seen the eager faces, heard the excited talk, when they had first chased that privateer – men like Dysart, Ridley and Costello would happily slaughter any Frenchman that Barclay told them to, quite unable to grasp that the same trick was being played by some foreign authority on their opponents. If they were not prepared to alleviate their own lot, to raise themselves from the dearth that such a life imposed, was it worth one drop of breath to persuade them to try? That had been an ever-growing doubt in the last few years, from the point where he had stopped believing everything his father said, and began to have the doubts natural to a growing intelligence.

He could imagine the scene at his back, Costello setting himself for the blow, legs spread for purchase, arm well back to maximise the strength of the cut. And he heard it before it struck, the sound reminiscent of a venomous snake he had once seen in a Parisian fanum of natural wonders, and to him just as deadly. The sting, as the nine tails struck home made him shudder and bite hard on the leather. Yet Pearce knew himself to be shocked more than pained, for the feeling across his back was one of a spreading numbness, not the agony he had anticipated. The next blow came while that thought was still in his mind.

Pearce had been beaten in every one of the many schools he had attended, for fighting, for impudence, or some other misdemeanour, with varying degrees of hurt dependent on the cruelty of the pedagogue determined to quell his rebellious nature. Such whippings had been administered to his bared posterior not his back, but he could recall right now, as more blows landed on him, that, while he was smarting, he had experienced worse pain than this. The sound of heavy breathing behind him testified to the amount of effort being expended by Costello, but that was not being replicated on his own flesh. Had all those tales he had heard about naval punishment been so much stuff – or might he find that the pain would come later, that his skin was not as whole as he supposed, but a mass of bleeding lacerations that would suppurate for weeks before healing.

Michael O'Hagan was seething, on the balls of his feet, glaring at the captain, his heart pounding as he fought his own demons. He wanted to rush across the deck and lift Barclay up by the neck, which he would then break before slinging him overboard to drown in green water. Yet mad as Michael was, the line of marines acted as a check on his desires – he would only get a musket ball for his pains, long before he could kill Ralph Barclay, and what good would that do? He took comfort in conjuring up the ways he would employ to dispose of the bastard should a future chance occur.

Charlie Taverner wasn't interested in the captain – he was more concerned with the punishment. So far the victim had not cried out, an achievement Taverner thought he would be unable to replicate. He was jerking as much as Pearce, especially when the fourth blow brought real pain, a cry stifled by that leather strap, striking as it did in a place already assailed, and as the number rose so did the hurt. Each time Taverner heard the numeral and observed John Pearce's body coil up in anticipation, he winced himself at the spasm which followed the thwack of contact.

Rufus still had his eyes closed, and what he saw behind those lids was much worse than the reality. He too had heard of the horrors of a naval flogging, of the cuts inflicted by the cat that, once a blow had landed repeatedly on the same spot, opened the skin to expose the white bones of the victim's ribs. The John Pearce in his imagination was no longer standing, but was slumped, hanging on the lashings that tied him to the grating, while his own blood formed a pool around his bare feet, and bits of his flesh flew in all directions as the cat o' nine tails slashed back and forth.

Cornelius Gherson was fascinated by the spectacle, not at all squeamish about the pain being visited on his messmate, even a little disappointed that there was not more in the way

346

of gore. The humbling of Pearce he could easily endure, for before him was a fellow too full of himself, by far, prone to giving out orders as if he had some kind of authority and probing into matters which were none of his concern. The disbelief that had greeted his attempt to explain the events of the previous night – that mere curiosity had got him into trouble – had been particularly galling. Doubly galling was the way the others had responded when they tired of his grunts, Taverner almost calling him a liar to his face and that stripling Dommet making a snide reference to cats and nine lives.

He was not about to tell any of them what he had overheard, the sound of a group of sailors talking treason, that gambling was just a cover for an activity that would see them damned by a man like Barclay or any other captain for that matter. They would have accepted his explanation for his presence, that he had been attracted by the sound of dice, if the boy Dent had not observed the length of time he had eavesdropped on the quiet conversation taking place in the cutter. That was another gripe to lay against Pearce. It was his feud with the boy that had endangered the whole mess and nearly got him killed.

And what drivel he had overheard, from men whose ignorance was staggering; talk of rights and abuses, and ways to make life in general, and particularly that aboard ship, better for the common sailor, of pay not raised for a hundred years or more, captains too fond of the lash and pursers who cheated on their accounts. Half-baked notions he had thought as he listened; useful information though in the strange world in which he now found himself, particularly the obvious fact that while such forbidden talk might be kept from those in authority, it must be known and tolerated amongst the experienced members of the crew. His friend Molly had evinced no surprise when Gherson asked him to convey to the men who had nearly dumped him into the sea that their secret was safe, even from those with whom he shared a mess table.

Another thwack brought him back to the present, and to the notion that what was happening on this deck barely rated against the pleasure he had derived from a bloody cockfight or a decent bear baiting in which dogs had torn at the fur and flesh of the bear. It could not hold a candle to a pair of Bull Mastiffs at each other's throats. There was a moment in which, seeing the bosun's mate prepare another swing, he had to restrain himself from crying out encouragement, as he would have done at any one of those spectacles.

Emily Barclay looked at the line of indifferent marines, men who had the air of having witnessed much of this before, since she did not want to look at the punishment being inflicted because of her. Each administered blow was like a lash on her conscience. She knew each time the cat landed her husband's eyes flicked in her direction, so she set her face not to react in any way. But inside it seemed the rhythm of the blows matched that of her heart, the thudding of which felt just as heavy.

'Pray I have the courage to resist this, when I have power to command it.'

Digby said these words over and over in his mind. He could not speak them, for to do so would diminish him in the eyes of his fellow officers. It was not a thought he had often, when he dreamt of promotion and command. But along with the pleasurable anticipation of privacy, of the space of his own cabin, of the power of decision in battle, lay this: punishment was held by the more enlightened to make a good man bad and a bad man worse. That he would have to order it, if only to contain the endemic drunks who took the flogging as part of the whole, hard bargains who would take a dozen without complaint, did not ease his mind.

This was different. Pearce was no hard case who had spent a life at sea and could walk straight from the cat to his duty. What would it do to him? Would he become a menace like Devenow, a bully who was as lazy as he was vindictive? Henry Digby hoped that he would not, just as he hoped he would, in the future, have the courage with such men to hand out punishment that was deserved, and the wisdom to eschew it when it was not.

Time had stopped for Pearce, for he was now feeling pain. Not what he thought he would feel, but no part of his back had escaped the twenty lashes he had endured. The pressure was kept up by switching the bosun's mates after the first dozen – Ridley was flogging him now. And while he was no believer in God he prayed for a release from this. His thighs ached from the need to hold up his body, his jaw clamped on that leather strap from the need to deny Barclay the satisfaction of seeing him fold, and he could feel the pressure increasing on his wrists as he fought to maintain his upright position.

Ralph Barclay knew he had been humbugged, but he could no more show the fact than say anything. Seething inside, he had to maintain on his face the austere indifference of the commander who could observe pain without emotion, the same pose he would assume in battle when shot, shell and splinters were flying round his ears. But it was hard, made more so by the way he could not prevent himself from glancing in the direction of his wife. He could remain aloof from his own frustration, he could remain remote from the feelings of the men who stood on this deck, but he could not maintain indifference with Emily. That was impossible, even though he knew just how much it weakened him in his own estimation.

'Twenty-four sir,' said the Bosun, stepping forward to take the cat 'o nine tails from Ridley.

Lost in that last thought, Ralph Barclay had to drag himself back to the present, before turning to the surgeon. 'Very well, cut him down. Mr Lutyens I hand him over to your care. I would see him well and back at his duties with some despatch. Carry on, Mr Roscoe.'

Then he looked at the deck, and the tarpaulin that had been spread to catch the blood. After a normal flogging he would have added the need to clean that up. He did not have to do that now – there wasn't any.

'Humbugged,' he said under his breath, before looking up towards his wife, who probably thought she had witnessed the real thing. 'I think, Mrs Barclay, that you would be best off the deck, as it is about to be cleaned.'

As Emily obliged, without looking at him, he added, 'Mr Roscoe, send in the cutter to bring off Mr Collins.'

CHAPTER FOURTEEN

Pearce was not cut down, he was untied, and, aware that he was the object of much scrutiny he managed to walk to the companionway, stiff but upright, Ridley and Costello at either side holding him as if he was on the point of collapse. But Pearce was far from that, being released had restored his own faith in his ability to walk away from what had happened on his own two legs. Behind him he heard the orders given that got the men back to their duties, those on deck resuming the tasks they had been engaged in before the flogging, the watch off duty trailing down to the maindeck. Again the able and ordinary seamen who had either ignored or guyed him the past few days were looking at him directly with sympathy – one or two even smiled as he went further down to the surgeon's quarters on the orlop.

'Your shirt, mate,' said Ridley. Then he grinned. 'I should think old Barclay is seething by now, you not bein' at all cut.'

'No blood?' asked Pearce, gingerly moving his shoulders, not far, for to do so brought a stinging sensation.

'None, though your back be as red as a monkey's arse.'

'We laid into you hard, mind,' said Costello. 'Had to put up a show.'

Pearce eased himself on to a chest, and he sat there hunched over. 'I don't understand.'

'You wouldn't, you being such a damned lubber,' sneered Ridley, 'and, I will add, as useless aboard ship as a whore without a hole.'

'If you'd been caught off Deal,' Costello added, 'I doubt you'd be talking now, nor for a good week after.'

Pearce looked at the pair, both smiling, the quizzical expression on his face plain evidence that he was still confused. Ridley sat opposite him, and hunched forward, his voice quiet. 'Not all cat o' nine tails come the same, and, since it be a new one for each man to punish, it depends on who's making 'em as to how much damage they do.'

'Have you got it now?' asked Costello.

'I think so,' Pearce replied, in a far from convincing tone.

'Ain't got a clue, Ridley,' Costello responded. 'Not a bloody inkling has he.'

'We, or the Bosun hisself, makes up the cat,' said Ridley, earnestly, 'a new one for each flogging. And if'n we want to we can choose fresh hemp to make it, or go for a harder rope.'

'And we can soak it an' dry it,' added Costello, 'till it gets real nippy, and even treat it with a touch of pitch if we like. The one that does the damage is the thieves' cat, 'cause that has knots in the tails, and is made for any grass-combing bugger who steals from his mates and is caught.'

'What you just had,' Ridley added, 'was made special from hemp, and soft. Mind we blacked it up a bit to make it look like the proper article.'

'It still hurt,' Pearce protested. He nearly added something about the blow to his pride, but held back – these fellows would not care a hoot about that.

'That ain't pain, mate,' Ridley scoffed. 'Even a common cat would have had you hanging by the thumbs. But the feeling aboard was that old Barclay was coming it a bit high, that he can't have his missus parading around the deck, her bein' as pretty as she be, without she catches the odd eye, and bein' she's sociable, will be on the receiving end of the odd comment. That if he is goin' to flog for that, then there is not a man aboard who won't feel the gratin' on his cheek at some time this commission.'

Costello's voice had a lot of satisfaction in it. 'That was our way of telling him, carry on, mate, but it won't strike no fear.'

'That's very interesting,' said Lutyens, appearing in the doorway.

Ridley was on his feet in a flash. 'Now don't you go spreading that round the wardroom, Mr Lutyens.'

The surgeon put his head to one side, not responding to Ridley's worried expression. 'You did not say so, Ridley, but you implied that the captain would have seen through your ruse?'

'He would have, your honour, lest he be blind.'

'Then I imagine that everyone in the wardroom will have observed the same.'

'Some will, some are too callow,' said Costello. 'But if you say 'owt it will become a topic. If that happens it will get to Barclay's ears at some point and he will have to come out and do something.'

'At a cost to all and sundry,' added Ridley.

Lutyens produced a quite singular smile. 'You can scarce comprehend how much pleasure silence will give me, as I try to discern who has made the link and who has not. Nothing affords as much gratification as watching grown men sniff round a commonality that no one may voice. Now, if you will be so good as to leave me with my patient.'

Ridley asked his questions in a fading voice as they made their way out. 'Is that bugger odd, Costello, or is it just me?'

'No, mate, he's as daft as a brush, and as creepy as a spider.'

Lutyens smiled at Pearce. 'I see the men lack certain comprehensions.'

'I hazard,' Pearce replied, 'that you might find them wiser than you think.'

'I do hope so. Now please lie down so that I can examine your back. Ah! Very red indeed, and,' as Pearce winced, 'sore to the touch. I fear we have just observed a barbaric ritual, though there was an early Greek philosopher who held that humans had to be driven to goodness like a donkey to the plough.'

'Heraclitus,' Pearce replied, without thinking.

Lutyens' voice rose in surprise. 'You know the philosophers?'

'No.'

Pearce was cursing himself for his lapse, especially with one as watchful as this surgeon. If he had had a fractured education, with little formal schooling, he had learnt much from a father who, having educated himself, took endless pains to teach his only son. John Pearce might know little formal Greek or Latin, but he had discussed a great deal of philosophy as Adam Pearce searched endlessly for the key to unlock the means to improve the lot of his fellow humans. Heraclitus was one of the villains of philosophical history, a misanthrope who had shown scant regard for his fellow man, cruel even by the standards of Ancient Greece. But whatever he knew and didn't know was not something to share with this man, who was closer to authority than he was to those before the mast.

Lutyens' voice bore within it a deep degree of irony. 'You know nothing of philosophy yet name one of the more obscure in the pantheon. If you know of Heraclitus, you must also know of Socrates, Aristotle and Plato. I fancy I am not being told the truth, John Pearce.'

His patient shot him a look, and the surgeon responded by saying. 'Your true name is no mystery on any part of the ship now.' He followed that with a shout for some fresh water. 'For I need,' as he said to his patient, 'to soak some dried comfrey that I will apply to your back. Do you know anything of medicinal herbs, Pearce?' That was followed by a grunt, as he turned to open another chest, his voice going hollow as he knelt down to search through it. 'And would you tell me if you did? You would probably gabble the Latin tag for Poison Ivy then deny you had any knowledge of what you just said.'

'I don't know anything,' Pearce insisted.

Lutyens' voice took on an injured tone. 'It annoys me that you should take such an attitude.'

'I can't imagine why.'

'It may surprise you to know that I have an abiding interest in my fellow-man.'

Pearce wanted to say that there was little shock in that statement; the way he crept about the ship, popping up in all sorts of odd places, was unnerving, only marginally less so than the cold way he seemed to examine anyone who caught his eye. Suddenly Lutyens' fish-like face was right in front of Pearce's, the surgeon squatting to speak to him.

'And I have watched you more than most, as being part of a section of the crew in which I have an especially deep curiosity. You are a pressed man, taken against your will, and you are no sailor.'

'I think I know that.'

'Shall I tell you what I have observed, Pearce?'

It was painful to shrug, better to stay still, so Pearce's pretence at an indifferent response had to be made with his eyebrows.

'Water, your honour,' said a voice.

'Put it down and ask the sail maker if either he or one of his mates will attend upon me.' The wooden bucket was right before Pearce's eyes as Lutyens stood up, and he watched the surgeon dunk into it a large handful of dry, dark green leaves, pressing them down until they were submerged, his voice carrying on in that hurt tone.

'What I have observed?' Lutyens asked himself. 'I will tell you, shall I, about your mess table. O'Hagan, the Irishman, I like, for he is a genial soul when not being practised upon and the fact that he has beaten the resident bully is to be applauded. The Taverner fellow I would be careful to trust, unlike Gherson who I would not trust at all. That name inclines me to believe he is of Huguenot stock, you know, and slimy in the extreme.'

The need to defend him as a messmate was automatic, and given what he truly thought of the man, quite convincing. 'You damn him for his antecedents? Does merely being a descendant of a French Protestant who fled a Catholic massacre make him slimy? You might as well accuse King Louis and say he deserved to lose his head for it.'

Lutyens positively purred, like a man who had sprung a trap. 'I wonder how many common seamen could conjure up a memory of St Bartholomew's Night?'

Pearce had exposed himself again and he knew it. 'Anyone who has knowledge of their religion.'

'No, John Pearce, it is too long past. That massacre took place two hundred and fifty years ago, and even a pious religious memory would scarce include a knowledge of the Bourbon bloodline.'

'Simpson, sailmaker's mate, your honour. I was sent for.'

Pearce turned his head, even though to do so stretched the skin on his back. Simpson looked down at him and winked, another man who would have ignored him before the flogging.

'Ah yes,' Lutyens cried. 'I require you to make me up a sort of apron, from very light canvas, one that fits on the back not the front of the person wearing it.'

'The back,' the sailmaker enquired, in a voice that implied, 'I have been asked for some daft things in my time, but...'

'Yes,' Lutyens insisted, 'it will need ties down the side, shall we venture to be nautical and call them reefs, the whole to act as a compress to keep in place what I am going to apply to this fellow's back.'

'Like a poultice, you mean, your honour?'

'The very word, my man! How astoundingly apt. It would aid the efficacy of the thing if it was impermeable.'

'What's that mean?' asked Simpson

'Proof against water.'

'I could lard it with some slush from the cook,' the fellow replied. 'Can I say you will pay the price?'

'Make it so, Mr Simpson,' said Lutyens in a happy tone. 'A double-reefed affair, in the nautical vernacular, an invention which will no doubt be handed down to grateful posterity as a Lutyens.'

The sailmaker responded in a jocose tone of voice. 'Since I be cutting and sowing the bugger, your honour, should it not be termed a Simpson?' Lutyens barked a laugh, and Simpson added, 'Be with you in half a glass, your honour.'

'I would not have had to explain impermeable to you, John Pearce, would I now? Again you are silent but you fail to realise that from the very first, to me, you were singular, made so by the look in your eye.'

'That was hatred.'

'Hardly misplaced,' the surgeon replied in a softer, almost regretful tone. 'And I daresay you see me as an integral part of the abusive system. You do not reply to that, I observe, so I can take that as a yes.'

It wasn't, but neither could Pearce honestly say no. To him all authority was suspect, even Lieutenant Digby, who had been as kindly as his fellow officers were harsh. Was he wrong about Lutyens? The exchange with Simpson had been as that between two shipmates who knew each other well. The sailmaker had evinced no fear of the surgeon as a superior being.

'Perhaps I should not treat you,' the surgeon sighed. 'Perhaps in pain you would be a man less troublesome, for I mean to ask you some questions.'

'Not much point, Mr Lutyens, in asking of a man who knows nothing.'

Lutyens knelt down again to look him in the eye. 'You know that Captain Barclay only has licence to press men bred to the sea.'

Pearce wished he was upright, being tall enough to command the surgeon, perhaps to impose himself, for this talk was heading in an uncomfortable direction. 'Knowing that made no odds.'

'You know,' Lutyens insisted, 'that there are two ways to avoid even a press as illegal as the one that took you up. The first is an exemption from the Admiralty.'

'Which I do not possess.'

'Prevarication, sir,' Lutyens spluttered, 'and damned annoying for being so! The second reason, as you equally well know, is to claim that you are a gentleman and no seaman. How do you establish that you are such? Not by the contents of your purse but by the manner of your speech and the depth of your connections. No captain, even one as foolish as Barclay, would take up and hold an educated man, for to do so would see him in the dock himself as soon as a properly written letter arrived in the right quarter, one that would force the naval powers to act.'

A slow blink had to do service for the absence of a shrug. Pearce was thinking of his letter, hopefully winging its way to old John Wilkes, to set off a bomb under Barclay and his arrogance.

'You can write,' Lutyens continued, 'and before you deny it the purser told me that your first request to him once he had issued you with your slops was for a quill, wax, ink and paper. What for? Not to make lists, so I surmise you wrote a letter. The question is, did you manage to get such a letter off the ship?'

Lutyens gave him a chance to respond, a chance that Pearce declined to take.

'Had you made a protest to Barclay and established your status you would not be here now. But you did not – you refused even to give your proper name when you first came aboard and you would still be called John Truculence if one of your fellow pressed men had not let slip the name Pearce.

You were singular from the very first; you show a defiance to the officers and the trained seamen that comes, to my mind, not from temper but from a feeling of superiority. You casually allude to Heraclitus and demonstrate that not only do you know that Henry of Navarre was Protestant but that he was the first Bourbon King of France and ancestor to the late King Louis. So I am wondering, John Pearce, why you do not wish to use that name, just as I am wondering what it is that prevents you from bearding Captain Barclay and establishing that for him to keep you aboard is to risk his whole career.'

'Do you think that comfrey has soaked long enough?'

Lutyens smiled, seeming to imply that he now knew something that had hitherto been a mystery, then stood, moving towards another locked chest, opened by a large key, from which he extracted a brown stopped bottle. A small measure of the contents was poured into a glass etched with markings, the whole presented to Pearce to drink.

'A combination of medicine ancient and modern, will set you up famously and, as the captain requested, in short order.'

Pearce sniffed it. 'Laudanum?'

'You know the tincture?'

Pearce had dosed his father with laudanum often, to ease the pain of an internal affliction that would respond to no other palliative, just as he knew of people who took it in daily doses. It would make him drowsy, perhaps even senseless, but he also reckoned that it would make him forget the stinging of his back, as well as his present situation. The thought of a degree of oblivion was a welcome one, a period when he would not recall that he was a pressed seaman, nor think of the way he had deserted his father in Paris, of an escape which was, for the present, impossible. Raising himself on one elbow, Pearce threw his head back and downed the contents.

'Excellent,' said Lutyens, almost purring with pleasure. 'Once that has touched upon the vital spirit, for there is nothing like an opiate to bring such a thing to fruition, we can continue our conversation.'

The feeling of relief was immediate, a sensation spreading through his limbs that seemed able to relax each muscle in turn. The cold of the damp comfrey leaves being spread on his bruised back was soothing in itself, but Pearce knew that was not the root cause of his increasing comfort. A delicious numbness worked its way up from his kidneys to his shoulders, through his neck and into his head so that even his jaw seemed altered, though he had not thought it clenched. He could hear Lutyens singing softly, too low for any words to be discernible, yet soothing in the sound. Sleep seemed possible and that happy thought as he closed his eyes, brought a smile to his face.

'So, John Pearce,' Lutyens whispered in his ear, pencil poised over his notebook, 'what of Plato?'

'A foolish man, or so my father thought. The Republic is nothing less than a paean to the Spartans, who lived off the back of slavery...'

Lutyens interrupted gently, 'Your father?'

That produced a frown, as though the question was difficult. After a lengthy pause the reply came. 'Adam Pearce.'

The surgeon had been holding his breath, fearing he had gone too far too soon. 'How silly of me. Is he not a friend to Tom Paine the radical pamphleteer?'

'Friend no, but they share many of the same notions.'

'What would they be?'

What followed was mumbled and far from coherent. Words were being dredged from Pearce's mind that were not really his own, but those he had heard from his father's lips; each person's right to the fruits of his labours, an end to tithes both feudal and clerical, ramblings on the iniquities of Kings, courts, titles, prelates as well as the hereditary principle, and the manifest failure of those who removed monarchs to make any change to the lot of the common man. Lutyens only half listened, for he had heard it all before, had indeed debated such notions with his friends, as aware as any man that the world in which he existed was riddled with manifest imperfections. But that was not really what interested him, and he happily let his patient ramble only so that he would become comfortable in a confessional state.

It was for moments like this that Charles Lutyens had chosen the Navy and this ship. He knew himself to be over-qualified for such a lowly post, but that mattered not for the position was a means to an end. A surgeon he might be, but his interest lay not in the corporeal human body, with its mess of blood, tendons, tissues and bone, but in the brain, the cerebral part that controlled all those moving parts. He was enough of a student of Voltaire to scoff at any notion that the heart had any dominion over a man's actions, sure as a rationalist that the head was the seat of all emotion. But it was not a surgical interest – he had trepanned enough cadavers in his training to be bored with the soapy mass of tissue contained in the skull. His fascination went deeper than the knife!

The Sick and Hurt Board of King George's Navy had not enquired too deeply into his competence or his motives; there was a war on, fleets fitting out and no excess of qualified medical men queuing to serve in the King's Navy, especially in the smaller vessels. Here was one not only willing but eager, a fellow who had powerful connections, which wended though his Lutheran pastor father all the way to a royal family who often worshipped at his church. Lutyens had asked for a frigate because big ships carried too many men for his purpose and were rarely in action. If they did not comprehend the reason for the request, the officials at the Sick and Hurt Board were too grateful for the offer of his services to refuse.

Already he had examined and made notes on those with whom he messed, the members of the wardroom; lieutenants Roscoe, Thrale and Digby in that order of seniority were satisfyingly different, as was the pun-obsessed marine officer, Holbrook. The Purser seemed a slippery cove, almost too true to type, while the Master, Mr Collins, was a worrier. The eight midshipmen and master's mates who shared the overcrowded midshipman's berth had eluded him somewhat, but all sorts of skulduggery was going on in that quarter, certainly bullying, perhaps theft, and quite possibly buggery. It was interesting to reflect that every wardroom officer had progressed from what they commonly referred to as 'that damned filthy bearpit'. Thus he would be given a chance to probe the scars such surroundings created at the same time as he observed the long-term effects on those who had endured them.

The crew he was slowly getting to know – some because of the numerous cases of the pox aboard. Volunteers or the first takings of the Impress Service, men bred to the sea, would repay close study. What made such people volunteer for a duty that was by common repute so harsh? But men such as Pearce were like the philosopher's stone; fellows forced to serve in the King's Navy, brought aboard by a system universally condemned, but one that could not be sacrificed when Britain went to war, men who, when it came to the moment, were reputed to fight with as much tenacity as those who had come aboard of their own free will. From the whole he hoped to discern attitudes and motives that would be at the kernel of the investigations he was here to undertake.

Then there was the captain. Was he a mass of contradictions, or just a product of the service that had created him? Lutyens had learnt from those members of the crew with whom he had spoken that they saw nothing abnormal in the way Barclay behaved, though it had been obvious such an opinion had been dented by the flogging of Pearce. Watching intently as the cat swung, he had felt the discontent amongst the crew, men too wise to show it in their faces, for they did not want to join the victim at the grating. There was no doubt in Lutyens' mind that Barclay was aware of the crew's displeasure, yet it had no effect on his actions. And finally there were the intricacies of the captain's marriage – a whole other area of enquiry that Lutyens had never anticipated.

By studying men in the enclosed setting of a ship of war, over an extended period, Charles Lutyens hoped to find many things. Could men be classified as type? Was there a measurable index of types? Why did men indulge in acts of cruelty and kindness, often both in the space of a few minutes? Why did they fight? What caused men to follow other mere mortals, for it had to be more than simple rank? What did leaders have that singled them out? He would make an enquiry into motives and actions, putting the whole together in a carefully written study. And perhaps he would acquire fame from passing on his observations on the truth of the human condition as it applied to the fighting seaman. But now, taking up his notebook and finding the passages that related to his present patient, he would, by gentle questioning, get to the truth about John Pearce.

Pearce was still talking as Lutyens read his notes, and in doing so found that he had scribbled more on this man than any other on the ship outside the wardroom; the fact that he had marked him at once as different from the rest of the pressed men, the singular reality of his observation that although older than Pearce he had felt to be a junior in his presence. Lutyens found himself slightly embarrassed to discover that he had described Pearce as attractive, which was surely a misnomer, and he searched for what he had really meant, a word to describe the way Pearce attracted men to him. He scored out attractive and replaced it with forceful. Then he renewed his questioning.

'Born in?'

'London.'

'Mother?'

'Dead.'

'Brothers and sisters?'

'None.'

'School?'

'By the score but never for long.'

'Father?'

'A good man, but fixated by the lot of his fellow man.'

'Do you love him?'

'With all my heart.'

Lutyens saw tears fill the corner of Pearce's eyes and gentle prodding produced the information that the son felt he had failed his father, deserted him, allowed him to insist on flight for only one, too ready to accept the excuse that he was too ill to travel. That unlocked the thorny emotions of their relationship:

mostly a difference of opinion over the way ideas translated into actions. This exposed another strong influence, the teachings in philosophy, rhetoric and law he had received from his tutor, the Abbé Morlant. His life in Paris had not all been dry study; there had been women too, numerous and varied in age and social station. John Pearce had received schooling in riding and fencing, the paradox being that his levelling father was determined his son would have the attributes of the gentlemen he so despised, his excuse being that he wanted these things for all men.

'Your honour.'

Lutyens turned to see the sailmaker standing in the doorway, looking at Pearce's leaf-covered back, a quizzical expression on his face, as the surgeon put a finger to his lips to ensure silence. Simpson held up his manufacture, pale brown canvas of a light texture, shining with the cook's slush, and with the requisite ties hanging off.

'You'll need a hand to get it on, with him being dead weight by the look.'

Pearce was still rambling, fortunately in a voice so low that only an ear close by could pick it up. It was not that Lutyens mistrusted Simpson – he was wary of everyone. But let one word of what he was learning here get out and it would be all over the ship in a trice. And the look in Simpson's eye, as he looked down on Pearce, was one of deep curiosity, which made Lutyens question if he was the only person aboard who harboured doubts about this patient.

'Leave it. I will call for help when I need it.'

Simpson looked far from pleased, and even less so when the surgeon came out from his small cabin to ensure that he moved away. Then he went back to sit with John Pearce.

* * *

Ralph Barclay had on his desk a drawing of the observations the master had made, showing as notations what they knew regarding the depth of water and what hazards lay in their path in the way of rocks and sandbars. The information Collins had brought back with him only served to underline the folly of trying to take his ship into the estuary.

Thankfully Collins had not observed any preparations for a stout attempt to defend the place – a modicum of activity around the bastion, but nothing to suggest the place was being made ready to repulse an attack. Nothing untoward either aboard the vessels except the comings and goings between ship and shore. Barclay had to believe his enemy reckoned himself secure, so a boat attack under such circumstances stood a good chance of success. In a previous commission, with officers he trusted, he would most certainly have invited them to a conference to discuss the raid, that followed by a good dinner in which they would be free to air their opinions. Ralph Barclay could not bring himself to do that now. The plan was his, and his alone. He was, for once, aware of that sense of isolation that afflicted all captains – the obverse side of the privilege bestowed by rank.

It was doubly galling that the one person he should have been able to talk to, not in a tactical sense but merely as a sounding board, he could not. Emily would keep referring, obliquely but doggedly, to the incident that had taken place that morning on deck, and much as he did not wish to discuss the matter he was finally forced to respond – to tell her that in matters of discipline she was not allowed to even comment, never mind disagree. Her statement, that that being the case, she would say 'nothing at all', was denied any response by her huffy departure, followed by the immediate entrance of those who would be taking part in the raid.

'Gentlemen, this will be a cutting out operation with boats.'

Ralph Barclay looked at each face in turn then, and saw nothing, neither approval not divergence of opinion. He had been about to explain his thinking, but such bland acceptance killed off the notion, and he confined himself to outlining the salient points of the defence and how he wished to confound them.

'Mr Roscoe, your task is to cause a diversion by attacking that bastion, with Mr Thrale in support. I wish you to land where you will not be seen,' Barclay jabbed at the rough-drawn map, indicating a small promontory on the western shore that would provide a degree of cover for Roscoe to land his men. 'I have marked the spot here, which will allow you to get ashore unobserved. In the dark you should be able to get right up to the walls without alerting them. I want noise and confusion, our enemies thinking those guns the main object of our endeavour, that by taking the stronghold we intend to use the cannon against the *Mercedes* and render the position untenable, driving them from the anchorage. With luck they will rush to aid its defence. That will render my task of taking the ships easier, for once they depart I can board.'

'Can the cannon on that bastion be brought to bear on the anchorage?' asked Roscoe.

'I would think it likely.'

'Then, sir, does that not, in fact, present the best means of recapture?'

Barclay waved an impatient arm across the table. 'Only if we could take and hold such a position, Mr Roscoe! That means taking on the town as well as the crew of the privateer, and quite possibly troops from the interior. I doubt we have the number to achieve that and we certainly do not have the time. No, it must be a diversion only, though I intend you should take with you the means to destroy the position, gunpowder to blast down the walls and spikes for the cannon. It would be an advantage to our nation to make it untenable for future use.'

'Then would I be allowed to state my desire to lead the main assault, sir, that is the boat attack?'

'Your zeal will be noted,' Barclay said, 'but I have given myself that duty.'

Roscoe gave him a cold look. It was Gould and *Firefly* all over again. Barclay knew he was taking to himself a duty that should have gone to his Premier. Ship's captains generally stayed aboard and sent in an assault – giving their inferior officers a chance at distinction – they did not, themselves, lead them. But then not all faced possible disgrace, as did he.

'All three boats will act in unison, and we will only part company once we are inside the arms of the estuary. Mr Collins has given half an hour before midnight as the hour of high tide. Your assault, Mr Roscoe, begins at midnight and provides the signal for mine. I intend to cut the ship's cables and drift out of the anchorage on a falling tide.'

There were nods of agreement. The wind had shifted throughout the day, becoming more northerly and breaking up the cloud cover, so the possibility existed that it would be foul for an exit.

'Mr Farmiloe will accompany me, Mr Craddock as senior midshipman to second you Mr Roscoe, Mr Burns to second Mr Thrale.'

It was annoying the way the boy Burns blanched at that; he almost seemed to shiver with dread, which was unbecoming for one related to him by marriage.

'Mr Digby, you will stay aboard and command the ship with the assistance of Mr Collins. You will keep a sharp lookout for either ship coming out. If there is no lantern on either at the foremast they are still in the possession of the enemy and you may, as you see fit, engage them. Now I suggest we commit what the master has noted to memory, for we will begin and end this action in darkness.'

None present could be in any doubt that it was a desperate throw, but even if what they were about had been caused by their captain's recklessness they were keen to go in. What it presented to these officers and the mids who would accompany them was priceless in a world with too many applicants chasing too few berths – any chance for glory was also a chance for promotion. Succeed, and every man would be lauded, fail and only Barclay would suffer ignominy.

Pearce slept throughout the day, a blissful eight continuous hours, his back coated with the soothing comfrey, for once not damned by the need to man his watch. Lutyens let him be, more taken with the paradox he was witnessing amongst the crew, one he alluded to when Pearce awoke, but only after he had enquired about his condition.

The patient eased his back, feeling the skin still tight, itching rather than stinging, and beneath the skin bones that carried a bearable ache. And he felt refreshed, almost like a different person, more alert after a slumber that went beyond the usual three and a half hours.

'I can scarce credit that I was at that grating, let alone that it is only half a day past.'

'Old remedies, Pearce,' Lutyens insisted, 'they never fail. Comfrey was known to the ancient world as a palliative, yet few medical men use it now. But go to the country and you will find the common village healer swears by it. Laudanum, too, comes from a natural source, a variety of poppy. I cannot think why there is such a desire in medicinal circles for innovation when we have to hand so many well-tried cures.'

Pearce was tempted to disagree but Lutyens had moved on to discuss the forthcoming attempt to cut out the Indiaman, openly perplexed by the attitude of the crew.

'I cannot fathom it, Pearce,' eyes alight as he hooted at the expression. 'Salty is it not?' Then he adopted a more serious tone. 'It is plain that the crew are indifferent to Captain Barclay – there is no air of him having inspired them to attempt exemplary deeds. Yet what do I witness as preparations go ahead for this adventure: a heightened state, a glow in the eyes of many, impatience! They shake their heads at what has happened so far,' the voice dropped to a conspiratorial tone, 'I do believe they think Barclay a fool to have been so guyed by the Frenchman, even more of a fool to increase the stakes to try and win all on a throw. Yet they are afire to fight.'

Pearce wondered if he should reply, just as he wondered why this surgeon wished to engage him in conversation on such a topic. His recollection of the time since he had entered this sickbay was vague, but he had a nagging suspicion that he had talked a great deal, that he might have told Lutyens more about himself than he wished.

'Come, John Pearce, you must, for all love, have an opinion.'

'There are those who love nothing more than a scrap.'

Lutyens bowed, leaning forward towards his seated patient, his voice insistent.

'Are you one of them, Pearce?'

'I will fight if I have a reason to do so, but I have always thought it foolish to seek one out.'

'My point! Surely a man must have a motive to wish to

fight, to face death or disfigurement, especially for a cause that will not improve his life one jot. Or is the reasoning and need of another, or some notion of patriotism, sufficient?'

'Perhaps it is the ship,' Pearce said, for he had observed that the sailors aboard talked of it fondly. 'They have a collective love of this vessel, of its reputation...'

'I hazard, not enough,' Lutyens interrupted, with an impatient scowl, which annoyed Pearce enough to produce a sharp response.

'...Or perhaps the life they lead is so dire in its prospect that anything, including their own mortality, is forfeit in the name of excitement or some false notion that they are on the verge of a wealth that will bring them ease and comfort. Narrow horizons make men prey to all sorts of designs, and they usually find whatever sacrifice they endure is more for the benefit of another than themselves.'

'That, I suspect, is precisely what Adam Pearce would say?'

Tempted to say, 'Who?' Pearce was stopped by the knowing look in the surgeon's eye, more so when he added, 'Laudanum eases more than pain.'

'I have seen what it does, Mr Lutyens,' Pearce said guardedly, and indeed having listened to his father's ramblings under the influence of the opiate, he knew he might have performed likewise. 'But I would be cautious about any revelations made. They are more likely to be invention than fact.'

Lutyens was amused. 'Indeed?'

'Am I free to go?'

'You are if you can stand and walk.'

Pearce felt a deeper ache in his back as he pulled himself to his feet, yet felt better for being upright and so much taller than Lutyens. Sitting, he had considered himself at the man's mercy. Looking down on him he felt less so.

'I do agree with you,' Lutyens purred, 'regarding revelations made under the influence of laudanum. To pass them on would be very unwise. Besides, it is no one else's business, is it?'

A slight nod was all Pearce would allow himself.

'You ain't never seen a man hacked about, have you lad?' said Molly, with a heavy grimace. 'Horrible it be, truly horrible.'

'Blood everywhere,' added his messmate, Foley, 'with great dark gashes that the flies love to feed on. And the eyes, dead, like bits of glass.'

'Cannon shot is worse, mind,' Molly continued, 'cut a man in half that will. Why I've seen men carried below in two bits, top bit screaming and the legs still twitching ten feet away on the deck.'

'Carried below,' cried Foley, 'though they were scarce to last. Tossed them through a gunport then, we did, for there's no ceremony in the midst of a sea fight. In warm water too, so it weren't no burial they had but the makings of a meal for the sharks. Makes you wonder if it be part of God's purpose, one of his creatures gifting sustenance to another.'

'Leastways we won't have splinters, Foley,' said Molly, gravely, ''cause if there's 'owt to turn your stomach it be a shard of wood slicing through flesh like a butcher's hatchet.'

Cornelius Gherson had been terrified before sitting down but the words he was listening to made him shake even more. Selected with the rest of Number Twelve Mess to go ashore, Pearce excepted, he was searching desperately for a way out, because all he could envisage in his imagination was his body riddled with musket balls, pierced by endless pikes, slashed by dozens of cutlasses, or torn to shreds by a cannon shot. The thought that

Pearce could escape such a fate merely by being the victim of a flogging made him furious. His dilemma was made doubly hard by the need to appear ardent, for all around him the crew of *Brilliant* was engaged in bloodcurdling threats against those they would meet this night. Molly, who had spotted his dread as easy as anyone with eyes, was having great fun stoking his fears.

'Mind, not every man I ever served with was as hearty for a fight as this crew. Seen men run below when it gets too warm on deck.'

'Must be hard to live with that, Molly,' hissed Foley, 'knowing that when it came to it, you ain't got the liver for a scrap.'

'Run below,' said Gherson, with a wholly false laugh. 'No one can do that tonight.'

'Some will duck out for certain,' Molly replied, 'when the fur begins to fly. Being dark, no one will see.'

'They say there are three parties going in,' Gherson asked, his voice eager, 'which one do you reckon will be the hottest?'

'Roscoe's, no doubt, with old Taffrail alongside him.' Taffrail was Lieutenant Thrale's nickname, due to him being as deaf as the posts that made up the stern rails. 'Barclay's gone and given hisself the easy part, I reckon.'

'How so?'

Molly had to think hard to make it sound convincing. But Gherson was a willing fool, quite capable of believing that the crew of the privateer, 'would be ashore most like'; that Roscoe and Thrale were facing cannon behind stone, which 'was a damn sight worse than wood'; that with a tide like the one in these parts, a cut hawser would see them sail out 'as easy as kiss my hand.'

'I want to take your place, Ben.'

Ben Walker fixed his messmate with those bright, bird-like

eyes, examining Pearce's face as he tried to figure out why he was being asked to stand aside, to let Pearce go in his place. He had been picked out as the one in their group most content to be at sea, yet surely with the wit to see what was in store for a goodly number of those going into action. Ben's silence had marked him out for Pearce as a thinker, and in his experience such men were less ruled by the excitability common to the herd.

'You ain't fit for it,' he drawled.

'I'll manage,' Pearce insisted, more in hope than certainty.

'I'm not afeart.'

'No one says you are, Ben. But I have something to gain by going, and you do not.'

Ben Walker wanted an explanation – it was there in his expression, but Pearce had no intention of giving him one. Let his own mind work on what he might lose or gain; if that was insufficient, he would lean on young Rufus, then Gherson, who would certainly try to extract a money fee.

'Trust me, Ben. Just like you I have secrets. I see it as no business of mine to pry into yours, but if you want to share confidences…'

Pearce left the rest up in the air, and was relieved when Ben said, 'We've been put under that deaf old arse Thrale.' Clearly revelation was not an avenue he wished to go down.

Neither Pearce nor Ben knew the details; they were confined to the officers and leading hands. But the outline of tonight's business was common gossip. 'I know, just as I know faces and names mean nothing. Thrale will be content if he has the number of men required, that is if he has the wit to count.'

Ben Walker looked at the deck planking, his head moving from side to side as he ruminated on what Pearce had asked. 'Would what you are asking for be the act of a friend?'

'Yes, Ben, it would.'

'I count you as a friend. The way you looked after Abel. Well.'

Pearce had to fix his face then, because that openly stated sentiment touched him deeply. 'I am grateful for that.'

Walker nodded. 'Then as a friend, and for Abel's memory.'

Sea chests had been hauled out of the holds and opened so that those who needed shoes and coats could get at them. In the crush and confusion of forty men identifying their property no one had paid any attention to Pearce as he found the one that contained his possessions, taking out his half-length boots and his collarless coat. He felt immediately that the weight was wrong, and, plunging his hand into the inside pocket were he had left his purse, he discovered it to be empty. A silent curse was all he could employ – there was no time for speculation – his money was gone, and he had to be gone as well to avoid discovery.

'You're mad,' whispered Michael O'Hagan, as, minutes later they queued on the moonlit upper deck for their weapons. 'Mind, I never doubted that was true.'

Those were no words that a man in a trough of doubt wanted to hear – no money made what he contemplated even harder – so when Pearce emphatically replied it was as much to steel his own resolve as to answer the Irishman. 'That Michael, is the coast of France.'

'It might be the gates of Hell.'

'Pearce?' demanded Dysart, peering as he identified him. 'What in the name o' Christ are you doing here?'

'You wouldn't deny me the chance to fight would you?'

Dysart gave him an arch look. 'I wouldna have thought this one yours.'

'It's in my blood,' Pearce insisted.

Dysart had been given a length of linstock, which he began

to wrap round his waist as Pearce elbowed his way to the pile of weapons, where he selected a tomahawk and a vicious short-bladed knife. Returning to join the two Celts, he added, 'They know all about fighting Scots over yonder, and they hold us to be mad in battle. The French even have an expression for it, *le furieux ecoissais*.'

Dysart grinned, juggling the flints that would be used to spark the slow-match, before stowing them deep in his pocket. 'Christ, Barclay will bust a gut if he finds oot a man he flogged in the morning was fit tae fight the same bluddy night.'

'Then let's hope it is something the surgeon cannot cure.'

'Amen to that,' Dysart replied, before adding. 'Taverner, Dommet, get that wee barrel of gunpowder.' Dysart then looked back at Pearce. 'So you might no just be going for a mad battle?'

Pearce just put a finger to his lips, as the command came to get the boats over the side. There was a nervous moment when Lieutenant Digby spotted him, his raised eyebrows testimony to his surprise. The pair locked eyes, before Digby nodded, then looked away.

'Where's Corny?' asked Rufus.

'Gherson,' Charlie Taverner snorted, probably hiding in the heads. 'The way he was shitting himself it be just as well.'

'Happen he's learnt his lesson from the other night,' said Rufus.

'Don't go wagering anything on that,' Taverner replied, as he went over the side into the boat.

Stiffly, Pearce followed him down.

'A trip around the bay,' hooted Michael, as he came last, by his loud proclamation taking any curious eyes off Pearce. 'Now, would we not have paid good money for such a treat, and here we are getting it for free. Sure, it's a grand life.'

CHAPTER FIFTEEN

The first strokes of the oar had made Pearce wince, but the constant movement slowly warmed his muscles, which caused the pain to ease into a dull ache. It was there, it was nagging, but thankfully it was bearable. Ridley and Costello had done him a great favour with their bogus, lightweight cat, and he had to believe that such a thing could not have been carried out without the connivance of the Bosun himself. Sykes, who had hauled him out of the water off Deal but declined to hand him over for punishment had to be in on the secret. Kemp had been kept away from that cat o' nine tails. Maybe Sykes had made sure the other warrant officers shared his sentiment.

Reflecting on that, Pearce was obliged to acknowledge that there were good men in King George's Navy as well as bad, just the same as existed in all walks of life. It was wrong to judge the whole by the likes of Barclay, Kemp and Sam Devenow. Time aboard might have revealed more kindness than contempt, and he would have made friends for sure, because all his life, in all the situations in which he had found himself that is what had happened. But it was not a notion he wished to put to the test – if he never saw another sailor in his life he would rest content. He turned his thinking to ways of getting away from this crowd of fighting men once ashore, adjusting what he had planned previously to the new condition he now found himself in – pennilessness.

The moon disappeared behind a large cloud, and the party in the cutter was thrown into near total darkness, with only the silver edging of the overhead black mass showing any light. When the moon did reappear, after what seemed an interminable gap, to bathe the sea in a pale glow, none of the other boats, which should have shown as silhouettes, were visible. Nor could they hear the sound of dipping oars, any coughing, the clink of metal or a voice checking for their presence.

Pearce and his companions rowed on, only their heavy breathing audible, while Lieutenant Thrale, one hand on the tiller, swung his head all around in a desperate search for company. Seeing none, he racked the sky, finger half raised to test the wind as he tried to discern his course by starlight, his lined old face even more creased by worry. Pearce half hoped they were lost; that they would land in the wrong place. The prospect of a fight, with an intoxicating tot of rum to fire the spirit, might be exhilarating to those with no imagination, but this was no fairground bout they were rowing towards, it was an enemy who would try to maim or kill them, an enemy who would not ask the nature of his sentiments first should he be forced into a confrontation.

'Can you hear that noise, sir?' Midshipman Burns called from the prow, a tremulous note in his piping, young boy's voice.

'Where away?' Thrale replied, tucking the tiller under his arm, hat lifted and a hand cupped to his ear.

'Dead ahead, I reckon,' said Burns. 'Breaking water.'

With the beating of his own heart and panting bodies around him, Pearce could hear nothing. Judging by the expression on Thrale's face, curious, anxious but unconvinced, neither could he, but that was likely due to the degree of his deafness.

'No,' Thrale insisted, 'to starboard. It will be the rocks Captain Barclay alluded to.'

'Rocks,' hissed Michael O'Hagan, 'what flippin' rocks?'

'Silence there,' barked Thrale, before dropping his voice. 'Sound deceives at sea, Mr Burns, plays tricks upon the untried ear, the sirens of ancient times were noted for it. What seems hard by can be a league distant. Pay no heed to the noise, just keep your eyes peeled for the western beach. Lieutenant Roscoe might already be ashore. If we do not get cracking he will head off for that bastion without us.'

He added, for the whole eight-man crew of rowers, and no doubt intended to include the fighters as well, in a voice that tried and failed to be uplifting, 'Bend to your oars, lads, otherwise we will miss out on any glory.'

'Glory,' Pearce scoffed, softly, so that only Michael beside him could hear.

'Sure,' Michael replied, his voice just as low, 'I been told by those staying aboard that we could all die trying to save Barclay's name.'

'The noise increases, sir,' Burns called.

Thrale had been trying to look at his fob watch to see if he was late, cursing the next huge cloud that had blown in to obscure the moon, but he tried a cupped hand again, then nodded, as if having finally located the sound. 'Well to starboard, Burns, I'm sure of it, and my watch, as well as the motion of the boat, tells me we must be getting close to shore.'

The run of the sea had changed, no longer the big, steady rising and falling swell of the open sea, but waves kicking to sharper peaks as they shelved in shallow water, lifting and dropping the prow in a more deliberate fashion. Pearce could hear the sound now, the crash of breaking water, and though he had no way of being sure, it did not sound to him as if it was well off to his right. He would have shrugged had he not been occupied on the oars, for it was none of his concern. The rowing became harder as the boat rode the increasing swell. The water was shoaling fast – sometimes enough to leave an oar free when it should be dipped, in a sea becoming disturbed enough to require the blades to back up a tiller that had become near useless at controlling the course of the cutter.

'I saw a flash of white, sir.'

'Come Mr Burns, even someone as green as you must know that white water signifies waves breaking upon the beach.'

'It is not like that, sir,' Burns squeaked, 'and the noise is much louder.'

'True,' Thrale replied in a reassuring voice. 'Perhaps we are closer to the rocks than intended – I have come off my reckoning a trifle. But be assured we will shave them and they border sand that stretches for half a mile, which will mean a slower approach than I had hoped, indeed we must bend to or we will struggle to get to the action before it is joined. Now I require no more talking, for even with the sound you allude to there may be people on shore who will hear you.'

The sea state was growing increasingly disturbed, not just

rising and falling but eddying suddenly, creating unpredictable troughs and peaks. And the sound of water breaking on rocks had risen from a distant to a very present and steady roar. Dysart spoke up suddenly, his voice anxious, but respectful. 'I reckon there be rocks under our keel, your honour, an' some of them might be more dead ahead that yer allowing for.'

'Is that Dysart?' Thrale growled, recognising the distinct Scots accent. 'Talking when I have ordered silence?'

'Aye, sir,' the Scotsman replied, his voice raised against the noise of the waves. 'But ah speak for every able hand aboard, when ah say it wid be prudent tae come aboot and get tae calmer water where we can check our position.'

Thrale barked loudly then, ignoring his own injunction to be quiet. 'Damn your impertinence, you will speak yourself to a grating, I tell you. Rowers, bend hard, I want to be driven up that beach when we strike sand, lest we broach to and get cast back into the spume.'

Thrale took off his hat again, and, laying it in his lap, he began to strike the crown like a cask, in a tempo that he wanted the men on the oars to replicate. Having already pulled for near an hour they were too tired to respond, which only enraged the old lieutenant, and made him strike at his hat more ferociously.

'Rocks!' Burns yelled. 'Dead ahead.'

If Thrale had reacted immediately they might have got clear. But instead he half-stood, swaying and hatless, peering into the gloom ahead, his mouth moving soundlessly as if he could not think of what to say. The boat was now bucking like a fickle horse in water that had no pattern to it. But the sound was unmistakable, and now it seemed to surround and envelop them rather than come from any given direction.

'To larboard,' Thrale shouted eventually, falling back to sit down and pushing hard on the tiller, 'boat your oars. Starboard oars, haul away hard.'

They tried to turn using one set of oars, and get the prow pointing out to sea again, but it was too late – the surf was too strong and it acted on a boat turned sideways to deny all attempts to get the head round, at the same time carrying them in further towards the shore. They were in surf now – a maelstrom that could only be a few dozen yards away from safety, but there was no choice but to let the head fall off again for they risked being be upended into the sea. Dysart started yelling to reverse the boat, in an attempt to get out stern first, setting an example himself by grabbing the end of Pearce's oar. He, like everyone else, was now standing, trying to exert enough pressure on an oar to get them clear. Burns was squealing fearfully and uselessly, bent over in the prow, while Thrale was yelling a set of conflicting instructions that no one was listening to.

The first rock they touched ground along the keel, a hard rasping noise, lifting the middle of the boat and sending everyone off balance. Shouting was drowned by the noise of the crashing Atlantic Ocean as it met the French coast – not even a yell of panic-stricken fear could travel further than the next ear. That useless thought filled Pearce's mind as he struggled to get back into position to row. This water stretched thousands of miles west, south and north – the waves that threatened them might have come from the Americas – and the old fool Thrale had managed to find one of the few spots in that mass which was deadly.

With his back to the shore Pearce could not see what was coming. Right by his ear Michael O'Hagan was bellowing his prayers to every saint or saviour in the papist pantheon. In front of Pearce, Charlie and Rufus, having been thrown down by the grounding keel, were on their feet again, but not rowing, not attempting to regain control of their oars. Instead, they were looking past Pearce and Michael with faces full of dread.

'The little shit has jumped!' yelled Taverner, pointing to the prow in a way that made it impossible for Pearce not to look. Burns was not there now, but as the boat dropped into a trough of swirling spume he could see the flailing arms in the water as the midshipman fought to stay afloat and swim. If they had ever had a chance of getting to safety Burns' action condemned it, for Charlie Taverner must have reckoned that the boy had seen a route to salvation and taken it ahead of the rest of the boat crew. Charlie grabbed Rufus and yelled in his ear, a second before they both went overboard. They could not swim but they took over with them one of the small barrels of powder, which, if they could maintain their grip, with the ropes that had been attached to carry it, they must believe would keep them afloat.

Water was flying around their heads now, making it difficult to see and almost impossible to think. Voices were yelling but if they were making any sense it was being carried away on the noise of wind and water being dashed against rocks. High white sheets of spume were visible now in light of a moon carried clear of the black cloud that had obscured it. The phosphorescence made the prospect almost as light as day, illuminating the desperate degree of danger they were now in.

Ahead lay glistening black boulders, their looming shapes rendered fantastical by the silver light that glistened on their wet surfaces. The cutter was being tossed about like a cork, and it was bound to capsize, if it did not break up on the submerged rocks that were crashing into the keel. Strakes of planking were already stove in and the bottom was filling with water, which was at least acting to give those still in the boat a modicum of stability. Whatever order should have existed was absent, and to Pearce it was clear that while Burns might have been pre-emptive in his panic-stricken leap, it was the only safe option now. He must jump now or wait until the rocks ahead smashed the boat to matchwood; hard unyielding stone that would sunder human flesh to a bloody pulp.

Pearce got hold of Michael O'Hagan's shirt collar and hauled his ear close. 'We're going over, Michael. Do not, whatever you do cling to me. I will hold you.'

'Jesus.'

'I swear on your Jesus, if you clutch on to me you will take us both to perdition.'

Pearce had to pull him over, because Michael could not bring himself to jump, in his mind hanging on to that last hope of life that existed with something solid beneath his feet. They did not get as clear of the side of the boat as Pearce wished, and it swung on a surge of seawater, crashing into them both so that they went under. Pearce felt what he dreaded, Michael's hands scrabbling for a grip on his clothing. The combined weight of himself and the Irishman took them deeper. Punching in water was useless, so Pearce did the only thing that he thought might make Michael let go – he bit him as hard as he could, with no idea of where he had sunk his teeth. He thought it was into his friend's head.

He managed to get one hand clear, and with some effort Pearce tore at the other to get Michael to release him just as they surfaced. Turning on to his back and dragging the floating

Irishman on to his belly, he stopped him from regaining his fatal grip. There was no way of knowing what was behind him, but despite the rocks he knew that floating was the only option, the waves would carry them in. There were rocks for certain, but he hoped for a gap or a boulder of a shape that would not maim them, break some bone or smash a skull, for that meant certain death. Each time he tried to turn and look, he faced two problems – Michael started to panic, and the furious surf and spume blocked any clear view of what lay ahead.

Something solid touched Pearce's foot, a rock he thought, and he pushed his boot down on it, wondering as he did so why he had lacked the sense to kick them off before jumping into the water. A wave rolled over his head, filling his mouth, thumping his back into a higher part of that which was under his foot. The pain brought back fierce concentration as he tried to get some purchase. With one foot pressed down, the next surging wave spun his body sideways, Michael still on his chest, then threw him into something so hard and unforgiving that he felt himself winded. The grip he had on the Irishman was lost, and it took a fumbling, groping hand to get hold of his clothing. Pearce was face down in the water now, one hand thrusting and hauling like mad as he tried to drag his friend, with what little purchase he could get with his feet, to a point where he hoped they could both get their heads above water long enough to breathe.

With lungs near to bursting, Pearce's head came clear enough for him to gulp in a huge mouthful of air mixed with seawater. His whole body was now lying on what seemed like a flat but angled piece of rock. An outstretched hand found a small crevice, which allowed him to grip and haul. He got his head clear for another gulp of air, burying the knowledge that filled his mind: he could almost certainly get himself to safety if he let go of Michael O'Hagan. But just as the Irishman had aided him without question, Pearce could not put his own salvation first.

Pearce struggled an inch at a time up the slippery rock, until he could get O'Hagan's head up out of the water. He tried shouting when he managed that, half the time spitting out seawater, trying to tell the Irishman that if he turned over and stretched out his hand he could save himself, but Michael had surrendered to Pearce and stayed like a dead weight on the end of his arm.

Was it seconds, or minutes before he felt them safe? Pearce had no idea, but he did know that the boat must have struck by now, which would mean men in the water who could not swim, men he had shared the main-deck with, men who had guyed him, but this very day had shown him sympathy too, men who could not be left to their fate while he had breath to save them. Michael O'Hagan was clear of the water now, too high up the rock to be dragged in by the undertow of a wave. As Pearce got on to his hands and knees, a high-pitched scream made him look back into the water, just in time to see the bobbing head of young Martin Dent. Kicking off his boots he made his way unsteadily down the slippery rock, then knelt and held out his hand.

There was a moment, as a crest brought Martin towards him, when he thought to withdraw it, to let the murdering little bastard who had so tormented him drown, but he could not. Their hands met, Pearce gripped and pulled, then, standing upright with the water breaking round his knees, he lifted Martin up by his shirt front, looking into the boy's terrified eyes with deep loathing. Then he threw him up the rock, with the fond wish that as he landed he might break something.

He peered out again, sure he could see waving arms, and he slipped back into the water. If the moon had gone again he would not have saved Dysart, who had stayed on the boat when everyone else had jumped, hanging on to a ragged, splintered gunwale as it smashed into the higher boulders. A bigger wave hit the side and tipped it over, throwing Dysart, arms flailing, screaming in terror, into the water. Going to get him nearly did for Pearce as the cutter bounced back out again, a metal rowlock sliding along his cheek as what was left of it was upended. Whether it hit Dysart he didn't know – the Scotsman came up to the surface on his own lungful of air just long enough for Pearce to grab him. But he didn't struggle, which made Pearce wonder if he was still alive. It didn't matter for there was no way to find out in the water, and, sure now of where he was headed, Pearce struck out for the rock where he had left O'Hagan.

It was less of struggle to get the little Scotsman up to safety, and having hauled Dysart out, Pearce went to look for more survivors. He did not plunge back in, for he could see nothing else – no hand, head or body in the water. Instead he stood, ear cocked for a cry of distress, aware that the breeze, which on dry land was the clement wind they had experienced in easier water, was slowly freezing him to the marrow. But the greater distress was internal, as he looked into the small gap through which the boat had careered. There was nothing floating there at all now, not wood, nor any member of the ship's crew.

The loud boom of an explosion made him look right up the estuary, and he saw the last trace of orange light as the flare of a fired cannon faded. Another boom followed, that and the faint crack of musketry. The darkness was lit again and again in the next few minutes as the attack he was supposed to be part of went in with only half the intended force. Shivering, Pearce conjured up an image of what might be happening, but, try as he might, he could not wish death upon anyone, even Barclay or Roscoe, because loss of life was an uncertain thing, and it was as likely to take those he liked or esteemed as anyone he hated. The only certainty was that he could do nothing to effect matters. Aid was needed here for those who had survived the wreck. How many were there? Did they have wounds that required attention? How could he create some heat, a fire that would keep men from dying of cold without sending out a signal to the locals that there was a distressed party of British sailors on their shore? Many questions filled his brain, but he found no answers.

If he felt any despair that was relieved by the voice of Michael O'Hagan, moaning, 'The bastard bit me, I swear to Jesus right to the fecking cheekbone, he bit me.'

'Bend to your oars, softly now,' hissed Ralph Barclay, 'and no sound.'

The first gun had just fired from the bastion, a defence he had slipped by in complete silence, to get to the point upriver from where he could mount the real assault. The tension of waiting had been unbearable, but not as bad as that which he had suffered up to this point. He had had time in which to reappraise yet again all the things that had gone wrong in the last two days. At one point he had concluded that death here in this obscure French inlet might be preferable to facing the wrath of his superiors or the disdain of a wife who could not understand that he was not a cruel man but a King's officer with a job to do and scant resources to succeed.

The masts of the two ships, sitting in deep water, were silhouetted against the sky, those of the *Lady Harrington* at the rear standing higher than those of the lantern-lit privateer. He was tempted to go for money instead of glory – one ship instead of both. Ralph Barclay suppressed the thought now, as he had before, and took a tighter grip on the tiller as if to stiffen his resolve. He was surprised that, although there seemed plenty of activity on shore, waving lanterns and the like, there was no sign of any reaction aboard the two vessels. Could it be that the entire crew of the privateer was ashore?

The cutter drifted in silently, slipping into the pool of light cast by the lanterns that hung either end of the empty deck, a moment when no one breathed. Surely they would have at least an anchor watch on deck who would spot their approach? Nothing happened, and Ralph Barclay was left to conclude that he had been over-anxious. The Frenchmen was so cock a' hoop with their capture, and so convinced that *Brilliant* was a dog of a ship and its captain a nincompoop, that no notion of a raid had entered their minds.

Cornelius Gherson was becoming calmer by the second, thanking Molly for the advice he had given. Getting into this boat had been easy in the dark, and no one aboard questioned the presence of an extra fighter. The booming and crackling sounds from the shore were reassuring too; let the others of his mess face shot and shell, he would sail out on the enemy ship, claim a simple mistake in choosing the wrong boat and be able to look them in the eye with conviction. Had he been upright and walking he would have done so with a swagger.

Richard Farmiloe stood in the prow, pistols tucked in his

belt, cutlass raised and feeling very exposed. The attacking party anticipated boarding nets, and being tall, it was his job to slash at them and create a gap while the rest of the men in the boat came forward to board. Behind him stood a sailor with a grappling iron that would provide a means to clamber up to the higher deck, and could be used to lash them to the enemy ship.

He would be the first man into action and that had made Farmiloe swallow hard when, still aboard the frigate, he had imagined what it might be like. Now that he was here and it was about to happen the youngster was easier in his mind, though aware that his mouth was exceedingly dry and his heart was pounding in his chest, either through fear, excitement or a combination of both. He had fully expected, in an approach that was going to take a minute or more, to see some men brought on deck by the noise created by Roscoe's attack, but it was still empty. Surely the privateersmen could not have left their ship entirely unguarded. And if it was guarded, why was there no curiosity? He was aware of the muffled oars, which did not sound quiet to him, but noisy enough to act like a signal. Gripped with a sudden renewed bout of fear, he wanted to turn and yell at the oarsmen to be bloody quiet, until he realised, as another cannon boomed out from downriver, that he was being foolish.

'Back your oars,' murmured Ralph Barclay, and what little way was eased as the rowers steadied them in the water, while those set to board half-raised themselves in preparation. The command to boat oars was unnecessary, the men could see they were close to the privateer's side. He saw Farmiloe reach out a hand to slow the prow into the privateer's hull, could almost feel the pressure on the boy's thighs as he strained to hold a heavy boat and thirty men to a pace that would make it touch the ship's side in silence.

No boarding nets, thought Richard Farmiloe as the cork fender on the prow touched, and the man behind him swung the grappling iron out and up to crunch noisily on to the French bulwark. Ralph Barclay was thinking that this was going to be easy – that all his concerns would evaporate as they sailed this ship out to join *Brilliant*. God, the crew might even cheer him, admirals would court him and surely Emily would come to see that the end justified the means, that the discipline he had imposed directly affected the way every member of his ship's company had behaved in action.

That ease was blown away with the head of the marine officer in front of him, as a heavy musket ball, fired at point blank range, entered one side of the fellow's skull and removed the other, the impact sending Lieutenant Holbrook's body over the side. Lost in his reverie Ralph Barclay had neither heard nor seen the nearest gun ports swing open, but he could see now the orange tongues of flame as they were discharged into men who were, quite literally, sitting ducks.

'Marines,' he yelled, 'return fire. Mr Farmiloe, get on that deck at the double.'

Please God, Ralph Barclay thought, let the French not have pre-loaded their muskets. If they had laid-by muskets ready to fire, and therefore did not need to reload the ones they had just discharged, most of the men in this boat, including himself, would die. Gherson had dived for the bottom of the boat, screaming out in fear, left by those too occupied to notice or care. Richard Farmiloe was halfway up the side, suspended on a rope when the first defender appeared on deck, and in no position to react to the man's presence. His cutlass was hanging on the lanyard that secured it to his wrist and he could not use his pistols without surrendering his grip. Ralph Barclay took very careful aim, ignoring the other shots that were flying around and cracking in his ears, and as the man raised a tomahawk to slice down on Farmiloe's head, he put a ball in him that sent him flying backwards into a crowd of men behind him.

His own voice seemed strangely different as he heard himself shout, 'Hale, get us out of here, Mr Farmiloe, let go.'

There was no point in even trying to proceed – the men on the deck outnumbered his and they had such an advantage that, had he had ten times the number, prudence would have dictated withdrawal. The boy dropped untidily back into the launch as his Captain's next order was calmly given, an instruction to the marines to 'maintain fire, steady now'. Hale's voice mixed with Barclay's as the coxswain ordered the boat crew to 'haul off with all speed.'

It was less tidy than Ralph Barclay would have wished. The marines were having difficulty reloading in the confines of the boat and the oars did not hit the water with the required precision, but Farmiloe had got to his feet and made the initial push that got the boat underway, while all those who had been waiting to board threw whatever they had come with, axes, pikes, cutlasses and clubs, at the open gun ports to stop those inside from firing another volley.

Ralph Barclay fired off his own second pistol as they drifted by an open port, just as the tip of a musket poked out, followed by a grinning head. The grin took the musket ball, the mouth, made visible by the flash, going from glistening teeth to a gaping black hole, and the look in the Frenchman's eyes, which had been eager, going out like a snuffed candle. The next head that came up he tried to crown with the butt, overbalancing in the process and nearly falling overboard as his intended target ducked and grabbed the pistol. Barclay was only saved by one of his marines poking the sod under the arm with a bayonet, which forced him to release the weapon.

All about him men were shouting, screaming with wounds or passion in both English and French. Musket balls, those that did not find flesh, were spattering the water. Ralph Barclay stood up then and offered himself as a target, never quite sure as he was furiously rowed out of the arc of danger whether the fact that he was untouched meant his luck had held or deserted him, for there would be no cheering crew now, nor a suddenly transformed wife. He would go back aboard trounced for the third time in two days, to a silence punctuated only by the cries of the wounded, the groans of amputees, and probably the sound of divine service as shrouded bodies were committed to the deep. But worse he would have to sit down and write a report on the action, one that would condemn him even more than the one he been forced to compose when the privateer took the *Lady Harrington* from right under his nose.

The noises around him had fallen to panting, cursing and moaning, with one exception. 'Who is that screaming like a girl, Mr Farmiloe? If he is wounded, help him, if he is not, in the name of God shut him up.'

Huddled in the bottom of the boat, Cornelius Gherson stuck his fist into his mouth to stop his squealing. But he could not stop the shaking of his body, nor the occasional sob that escaped his fingers. Lemuel Hale managed to kick him hard with the toe of his shoe.

'Stow it, in the name of Christ, or we'll tip you overboard.'

* * *

The rock they were on was high enough, and wide enough in its girth, to provide a degree of security and Pearce could see, now that he had the chance to look, that they were close to a larger formation, which loomed in silhouette against the night sky, showing what he thought to be treetops. Peering hard, he could just observe a kind of rock causeway leading to that, which though dashed by breaking waves, seemed to be nearly clear of the water.

The call '*Brilliant*', one that John Pearce never ever thought he would make, brought to life the other survivors. Burns, who had jumped first and thus stayed out of the most disturbed area of water, crawled sheepishly forward, probably fearing a drubbing from Thrale for what could be perceived as an act of cowardice. He was no more daring faced with Pearce, who, nominally his inferior, had to tell the boy to join Martin Dent and Michael O'Hagan round in the lee of the rocks where they were sheltering out of the wind, trying to make a moaning, obviously hurt, Dysart comfortable.

'Mr Thrale?' Burns squeaked.

'No sign of him, but that does not mean he has perished. He may have found safety elsewhere.'

Charlie Taverner and Rufus Dommet, who called back to Pearce's repeated shout, were clasping on to rocks in an exposed position, next to the barrel that had kept them afloat, still with hands on it as though they feared even on dry land to break contact. They too had to be urged to look to their welfare and follow the others. Before joining them, Pearce climbed as high as he could on the boulders, calling out to sea and in both directions in a last forlorn attempt to find survivors. No shouts came from out of the water or off the other rocks. The rest of the men on the oars, if they did not respond to his call, like Thrale, might still have made it to the shore, but any search for them would have to wait till first light. The marines, festooned with ammunition and grenades would have had the least chance, weighed down by their heavy red coats and equipment.

Upriver the cracking of muskets had intensified for a while before dying away, leaving only the dull boom of an occasional cannon. Had they succeeded or had they failed? Was Barclay at that very moment conning his capture out of the narrows of the anchorage into the wider estuary? If he was, how could they signal they were here, and should Pearce even try? It was quickly obvious to Pearce that if he could cope on French soil, most of the others would not, and he could not just abandon them. If he could get them back aboard ship he would be free to go his own way.

'Mr Burns,' he called down, 'tell me about this attack.'

There was no reply, so Pearce jumped down, crawled out of the wind, and peered into the dark recess where the survivors were sheltering. 'Mr Burns, without Lieutenant Thrale here you are in charge.' Burns groaned, so Pearce added, 'Which does not inspire me any more than it does you, but it is the case. We have to make contact with the rest of the cutting out party, or you will all be stuck here. Now tell me what you know.'

It wasn't coherent, for Burns was shivering with cold as well as confused, but Pearce got a bare outline of what Barclay had planned, the name of the town, Lézardrieux and something of the layout of the estuary, the most important fact being that the whole affair had been timed to coincide with the tides. Looking at the spume still smashing off the rocks below his feet it was difficult to believe the tide was turning, but it must be, and the situation could only get better as time wore on.

'How far up the estuary was Mr Roscoe required to beach his boat?'

Pearce got a slight sob in reply, hardly surprising from a boy only twelve years old. There was no hope of any leadership from that quarter, but a hard jab produced the required information.

'Michael, how are you?'

'Wet, freezing cold and not sure if I'm in heaven, hell or limbo.'

'Dysart?'

'Worse,' Michael said. 'I don't think he is conscious.'

'I'm going to try and get up the estuary to look for Roscoe. Has anybody got flints?'

Dysart's weak voice came out of the darkness, to deny what O'Hagan thought. 'I have. Or I had them when I went into that boat.'

'Then it would be an idea, Michael, to come with me and look for driftwood.' He handed over his short knife, which, stuck in his waistband, had survived. 'I am sure there are trees yonder, and that means kindling. You can cut some larger branches if this will suffice.'

'In the dark?'

'We need a fire if we are not to perish from cold. And it should be one that can be seen from the water, so that it will act as a signal, though it should be facing the sea so that it is hidden from the French.'

There was a great deal more Pearce could have said, but he lacked the time – let them figure out, themselves, what needed to be done. If the gunfire had slackened, with even the cannon now silent, that meant that the action had been terminated.

Barring complete failure the diversionary attackers would be running back for their boat, and once there they would not linger, but shove off hastily to get free of any pursuit. Crossing the rock causeway was not easy, and he and Michael had to hold on to each other several times to steady themselves against the waves rushing around their legs, or at others just to get across great bone dry boulders smoothed by centuries of wind. Finally Pearce dropped into a gap and felt sand underfoot, while in his nostrils, which had been full of the tang of the sea, he could smell wood.

'Jaysus, I have no desire to try and get back to the others on my own.'

'The tide is falling, Michael, it will get easier.'

'For a fish maybe.'

'If the water recedes enough, it would be a good idea to get everyone off that rock.'

'You're right,' the Irishman replied, though without much force. For the first time Pearce thought he detected a note of despair in a man he had come to see as a fount of optimism.

'Are you going to be all right, Michael?'

'Mother of God, of course I am. Have I not got good earth under my feet? Don't have a care for me, John-boy, have a care for yourself.'

'I will, Michael.'

'We will see you soon,' The Irishman said, in a tone that Pearce could hardly fail to register. It was more of a question than a statement.

'Very soon, friend.'

Pearce had to move slowly, with a mixture of sand and stones to negotiate, but at least he was in the lee of the rocks which had destroyed the boat, so when he was obliged to enter water, though cold, it was calm by comparison to the open sea, gentle breaking waves instead of a torrent. He was vaguely aware of moving in an arc in the direction he wanted to go, until he found himself looking at the sea breaking without tumult over a spit of sand, with just enough light to tell him that he was on an island and that sandbar was his route to the main shore.

Once over that, he jogged, soft sand slowing him until he trended down to where the top of the waves petered out on the shore. There the wet sand, glistening in the moonlight, gave him a firmer surface and he was able to run. His thoughts were a jumble – should he even be doing this – could he get from this part of France to a place where he could cross back to England? If he could, what would he use to pay for his passage, for he had no faith that someone would gift him a crossing, and he certainly did not have the skill to steal a boat and make the journey himself.

Should he try to return to Paris, to his father? He had no papers to travel and given the number of times he had been stopped by nervous National Guardsmen just three weeks previously between Paris and Calais, that could be a more difficult journey than traversing the Channel. And that too would require money. What if others had no desire to go back aboard – Charlie and Rufus? He thought he could manage Michael if he wanted to come with him – an Irishman could easily plead a visceral hatred of England – but any more might make the very necessary task of evasion impossible.

He was breathing very hard by the time he saw the faint pinpoint of light reflecting off something metal, so that the shout he tried was not as powerful as he wished. Clearly he was too distant to be heard so he concentrated on trying to increase his speed, trying to ignore the sharp pain of the stitch in his side. The crack of a musket, distant but clear, made him slow abruptly, and at half pace he saw a series of flashes in the far distance, then heard the cracks as fire was returned.

That had to be Roscoe retreating, firing off volleys at some form of pursuit, which spurred him on to run flat out, now far from cold, the damp on his face and his body slick with sweat. Pearce got more of an impression of what was happening ahead than a clear picture. Ragged flashes were followed, at regular intervals, by steady volleys of musketry, as Roscoe's marines returned a disciplined fire. Pearce only saw the outline of Roscoe's boat as it was pushed into the water, the silhouette like a dark dot on a silvered mirror. Now that the marines from *Brilliant* were side on he could see the long tongues of flame from their weapons streaking out towards the shore, where random shooting was flashing in reply.

That made him stop – if he ran on he would only get closer to the pursuers. Standing, gasping for breath, he found it hard to think clearly, but it was obvious that once Roscoe had cleared the shore he would turn his boats to head out to sea. That would bring him parallel to the point where Pearce was standing. Could he swim out and stop them? Not likely, the distance might be too great and who would see a bobbing head in the water? But at night a shout should easily carry the distance, and once he had been seen and identified they could row in to pick him up, which would allow him to take Roscoe to the point where the others were sheltering at a pace no pursuit on foot could match. Once there, in darkness, he was sure he could disappear.

Pearce stripped off his coat and shirt, the latter he needed to signal with, and stood waiting, letting his breathing ease until it was normal. The firing had stopped completely now, and the only sounds were lapping waves and the wind brushing past his ears. Now the boat was visible, no marines standing now. They were probably hunched over – happy to be alive and safe, thanking God.

'Brilliant,' Pearce yelled, waving his shirt, waiting a few seconds for a response before yelling again. The third shout and wave got a response, a volley of musket fire that made him dash for the tree line to his rear with sand spurting all around him as the balls struck. Cursing, standing behind a trunk too thin for true protection, he called down all the gods in creation on Roscoe's thick skull. Looking out again he saw the boat continue on its way, the occupants unaware that they had very nearly killed one of their own, also blissfully unaware that they had abandoned at least seven of their own crew.

He got back to find that they had rowed by without any of his party spotting or hailing them, because Michael, seeing the way across getting easier by the minute, had done as Pearce suggested and fetched everyone on to the more comfortable shore. It was thickly wooded and lighting a fire had been easy. There was kindling in abundance, though the cut branches, being damp, tended to make for a great deal of smoke and not too much flame. Pearce set another fire going on the dry rocks, facing seaward to act as a beacon, but with no result. How had the attack fared? When the moon was showing it had revealed no sign of any ship heading out to sea. That did not mean, with any certainty, that Barclay had failed, but it certainly did not point up that he had succeeded.

Dysart had a broken arm, and a big gash on his head, but no one else seemed to have suffered anything more than scratches and a bit of bruising. Pearce could feel dried blood on his face, but he suspected underneath that was a scratch, and his back, though it ached abominably, had to be borne. A search of the beach had revealed no more survivors and the firelight had brought no one in.

'They would not have seen you, Pearce,' said Michael, a more amenable soul now that he had heat, though the glow highlighted the deep teeth marks on his cheek, 'with your back against the dark shore.'

'Michael, no sweet words will make me feel less angry. What Frenchman is going to shout the name of their own ship at a passing boat?'

'With the wind in your face the shout might not have carried with clarity.'

Pearce growled, 'I don't even know why I did it. What have we, me most of all, got to gain by going back aboard that damned ship?'

'I would care to hear what in the name of Holy Mary we can do else?'

'Surrender,' Pearce replied, without adding that he was thinking of them, not himself. 'Hand ourselves over to the French. Tell them we are pressed seamen looking to be free.'

'And what then?' Michael demanded. 'Will it be a life of ease and comfort?'

'The Frogs are not good with captures,' said Dysart, who was laid out, his arm secured by two reasonably straight bits of branch bound by his own torn shirtsleeve. 'When we take a Frenchman he is offered a chance to join.'

'To fight against his own?' asked Pearce.

'To some that is better than confinement in a prison hulk, where yer like to expire frae some fever. At least we dinna work them to death as the French dae. Galley slaves have a better life than a French prisoner.'

Dysart rambled on, telling tales of men digging to sink pylons up to their necks in water, of sailors scraping out rat-infested sewers and other delights in a voice that had a strong hint of tale telling about it, underlined by the way the others sat forward to listen, their faces in the few flames showing the requisite level of horror at each revelation of French perfidy. Pearce was not certain, but he suspected the French treated their prisoners in much the same manner as the British, and that if he had been talking to a Frenchman fearing capture, he would hear the same lurid tale in reverse.

Surrender, claiming to be pressed and seeking sanctuary, was not really an option anyway, simply because, as any fool could see, they would not be believed. Had they rowed into the port in an intact boat with a white flag aloft, and singing the praises of the Revolution – perhaps. But to walk in on foot, in the condition they were in, after an assault had been mounted to take back that Indiaman, would leave no one in any doubt as to how they came to be here. Staring into the flames, as Dysart droned on, he contemplated once more the idea of making for Paris, enjoying a short romantic daydream in which he would confound the whole rotten structure of Revolutionary authority and rescue his father. But he soon realised the process of his thoughts was a fantasy – how could he leave this lot here, when, with his ability to speak French he was very likely the only one who could even attempt to get them out of their predicament?

'Am I right in saying the only option we have is to get back aboard *Brilliant*?'

Looking round the faces, Pearce could see that such an option appealed to Burns, Martin Dent, Dysart and Rufus, but not to Charlie Taverner or Michael. And it certainly did not appeal to him. What was also obvious was that the latter pair had no other suggestion to make. The misery of the thought provided no other solution.

'We need a boat,' Dysart insisted, clearly aware of the reluctance of the pressed men. 'But as to getting back aboard *Brilliant*, why I doubt she would still be about. Even if he has cut out that privateer, Barclay can't hang about here. He will luff up for the convoy and rejoin.'

'Without looking for us?' asked Charlie.

Dysart didn't answer – he didn't have to. A man like Ralph Barclay, with no Lieutenant Thrale and no cutter in evidence, would assume them lost, and write them off as dead in the execution of their duties. He was not the type for a sentimental search to see if they had survived.

'My aunt might ask him to search,' said Burns, without much conviction.

'Your aunt?' Pearce asked, confused.

'The captain's wife.'

Pearce was mildly surprised at the information and had to force himself to think of the present. His voice was full of irony, as he challenged the Scotsman. 'So what you're saying Dysart is that not only do we need a boat, we need one that will get us to England? Will another frigate do?'

Even wounded, Dysart could summon up some venom. 'Anything that can step a single mast will do, and anything bigger will not, 'cause you lot are as useless as Barbary monkeys.' He calmed down a bit, taken with the problem. 'A small fishing smack can manage, telling you lot what tae do, but better than that would be something no much bigger than the gig, as I say it has tae step a mast. If *Brilliant* be still aboot then come the morning we might spy her in the offing. Happen she'll respond tae a signal.'

Dysart went on, weaving, to Pearce's way of thinking, as much of a fantasy as he had when he was talking about the French treatment of prisoners. The fact that he quite liked the man did not blind Pearce to the thought that the Scotsman was so wedded to storytelling that he could talk himself into anything. What was more worrying was the way he seemed to be able to convince the others that stealing a boat was not only possible, it was easy, as easy as putting to sea without food and water, and, if they did not find *Brilliant* or some other British ship, of sailing up the French coast in sight of land till they reached the Dover narrows, where they could just port the tiller and sail in, 'nae bother'.

'And where,' Pearce asked, trying to inject some sense into things, 'are we to find this miracle boat?'

'We're no mair than a long walk from one, Pearce, and you ken it. Just as ye ken, that wi' you knowing the Frog lingo, you are the man to go look for it.'

CHAPTER SIXTEEN

Dawn revealed three corpses on the strand of what was now a long, deep and benign beach: Thrale and two marines were only identifiable by their coats, the old blue one of the lieutenant and the red ones of the marines, all three nearly shredded to rags by the rocks and the seabed. The bodies, particularly about the head, were in a worse condition than the clothing, evidence of the violence of their death. Pearce and Michael O'Hagan climbed the rose-coloured rocks which, with the tide slack, were now clear of any water right to their base, bar the odd wind-ruffled pool. The very peak, shaped like a chimney and smoothed by eons of time, was inaccessible to them, but they got high enough for a good view out to sea, and Michael was able to lift Martin Dent even higher so that he could scrabble onto the top.

Further out, waves broke over black boulders, that last night had been under their keel, yet between them and the shore was nothing that denoted danger. How could this small, sandy cove, lying like a horseshoe in the centre of the rocks, be any kind of hazard? Yet it had been just that; the whole mass of water had been white, the spume had flown everywhere, and the sucking sound as the waves retreated, loud enough to mask the cries of the drowning, had been like the sound of hell incarnate.

Somewhere out at sea they would be mourning the loss. Barclay's wife would very likely be crying for her nephew. Would she shed a tear for Pearce? Would she even notice that he was no longer aboard? Lutyens would, and Pearce wondered what he would have made of the man in other circumstances. He had his father's capacity for debate, and Lutyens had come across, as he recalled their sparring conversation, like a man who enjoyed the cut and thrust of that activity. Like a thought dragged from slumber, he had a sudden memory of talking about Plato, Spartans and Ancient Greece, without being sure why.

'Surgeon Lutyens conjuring up what happened, would no doubt quiz me about Charybdis,' he said suddenly.

'And what,' asked Michael, 'is that when it's about?'

'Part of the twin sea hazards of antiquity, Michael, a sea monster called Scylla, with six heads and a ring of barking dogs, very close to a whirlpool big enough to consume a ship whole. Odysseus and the Argonauts had to sail between them to get home from Troy.'

'Would that be anywhere near here?'

Pearce laughed. 'No one knows. According to Homer it took Odysseus ten years to reach his home island, and there is not a scholar born who could lay out his route.'

'God pray it does not take us ten years.'

Putting out of his mind the thought that somewhere out in that water were the bodies of dozens of other men, Pearce shouted up to Martin, 'What do you see?'

'Nothing.'

The boy might be a pest, but he was nimble and he had the best eyes of them all. There was no sign of HMS *Brilliant* on the horizon, nor of any boat that might be looking for a sign of them, and though time and turns at sleeping had led to a more sober appreciation of what was and was not possible, it was undeniable that a look into Lézardrieux could do no harm and might do some good. What Pearce found interesting to measure, as they gathered themselves for the long walk along the line of trees that fringed the beach, was the degree of faith each had in the notion.

On dry land again, Charlie Taverner was almost cheerful, and kept insisting that 'something would turn up'. Rufus, who had great faith in Charlie, was carried along by that notion, though unable to show any optimism on his worrier's face. Dysart, in pain from his broken arm, had set his stall out with his tale-telling and was very much of the positive wing. It was impossible to know what Burns thought because he was determined to remain as inconspicuous as possible, lest someone remind him that, as a young gentlemen and midshipman, he had the responsibilities of an officer and should be leading the enterprise instead of trying as hard as possible to bring up the rear. Martin Dent, Pearce reckoned, was too busy to say anything, wondering whether being rescued by a man he hated obliged him to change his tune. Only Michael O'Hagan looked at it rationally. It was a chance and no more than that, and it would be foolish not to explore it.

The only one who had no faith at all in their rescue, as they spied the first signs of human habitation – lines of smoke rising into the cold morning air behind a dilapidated and seemingly deserted stone bastion – was the man who insisted they get into the trees and out of sight, the man who stayed on the beach, trying to make his hair, his face and his sea stained clothes look half respectable, the man who would have to carry it out, and who could not make up his mind what to do if he did.

The remaining officers and crew of HMS *Brilliant* had stood to quarters at dawn with a greater degree of concentration than had attended that ceremony on most mornings. Depleted by their losses, those who had taken part in the cutting out operation were exhausted from their efforts. Each aboard was aware that the French might try a stroke of their own, hoping to catch the British frigate unawares, when she was too busy licking her wounds to be prepared for a battle. It was a long wait – interrupted only by the ship going about at every turn of the half hour glass, with the early-March sky not beginning to lighten till after six, two hours knelt by the cast off guns, with the cries of the wounded and those being attended by the surgeon welling up from the cockpit below. No crack sail drill attended the ship's manoeuvres – each time *Brilliant* wore it was in a wide and gentle arc, for there were too few hands now to work the cannon and the top hamper with anything like speed and efficiency.

Each cry from below tore at Ralph Barclay's core, every moan an audible reminder of the depth of his failure. His Premier, Roscoe, was clinging to life by a thread, having taken a musket ball in the chest; his second lieutenant was missing along with the whole of his raiding party who had never even made his rendezvous; and he himself had returned to his frigate with half the crew of the longboat bearing wounds of varying degrees of seriousness, having left behind in that inlet two dead sailors and his marine officer, Holbrook, with half his head blown away. The total bill, if Thrale did not show up, was a loss of twenty-eight men either dead or missing, and a dozen wounded. He had heard of fleet actions where the butcher's bill on a line of battle ship had been lighter than that!

Ralph Barclay stood silently straining towards a shore he could not see, with Digby, now acting as Premier, in company, praying that he would hear a cry to tell him Thrale had returned. On the forecastle and the main-deck, midshipmen were carrying out the duties of commissioned officers, taking acting-lieutenant rank, overseeing what guns they could man, and which mute sailors would work them. The lack of chatter was nothing to do with discipline. Ralph Barclay reckoned it was more to do with a degree of disenchantment – the mood of men who had talked up and mentally spent the money to be made from the capture of the privateer and the Indiaman, only to have that dream snatched away. Now they were mourning mates lost, or thanking their lucky stars that they had not been chosen to participate in such a fiasco.

Try as he might, Ralph Barclay could not see how to compose a despatch that would put what had happened in a favourable light. From the moment he had left the convoy to pursue that privateer he had been on the very fringe of his orders. If Roscoe survived he would be loud in his declaration that the chase should have gone to Gould in *Firefly*. How could he explain that, never mind losing her at night, he had rediscovered her in the morning cutting out one of the ships he was tasked to protect – and a valuable East Indiaman at that? To have chased her and failed to come up before they found a safe anchorage would not read well either. A frigate should have the heels of both a barque and an Indiaman, and his attempt at cutting out had been a failure.

'Can I stand the men down, sir?' asked Digby.

Lost in his thoughts, Barclay had not noticed that the sky had gone grey enough to give a sight of the empty sea around *Brilliant*. He stood, without replying, until the lookout above called down that he had caught the first glimpse of the shore, which in this light would be no more than an indistinct line of a darker grey than sky and sea.

'Make it so, Mr Digby.'

'Permission to remove the members of the raiding party from normal watch duties?'

Something of Ralph Barclay's old self resurfaced then. 'What an odd notion, Mr Digby. Is this not a ship of war?'

'It is, sir.'

'Then kindly bear that in mind. Order and discipline must be maintained.'

Digby's voice had a trace of despondency in it as he added, 'Including the deck, sir?'

'Very much so, Mr Digby! I fear we shall be witness to a few funerals this day. I would not sully the bravery of those who have given their lives for their country by despatching them to a sea grave from an unclean deck.'

'And the course, sir?' asked Collins.

Barclay looked aloft at the suit of sails, then at a course that was taking them away from any chance of being spotted from the shore. 'What we are about at present will suffice. We must let the full daylight come so that we can make a judgement about what to do.' That he felt the need to explain himself was a good indication of how his position had been undermined by his failure. 'Our friend may try to run for St Malo and if he does I intend to have him. We want sharp eyes in the tops

Mr Digby, for if a sail appears I want to know immediately. If you need me, I will be below in the cockpit.'

'Our friend,' Digby said softly as Barclay disappeared, 'can sit snug for an eternity. We cannot.'

'Amen,' moaned the master.

Orders were issued to house the guns, the timbers rumbling as they were run up on their breechings to be bowsed tight against gun ports. The powder monkeys returned the cartridges to the gunner, while the gunner's mates collected the flintlocks. Smoking linstock, there to fire the cannon should the flintlocks fail, was dowsed: rammers, swabs and wormers again lodged away and the task of sweeping up the sand that had been spread on the deck began. Forward, the cook was lighting his coppers to prepare the men's breakfast, while on the upper deck the task of sanding, holystoning, sweeping, washing and flogging dry the deck planking was under way for the watch on duty. Below, those off duty were listening to the tales of the men who had survived, including those of that pretty landsman Cornelius Gherson, who had, it appeared, not only been in the thick of things but had been instrumental in getting the whole party out of trouble, spinning a thrilling tale of personal and collective bravery.

HMS *Brilliant* cruised the Brittany shore, more than hull down so that she was invisible from land. Only the lookouts aloft were able to spy the coastline, which was also close enough to espy a ship's topmast, each half leg of her course taking her past the point that marked the Estuary de Trieux. It could have been any day at sea if someone could have quieted the keening sound of a man losing his arm two decks below.

Crouched low in the confined space of the cockpit, Ralph Barclay watched Lutyens work with only half a mind – most of his attention was on his wife who looked tired and haggard from a night awake and an early morning. Like Mrs Railton, the gunner's wife, she had spent three whole hours helping the surgeon. A sheen of sweat covered her brow, wisps of hair were escaping from under her cap, and black blood stained her apron. If she had ever had a fear of gore it had gone now. Nor did the writhing figure on the table, biting so hard on the leather strap in his mouth that his neck veins looked set to burst, evoke even a blink of sympathy. The cut had been made and the saw was now rasping through the bone, too slowly for Barclay's liking. And when Lutyens finished lopping off the arm, leaving an untidy stump and several flaps of bloody skin, Emily took the appendage off him and tossed it into the nearby tub as though it was a piece of wood for the fire.

Three bodies lay to one side, men who had come aboard alive and had expired on that table. Was that really due to their wounds or to the poor care they had received from Lutyens? Was Emily any better, having never had even a modicum of training in the art of nursing a wounded man? She did look at him once, but it was hard to tell in that lined and tired face if there was any regard, and once more he was struck by his own inability to communicate with her. Why could he not explain to Emily his hopes and aspirations in a way that would gain her support? Why could she not see that though life at sea was harsh, authority was a necessity? No one could be safe in a ship that was a debating chamber, and sailors knew the risks they ran when they transgressed, and were well able to accept the punishment that was doled out for their misdemeanours.

Worse, as far as her husband was concerned, Emily's cousin, young Toby Burns had not returned, and it would be his task to tell her, and no doubt to bear the brunt of a look that would lay the blame at his door. She had come down here as soon as the first of the wounded from Roscoe's party had been brought aboard, so had no idea of what had transpired since. He recalled the boy's face when he had been informed that he was to be part of the raid – fear and dread. Again he was in a quandary; it was his job to make a man of Toby Burns, not to mollycoddle him. If the youngster risked death in the process, then that was part of his duty. Ralph Barclay saw a young man who needed to prosper in the service if he was ever, one day, to enjoy commissioned rank. Emily, no doubt, saw the child who had visited her home to play – a little boy, frightened of heights, his fellow mids, and any thought of battle.

Lutyens was stitching his patient up and he was having the devil's own job of getting the ligature that would allow the wound to discharge to stay inside his ham-fisted attempts with the needle. Ralph Barclay had learnt about stitching as a young man, it being held necessary that a midshipman should know how to cut out, sow and make a sail. Watching Lutyens losing his thread, or getting it wound around the wrong part of his fingers, he reckoned the surgeon would never have passed that particular test. That was a thought obviously shared by Mrs Railton, who was looking at the deck beams above her head with despair.

'Mr Lutyens,' he asked, when the surgeon had finished, 'I must ask you what the chances are for Lieutenant Roscoe?'

Lutyens looked up, his face as tired as Emily's, his eyes seeming out of focus as though the question was strange to him. His fine, normally curly, ginger hair was flat now, and wet from perspiration, making him appear even more odd, an impression not aided by the lantern light by which he was working.

'The ball has been extracted, and I am informed he took the precaution of donning fresh linen before leaving the ship, so it may be possible to avoid corruption in the wound.' He looked down at the man he had been working on, who had finally passed out from the pain, the leather strap marked by the bite of his teeth now lolling out of his open mouth. 'In the end, Captain, like this fellow here, it is his vital spirit that will decide his fate.'

'I will send a party to remove the dead,' Barclay said.

'Thank you.'

'Emily, I think you have done enough here.'

'Your husband is right, Mrs Barclay,' said Lutyens. 'We all need some rest.'

'And I am here, ma'am,' added Mrs Railton, with a kindly look, 'to aid Mr Lutyens.'

Emily nodded, and put out a hand to gently touch that of the squat gunner's wife. She then preceded her husband out of an area that looked very like a charnel house. Ralph Barclay waited until they were on deck, and the breeze had begun to refresh her, before he told her that Burns was missing.

'I have no idea what became of them. No word has come from any of Thrale's party.' He saw the tears begin to course down her face, tears that she had not shed over bleeding, screaming bodies, but that could be brought forth by the contemplation of the unknown fate of a boy like Burns. That made him add hastily. 'Which leads me to suspect, my dear, that they must have landed, but in the wrong place, and, trying to catch up with the others, may have fallen captive to the men defending the port.'

'Or killed.'

'No,' Ralph Barclay replied, thinking that if he had kept

Burns with him at least he would know. Why had he entrusted the boy to that old fool Thrale, who could barely navigate his way around the wardroom let alone the Brittany shore? Had it just been a notion to demonstrate no favouritism, or had the thought of Burns along with him, quite possibly freezing in action, determined him to send the boy with another? 'There are no reports of any shots after the boats left the beach, no sight nor sound of a fight.'

'So he will be a captive?' There was no joy in the question, and she would not look at him.

'I cannot say I hope so, my dear, for that is not the case. But if he is, then that is a better fate than the lot of those we will bury today. He wears his blue coat, the French will know him for what he is, a young gentleman, and will treat him accordingly.'

Ralph Barclay put as much emphasis into the words as he could, well aware that he was talking of a France that had died in 1789. What it was like now for prisoners of war would be anyone's guess.

'The rules of warfare oblige the enemy to inform us of any officers they are holding; we do the same, and that includes midshipmen. In the previous wars with France there has always been a cartel that runs between Dover and Calais for the exchange of prisoners. If he has been taken, he could be back in England within the year. I will not say that his life will be snug till then, but he will not be ill treated.'

'I should tell Mrs Railton of this, since he sleeps...slept...in her quarters. I cannot think but that she was fond of him.'

Emily shivered, as though the contemplation of that was fearful. Ralph Barclay took her arm and led her off the deck to the door of his own cabin. There was still a marine to open it, but something told him not to follow her through.

'Mr Digby.'

'Sir.'

'We will commence the burials once everyone has breakfasted. Please detail the necessary hands to sew the dead into their shrouds.'

He followed that with a long, sad look towards the Brittany shoreline, wondering if burials were taking place there as well.

Pearce had to take a long detour through the trees to avoid that bastion; it looked deserted but he could not be sure. His route took him uphill, then brought him back down a slope into the waterside part of Lézardrieux. From here he had a good view of the hill on the other side that rose towards a church – complete with bell tower – which dominated the anchorage. There were hills behind the town too, so that the whole area was well protected from the elements.

When he first heard the locals speak he realised that while he might know Paris, he did not know France. He had heard plenty of regional accents in the capital, and he knew from visits to the Jacobin Club that there were Bretons in the mix, for it was they who had founded that radical institution. But they had been educated men; they had not spoken the common argot of the citizens of this place, which, when he heard it, seemed so accented as to bear little resemblance to the national tongue. Indeed many spoke a language that was wholly different, making him fear to engage in conversation. His appearance proved less of a worry. His torn topcoat and scuffed boots blended in with the locals who were, in many cases, as badly dressed as he, and seemingly living in a community to which a razor had never been introduced, so numerous were the beards.

The open sea was just visible at the end of the long inlet and the fishing port was built on the flat littoral, facing a high wooded bank on the other. There was deep water in the middle, with great baulks of timbers sunk as pylons, but, with the tide out deep, mud banks lay between ship and shore. The buildings were huddled together, just back from the shoreline, lacking any pattern – a couple of high structures, warehouses with joists above the lofts, houses in the main, but with a pair of taverns identifiable by their swinging signs. Some form of market was in progress on the hard-packed earth that passed for a quayside, and soon Pearce was in amongst the bustle of a living community.

The smells were those of a fishing port – the strong odours of recent catches being dried, one great container, flat and round, full of tiny dead silver fish, creating a stench so powerful as to make Pearce gag. The clean sea tang of still live crabs and crayfish crawling over each other in great tubs was a welcome relief. Harder to bear, to a man who had not eaten, were the smells of the bubbling marmites of fisherman's food, the heads and tails of gutted fish slung into a constantly cooking pot. The odour of fresh baking, as he passed an open window, exercised an even greater pull on Pearce's empty gut, as well as his emotions. What was it about the smell of bread that conjured up an image of hearth, home and sound prosperity?

He reckoned they would be breakfasting aboard *Brilliant* about now, and that thought made him hanker – for the briefest moment – to be back aboard ship, for there was something to be said for regular meals even if the fare was monotonous and lacking in taste. The thought of the money that had gone missing made him curse, but he was well aware that even if he had it, to proffer English copper and silver to satisfy his craving would hardly aid anonymity, testing enough when he felt that everyone must be looking at him, a stranger in what had to be a close-knit community.

Eventually curiosity overtook trepidation as Pearce realised he was not an object of suspicion – quite possibly they thought him one of the privateers. If anyone looked at him it was a passing glance rather than any form of deep enquiry, and his obligatory *bonjour citoyen* seemed good enough to allay any mistrust. It was a greeting he calculated would be safe given the prevalence of tricolours in windows and on the hats of the citizenry. Clearly Lézardrieux – unlike many parts of western France – was loyal to the Revolution.

The two vessels lay at anchor in the midstream, confirming what he had suspected: that Barclay had failed in his attempt to capture the privateer. Indeed so unscathed did that ship look that Pearce wondered if the captain had even got near enough to make his planned assault. Close to, he could read the lettering on the counter – *Mercedes* and St Malo. The *Lady Harrington* was in the same state in which the crew of HMS *Brilliant* had last seen her, with damaged bulwarks and shattered stern decoration. Neither ship was of much use to him, his examination being mere curiosity. His instructions were to look out for something big enough to take the stranded party, but not so big that they could not manage her.

The rest of the boats in the river, or lying in the exposed mud of the low tide were inshore fishing smacks, with single masts, in no way big enough to hold a party of seven nor to survive any sea that took them far from the shore. Small rowboats either tied up to a riverside bollard or scuttling about in the water were of no use at all. The bigger boats, those belonging to the Indiaman and the *Mercedes*, of the same size as those he had hauled on and off HMS *Brilliant* and perfect for the task, were tied up by their sides, out of reach beyond the broad band of brown mud.

A small knot of people had formed by one of the cables that attached the French ship to the shore, and though it was risky to get too close and chance a conversation, Pearce went to look, because between their legs he was sure he had seen a dash of red.

The dead marine officer had lost half his head and the other side was so damaged that it was unrecognisable. He lay, flat on his back, legs splayed, the belt and breeches that had once been pipe clayed so white now streaked dark brown with dried mud. The red coat was covered with dark stains, too, which made Pearce wonder until one of the group looking at the cadaver sent a long streak of tobacco spit on to the corpse. That was followed by a casual kick, a grunt of 'cochon', before the man moved off to be replaced by another citizen ready to abuse a lifeless enemy. Pearce moved swiftly away himself lest he be obliged to do likewise. The English voice, exclaiming, 'Poor bastard', almost stopped him in his tracks.

The temptation to spin round and look was overwhelming but had to be resisted, and Pearce waited until he was yards away before he risked a backward glance. Which of the men round the body had spoken? There was nothing to distinguish a Frenchman from a Briton. The solution lay in the lack of abuse, as a pair, nudged by a fellow wearing a tricolour cockade and carrying a pistol, moved away without delivering either spittle or a kick, looking sad rather than satisfied. Pearce, falling in behind, noticed the taller one of the pair had a pronounced limp, while the other had an empty sleeve. Wounded men? But not from *Brilliant*, because their faces were unfamiliar, which could mean they were from the *Lady Harrington*, part of the Indiaman's crew. Yet they passed the merchant ship without making any move to signal for a boat to go aboard, turning instead into an alley that led off the quay, then into several others until Pearce was unsure in which direction they were finally headed.

The sight of another armed guard holding a musket and sporting the obligatory tricolour, slouched by a doorway, made Pearce slip out of view, hiding in an angle where one building protruded further than another. He heard indistinct words exchanged and the rattle of keys, the sound of a lock being eased, the creaking of an opening door followed by slamming and relocking. Peering out he saw the two Frenchmen exchange a few words, before the one who had escorted the prisoners to this place moved off, with no sign of the men he had been guarding, leaving what was clearly a sentinel still in place.

He was gone while the stationary Frenchman was still looking at his colleague's back, turning right and right again in the hope of coming to a point of contact at the rear. All he encountered was high unbroken walls, under some kind of enclosed bridge, and another right turn brought him to the far end of the original alleyway where he could look back on the sentry, who was now leaning on the wall, head down as if half asleep.

If this was a place of confinement they had chosen it well, a house with only one door at ground level, though Pearce decided to check on that by walking past the sentry, who lifted a sleepy head to acknowledge his approach, but made no comment. There was a window, impossible to see from a few feet away, barred and shuttered, which meant little since, if it was a way to talk to those inside, it was so close to the man guarding the door that no communication could take place without him hearing the exchange. The act of talking to the sentry was completely spontaneous, seemingly unbidden, and one that later would make John Pearce wonder if he was tainted with a touch of madness.

'Good day, citizen.'

The head lifted and the eyes were on him, but there was no unease in them, more the light of a bored man happy to engage in conversation. The reply was equable, without being overly friendly, though the fellow did straighten and take a firmer grip on his musket. 'Good day to you, citizen.'

There was a fraction of a second when Pearce thought to just walk on, but he had created an opening and if he did not exploit it, it might never happen again. And his mind was racing on another level; behind that shutter were British sailors. Dysart was no doubt right when he insisted that all they could manage was a single-masted boat; that even a large enough fishing smack, with him a one winged bird, might prove beyond their competence. But that did not apply to the men from the *Lady Harrington*. They could handle anything, for even he, a lubber, knew that the East India Company, the richest trading cartel in Britain, was fussy in its crews and with the wages it paid, it could afford to be. Wages, food, the two words seemed to clash in his head.

'Is this where they are confining the English prisoners, citizen?'

'It is, citizen.'

Pearce took two paces back, peering at the shuttered and barred window, suddenly assailed by less sanguine thoughts. These men were locked up and guarded – not very well guarded – but by an armed man none the less. He and the other survivors of Thrale's party would not only have to get them out of their confinement, but get them aboard a boat big enough to accommodate them all, something like the cutter he had come ashore in. Such a boat lay alongside the *Lady Harrington*, one that could get them back to England, and the men to sail it were feet away.

'Are they being fed?'

The sentry shrugged. 'They brought some victuals with them when they came ashore.'

'Fresh food would be better. Who do I speak to about providing them grub?'

'Search me, citizen,' the sentry replied, to a fellow who was wondering from where those words had surfaced. It was the only thing he could think of, and seemed directly linked to his own lack of funds and his empty gut. It also sounded lame and stupid, though the sentry didn't seem to think so, which emboldened Pearce to keep going.

'I was thinking to bid for it?'

'It won't be worth much, citizen, they're off to St Malo as soon as that English pig and his warship clear the coast.'

Pearce grunted. 'A little is a lot to a man who has next to nothing.'

'Where you from?' the sentry asked, a trifle more animated in the way he looked Pearce up and down.

That, since he had heard the local dialect, was a dreaded question, yet with only one answer, given the city where he had learnt his French.

'Paris,' Pearce said, which produced a look of deep inquisitiveness that invited explanation. Parisians were not popular outside their city; they were held to be rude and arrogant. That was something Pearce knew to be true himself, having suffered from much Parisian condescension – a trait that had nothing to do with Revolutionary spirit.

'Wanted to be a sailor until I found it was no life for a

dog. Ran away, I did – young and stupid, then, citizen, wiser and poorer these days, and likely to be scraping for want of employment. Now there's a war on, and few ships setting out because of the English blockade, berths are hard to come by.' Pearce cocked his thumb. 'Any chance of a word.'

That really brought the sentry upright. 'A word?'

'I speak a bit of theirs. Landed cargoes over the water in the peace. Worked a few of their women as well, though they are smelly, ugly brutes.'

'They're not much different here, citizen, in case you ain't noticed,' the sentry with a bitter laugh. 'I know, I live with one.'

Pearce lifted a hand, making a fist with his middle finger out as if to knock on the shutter. There was a long pause while the sentry thought about it, before he gave another shrug and resumed his leaning position against the wall, which allowed Pearce's heart, which had seemed to move up into his mouth, to return, pounding, to where it belonged.

The rap on the shutter echoed down the narrow alley, as did the creak as it opened, and Pearce found himself looking into a rubicund face with a pair of questioning bright blue eyes and a long clay pipe clamped between the teeth. Having got this far on inspiration Pearce had no idea how to proceed. He could hardly just address the fellow in fluent English – even if the guard wouldn't understand a word, any ease with the language was bound to make him suspicious, so he asked lamely, *'Parlez-vous français?'*

'No, mate.'

Pearce pointed at the man. 'British', then at himself, 'friend'.

The reply was sarcastic. 'Why that be right nice.'

'Shut that fucking winder, Dusty, the draft is freezing my balls off.'

Pearce put a hand out to hold back the shutter, in case the injunction was obeyed, turned his back full on the sentry, put his shoulder against the wall and whispered, 'Don't shut it.'

'Who the...'

The finger to the lips shut him up, and Pearce said, 'HMS *Brilliant.*'

'You're having a laugh,' the man cried, turning back into the room. 'This arse claims to be one of those no good buggers from that frigate.'

'Well, if he is, tell him to bugger off,' came the reply, from a different voice, ''cause they's done enough harm as it is, the useless sods.'

'I need to talk,' Pearce insisted, with a jerk of the head back at the sentry. He followed that with a stream of louder, pleading French, on the subject of poverty, before dropping his voice once more, 'and he thinks I'm a frog.'

'Sounds like he has the right of it, mate.'

'You have to talk to me.'

'Talk? What about?'

That made Pearce angry. 'Anything, you dozy turd.'

That rubicund face went taut and but for the bars on the window Pearce might have found himself ducking away from a clout, but then the man he was talking to was pulled violently backwards and there was another face at the bars, a more battered affair, with a long nose, prominent cheekbones and one tooth in the middle of a wide mouth. 'He ain't no frog a'talking like that.'

'*Vous comprendez manger?*' asked Pearce, loudly, making a very obvious gesture with his fingers to his mouth, before adding softly, 'I'm supposed to be bidding for the job of feeding you.'

'Then you best go see that tight-fisted mate that took over

captaincy of our ship.' Pearce just shrugged, which made One Tooth continue with a subject clearly close to his heart. 'He's set himself up good and proper in the best tavern in the place, eating heartily and quaffing wine, while we are left to rot.'

'*Dit-moi* – tell me, just keep talking.'

'What's your game?'

'You're prisoners, right?'

'No, mate! We's here on one of them soddin' Grand Tours that rich folk take.'

John put his hand up to silence the sarcasm, before calling back over his shoulder. '*Il est tres difficile, mon ami. Les anglais sont des idiots, non? En particular cet homme avec un seul dent.*'

'*Tout les anglais, citoyen, sans exception,*' the sentry replied.

Pearce looked at One Tooth, whom he had just insulted, listening to a tirade against the East Indiaman's mate, who, after the captain had suffered a seizure and died, had got them into this mess by failing to come up with the convoy. Captured, he had seemingly abandoned his crew to their fate while seeking favours for himself, using the dead captain's private ventures as a bribe. St Malo was where these sailors would go, and to a future that, according to what Dysart had told him, even taking out the embellishment, was at the very least going to be damned unpleasant. Did these men share Dysart's view, that captured British seamen were put to toil that could best be described as slavery? If they did they would be desperate to escape.

This lazy sod leaning against the wall must have the key to that door – Pearce had heard it open and close – and it was hardly likely that fellow who had brought them here carried it with him. It was simple: clout the guard, open the door, free the crew of the Indiaman. And what then?

'How many are you?' One Tooth didn't like being interrupted, that was plain by the look on his face. So Pearce spoke quickly, hand held up, reeling off for the benefit of the sentry every French dish which he had ever heard of or tasted, before reverting to English. 'We have a party ashore from *Brilliant*. We're stranded – no boat – we can try and get you out…'

Pearce stopped, because One Tooth, judging by the look in his eye, could obviously guess the rest. 'How big a party?'

'Seven,' Pearce replied. No use saying that included two boys and a broken arm. 'You?'

'Twenty-five.'

'Wounded? I saw some wounded.'

'Two. Not bad enough to leave. Coin?' One Tooth demanded, rubbing thumb and forefinger together, to which Pearce shook his head.

'Wait.'

The babble of noise inside the room was silenced by a bark from One Tooth. 'Shut your gobs and listen.' His voice dropped then, becoming too soft to overhear, so Pearce turned back and engaged the guard in conversation, the man being unaware that the question posed to him about how long he was on duty had nothing to do with sympathy and everything to do with trying to put together some form of plan. Pearce's mind was racing. Darkness would be best – and the tide, like last night would be high. How to get his stranded party into the town without being seen, or at least arousing suspicion? Then they would have to free One Tooth and his mates. It would be a different guard from this one. Would he be as easy to fool? Could they gather any weapons?

'Froggie!'

One Tooth was back at the window, his hand cupped as he held it out through the bars. 'Money.'

'Not French?' said Pearce, looking at the small pile of shillings and sixpences in his hand, every one bearing the head of an English King.

'Makes no odds, mate. Take my word, they'll 'cept anything in a port as long as it's silver. A golden guinea is even better. Use it to buy grub, then come back here and see if that arse that's a'guarding us will let you inside. If we's to do 'owt we has to talk free.'

One Tooth, despite what Pearce had said earlier, was clearly no idiot. He was right about the money too, though the silver was not taken without being tested with a strong tooth and some murmuring, for he was obliged, because of those same coins, to lie about who he was, where he was from, and for whom he was buying. The idea of British prisoners eating at all was bad enough when, he was repeatedly informed, no fisherman dared go far out on what was a good day because that damned frigate was still in the offing.

The notion that some shit from Paris, and an impatient one at that, who ate almost as much as he purchased, was earning out of it, was worse. Pearce was as rude as anyone from the capital would have been, because time was not on his side. He bought, for prices that were an outrage, bread, cheese, some cooked fish and cider, taking, when any change was proffered, the useless paper assignats that were the debased currency of Revolutionary France.

Pearce listened too, and in doing so overheard several different versions of what had happened the night before, some too overly fantastic to be true. But the depth of Barclay's failure was obvious. His enemies had been waiting for him and had given *les rosbifs un nez sange*. The locals were proud that the little bastion that protected the anchorage, manned by their own citizens, had repulsed the English, unaware that taking the place had never figured in Barclay's plan. The crew of the *Mercedes* won less praise, probably because they were strangers, the general opinion being that if the locals had not stood firm, then the result might have been different.

Still, there was some pride that a Breton crew had bested the English, though the number of related British dead was many more than had tried to cut out the privateer. But the possibility existed, as Pearce listened to the reprise of every shot and cut from axe or cutlass, that not one of the main raiding party had got away alive. Against that there was only that one dead marine still laid out on the dockside, a magnet for more degradation, flies and scruffy looking dogs that would have fed on him if they had been allowed.

He made his way back to that alley, laden with food, doubts and images of a boat full of dead men drifting out to sea. He arrived back while the sentry he had spoken to would, according to his own reckoning, still be there. It took a silver shilling to get inside, where he found that One Tooth, along with his mates, had not wasted any time either.

'You've got to get clear before they change the guard,' One Tooth insisted, grabbing the food. 'Tide will be high when it's dark, don't know the exact time, but if we's to get our ship out of here...'

'Ship? I was thinking of the boats.'

'If'n you want to try and get clear in a boat, you's welcome to try, mate, that be some of the worst water in creation out there, no place for 'owt but a deep hull. The fall of the tide is fierce and sets up a right strong current, so as long as the

429

wind ain't dead foul and blowing a gale we can drift out.'

Pearce still could not believe he was hearing right. 'You want to take back the *Lady Harrington*?'

One Tooth grinned, making the single molar even more stark. 'One in the eye for them frog bastards and our mate an' all.'

'And where would you sail her if you did?'

'Why, back to England, you stupid arse. Where else?'

'Can you do that? I mean the navigation and all.'

'Ain't hard, mate. All we has to do is set a course straight north and we will run into the coast of England.'

Pearce was shaking his head, as One Tooth babbled on, making what seemed impossible sound as simple as tossing a coin. The prospect was tempting, the solution to his whole dilemma of getting both his whole party and himself away made even more sound – a ship instead of a boat.

'I would not want to meet our ship.'

'Neither would I, mate. King's ships is to be avoided lest you be in a convoy.'

If they could avoid *Brilliant* he had a chance to get back quickly to where he had been a week before, on British soil and in a position to help his father, a much better prospect than the notion of going to Paris or Calais. But Pearce still had to stop himself from being over-optimistic.

'We don't even know how many men are guarding your ship.'

Pearce was hustled to the door. 'Then you've got the rest of the day, mate, to find out.'

CHAPTER SEVENTEEN

Making his way back to the waterside with the remaining food, Pearce reckoned what was being proposed was impossible; until he considered the alternative, which was to do nothing and leave those men incarcerated until they were taken to St Malo. They could not get free without his aid, and he could not get to where he would ideally like to be without theirs. A long look at both ships on his way out of the port highlighted the first and most obvious problem: the *Mercedes* was downstream of the Indiaman. Did One Tooth know that? He must, and perhaps he had taken it into account. The next difficulty was one of which he was already aware; he would have to formulate any plan – the prisoners could not do so from their confinement and the rest of his party would be obliged to stay outside the place till after dark – and he did not feel tremendously confident of his ability to come up with something that had a chance of success.

The factors militating against a coup multiplied the more he gnawed at them. They had few weapons and their opponents would be armed. How alert would they be after last night?

They might have given *les rosbifs* a bloody nose, but could they be sure that Barclay would not try again? They might well be on the lookout for another raiding party, armed and waiting as they had apparently been the night before. These thoughts stayed with him as he trudged out to the woods, a heavy sack swinging over one shoulder.

His shipmates fell on the food, curious to know where he had got it but too hungry to really care about Pearce's replies. Huddled in a small clearing, out of sight and the wind, they were cold and tired as well as famished. Pearce waited until they had eaten before recounting his tale, which was received with varying degrees of disbelief.

'I must leave you again. If the French are getting ready to repel another assault, I will see it.'

'If they are?' asked Dysart.

'Then we must wait.'

Pearce walked down to the shore and looked up the inlet. That chimney-shaped rock onto which they had smashed marked the point where it joined the open sea. It was almost as if he could feel the presence of the frigate; the locals were sure *Brilliant* was still there. Why that should be Pearce could not fathom; no genius was required to deduce that the privateer held all the cards in any game that Barclay cared to play, being able to sit in Lézardrieux until doomsday if necessary. Bested three times already, only a fool, or a desperate man, would hang about to be embarrassed again. But seemingly he had, which meant not just escape from France; if they were to get to England they had to avoid Barclay as well.

'We ain't seen so much as a topsail,' Dysart insisted, when Pearce alluded to *Brilliant*.

'But the local folk must have. They were all moaning that they couldn't fish in deep water because of the English warship. And if she wasn't out there, if she was gone, I reckon that privateer would have upped his anchor and set a course for St Malo.'

'Upped his anchor and set a course,' O'Hagan exclaimed. 'Jaysus, you're beginning to sound like a proper tar, John-boy.'

Pearce grinned. 'God forbid.'

'Now, would that be the one you don't believe in?'

'The very same, Michael.'

'Sure, I'd want to be there the day you meet our maker.'

'If you don't mind, Michael, I'll leave you to represent me.'

Death! That brought forth an unpleasant image, that of the marine in Lézardrieux. If this went wrong it would be his body they were kicking and spitting at, be it dead inert meat or the repository of a soul. 'I might have to find some faith, Michael, for what I am proposing we do will require divine intervention.'

'Let me do the asking,' O'Hagan replied, putting an arm round Pearce's shoulders. 'Sure, I've had more practice, and I don't doubt more need.'

There was a lot to sort out, and Pearce worried that he had failed to think of everything. They needed an easy rendezvous, because he would be coming for them after dark. What weapons did they have? Apart from his knife, only what they had salvaged from the beach. Then he remembered the barrel of gunpowder that had helped Charlie Taverner and Rufus to get ashore, which they had left behind at that spot because it was too much trouble to carry. That led to an argument about who should go back and fetch it, solved by Michael saying that he would rather be busy and about some task than sitting on his arse all day with these miserable sods. Surprisingly, Martin Dent, with an embarrassed look at Pearce, offered to accompany him. The boy was mellowing.

The rest Pearce set to fashioning clubs from the ample deadwood that lay all around, with the caveat that they must be careful and stay out of sight.

O'Hagan and Martin Dent made their way back to the landing place through the trees, until the Irishman felt they were far enough away from Lézardrieux, and sight, to use the strand of beach. The silence between them was of the awkward kind: Michael not sure what to say to the boy, Dent showing signs of the kind of withdrawal that went with his age. In the end Martin was more at home in that state than an Irishman to whom a lengthy silence was anathema.

'Has anyone ever told you, boy, that you're a proper bane?' The words, delivered without rancour, were followed by a sideways look at a bowed head and hunched shoulders. 'I ache still from the blows that sod Devenow laid on me, and all because of you.'

Still, the boy wouldn't speak, refusing any form of eye contact as well. Michael put a hand out to ruffle his hair as a way of breaking the ice, only to have Martin skip sideways as if he was dodging a blow. 'Sure, something tells me you've felt a few clips in your time.'

Martin shrugged as he bent down to lift a large stone and throw it into the calm undisturbed water of the inlet, creating a huge splash that sent ripples streaming out for twenty feet.

'Perhaps not all of them were deserved, though I take leave to doubt it the way you carry on. We talked about chucking you over the side at our table. The whole mess was in favour, bar two.'

That got Martin's attention – not a look but a distinct stiffening of the shoulders.

'And would you be after believing John Pearce said no to that idea. Odd that, since you was so bent on doing him in. Saved your life too, though only the Holy Mother knows why.' Michael's voice hardened. 'Which I hope he don't live to regret.'

Finally goaded to reply, Martin's voice was muffled by his chin being on his chest. 'I ain't goin' to say sorry, if that's what you're asking.'

'Not even for the soul of poor old Abel Scrivens, who would have done you no harm?' Michael laid a hand on the boy's shoulder with just enough force to stop him and he turned his head, albeit with his chin still on his chest. 'For he was the other one who said no to dropping you in the drink.'

Martin's reply was spirited, like that of someone wrongly accused, and with a direct stare to support it. 'That were a mistake!'

'I don't doubt it, boy. Trouble is, old Abel ain't here to forgive you.' Martin Dent looked at O'Hagan a second time, fear in his eyes, leaving the Irishman unsure whether the fright was prompted by the idea of what he might do, or, less likely, some notion of eternal damnation. 'Probably would, too, kindly old gent like him.'

The repetition was a mumble. 'I said it were a mistake.'

Michael bent down himself and picked up a stone, flat and flint-like. 'Now that looks to me like a skimmer.' He launched the stone as he spoke. It hit the water flat and bounced four times before it sank. 'Jesus, that was a goer. In Ireland, where

I come from, they say if you can get a seven skimmer you're sure of salvation.'

Martin's doubtful expression almost made O'Hagan laugh, and that humour was in his voice as he said, 'You might as well try it, boy, for something tells me that the way you go on, you're destined for hell.'

That one activity, an attempt over fifteen minutes, ultimately unsuccessful, to find the magic seven-skimmer changed the whole nature of the relationship. Martin lost his reserve through competition, though Michael was startled at the amount of effort the boy put into winning. His concentration, tongue firmly lodged in his teeth, was total.

'How long you been a ship's boy?'

'I was born on one,' Martin replied, followed by a curse as he heaved a stone that sank straight away.

The rest of his tale emerged between the gasps of his endeavours; born to a sailor father he never knew and a mother who plied her trade in Portsmouth dockyard and the Spithead anchorage, a woman spoken of with no affection who was dead of drink and disease by the time he had survived five winters. A berth aboard a seventy-four followed, if you could call a few strakes of planking on a lower deck by such a name, a place where he was at least fed, where he learnt to make himself useful to the gunner as a powder monkey; to the Yeoman of the Sheets as a tyke who could top the highest point on the yards, and to the Bosun as a right handy nipper when the ship raised anchor and the cable was hauled in on the messenger. Another fellow, a marine, had taught him to rattle the side drum, and that, when he got aboard *Brilliant*, had got him the post of marine drummer.

'Have you lived ashore?'

'A fiver,' Martin hooted, as a fresh stone skimmed the water. 'Lived so when I was a bairn, for my Ma changed husbands regular, though I don't recall it now. Had to sometimes when a ship I was on paid off, but I allas got myself another berth damn quick, 'cause ashore is no life for a grown man, let alone a lad.'

Relating the nature of that life had Martin putting extra effort into stone throwing, which tended to spoil his shots rather than aid them. He had scrabbled through pig swill bins for food, fought for a deep doorway to sleep in of a night, nearly frozen to death in winter from want of a blanket, and been scared to sleep lest some other sod stole what little he had, 'like a pair of clogs, for which those grass-combing buggers would steal your eyes and come back for the holes!'

'That I have seen myself, boy.'

Martin Dent stopped suddenly, arm raised for another throw. 'Have you ever thrown a seven skimmer?'

Michael laughed and shook his head. 'Never, boyo. So when you get to hell, like as not I'll be waiting there for you, fists raised to give you the hiding I cannot, for your size, give you now.'

'I won't be so easy, mate,' Martin insisted, with the bravado of youth. 'I'll be a grown man and a match for the likes of you.'

'Maybe you will be a handful at that.' O'Hagan put an arm on the boy's shoulder, this time without engendering alarm. 'Enough of this, you and I best be on our way to get that gunpowder, or the others will reckon us taken.'

Martin Dent grinned then, which lit up his urchin face. 'Happen they'll reckon I've done you in.'

* * *

It was difficult for Pearce, in a fishing port made idle, to find a spot from which he could observe both the *Mercedes* and the *Lady Harrington* without drawing attention to himself. Any number of souls were sitting around on casks and wooden bollards, or on the gunwales of beached boats, yarning away. Wandering from place to place, he could only hope one solitary figure who sat down occasionally to whittle on a piece of wood was unlikely to be noticed. That assumption proved correct – he was left in peace by everyone except the odd curious urchin and an alarming number of sniffing dogs.

He had to move constantly because it was too cold to stay still. In doing so – time and again – he passed the tavern that housed what he reckoned must be most of the crew of the *Mercedes*, celebrating their great victory, by the sound of it. The mate of the *Lady Harrington* was probably inside; maybe he too was drinking himself senseless. Would he wake in the morning to find his ship gone?

The tide was in again and had raised both sailing vessels so that they towered over their surroundings, snubbing on their cables. The way they strained, upriver one minute, downriver some time after, told him at what point it ceased to rise and began to fall. The fishing boats stuck in the mud had been sucked free and lifted to float as well, and as a result activity had increased markedly, with fishermen working on nets and tackle. Pearce realised he was looking at the conditions that would prevail later – at about midnight – with the exception that the whole anchorage should be quiet, both on the water and on shore. Would there be a moon by which they could see their way? The sky was blue, with large, high and white clouds. The wind, which had picked up as the day went on, was coming in off the sea, which meant it was from a northerly direction. Would that wind fall as darkness descended?

Questions piled on questions, as the water in the inlet receded exposing mud once more, with solutions hard to come by. His confidence ebbed and flowed – nothing in his life had prepared him for this. He thought back to the previous night, to the abortive attack Barclay had made. Much as he hated to admit it, he knew that he would have to think like the captain of HMS *Brilliant*. That raid had been carried out working on a set of assumptions – that they turned out to be wrong was a consequence not of stupidity but of chance. He must operate on the same principles. There was no way success could be guaranteed. All he could do was slowly think each imagined situation through, eliminate the impossible and try to minimise the risks.

The chorus of voices from the waterside tavern rose and fell as the afternoon wore on, sounding ever more raucous as the men inside got steadily more drunk, with constant comings and goings between ship and shore that made counting the number of potential enemies difficult. The singing began to tail off as inebriation turned to stupor, and it seemed to Pearce there were fewer voices to chant what was, he thought, a very small repertoire: a mixture of sentimental ballads alternating with the same kind of vulgar and salacious chants he had heard all over his native land – songs of men with massive endowments, or of women with less than endearing habits. Occasionally he heard the sound of a fight, and once or twice that spread out onto the hard earth of the quay, making the locals, in their boats or just walking by, shake their heads.

The Frenchmen were sailors, who – just like their English counterparts – drank like fish and fought like idiots at any opportunity. Many of them must be incapable by now and would get more so before the night was over. But they would not all be drunk and he still did not know the size of any party aboard the Indiaman, for everyone aboard kept inside out of the cold wind, no doubt huddled close to the stove in the great cabin, the chimney of which was belching smoke into the afternoon sky. There was a train of smoke from the *Mercedes* too, which was worrying, given that they needed to pass her in a narrow channel where they could be close enough to each other to lob a gobbet of spit.

He took a walk through the alley where the prisoners were held, merely nodding to the fellow, a different one, guarding their door. He established that it was one man as before, and that the approach and passing of a strange face did not cause any more alarm than it had that morning. Then he went back to the shoreline, to watch the depth of mud between land and water lengthen. On the hill the church bell tolled the half and whole hour to a sun that was sinking inexorably in the west, taking with it what little warmth it had afforded and leaving Pearce chilled to the marrow.

He left before the last of the light went, to make his way back to his companions, the church bell tolling in his ears. It was an unhappy sound to a man who, in his heightened imagination, and well aware of how little he had actually been able to discover, could easily turn the clanging into a knell of doom.

'Where the hell is that Irish sod?' demanded Charlie Taverner, stepping to the edge of the trees and peering for the umpteenth time along the darkening shoreline. 'He should have been back with that powder an age past.'

'Ye can tell yer no' a sailor,' said Dysart, wincing as shifting his body made him aware of the pain in his arm.

Charlie did an impersonation of a sailor's gait, all bandy legs and rolling body. 'If I walk like this, Dysart, and swear and drink enough, I'll get taken for one, won't I, Rufus?'

The funny walk made Rufus laugh out loud, a sound that pleased Charlie no end and had him repeating the impersonation.

Dysart was less taken with it. 'At sea ye learn no' to fret, Taverner, for there is naught you can do. It's aw wind, tide and the lap of the gods, is that no right, Mr Burns?'

The midshipman sat toying with a rough-looking club. He looked at Dysart for a moment and nodded, though without much conviction. He had hardly said one word since coming ashore, and his face told anyone who cared to look that he had the weight of the world on his slender shoulders. Toby Burns did not speak for he feared his voice would betray his feelings. If being aboard HMS *Brilliant* had been less than salutary, what had happened here was hellish. All he could reflect on was home, of apples from the family orchard, or fishing in the nearby stream.

He thought of his clerical father delivering grace at the head of a table laden with food; of his mother, who treated him with a tenderness that he longed to experience now, arms that would envelop and comfort him, filling his nostrils with a smell of lemons that he could conjure up without effort. There had been school, which he hated, yet which now seemed a paradise compared to what he was living through. Would those who shared his classroom, who had been so envious of the position his relationship to Captain Barclay had earned him, covet this; the certainty of capture by a fiendish enemy who might well tear him limb from limb?

'I didn't have much to fret about till you and your lot came a-calling,' Charlie sighed.

''Cept not having a pot to piss in,' murmured Rufus.

'This ain't no better, Rufus.'

'No better than what?' asked Dysart.

Charlie looked at the Scotsman, with his spiky, sand-coloured hair, and that patch of skin red and angry where the surgeon has shaved it to tend to his head wound. Dysart had the kind of brows, near to invisible, and pallid complexion that exaggerated the nature of his pale-blue eyes. It suddenly occurred to Charlie that he might be old enough to have been one of his early victims, for rolling sailors had been a pastime amongst him and his mates a few years back; ashore, drunk and insensible they were easy meat even for fourteen-year-olds, provided you got to their purse before some greedy whore did.

'Ever been to London, Dysart?'

'Berthed at Wapping once or twice.'

'And had a jug in the Prospect of Whitby?'

Dysart grinned. 'I have that an aw.'

'My old stamping ground, that was, from the Fleet all the way down to Wapping Steps.'

'Fleeced many a mark thereabouts, didn't you, Charlie?'

Taverner glared at Rufus to shut him up. 'I would have found you easy meat and that's no error.'

'Was that your trade, Taverner?' asked Dysart, in a less friendly tone. 'Fleecing folk?'

'You has to make your way in the world, and with whatever means God gifts you. My tongue and my wits was mine.'

The temptation to explain was strong, especially in the face of the look of disapproval on the Scotsman's face. Taverner senior had laboured long, hard and honestly as a roofer all his life, only to end up dead not yet thirty under a pile of wood scaffold that collapsed under him and his workmates. Nothing came from the man who had put up that scaffold, or from the builder who had employed him to erect it, which left eight-year-old Charlie, his mother and his three younger sisters to fend for themselves. Honest toil never brought in enough – it was law-breaking, not law-abiding that had kept the family out of the workhouse, until age did for his mother and the girls grew old enough to fend for themselves. Those eight years had felt like a hundred. There was no point in even trying to justify such a life as he had led. You had to live it to know why it was as it was.

'Mister,' Charlie sneered, determined to change the subject, his arm pointed in the general direction of Burns. 'Did you not term him that?'

'I did,' Dysart replied, nonplussed, as the midshipman stiffened, for he discerned a threat in Taverner's tone.

'Here we are, stuck in the middle of nowhere, with no ship, and still, to you, this pup is mister.'

'Mr Burns is a young gentleman,' Dysart insisted, 'and that gets him the courtesy.'

'You'd be better off gifting him the toe of your boot.'

'Sure, a fine bunch you are.' O'Hagan's voice made everyone turn. He and young Martin stood silhouetted at the edge of the trees, the gunpowder barrel under one Irish arm. 'Nobody keeping watch.'

'We was just about to get a fire going,' said Charlie quickly, 'now that dusk is upon us.'

'Then I'd best put this powder well away from here, for any fire you light is likely to blow us to Kingdom Come.'

'Rufus, Mr Burns,' Charlie spat, 'it's time to fetch some kindling.'

When Pearce arrived they had a small blaze going, well back in the trees, and with no fear in what light was left that any smoke would give away their presence.

The rise of the tide indicated to Pearce that it was time to move. Thankful for a moon, they left the woods to pass silent and dark houses on the way into Lézardrieux, with only the odd barking dog to note their presence. Pearce and Michael were in the lead; Dysart, the two boys and the barrel of gunpowder behind, with Rufus and Charlie Taverner, very nervously bringing up the rear.

'Don't tiptoe,' Pearce insisted, 'walk normally but quietly and upright, for if you crouch you will look suspicious.'

Rufus and Burns had contrived clubs – pathetic affairs made of crooked wood, with stones lashed to the timber by strips of bark – and Pearce recalled with an odd feeling the way they had shown them to him for his approval, as though he was in all respects what he did not want to be, their leader. He had said kind words in praise of their efforts, feeling like a hypocrite, even more of one as he observed the way his approbation cheered them both. It was a sobering thought, that apart from Michael O'Hagan, they were not warriors, and his skill was in fisticuffs, not the use of weapons. Pearce certainly did not think of himself in that vein either – childhood scrapping did not count. He could use a sword, but had only ever done so in bloodless contests at a Parisian fencing school. Even if they had to be whispered, the need to share his concerns was overwhelming.

'We're a mite short on muscle, Michael.'

'We are that, John-boy.'

'Dysart would have been a fighter, but he's now useless with that broken arm. I would hazard that Charlie and Rufus have spent their lives avoiding any skirmish rather than engaging in one. Martin Dent is like Burns, too small to count, and here I am, a total impostor, leading them into a strange port in a strange land to rescue a group of men they don't know. And what do we have to do? Steal a huge and complex ship from under the noses of its captors. Am I mad or what?'

'Sure, anything for an easy life,' the Irishman replied.

Pearce felt the anger well up in his breast, but that died as he heard the chuckle that followed Michael's words. Unbidden, he felt his own laughter begin to bubble up, and it forced him to halt as it burst forth in serried splutters. Michael O'Hagan was laughing too, and making as much of a hash of maintaining a decent silence as Pearce. They ended up leaning on each other, hands on heaving shoulders, wheezing as they sought air from their pained and starved lungs, with an angry Dysart hissing at them to, 'Hud yer bluddy wheest, ye pair o' dozy sods.'

'Sorry,' Pearce gasped, forced to pound his chest in order to regain control.

'So ye should be, daft buggers.'

'Are you all right, Michael?'

'I will be, John-boy,' replied a panting O'Hagan, 'just give me a minute and I will be.'

'We'd best get moving.'

The wind had dropped as they sighted the topmasts of both vessels. Hearing the creaking of their timbers as they rode the incoming tide, a ripple of murmurs went down the line. Pearce led them to a deep doorway on the quayside that had been like

445

a coal-black recess even in the early evening light. At night it would, he hoped, keep those who would stay here safe from view, provided they did not speak and no one came to the place. He went off alone, to examine the ships.

The privateer was gloomily lit on the deck, but only chinks of light came from the casements of the Indiaman's great cabin, indicating that those who had drawn the short straw to stay aboard were still there. Apart from the stars, the lanterns outside the taverns provided the only light in the place. They were quieter now, and he was tempted to enter and see how many potential foes were still capable of reacting if the alarm was raised. But that would be unwise, though he hoped, from the low buzz of conversation coming through the wooden shutters, that it would be few. The rest of the fishing village appeared to be asleep.

'Come along, Michael,' Pearce said on his return. 'This is, I fear, a task for thee and me.'

'A club?' Michael asked.

Pearce smiled, wondering if his friend could see it by the light of the moon. 'I think nature has endowed you with what you need.'

The first problem arose when they entered the narrow passageway – the height of the buildings cutting out what little light existed.

'This will never do, John-boy. I cannot see my hand in front of my nose.'

'I am damned if I know what to do about it.'

A wave of weariness assailed Pearce then, a product of too little sleep and too much thinking, not helped by a resurgence of the numerous doubts that had flitted through his brain all day. It was a more certain hand that took his arm and led him back out to a point where the starlight and moon gave a glimmer of sight.

'Wait here.'

Michael moved away, heading for the nearest tavern, and Pearce had a heart-stopping moment when he thought that the Irishman was going to walk in and demand a candle. But he stopped outside, right under the light, and without waiting to calculate any risk he reached up and took hold of the iron bracket that attached the lantern to the wall. Slowly, wrenching back and forth, he detached it from its fixing. Holding it out, with the wooden dowels that had been sunk in the stone still fixed to the end of the bracket, he returned to join Pearce, and they set off up an alley in which they could now see where they were putting their feet.

As soon as they turned into the right alleyway Pearce felt a familiar sensation. He began to shake, and he wondered if it was evident in his voice as he started talking, not loudly but audibly in French, Michael's head bowed, pretending to listen. If it was the Irishman gave no sign, and as they approached the point where the sentry should have been, he laughed so loud that Pearce nearly had a seizure, which was doubled in its effect when he realised there was no one to hear it, no one guarding the prisoners – a fact that put paid to his trembling.

As he walked past the door, Pearce, under his breath, swore heartily in two languages, cursing his own stupidity for not realising that on a cold night no sentry would stand outside. He recalled from his visit earlier that day the interior doorway the sentinel had opened to give him access to the prisoners in the large room they occupied. He racked his brain but without success to try and recall if there was another room. Finally, because there was no choice, he tapped softly on the shutter, so that he could communicate with those inside. It swung open on a dark room, and One Tooth's face appeared at the window. The look Pearce got when he explained was eloquent testimony to the fact that he was not alone in thinking himself dense.

'Sentry sleeps, we reckon, in the corridor between the front door and ours. There ain't no other, and there's no way up a floor either from what we has seen, though the sound of feet give me to reckon there's habitation above us.'

'On his own?' asked Michael, which was answered with a nod.

The silence that followed was punctuated by an odd sound, a sort of low rattle that made Pearce move from the window to the door. The wood was too thick for any sound to penetrate but there was definitely something making a noise. It was only when he stood back, perplexed, that he realised it was coming from above his head. At the top of the studded oak door was a skylight, slightly ajar. Beckoning to Michael, he had himself lifted on a cupped hand, put his ear next to the gap and heard the unmistakable sound of snoring; he also caught a very strong whiff of a human being not overly fussy about washing.

A sleeping sentry, but where was the key – on his person or in the door? Running a hand into the gap at the top he felt for the cord that must hold the skylight in place, and, finding it in the centre, steadied both it and himself on the frame. He cut slowly with the edge of his knife until the string parted, at which point he began to lower the skylight. It did not go far, about six inches at the top, as it had a metal catch to stop it from being fully opened, a protection against thieves using the gap as a way of entry. He tried to push it aside but the metal was too thick and he could not apply enough pressure. Dropping down, he explained the problem to One Tooth.

'What's the state of the tide?'

'Coming to its peak, very likely.'

'Then you have to do something.'

That niggled Pearce – and he was close to saying so – but what was the point? A sentry asleep, suddenly awakened, was not going to be thinking as clearly as he should. This was no professional soldier but some layabout recruited into the local National Guard, given a worn blue coat, a hat and a big cockade. He had seen enough of them, often the scum of the earth, to have little respect for the breed. There was no way through that door unless the sentry opened it and he probably would not respond to a knock. But he might, just might, react to a row. Then he paused, holding up his hand to stop One Tooth saying any more, because once they were committed there would be no going back. The noise he anticipated would certainly wake up more than the sentry – for there were the people who lived above. What would they do? There was no time to decide if he was right or wrong – he had to act!

John Pearce could hardly say that rioting was his speciality, but he had seen enough in his time – not least the night he was taken from the Pelican – to know that most people kept their shutters closed if they heard a disturbance outside. In France, or certainly in the Paris he had so recently left, that was doubly the case for fear of implication in something that might see a person in a tumbrel on the way to the guillotine. And really there was no choice, except to revert to the original idea of leaving the crew of the Indiaman to try for a boat on their own. They had a chance tonight that would not last.

'Pretend I'm your mate,' he said, taking the lantern from Michael.

'What?'

'You miserable swabs,' Pearce shouted, trying to be loud and slur his words at the same time. 'You can rot here in hell for all I care, I shall buy my way back from St Malo and set my feet on my own good hearth.'

He had to make a really sharp gesture to get a shocked One Tooth to reply, and his shouted response was not truly effective, more of a growl than a yell.

'Get them all shouting, man,' Pearce yelled, 'we need a commotion.'

One Tooth hesitated for a second then gestured to his shipmates, who had been standing back, no doubt hoping for their prison door to open. Within half a minute they were crowded at the window trading insults with Pearce, who was staggering around like a drunk. Michael, unbidden, had placed himself on the jamb side of the door, one fist raised to clout the sentry if he showed his face.

The door only opened a crack, and showed nothing more than a nose, but Michael dropped both fist and shoulder then hit it with all the force he could muster, sending the man at the rear flying back into the wall behind, his musket clattering along the flagged floor. Michael was through and on him before the poor soul realised what had happened. Unable to deliver the kind of blow he would like, Michael was reduced to scrabbling about the man's body for his throat, ignoring the screaming pleas in French for mercy. The lantern saved the fellow's life, for it illuminated him seconds after Michael got his hands round his neck. The sentry's eyes were already popping from his head, his face going a dark red colour, as Pearce intervened, shouting to O'Hagan that the keys were more important.

Michael let the man go and he fell sobbing into a heap.

Pearce lent over him, loudly demanding '*les clés*,' and giving him several rough shakes to keep him frightened. Michael picked up the musket and jammed the weapon against his head.

'*La porte, dans la porte*,' he cried, a feeble finger trying to point to the door, which revealed a pair of large keys on a ring, one in the lock. Pearce grabbed at them, and found that his hands were shaking as he tried to open the interior door. He had to take a deep breath to get the key in the lock, only to find that he had inserted the wrong one. Cursing, he tried the other and the door swung open to reveal a group of anxious sailors. They could not see but only hear what was going on, and they had fists raised, ready for a fight.

'Get him in here, Michael,' said Pearce. 'And somebody close those shutters and the outside door. I want his hat and his coat.'

That took a few seconds, not because the sentry resisted, merely because in his fearful state he could not comply. Pearce put on the large cockaded hat first and the blue coat next. He took the musket out of Michael's hands, said, 'Wait here,' and went back out through both doors, shutting the outer one behind him.

Those inside heard a tirade of French that meant nothing to them, followed by slurred but clear English, as John Pearce ordered away the imaginary mate of a captured East Indiaman. The last thing they heard, again incomprehensible, was Pearce assuring a couple of citoyens who had finally opened their shutters that it was nothing with which to concern themselves and that they should go back to bed. That done, he came back inside, to find the sentry trussed and gagged with the shreds of his own shirt. Michael was standing over him, the bayonet that had been on the man's belt now in his hand, his powder horn and cartridge case over his shoulders. The only thing that had not changed were the Frenchman's eyes, which were those of a fellow still convinced he was about to die.

'We wait,' Pearce insisted.

'Why?' demanded One Tooth.

'Let those who looked out settle.'

Pearce stood by the open door for several minutes, the trembling returning as he wondered at his own audacity, while simultaneously questioning where the inspiration had come from to act as he did. When he was sure it was totally quiet he came inside and beckoned to One Tooth.

'Michael will go ahead, and fetch the rest of our party. You should leave in small groups to keep the noise down, and no running for the noise will echo off the alley walls. It is down to the end and turn right for the quay, but stay in the dark until we are sure we can get a boat to take us out to the ship.'

One Tooth looked amazed. 'You mean you ain't yet got a boat?'

'No, I dammed well have not,' Pearce growled, looking round the assembled sailors, who were of all shapes and sizes. He was thinking that if they were like the man who appeared to lead them then he, like their mate, would be tempted to leave them behind. 'Now, I want to know who are your fighters, because they are the ones that we will have to put aboard.'

'You'll be with us,' said the round, pink-faced fellow called Dusty who had first come to the window. 'And you is Navy.'

'You know the ship, we don't. We think there is somebody in the main cabin but we can't be sure.'

'All day,' moaned One Tooth, 'and that is all you've discovered.'

Pearce lost it then, and grabbed the man by the front of his shirt. 'If you want to hang on to your last fang, mate, you will stow it.'

'There you go again,' said Michael, moving into separate them, 'sounding like a tar.' He had to stand foursquare before One Tooth, who looked set to take Pearce up on his offer of a scrap. 'And don't you go threatening to clout anybody. That, John-boy, is my job.'

One Tooth was no fool. Pearce he might be able to match but this Paddy towering over him was way too much of a handful. His whole body changed shape, the shoulders dropped and his head tipped, smiling to one side as he said, 'We shouldn't be a'squabblin' boys. We's in this together, is we not?'

'Right, give us a layout of the ship, and let's decide who is going to do what.'

Getting twenty-five men down the alley in what should have been silence tested Pearce's patience even more. They sounded, to his sensitive ears, like a herd of bullocks that had found a hole in a fence and run for freedom. But they made the quay without incident or alarm and joined Michael and the others, whom he had brought into the darkness of the alley.

'There was some shouting to the ship,' said Taverner. 'God knows what they were saying, but a boat has come in.'

A sudden noise made Pearce edge out, to see a group of four men stagger from the now-dark front of the tavern, two holding each other upright, the others looking in need of the same support. They lurched towards the water's edge, occasionally stopping for a drunken exchange of insults, and lowered themselves with little skill into the small boat. A bored-looking oarsman sat hanging on to the sticks, looking balefully at his inebriated companions.

'Did that fellow in the boat see you?' he whispered to those behind him.

'If he did,' Taverner replied, 'he paid us no heed.'

'We didna try to hide,' Dysart added, 'like you said, we acted normal.'

The oarsman cast off with some difficulty, for his shipmates insisted on helping. They rowed noisily and aimlessly out into the midstream. Pearce could hear the sober one cursing his mates to let him row, but they paid no heed and it took an age for them to get to entry port on *Lady Harrington*, which they clattered into in a fashion that seemed designed to wake everyone aboard. The time they took to get on to the ship was even longer, took several attempts and just as many fallbacks, before they crawled on to the deck followed by the disgruntled fellow sent to fetch them.

'Not every one of our foes is drunk,' said Pearce.

'We have to move swiftly,' insisted One Tooth, 'or we'll forfeit the run of the tide.'

'A minute or two more,' said Pearce. 'Let them get below.'

If it was a minute or two it seemed an eternity, one in which Pearce wondered why he was making all the decisions, a task he had assumed would cease once the crew of the *Harrington* gained freedom. But they were like his shipmates, quite happy to let him assume the responsibility. Why? Fear or habit, he could not tell, and decided right now it didn't matter – if no one else had a clear purpose he did! Finally the French sailors and their drunken exchanges were no more, and the whole area was again silent. Pearce, feeling very vulnerable, with One Tooth behind him, moved out to the edge, looking at the ship and the water in between, but mostly at a pair of boats tied up to the side of the Indiaman.

'That cutter by the entry port will do nicely to get us out of there,' whispered One Tooth, pointing to the larger of the pair. 'The jolly boat they just used is too small.'

Pearce pointed further down the estuary, to where the fishing fleet was gathered, some on lines that would allow them to be dragged in. 'What about one of these fishing smacks, they're tied to the shore.'

'Too risky, mate! Lots of fisher folk will have a dog chained on board at night. That's how they keep them secure and make sure no bugger steals 'em. Only have to set one of them barking and they'll all be off, raising Cain and their owners. No, the cutter be best.'

'Would I be right in thinking you can swim?'

'Never in life, brother, water is mortal to mere flesh. Can't any of your lot oblige?'

'Well, I hope when we get aboard you damn well know how to sail a ship,' Pearce growled.

Pearce was in the water in a minute, breasting out, the cold near heart-stopping in its intensity. Getting aboard the cutter proved impossible, the gunwales were too high out of the water and if he tried to lift himself he risked clattering noisily into the ship. Treading water, he tried to undo the painter, but the knot was too difficult. Hanging on with one hand, he got his knife out of his waistband. It took an age to slice through the rope, but it parted eventually. Lying back, he began to swim, towing the cutter very slowly behind him.

One Tooth was as grateful as ever. 'Christ, you took your time.'

'Shut up,' Pearce snapped, as he stood up, water dripping from his clothing. 'Just get in.'

The *Harrington*s took their places without talking. Pearce was followed by Charlie and Rufus, still carrying their cask of gunpowder. He helped Dysart aboard, took station in the prow with Michael and his musket and prepared to hand off the cutter when they reached the side of the ship.

'Mr Burns, I want you first aboard, keeping a lookout. Get to the upper deck, and keep an eye on the cabin door.'

'John-boy,' said Michael. 'Send Martin.'

'Is that wise?'

'If Martin wanted to betray us, he's had all day to do it. He could do it now.'

'Not if he wants to live.'

'I will vouch for him.'

Both men looked at the boy, who was looking at Pearce, almost pleading to be trusted. Pearce nodded, then added, 'Martin, you go with him.'

'Jackets off, lads,' hissed One Tooth, 'and make fenders.'

Those not rowing obliged, removing their coats, rolling and draping them over one side of the cutter so that when it touched, side on, it did so in silence. Pearce took hold of a manrope on one edge of the entry port to hold it close, One Tooth the other. Martin, shoeless, was already gone, skipping over the side with ease and disappearing into the darkness of the deck, followed with more circumspection by Midshipman Burns. Slowly, too noisily for Pearce's liking, the rest began to follow.

'Rufus, Charlie, stay in the cutter with Dysart, and man the oars. If this goes wrong we might need this sod to get out of here.'

Pearce went aboard and joined a clutch of whispering sailors. One Tooth was sending some to find axes. They would go the hawser on the maindeck that held the Indiaman to the baulks, and, once the commotion started, cut the ship free regardless.

'Two of you get yourself a place near the wheel, for once she's free she might well run aground.'

'Where can I get a weapon?' asked Pearce.

'Outside the main cabin, which is where we are headed, right after we've seen to the forepeak.'

Rocking on the gentle swell, ropes creaking and timbers working, the *Lady Harrington* made enough noise to cover the movement of twenty-odd barefoot souls as they went forward, One Tooth explaining to Pearce that the drunks should be berthed in what had been the original crew's accommodation. The snores told him the man was right long before they reached the door. There was no point in asking where the *Harrington*s had got the belaying pins – they had them and used them. A series of heavy thuds induced silence in an area so familiar that they could work by sound alone.

Then they went forward, using the companionway to the upper deck, where they found Martin Dent and the two men allotted to the wheel lying just out of sight. Martin indicated to Pearce that he should have a look, and, raising his head above the level of the planking, he saw that the door of the cabin was ajar. There was light spilling out under the peak of the poop, though the bulkhead was in shadow, and the babble of conversation told him that there were a lot of people in there.

'Martin, where's Burns?'

'Don't know. He came aboard but that's the last I saw of 'im.'

'Damn that boy!'

'Weapons were on the rack by the cabin door,' hissed One Tooth.

Pearce thought of *Brilliant* and the pikes and weapons stored in various parts of the ship. 'Locked?'

'Course,' One Tooth replied. 'No master in his right mind would leave them undone.'

'Keys?'

'In the cabin, or they were. But we had 'em out to fight the Frogs.'

Michael came up beside Pearce and, nodding, aimed his loaded musket at the doorway. Crawling forward towards that yellow streak of light, Pearce realised he was trembling again – from fear or anticipation he did not know, but it was enough to make him stop for a moment, again assailed by the notion that he, who thought himself a talker rather than a doer, was not cut out for this.

Terror or desperation drove him on and he made the bulkhead in front of the cabin, then ran his hands along the wooden wall: too fast, for his hand dislodged a sword, not locked away as One Tooth supposed, but loose in its groove. The weapon clattered to the deck and the talk inside the cabin stopped abruptly. Pearce grabbed the sword by the blade – heavy and cold to the touch – and tried to scrabble away in silence towards the steps that led to the poop, just as a Frenchman came through the door, looking left and right and calling out enquiringly.

Pearce would never know if his attempt at concealment could have succeeded, because from below came a great thud, quickly followed by a second. He only found out later that the pair set to axe through the hawser, who had become impatient, had started on their task without an order to do so. It made no odds; to the men in that cabin the sound signalled danger, and a dozen of them, all armed, rushed on deck, one having the sense to let off a pistol into the air, the quickest way to give the general alarm.

CHAPTER EIGHTEEN

Michael fired off his weapon inside the same second, and with a group to aim for he could not miss – a man groaned, spun away, and fell. Michael had the bayonet on the end of that weapon as well, but that still left One Tooth and his party unarmed against men with swords and pistols. Knife in one hand, heavy unwieldy cutlass in the other, Pearce had to attack them from the side, ghostly shapes illuminated by the moonlight, or standing in the streak of lantern light coming through the cabin door. Surprise won him a momentary advantage, and he managed to club more than slice at one fellow holding out and aiming a pistol. The hilt of the weapon served to chin another, and he could hear, as well as the continued thudding from below, a wild Irish yell as Michael O'Hagan came to his aid, musket out and blade aiming for the nearest body.

Pearce threw his knife to distract the man who wanted to shoot Michael, but not being a throwing weapon it hit him on the shoulder and clattered to the deck. It was sufficient to spoil his aim, though, and he missed with his shot, which went wide of Michael and lodged itself in one of the *Harrington*s, who fell back down the companionway. They were not coming on, One Tooth and his mates, which left both Pearce and Michael isolated. Martin Dent was made of better material – he had slid forward to catch hold of Pearce's knife, and, back on his feet, staying low, was slicing away at any leg that came in range. The Irishman was jabbing away, the sheer fury of his action driving his opponents back. The sword Pearce was wielding was not one for elegance, nothing like the épées or light sabres he had learnt to use at his fencing lessons. This was more a bone-breaking club, heavy and damned difficult to use when the bearer was outnumbered. But he swung it above and around his head with gusto, trying at the same time to count the numbers he was fighting and the effect of that first warning pistol shot.

'*Harrington*s, move,' he yelled, 'or we're all done.'

There was a curious sensation of clarity. Even as he fought, Pearce seemed to be able to see in limited light where the next and most dangerous assault was coming from, to parry it or produce a blow that wounded the attacker; this at the same time as he was calling out for assistance – and that damned trembling sensation was gone now. He could also observe that his foes had exhausted their combustible weapons. Could not One Tooth and his mates realise this – that it was sword against anything they could muster, and that these Frenchmen were sluggish? The only two who appeared were Charlie Taverner and Rufus, armed with nothing more than belaying pins, but coming up behind those fighting their messmates and using their weapons to good effect. They created a bit of space, so Pearce was able to back up to the sword rack and grab another weapon. This he slid as hard as he could down the deck so that it lay beyond the fight, and Charlie, who had seen it pass, was quick enough to go for it, then get up just in time to stop another enemy braining Rufus with his pistol butt.

Pearce was grabbing as many swords as he could, in between parrying blows, chucking them overhead or under feet, and slowly, armed, the *Harrington*s emerged to engage in the fight. Pearce was aware that the thudding below had ceased, which meant that either their labours had been interrupted or the ship was free of the shore.

'Martin, below! Find out what's happening.'

The boy slipped away, not without a jab to the groin of one Frenchman that produced a high pain-filled scream. Now the attackers outnumbered the defenders. None too soon, for wielding that heavy cutlass had exhausted Pearce, and Michael had taken several blows and was much slower in his responses than he had been at the outset. The speed with which the fighting stopped had Pearce on his knees for the first time; he had lunged at a Frenchman only to avert his blade quickly as the man dropped his weapon and put his hands up high. He lifted his head to see Charlie Taverner, Rufus and One Tooth pushing those who had surrendered against the cabin bulkhead.

'Get the swords still in the rack,' he shouted.

'The hawsers are cut,' yelled Martin Dent, only his head showing at deck level.

'You two,' shouted One Tooth, pointing, 'get on that bloody wheel. Two more in the bows to give us a course, and the rest get capstan bars to fend us past that damned Frenchman.'

A ball took the *Harrington* standing next to One Tooth, hitting him on the shoulder so that he spun round and dropped to the deck. Pearce looked to Michael to load his piece, but

461

the Irishman had already done so, and had his musket aimed over the side to return fire to the shore. Others had picked up dropped pistols and were looking for the means to reload them.

'Charlie, get Dysart out of the cutter, but leave it lashed on just in case.' As Charlie moved he saw Rufus on his knees, head down, and ran to lift him. 'Rufus, are you all right?'

'Bugger booted me right in the balls,' he said, lifting his head with a grimace of pain.

'And there's me thinkin' you didn't have any,' Charlie hooted, as he moved away.

Following his gaze, Pearce found himself looking into a row of angry eyes. There were eight still on their feet, not all without wounds but too dangerous to leave to their own devices. Rope them! With what? Confine them! Where was secure? The solution flew in the face of everything his father had ever tried to teach him.

'Get up, Rufus. Gather some men, and throw those bastards overboard.'

'Axes?' The shout came from the bows. 'We've run foul of the French mainmast rigging.'

As men rushed forward, carrying swords rather than axes, Dysart appeared with Midshipman Burns in tow. They were just in time to see Rufus Dommet, with the aid of a *Harrington*, heaving the man who had kicked him over the side, his yell of alarm killed by the splash as he entered the water.

'Anyone got a loaded pistol?' Pearce called.

'Me,' a *Harrington* replied.

'Give it here!'

Pearce took it, went to the Frenchman nearest the side, and in his own language with the pistol at his head, invited him to jump, the task made harder when a musket ball removed a piece of the bulwark right under his nose. Oddly enough that sped the men over, and splash followed splash until the deck was clear.

Michael got off an occasional shot. Forward, axes and swords were hacking at the point where the rigging had fouled. Free now to look, those on the quarterdeck could see the current was swinging the stern round to a point where it would run them ashore to a quayside crowded with yelling Frenchman, some bearing torches, others so drunk they were unable to shake their fist without falling over. It would be fatal to get near them, for enough of those numerous enemies were sufficiently sober to cause trouble – a pair with muskets and the powder to load them were already doing so.

'Michael, I need those guns silenced.'

'Then you'd best come and aim this thing yourself, John-boy, for it is of little use in my hands.'

'Let me,' said Martin Dent, putting a hand on the weapon.

'It will blow you off your feet,' Michael scoffed, but he did let the boy take it, and Martin laid it on the bulwark and took aim, slowly squeezing the trigger. Michael was right, the discharge threw Martin backwards, but there was an immediate scream from the nearby shore that meant he had found a target in the yelling crowd of drunks.

'Look,' said One Tooth, pointing forward. Pearce followed his finger, to see two things. That a fight was going on between the anchor watch of the *Mercedes*, and at the same time a party of the shore-side Frenchmen with torches was making its way down the quay to commandeer fishing boats. 'We can't fight them all if they get aboard.'

There was a hiatus, with no one doing much from the shore

to impede their progress. Firing had stopped, the only activity taking place in the bows, where the Frenchmen were trying and failing to get lines on the *Lady Harrington* so that they could lash her off to their stationary ship. Those on shore must have been pinning their hopes on a number of men getting aboard, sufficient to take back the prize.

'Then we must ensure they do not.' Suddenly Pearce added, 'What is your damned name, anyway?'

'Twyman.'

'Everyone forward to keep the crew of that ship off our deck,' said Pearce, his mind going back to the chase that had started this whole affair. 'Twyman, have you got a cannon we can aim forward on those boats?'

'With the swing on the barky any one of the side armament will do.'

'Powder, balls?'

'Balls should still be by the guns, though they might have emptied the magazine.'

'Send someone to look. Dysart, that barrel of powder?'

'Still in the cutter.'

'Burns, go with Martin and fetch it.' The midshipman stood stock still, until Pearce shouted. 'You must do something, boy!'

'I'll go,' said Rufus. 'Me and Charlie, it's sort of ours like.'

'Slowmatch, Dysart.'

'Aye. Roond ma waist still.'

'Well, get your flints on it and get it lit.'

'We're clear forrard,' came the cry.

'On the wheel, keep us that way,' shouted Twyman.

Pearce went down the starboard gangway to look at the guns, aware that the ship was moving – slowly, but it was moving, running out on the falling tide. On the opposite deck the *Harrington*s were fending off with their capstan bars. The Frenchmen opposing them could have used a cannon – not more than one for they were too few. Was it that they were stupid, or did they fear to damage their prize? What difference did it make?

Being an East Indiaman, the ship was well armed, with half a dozen long nines a side. Twyman was right, there were balls left in the garlands, and within a minute he had a flintlock to fire the piece, the ship's own powder in cartridges, swab and rammers, linstock burning slowly in case the flint didn't fire, two buckets of water and his own mates as gun crew.

'Martin, you're powder monkey. Let go of the breechings. Open the port. Michael, Rufus, Charlie, on the tackle. Mr Twyman we need more hands.' Charlie didn't wait – he was already swabbing the gun just in case it had been fired when the East Indiaman had been taken. Dysart showed Pearce how to attach the flintlock while a cartridge was picked, the touchhole covered and the rest rammed down the barrel with the ball.

'Now all ye have to dae,' instructed Dysart, handing Pearce the firing line, 'is look doon the piece, point it where you want the ball tae go, and pull this hard.'

'You know what you're doing, Dysart.'

'Aye. But I'm no up tae bein' the gun captain, Pearce, especially no with this gammy arm. You are.'

It was an odd way for the Scot to say he was grateful, but that, judging by the look on his face, was what it amounted to. Pearce realised that he was, and had been, enjoying himself; his blood had been racing for an age now, a strange and compelling feeling that had first surfaced when he started fighting, and had still not diminished. Leaning down, picking out one of the bobbing torches as a target, he called for the gun carriage to be levered round as far forward as the cannon would bear. They had to take the quoin out and reverse it to depress the muzzle, but the time came when one torch was in sight right down the line of the cannon.

'Stand clear,' said Pearce, stepping back himself so that he was holding on to three feet of firing lanyard, his own arm fully stretched. He pulled, saw the spark, then jumped even further back as the cannon fired, sending out an orange tongue of flame that lit the night sky, and a solid ball that crunched into a berthed fishing boat and turned it to matchwood, as the gun shot back into its straining breechings.

'Reload,' Pearce shouted.

'We're clearing the *Mercedes*.'

That shout made Pearce look aft to where the privateer's foredeck was slowly, for they were still drifting, but surely coming abreast of the *Lady Harrington*'s poop. Behind him, amidships and well away from the powder, he could see the slowmatch fizzing as it burnt into a tub of sand. Dysart was sitting on the small barrel of gunpowder they had fetched aboard, with his broken arm sticking straight out. The ropes which had carried the barrel were still there, loops of hemp that were too tempting to resist.

'Dysart, can you make that barrel you're sitting on live?' The questioning look made Pearce continue. 'I think a little bit of that slowmatch, inserted, might make it into a useful bomb. Only you can tell what would happen if that went off on an enemy deck.'

'Why, it wid be terrible.'

'Can I ask you to make it so?'

The cannon was reloaded, Pearce had it hauled up, adjusted his aim and elevation, them pulled the firing lanyard again. This time, with shortened range, the effect was even more devastating, as the ball sliced through the flimsy scantlings of the small fishing boats, sending slivers of wood in all directions and bringing in its wake the satisfying sound of men receiving wounds.

'That cleared the buggers,' shouted Charlie Taverner, looking over the bulwarks, 'and some of them have taken splinters.'

Pearce moved forward to follow Charlie's finger, and to see the privateersmen seeking cover, with the exception of those half dozen writhing on the ground.

'Mr Burns, sir,' called Dysart, 'will you oblige me by turning this wee barrel on its side.'

Pearce turned to look at that. The boy did not respond, indeed he seemed to be getting ready to slink away again. Pearce's harsh tone stopped him. 'Move, Mr Burns! You wear an officer's coat. It would benefit us all greatly if, just this once, you were to behave like one.'

Pearce's censure brought compliance – slow, not enthusiastic, but forward movement nonetheless. With the barrel on its side, Dysart handed Burns a knife, with which the boy went to work on the bung, creating a hole down the side of the cork into which the Scotsman could feed his linstock, all the while talking the young midshipman through.

'We want it cut short, Mr Burns, very short, an inch showing and nae mair.'

A cry came from the men on the wheel. '*Mercedes* has cut her cable.'

Pearce was forced to leave off gun-laying to find out from Twyman what that meant.

'They are lighter than us, a shallower draught, so they might drift out with greater speed.'

'So?'

'They will hope to foul us, run their bowsprit over our rail, snare us on lines and act as a sheet anchor so that we drift into the shore.'

'Then,' said Pearce emphatically, 'I think spoiling their game comes first. Charlie, Rufus, you said that powder barrel was yours.'

'It is, Pearce,' shouted Charlie, for the first time in an age his face happy, something like it had been that night in the Pelican. 'It most surely is.'

Pearce wanted to light the slowmatch before they moved from the gangway, but Dysart had too healthy a respect for powder to let him. He insisted on patience until the entire party was on the poop. Then, and only then, would he take the small piece of linstock, already burning, and apply it to the bare inch left exposed.

'The honour,' Pearce said to his two messmates, 'is yours.'

'Dinna rush,' warned Dysart. 'See how slow it burns.'

What crew remained on the *Mercedes* must have sensed something coming, even if they could not see what it was. Those who could be spared took up position to fire a couple of muskets at the party on the Indiaman's poop, but they were rebuffed by a fusillade, led by Michael O'Hagan, made by his musket and numerous captured pistols.

'Get ready,' warned Dysart as the burning fuse reached the very edge of the bung. Charlie and Rufus lifted the barrel by the ropes and started to swing, with the Scotsman intoning an interminable *one-twa-three* for the throw. On three, the two Pelicans gave a mighty heave backwards, then forwards, and slung the barrel of powder, its fuse fizzing angrily, onto the privateer's deck.

'Now get doon,' the Scotsman ordered.

It was as well they obliged. Almost as soon as the barrel hit the enemy deck, following no more than a couple of rolls, it went off, a great crashing explosion that tore lumps out of the French ship. Flaming staves rose into the rigging and lodged there, setting light to tarred rope wherever they came into contact. It seemed only minutes until the *Mercedes* was ablaze all along her forepeak, those who had been left aboard no longer seeking to close her in on the Indiaman. Now they were looking for a way to survive.

'Back on the gun,' Pearce shouted, finding he had to drag some away from the terrifying sight.

'Aye, aye, Captain,' called Charlie.

Pearce grinned, and in doing so realised how tense he had been. 'Only a gun captain, Charlie.'

They got off one more shot, that one aimed at a target that lay astern of the ship, and this time the ball landed on the shore to bounce along, sending Frenchmen flying in all directions.

'I never wanted to be a sailor, Michael,' said Pearce, leaning wearily on the Irishman's shoulder. 'But right now I would be happy to change places.'

'Only a fool would believe that, John-boy,' Michael replied, 'an omadhaun in the Erse.'

'Is that what it means, a fool?'

'Aye, though one tinged with madness.'

'Then I have found my true rating.'

The flash of the exploding powder that set in motion the destruction of the *Mercedes* lit the night sky and was visible for fifty miles, brilliant fading to constant, reflected off the cloud cover. Lieutenant Digby, who had the watch aboard HMS *Brilliant,* deliberated about waking his captain, worried that a man who seemed to have clutched at so many straws would do likewise with this. He knew that the frigate should not be here, three days sailing at least from the convoy. If Gould had obeyed his instructions and cleared the great headland at Ushant he would be well on his way to passing Brest and entering the Bay of Biscay. But reluctant as he was, he had no choice – Barclay's standing orders were quite specific.

'It came from the Estuary de Trieux?' Barclay demanded, night glass to his eye, nightshirt flapping in the breeze.

'I can only report that the explosion came from the general direction, sir.'

'An opinion, Mr Digby.'

'I feel obliged to decline to give one, sir. It could be anything.'

'And what, sir,' Barclay enquired drily, passing the lieutenant his telescope, 'would you say that was?'

Digby looked, not knowing whether to be pleased or despairing about the orange glow that tinged the sky. 'Fire, sir.'

'A large fire, sir, perhaps even a ship fire?'

'We cannot assume that, Captain Barclay.'

'No Mr Digby, we cannot. But I think we are obliged to investigate. Please set me a course for the mouth of that estuary. I want to be close inshore by dawn.'

'Aye, aye, sir.'

Unbeknown to Pearce, Twyman had been busy getting some kind of sail on the ship that would enable the helmsman to hold her head steady. Firing his cannon, watching the gunpowder bomb and the subsequent fire, he had not even been aware that men had gone aloft. They had rigged a jib and the gaff, as well as a topsail that could be braced round into what were now light airs. With this the *Lady Harrington* could set and maintain a course, with the added advantage that the topsail, backed, could slow their progress down the channel, very necessary if they did not wish to run aground.

Nor was he aware, as a nautical novice, just how swiftly the tide fell in the bight of Brittany, the speed with which the water exited from this estuary. At the mouth of the inlet it was like a tidal race, a cataract that met the incoming seawater, breaking over rocks in abundance, to create a maelstrom of white water, something the locals avoided like the plague.

'I need hands on the braces,' Twyman yelled. 'For if we don't have sails set right we could broach to in that water, an' that don't take no account of the rocks.'

He had caught Pearce cold; he was still, like his shipmates, basking in the glow of the martial success. One Tooth Twyman had no tact at all, so when he yelled at them for some activity it was well larded with expletives.

'Are we being required,' Michael scoffed, with an expression that boded argument, 'to do willingly what we hated to do for Barclay?'

'We are,' Pearce replied, 'and I fear we must.'

In a voice full of irony he simulated what he had heard on *Brilliant*. 'So clap on to them falls, me hearties, an' pull like the very devil.'

Which the Pelicans did, their spirits as high as his, running to where they were told, hauling on ropes like demons, aware that Martin Dent was aloft doing what he did best on *Brilliant*, handling the highest sails, while Mr Burns was likewise replicating his naval behaviour, standing by the wheel being utterly useless. Dysart, with only one good arm, had taken on the task of ensuring that ropes were properly attached to their cleats, that they would not fly off and endanger the whole ship.

The Indiaman hit the disturbed water to rear and buck like a horse, with Twyman and two others fighting a wheel that wanted to rip itself out of their hands. The bows dipped alarmingly, and the long bowsprit shot well east. Pearce and his mates raced to loosen one set of braces, then ran with equal alacrity to tighten those on the larboard side. The wind on the sails, in that configuration, brought the head round and the *Lady Harrington* ploughed out into less tempestuous waters.

The boom, and the shock that hit them seconds later, took everyone aboard by surprise. They had been too busy seeing to the needs of their ship to think of what was happening to the *Mercedes*, illuminated like a torch by the flames that ran through her sails and rigging. The hull had been ablaze too and as the flames reached her store of gunpowder she simply blew up, a great cataclysmic explosion that sent most of the decks skywards, while the scantlings were blown out to reveal the fiery red ball that was the seat of the blast.

'Jesus,' said Michael, crossing himself.

'Fire got the magazine,' said Dysart.

There was a moment of uncertainty for Pearce; part elation, part regret at the death of a ship and quite possibly several men aboard her, pride at what they had achieved tugging at every pacifist tenet he had ever been taught. If that had been *Brilliant* and Barclay would he care so much? That was a thought that brought him abruptly back to consideration of the next dilemma.

'Twyman,' he shouted, 'is it possible to set a course that would take us east?'

'Whatever for?'

Pearce looked out into the inky western darkness of the sea, lit only by a streak of moonlight. 'I think our frigate is out to the west, and I have good reasons for wanting to avoid her.'

'Then if that's what you want you'd best get back on those bloody falls and haul away on command, though I won't put the helm down till we are well clear of that damned shore.'

Once on a settled course, sailing easy, everyone aboard could relax and count the cost of what they had done. They had one *Harrington* dead; the two wounded were brought in to rest in what had been the Indiaman captain's sleeping cabin and rendered what aid was possible. It was not much, and worryingly, Michael identified one fellow who had saved his life as critical. It was that smooth-faced cove that Pearce had first met at their prison window, the one known as Dusty.

'Seen it before, John-boy, that lack of colour. Poor sod can barely breathe. He needs a medical man.'

'How long, Twyman, till we raise the home shore?'

'God alone has knowledge of that, mate, and if you was a sailor you would know better than to ask. The wind will decide. If it favours us, and the weather stays clear, two to four days. But I've been stuck in this stretch of water for a whole fortnight, beating up the Channel into the teeth of an endless easterly, and that with a full crew of hands.'

'I would hate to be responsible for anyone's death.'

'We's all got to go sometime,' Twyman replied, heartlessly.

Pearce was now feeling guilty, his mood black, not only

about the remarkably few casualties they had suffered, but also about those amongst the Frenchmen – he was sure he had killed more than one – which he knew to be absurd. They would have killed him if they could, and probably celebrated the fact of doing so. But being irrational did not make that emotion any easier to avoid. He was assailed by the stupidity of some of the decisions he had made, easily able to imagine the consequences had the whole party not been favoured with remarkable good luck. Added to that was the certain knowledge that he had risked a great many lives to achieve an utterly selfish end – his own return to England. The excuse that he was acting for them collectively was now, obviously, so much moonshine. His mood rendered him uncommunicative, which did not register with the crew of the Indiaman, but offended those with whom he had come ashore.

'Anybody wid think we lost,' moaned Dysart, unaware that the look Pearce gave him was not one of annoyance, but yet another twinge of conscience; if the Scotsman was not to lose the full use of his arm for life, he needed a surgeon as well.

Sitting in the capacious main cabin, his mood was not helped by his surroundings. Pearce could only wonder at the area allotted to the man who ran the ship compared to that given to everyone else. The whole space, which could fore and aft be divided in two, seemed to occupy a third of the length of the vessel. The captain had his own privy and a separate space for his bed. The furniture would have graced any salon at home and the quality of the late captain's private stores – the Frenchmen aboard had been heavily at the wine – reeked of easy wealth.

'He was of a high colour, mind,' said Twyman, talking of the previous occupant, while happily occupying his chair. 'And choleric, forever yelling and going blue with it. So when he had his seizure none of us were like to be shocked.'

'What happens to the ship now?'

'God knows,' Twyman replied, his single fang gnawing at his lower lip. 'Sail into an English port, send a note to the owners and see what happens.'

'Some of us would need to be put ashore prior to that.'

'Was you pressed?' Pearce nodded, as Twyman added, 'And freshly so judging by your skills.'

'Not much more than a week ago,' Pearce replied, 'though it feels like a lifetime.'

The thought of his destination had obviously made Twyman gloomy, but he brightened considerably when responding to Pearce's request. 'I'd be an ungrateful swab if I couldn't manage that, mate. Don't you fret, I'll get you clear.'

'Lying one-toothed bastard,' said Dysart, when Pearce accosted him to ask him what he wanted to do – come ashore with them or stay on the ship. He kicked the bulwark by which they were standing. 'The bugger is salvage at least.'

'So?'

'The value o' the ship and the cargo has tae be redeemed by the insurers – them bastards that tak their coffee at Lloyds. It's worth thousands, maybe tens of, since we dinna know the cargo. Nae wonder he's happy to get you off the bluddy thing so you'll no get a share.'

'Are you sure?' asked Pearce, feeling rather foolish.

'As sure as a canny straighten my arm,' Dysart responded, his normally kindly face a mask of real fury. 'That's the law o' the sea, man. You wouldna credit it, would ye? Having saved the bastard's arse, he wants tae diddle you oot of ony reward.'

'It's not one we could claim anyway Dysart, since we intend to desert.'

'Well, dinna tae it near to any naval port, for the sake of Christ. There's an army of glass-combing buggers in them towns that'll spot you in nae time an' will hand you o'er for a bounty.'

'I will have to talk with Charlie, Rufus and Michael, and see what they want to do.'

Dysart's voice was soft now, fatherly even. 'Just remember, Pearce, drop anchor in this and you and yer friends are safe, 'cause you're no deserters. Yer still Navy and you might also be in for a right good dose of coin when this barky is condemned.'

'And then?'

'I grant ye that's no sae nice. You'll be sent aboard another man-o'-war.'

'It's not worth it,' Pearce replied.

The lookout on HMS *Brilliant* called at dawn. 'Sail ho! Ship bearing due west. I just picked up the masthead on the rise.'

'Bugger's run for St Malo,' Barclay spat.

For the first time in forty-eight hours he felt able to look and act as he should, like a senior Post Captain, giving the eye to his deck officers instead of avoiding contact. If he had not insisted on closing the Estuary de Trieux they would have missed the enemy.

The next call came fifteen minutes later. 'Looks like the India ship, your honour.'

'There might be two sail.'

It was a good five minutes before the lookout responded, a period in which Ralph Barclay swung between euphoria and despair, hope rising only to be killed off by pessimism, the feeling that all his hopes, dashed more than once, were about to be sunk again.

'There's only one ship to see and it is definitely the Indiaman, 'cause she is flying the company pennant.'

'No tricolour above it?'

'No.'

'Mr Collins, more sail.'

It was Martin Dent who spotted the frigate, sitting as he was on the crosstrees, right at the top of the *Lady Harrington*'s masts. His gleeful identification of HMS *Brilliant* was not shared on deck by anyone other than Dysart, and the mood deepened when Twyman denied the possibility of outrunning a frigate.

'You're sure?'

'As I stand here and breathe.'

Pearce looked towards the low line of land, just visible. 'How far offshore would you put us?'

'A good ten miles.'

'Could we take to a boat?' asked Charlie Taverner.

It was Dysart who replied, not Twyman, the Scot's face angry at what he saw as stupidity. 'You wouldna get two miles. Barclay's got boats an 'aw, and men who can row better than you daft buggers. Think what will happen if yer taken up as deserters. The first thing you'd face is the grating, and this time it will be a proper cat, no' some damp and useless hemp.'

The deck fell into silence, *Harrington*s and *Brilliant*s alike struck into silence. John Pearce was aware that others were waiting for him to make a decision, and that annoyed him – had he not done enough? But even as he deliberated on the ineptitude of his fellow men, he could not help but filter through the alternatives they faced. And the conclusion was as unpleasant as it was unwelcome.

'Twyman,' he said eventually, his voice heavy as he glanced around to what was a totally empty seascape, 'if we cannot outrun *Brilliant* then we had best heave to.' He answered the looks of disappointment with the words. 'That way, at least, the wounded men will get quick attention.'

'Let fly the sheets,' Twyman shouted, his face a mask, giving nothing away regarding his own feelings.

'John-boy,' asked Michael, with an enquiring look. 'You're sure?'

'No, Michael, I am as unsure as anyone on this deck.'

The Irishman pulled out the first belaying pin, releasing the mainsail to flap uselessly as the way came off the *Lady Harrington*.

The decision had been made and the emotions of those on board varied. Rufus put the best face on it, pointing out that they would be reunited with Ben Walker, which Charlie Taverner spoilt for him by mentioning Gherson. Charlie was looking glum, Pearce thought, like a man on his way to the guillotine or the gallows. Michael just looked angry.

'Sorry, Michael.'

'Sure, I have no idea what you are after saying that for.'

'I thought to get us free,' Pearce said, nagged once more by the thought of his true motives, and wondering why, having got clear of Lézardrieux, he hadn't asked to be put ashore at once. Too late now!

'Free. What is free, John-boy? The right to toil until your body fails, then to die in a gutter?'

Pearce gave him a tired smile. 'You're not recommending the Navy, are you?'

The Irishman shook his head. 'Not for you, and not on that there ship, 'cause all I can see for you there is trouble, enough trouble to see you dangle, for one day I swear that you will take a swing at Barclay.'

'The tree of liberty must from time to time be refreshed with the blood of tyrants.'

'What?'

'Thomas Jefferson, an American patriot, said something like that. I'm not sure I have the absolute right of it.'

Michael was not impressed by the quotation. 'Me, I care not where I am, a hull is as good as a ditch.' Pearce looked at him in disbelief, until he realised that the Irishman was speaking to reassure himself.

'It's not just you.'

'Charlie will sulk but survive, and Rufus, though he will haul on ropes for eternity and learn little, is as well off at sea as he is ashore.'

'Which leaves me as the problem.'

O'Hagan favoured Pearce with a huge grin, then put a hand on his shoulder. 'Sure, you're that all right, and one I am right glad I met.'

Brilliant was within hailing distance within the hour, with a boat in the water seconds after she hove to. Pearce could see Barclay in the sternsheets, and observed that the frigate captain was not going to come aboard without a strong party of red-coated marines. Lifting a telescope that he had borrowed from Twyman, he ranged over the deck of the man-o'-war, picking out the cloaked figure of the captain's wife, Lieutenant Digby and further forward, leaning over the rail, Ben Walker and Cornelius Gherson.

'Man ropes,' said Twyman. 'We need to rig man ropes for your captain to come aboard.'

'Those,' Pearce replied, bitterly, 'you can do yourself.'

A call brought one of the *Harrington*s to drop two lines over the side that looped through eyebolts and acted as the side of the ladder needed to get aboard at sea. Barclay climbed the wooden battens on the side of the ship with ease and came on deck with a look of deep curiosity. That he was not pleased to see Pearce was obvious by the glare aimed in his direction, nor was he about to favour anyone on the deck, *Brilliant*s or *Harrington*s, with a smile, though Dysart was worth a nod. But when he spotted Midshipman Burns by the wheel, a wave of relief swept over him.

'Mr Burns, an explanation if you please.'

'Sir,' the mid replied, stepping forward and lifting his hat.

'Who commands here?'

'Well, I do,' said Twyman.

Barclay looked him up and down, then called to Burns, 'Would I be right in assuming, young sir, that this ship was taken from under the noses of that dammed privateer?'

'Yes, sir.'

'By men from my ship?'

'Partly.'

Barclay glared at the boy. 'Partly?'

'We took it back with the help of the ship's own crew, sir.'

'Only right and proper, Mr Burns, but that does not alter the fact that this ship was in enemy hands for a full thirty-six hours.'

'She were not,' protested Twyman, 'not more'n twenty four.'

Barclay reacted as though Twyman had not spoken, his remarks still aimed at Burns. 'Which means, young sir, that this vessel became property of our enemies, and, retaken, is now a lawful prize of His Britannic Majesty, King George. And that means, Mr Burns, that until I myself set foot on this deck, you had the command here.' Then Barclay lifted his hat. 'And it behoves me, before superseding you, to give you your due salute.'

Burns had not the wit to reply, but he did, once more, lift his own hat.

'Thank you, Mr Burns. Now be so good as to escort me to your cabin.'

'I protest,' said Twyman.

'Noted,' Barclay replied, without giving the man a glance.

There was not a jaw that did not drop as Burns complied with his captain's request – taking Barclay to his cabin, and two marines, who took station at the cabin door, made sure no one, not even Twyman, could follow.

CHAPTER NINETEEN

When Barclay emerged he had the truth of the tale. Burns had not admitted how little he had personally achieved, nor did he over-praise the man who had actually led them. But then he didn't have to, for as Captain Barclay informed him he was the senior in the party, and even if he was only a slip of a mid, he was, by the very nature of his coat and rank, in command, so all the glory accrued to him.

'And I shall have pleasure in saying so in my despatch. I don't doubt it will be well received by higher authority. I would say, Mr Burns, that such a feat will make your name in the service. Now, oblige me by sending my barge back to *Brilliant* so we can get a proper prize crew aboard this vessel. And once that has been achieved it would give me great pleasure, nay pride, to invite you to dine with myself and Mrs Barclay.'

Then he looked to where Pearce stood, giving him that same baleful stare as he had the day he had first come aboard. 'Naturally, that will mean the return of the men you led to our own ship.'

'Mr Burns,' Pearce said, ignoring Barclay. 'We need the surgeon.'

Barclay said nothing till the midshipman repeated the request, and nodded once he did.

The whole ship knew the truth within ten minutes of their own men corning back aboard. Dysart and Martin Dent were quizzed rather than the Pelicans, which set up a buzz that had Hale calling on his captain, though unhappily, for his account did not make pleasant hearing. What he reported was not the truth, for it had grown in the telling, making gods out of mere mortals. What was galling was the frequency with which Pearce's name came up, especially since Emily Barclay could hear every word his coxswain was saying, having sat in uninvited to listen to the conversation. That forced the coxswain to filter what had been said about the behaviour of Midshipman Burns.

'Surely that is good news, husband,' said Emily, once Hale had departed. 'That a member of your crew should show such ability.'

Ralph Barclay waited for her to say 'volunteer', dreading that she might do so. He was seething inwardly, for the last two days with his wife had been hard indeed, and these were almost the first civil words she had spoken to him since he had flogged this man she seemed to want to hail as a hero. Emily was not unaware of the effect of her words; it had never occurred to her that she might have power inside her marriage, but the argument over that flogging, and the way her husband had acted since then, half blustering, half timid, was enough to show her that she had a substantial amount. The trouble was knowing how to use it; for certain it would be fatal to overplay her hand. Meekly applied pressure was forceful enough.

'You feel I should reward him?'

'Only, Captain Barclay, if you think that it is merited. It is, after all, beyond my competence to judge.'

It was difficult to reply in an even tone. 'Let me think on it.'

He scarce got time for that, for Twyman came aboard demanding to see him, insisting that he remove his prize crew forthwith, 'For at best, Captain Barclay, the *Lady Harrington* is salvage.'

'Salvage?' Barclay exploded. 'You are taken by that French dog, rescued from confinement by a party led by one of my midshipmen...' He had to stop then, for the look on this merchant seaman's face was too startled to continue.

'Midshipman. The little lily-livered bastard hid away the whole time.'

'Language, sir,' Barclay barked, glad that Emily had gone to the sickbay to assist Lutyens, and so would not hear these words. 'This interview is at an end now. You have just seen fit to insult a cousin of my own wife, a boy she holds dear to her breast.'

'It matters not who did what,' Twyman insisted. 'The ship was not in enemy hands for the required time.'

'I think, sir, that an Admiralty court will be the judge of that.'

Barclay did not really resent Twyman's anger or his insults. Nor did he mind the fact that he was lying about the time spent in captivity. After all, as a prize taken by a King's ship he would get not a penny; as salvage Twyman and his crew would do well, though they might be obliged in extreme

484

circumstances to share their good fortune with the crew of *Brilliant*. No one, least of all Barclay, could resent a fellow trying to fight his corner when there was money involved. Against that he had a degree of confidence. Ommaney and Druce would present his case to the Admiralty Prize Court at Lincoln's Inn with the kind of zeal occasioned by the notion of profit. The ship's insurers, coffee house vandals, would no doubt put up a good legal team as well. Twyman counted as nothing in the scheme of things. At best he would be given a chance to make a written submission, one that would not tally with that sent in by himself and Burns.

'I intend that your ship should sail back to an English port.'

'Under my direction,' Twyman insisted.

'No, sir! Under the hand of one of my officers.'

'This is an outrage.'

'You may term it so, I term it prudent.'

They argued for an hour and a half, back and forth, while Barclay, whose mind was firmly made up, so that he only had to respond by rebuttal, used the time to think. Time and again, as Twyman repeated the same grievance, altering the words only slightly, Ralph Barclay conjured up the face of John Pearce, very much with that look of belligerence he had displayed the morning he had been sworn in. The man was a menace, and Barclay wished he had left him in that alley by the Pelican. But he had not, and he was on his ship; what to do about him?

Without his wife aboard, it would have been easy; he had seen troublemakers flogged into submission before. But Emily would make his life a misery if he tried, and it was no comfort to him to know that she could, something she had already proved. Where did the shrew in her come from, for it had never before been evident? Yet she had found looks that made him feel like a scrub, silences that made him feel foolish, and attitudes that made him seethe with impotence.

Slowly, as Twyman ranted on, a solution presented itself, and having arrived at that he brought the argument to a conclusion by alluding to the possibility that the crewman from the Indiaman might find himself clapped in irons if he did not desist.

Hale came into the cabin as soon as the coast was clear, to fill in the bits of the story he had left out for the captain's wife: how her little cousin had behaved in action. It did not make for a pretty tale and added another layer of anxiety to Ralph Barclay's complex peregrinations.

'The captain wants to see you, Pearce,' said Lieutenant Digby, who was now confirmed as acting Premier.

Pearce looked up from his mess table, where he was once more obliged to take his ease, doubly uncomfortable because he was forever put to the blush with Taverner, Rufus and Michael singing his heroic praises, conscious that such praise had Gherson seething.

'Am I allowed to refuse?'

Digby had to suck in air – hard and audibly – through clenched teeth. Being acting Premier meant if he had no way of imposing discipline by dint of personality, he had no recourse to anything other than the Articles of War. Pearce should have leapt to his feet as soon as he addressed him – that he had not done so was in itself a punishable offence, but looking into those defiant eyes he knew that even that threat would not wash.

'Would you believe me if I said that it might be in your favour to do so?'

Pearce was aware that the exchange had not gone unnoticed by the rest of the crew, just as he knew how much he had challenged Digby's authority by staying seated. Given that Digby was the only officer who had remotely shown any kindness, Pearce knew that the man did not deserve it. Slowly he stood, and lifted his hand. Breathing stopped on the whole maindeck then, with men wondering if he was going to hit the acting Premier – the bugger was mad by all reckoning, so anything was possible – but Pearce put his fist to his forehead and gave him the required salute.

'Aye, aye, sir.'

'Follow me,' said Digby, turning away to hide his relief, quickly enough to see the eyes of the crew diverted.

Having sent for Pearce, Ralph Barclay had the task of asking his wife to leave the cabin, including the coach, were she was wont to spend her time. It was a delicate task because by doing so, he alluded to the notion that she might eavesdrop.

'I plead, my dear, the interests of the man himself, for we have seen that this Pearce has a high opinion and few manners. I fear he may say something untoward, and if it is overheard by you I would have no choice but to react.'

'I will happily take a turn on the deck. With your permission I may ask my cousin Mr Burns to join me. I am agog to hear of his adventures.'

'I shall send for him,' Barclay replied, thinking that to eavesdrop on that exchange would be illuminating.

Emily was on the windward side of the quarterdeck by the time Pearce came aft, barefooted and coatless again. That part of the quarterdeck was the preserve of the ship's captain, a place where he – and his wife – were allowed to walk undisturbed in the freshest air available. That her eye was on the man of the hour was not to be remarked upon; everyone on the ship was looking at him. All she got was a flick in her direction as Pearce crossed the divide, passing the mainmast towards the officer's preserve. She tried to respond with an expression of reassurance, sure as she was that her husband, faced with her disapproval, was about to mellow. Burns came trailing in Pearce's wake, but Emily Barclay did not observe the looks he got from the crew, which could hardly be said to be flattering.

'Mr Burns, come walk with me and tell me what you have been up to. I am sure now that you are a hero Captain Barclay would not mind.'

Burns still hesitated, for the windward side was sacrosanct when the captain or his lady graced the deck. It was Digby, turning from having delivered his charge, who saved his face, being one of the people aboard yet to be told the whole truth about the cutting out of the *Lady Harrington*. He said, 'Carry on, Mr Burns. I am sure the captain would have no objection.'

'Now, cousin,' Emily whispered, 'from the very beginning.'

Toby Burns had had time to think, had talked to the captain, heard himself referred to in heroic terms and faced and boasted to his fellow midshipmen. So he now had a story to tell that put him in a good light, from the very moment he had warned Lieutenant Thrale that he was off-course. Cousin Emily heard how his action had saved some of the crew; how, reluctant as he was, he had had to take command. She heard of the difficulty of one so young as he ordered about grown men to get them to act for their own sake in the face of their natural lethargy and their sense of despair. His role in the freeing of the prisoners was central – and he was working off what Pearce and O'Hagan had reprised of that affair – he being the only one small enough to slip through a skylight at the top of a securely locked door and attack the guard.

'He was asleep, cousin,' he added hastily. 'So it was not a difficult thing.'

'Were you not terrified?'

Chest puffed out, Burns replied, 'Petrified is a better word, but I knew I had to do my duty. So many men's lives depended on it.'

'And the taking of the ship, the destruction of the privateer, Toby?'

'The men must take praise for that, for I am only one; they fought like demons, outnumbered too. But I have a small hope that they would acknowledge that my plans and my instructions, plus the encouragement I gave them in battle, played some part in our success.'

The kiss that Cousin Emily planted on his cheek, the words that he was indeed a hero, were music to his ears.

Barclay kept Pearce waiting, going over the thoughts he had harboured earlier. The concern that was uppermost was not of his wife's disapproval, but the attitude of his crew when he had flogged the man; then, that moment on deck when Pearce had nearly struck him. He was aware that his men were not, on either occasion, with him. Sensitivity to the feelings of a crew was a paramount part of being a good commander, and Ralph Barclay had no doubt he was that.

'Fetch him in,' he said to Shenton, 'then I want everyone out of earshot, so make sure you tell Mr Digby to clear the poop.'

Both sets of eyes lifted to the skylight above Barclay's head, a fine place for a senior member of the crew to listen in on cabin gossip. There was a pause while this order was carried out, then the marine sentry showed Pearce in and escorted Shenton out. Still scruffy from his adventures, unshaven and his ducks streaked with everything from gunpowder smoke to mud, Pearce did not look like much to trouble a Post Captain. But he did trouble him, and in a way that undermined both Barclay's domestic and professional well being. There was no invitation to sit, just as Pearce gave no salute, keeping his balled fists firmly by his sides.

'Mr Burns told me you behaved well.'

He nodded slightly, unblinking; the man had presence – there was no doubt of that, but Barclay had dealt with people of greater merit than this rogue and was not about to be put off his stroke.

'I would be obliged if you would tell me how he behaved?'

'I think whatever he told you would be as close to the truth as you need to know.'

'Do you have any reason to feel that you should not be aboard this ship?'

'No more than ten or twenty others, and as to reasons I think you know them all.'

Barclay tapped his fingers on his desk, holding Pearce's look with his own. 'I am minded to show you some favour, for you and your fellows have helped Mr Burns to deliver to this ship a valuable prize. But I must warn you that insolence is not likely to aid that.'

'Let us just say then that I am not bred to the sea.'

'I am curious to know what you are bred to.'

'The freedom to choose my time of waking and sleeping, eating and washing.'

Ralph Barclay was getting nowhere. He was going to have this man off his ship, for reasons that had nothing to do with kindness, but he wanted Pearce to hint at some gratitude.

'I am minded to grant you that for which you ask.'

'That also applies to the men brought back aboard with me.'

Barclay laughed. 'You'll be asking me to free them too?'

Pearce stiffened then, though he tried to hide it. Was what Barclay said a slip of the tongue, or did he mean it? 'I speak of men who did just as much as I, maybe more, to retake the *Lady Harrington*.'

'I fear you must leave them behind.'

'No. If I go, those in my mess must go too.'

Inwardly Pearce was screaming at his own foolishness. He was being offered what he wanted most and turning it down.

'Am I to understand,' Barclay demanded, leaning forward with a smile of disbelief, 'that you would forfeit your own chance to be out of the Navy for them?'

God, thought Pearce, I'm as much of a gambler as this bastard before me, and just as likely to be a loser.

Had Pearce been able to see inside his opponent's mind, he would have found a confused train of thought added to a tinge of jealousy, which led inexorably to a clear conclusion for Ralph Barclay. How would the freeing of Pearce look to Emily? There was a nagging suspicion that she had taken a shine to this fellow, hence the jealousy. Then there were his officers and the crew. How would the discharge of one man, whom he had flogged for paying attention to his wife, be perceived, let alone the release of several when he was short-handed and clearly could not spare any men?

Pearce was looking hard at Barclay, trying to guess what he was thinking, when the captain suddenly smiled, then nodded, and said. 'Very well, you may go and tell your mess to collect their possessions. Please be so good as to ask Mr Burns to join me.' Barclay picked up a quill, looked at Pearce, looked down again, and said, 'That is all.'

'It's our reward for taking that ship,' said Pearce, when word came to get their dunnage together, 'and I think he sees us all as trouble.'

'I care not,' cooed Gherson, which earned him an old-fashioned look from Pearce, who when he had said his mess, had somehow forgotten that Corny was part of it.

Michael just beamed and said, 'I am going to go and kiss that bastard Devenow on his one good cheek.'

Charlie Taverner was speechless but happy, Rufus doubtful. The one who stuck was Ben Walker.

'I'll stay, if you don't mind.'

Charlie was shocked. 'We started together, Ben, we should stick together, mates.'

'In misfortune, Charlie,' Ben insisted, his eyes slightly wet. 'What are you going back to when you get ashore? The Liberties, or a life outside dodging tipstaff warrants?'

'I am not going back to that, Ben, I swear, nor to London. I'll find a place where I'm unknown. Time I put my back into some work, made a bit of myself. Maybe together it would be easier to prosper.'

'I wish you joy,' Ben replied, slowly shaking his head, a look of determination on his face. 'I'm staying.'

Dysart, now with his arm in a sling, called from the steps to the lower deck. 'Trunks are out of the hold. Come and get yer dunnage. And Pearce, Mr Lutyens says he wants a word.'

They made for the companionway, all except Pearce and Ben Walker. 'You're sure, Ben?'

'I am, Pearce. There's nowt for me ashore.' He let his eyes drift round the maindeck. 'Maybe if Abel was still alive, I might go, for he was wont to see to our care. Charlie, well I like him but he's no fellow to go relying on. Who knows, there might just be something here.'

'Ben, I have to ask you.' He put a hand up as Walker stiffened. 'And I know I have no right. But it would grieve me to go through life knowing you as I have without any inkling as to what kept you in the Liberties.'

'I have a notion to know what brought you there.'

'It's a long story, Ben, but I do face arrest. You?'

It took a while, a degree of thought, before Ben said, 'Twixt thee and me?'

'On my life, Ben.'

Walker's shoulders drooped, as if disclosure added a weight to his conscience rather than relieving it. 'A girl, Pearce. Love – another blade, handsome cove, tall like you and blue-eyed, a charmer. Then betrayal. I went too far to right matters, made them worse.'

Pearce didn't have to ask how far was too far. It was all in Ben Walker's slumped posture. 'Someone died?'

'Someone dear.'

'If Michael's God exists, I'm sure he will forgive you.'

'He'll have to, Pearce, for as sure as hell is hot I will never forgive myself.'

Lutyens looked out of his little surgery to ensure no prying ears before he spoke to Pearce.

'Here, take this letter.' Pearce made no move to accept the folded paper being proffered. 'If you don't, you will most certainly regret it.'

'Will I?'

'Damn, you're a hard man to help,' Lutyens replied, in an exasperated tone. 'This is to my father, and is about your father.'

'I'm not sure I like the sound of that.'

'You will when I tell you that my father is the Lutheran pastor of the Deutschkirke in London. You will be even more pleased if I tell you that Queen Charlotte, particularly, worships there often, the King less so. My father is highly regarded by both. Perhaps you will even mellow if I say that a plea can be made directly to His Majesty on your father's behalf from someone he trusts, which I hazard would be more effective than the same from some of his old radical friends.'

'I'm sorry,' said Pearce, holding out his hand for a letter that was pure gold. Farmer George only had to click his fingers to get a warrant lifted.

'I mention you as well,' Lutyens added, turning away, 'and I have asked that he extend to you both hospitality and his protection.'

'Why?'

Lutyens turned back, his voice thick and the strange consonants more pronounced, nailing what Pearce had thought at first, that English was not his native language. 'You are a strange fellow, Pearce, singular in fact. There are far too few like you. And no man should suffer merely for his bloodline, nor might I add for his beliefs. You should be free to do and say as you like, for if we are fighting anything we are in conflict with a tyranny in France that will not accept the right of any man to that.'

'That's sounds remarkably akin to the American Declaration of Independence.'

'That may be so. But it is what I have always believed. Now go, before I regret my altruism.'

* * *

'Here are your orders, Mr Burns, and a despatch for the Admiralty. You are to take our Indiaman into port and hand her over to whichever senior officer has the command on that station. Then you will deliver this packet to Whitehall.'

Barclay grinned, Pearce's letter was inside his own, and it would go into hands that knew how to exploit it; let the arrogant sod suck on that!

'To you will go the glory of the capture, as well as the complete destruction of an enemy privateer. Who knows, you may even get a Gazette to yourself and your exploits. Here also is a sealed request to any naval captain you encounter to leave your crew be – in short, not to press them. I have also enclosed papers of discharge for those in Pearce's mess, but I abjure you not to open them or hand them over until the fellows you will take with you are on dry land.'

Burns was not sure how to react. He was being given a ship to sail and he had no idea how to do it. Then he brightened. The crew of the *Lady Harrington* did – Twyman had shown that already – all he would be obliged to do was have a cruise.

'I have asked Mr Collins to allow you one of his senior master's mates to get you home.' Barclay stood up, and held out his hand. 'I will of course accompany you to the ship, but I would like to shake you by the hand now, a sort of private farewell.'

Burns' podgy mitt was sweaty, his grip fish-like, which made Barclay glad of his masterstroke. If Emily could be brought to show pity to a cove like Pearce, what would she do if young Burns got into trouble, which judging by his lack of both courage and ability was only a matter of time? And by sending him back to garner the credit for the capture of a

British ship and the destruction of an enemy he was doing the best he could for a relation by marriage by way of advancing his career.

The numbers that came to see them over the side touched Twelve Mess; Barclay had Toby Burns and the ubiquitous file of marines sharing his transport, while Pearce and his fellows were allotted the jolly boat. Martin Dent came close to Pearce, grabbing his coat and pulling at it, looking at him in a strange way before running for the rigging. It was only when he moved that Pearce felt the bulk in his pocket, and an investigative hand clutched at his missing purse. How the boy had got it mattered not – it had been returned, and he was sure contained the same near fifty guineas as when he had come aboard.

Dysart waved his one good hand as the boats pulled away, shouting, 'Scots wae hae,' and much to Cornelius Gherson's embarrassment Molly loudly called his name, and then blew him a kiss. Ben Walker did not show, which disappointed four in the boat, but Martin Dent was, by that time, in the very height of the tops, legs entwined round the crosstrees, both arms swinging a farewell.

On the poop, Emily Barclay, standing with Lutyens, had to stop herself from giving a parting wave to the pressed men, the same kind as she had given to her cousin. And she was proud, not for the fact that her views had prevailed, but because her husband, too long a bachelor, too long in the Navy, had come to see sense and to begin to act like the kind soul he truly was. At that moment, she was looking to the future, to marriage and life aboard ship, with great confidence.

* * *

'Right, Mr Twyman, I am putting aboard Mr Burns in command of the prize, and master's mate to sail her home.'

'You can do as you wish, Captain Barclay, it will make no odds. This vessel is salvage and that is that.'

'As I have said, a matter for the court.' Behind him Pearce and his party were coming aboard. Twyman had seen them approach, but was surprised to see them bearing ditty bags, for he had heard from their lips that *Brilliant* was short-handed. 'Here, I have gifted you five hands, not the best I grant you but good enough to haul on a rope. Plus a master's mate to undertake navigation, six men in all. You will oblige me by selecting the same number from your crew to take their place aboard my ship.'

'I'm damned if I will, sir. You're not at liberty to press from a convoy ship.'

'But you are no longer on convoy. You are setting sail for home waters.'

'But...'

'Marines,' was all Barclay said then, not loud, but it brought down a line of muskets nevertheless. 'As I say, Twyman, you choose. I do not wish to usurp the right to decide what men I shall take, but I will if I have to.'

The inference was plain; tally off some men, or you will be the first on in my boat.

Those left behind were still cursing Barclay's perfidy when the two vessels parted company, HMS *Brilliant* setting all sail to the west and her convoy, the *Lady Harrington*, as much as she could safely carry, to the northwest, the master's mate Barclay had sent aboard insisting that was necessary to avoid the deadly waters around the Channel Islands.

* * *

Standing by the shrouds after his breakfast, watching other members of the crew go aloft, Michael O'Hagan and Rufus Dommet included, Pearce was conscious of the trepidation that held him back, and that knowledge annoyed him. No one had challenged him and there was no authority ordering him to go against his own inclinations to keep his feet firmly rooted to the deck planking. Sailing the *Lady Harrington* was very different from sailing a frigate, not comfortable exactly, but leisurely in comparison to the loud and persistent demands to 'double up' that were such a feature of life aboard HMS *Brilliant*. Sails seemed to be set and taken in at a pace to suit the crew, not the demands of some naval captain's vanity. He had to assume that in bad weather things would be different; self-preservation would demand swift action, but on this short voyage home the weather was as benign as the discipline.

Pearce knew he could climb to the mainmast cap, and he could recall the feeling of superiority, indeed almost of pleasure, such an ascent had given him. But could he go higher, to the actual tops, a place where boys like Martin Dent could get to with ease; and if he could, why would he want to? He supposed he would – because of the devil in him; that trait his father so gently deplored, the need his son seemed to have to be better than other men: to ride a horse faster, to pin an opponent swiftly on the point of an épée or slash at his head guard with a sabre; to be the first to attempt a seduction, moving to introduce himself while others, his peers in age and aspiration, held back. As these thoughts filled his mind, Pearce was already climbing.

At the lower mast top he acknowledged an amused shake of the head from Michael O'Hagan, before placing a foot on the much narrower shrouds that led up to the tops, noting that they were less springy, more taut than those below.

They narrowed ever more as they passed the access point to the topmast, until at the cap they were no wider than his own shoulders, while at his feet only a few strands stretched crossways. The wind, gentle on deck, tugged at his clothing and chilled his body. Hauling himself on, he joined the fellow posted there as lookout in a space a third of the size of the platform below. The cap consisted of a mere three strakes of thick square timber, and at this height he was much more aware of the motion as the *Lady Harrington* dipped and rose on the ocean swell; aware, but not in any way alarmed.

As soon as he felt secure, both arms looped around the masthead, Pearce experienced a creeping feeling of exhilaration, with the wind strong on his face, the air clean and salt-free, knowing as he looked around that he could see for miles in every direction, while below the likes of Charlie Taverner and Gherson, who had flatly refused an invitation to join him, were mere specks on the deck. Burns was an even smaller dot, standing before a wheel that was held by the master's mate from *Brilliant*, closely shadowed by Twyman, who refused to yield the deck to Barclay's appointees. It occurred to Pearce that the little midshipman was another person who showed little inclination for climbing masts.

The shout of 'Sail Ho' right in his ear, nearly caused Pearce to lose his grip. He spun round to follow the outstretched arm of the lookout, which was pointing in a vaguely easterly direction, straining his eyes to see the object he had identified.

'Where away?' came the voice from the deck.

'North-east, I reckon,' the lookout shouted. As he did so something rose from the grey edge of the horizon, and Pearce saw the tip of a mast, maybe a sail, and most certainly a streaming triangular flag.

'She's showing a man-o'-war pennant.'

'Friend or foe?' Pearce asked the lookout.

The answer was grudging, for he was with a fellow who had seen his mates pressed in the Navy, to be replaced by a lot he considered useless buggers. 'Won't know that for an age yet, till she's hull up and maybe then she might be flyin' false colours.'

The commands from below had the yards moving and Pearce saw the prow of the *Lady Harrington* swing slightly westward. 'We'll keep as much water betwixt us and them till we're sure,' said the lookout.

If time at sea had little dimension at deck level, that sensation was even more apparent at the mainmast cap. To Pearce, little changed; the approaching vessel got bigger, but so slowly as to be almost imperceptible. Yet to the lookout features of the approaching ship were constantly being revealed. She was a line of battle ship, two-decked but too small for a seventy-four, and looked to be British. The flag at the main told him she was in a squadron commanded by a vice-admiral of the white. He gave the information tersely to Pearce that, if he had a brain in his head he would know the Navy had three squadrons, blue, red and white.

'Sweet sailer too,' the lookout added, 'she's coming up hand over fist and that on a bowline.' Pearce declined to respond; he thought that meant sailing into the wind but was not certain enough to say so.

'Pretty,' the lookout exclaimed as the prow of the warship swung across to another tack, the yards switching also. 'Sheeted home her yards as sweet as a nut, she did.'

In half an hour they knew for certain she was British; that she was a sixty-four gunner, and as soon as some of the crew on deck could make out her figurehead, a large white face over a blue cloak and a golden crown on the head, they could say for certain that she was HMS *Agamemnon*, and that the request to heave to was one that could safely be obeyed.

The captain who came aboard was slight of build, so much so that standing next to Midshipman Burns, speaking in what was a high, light voice, he nearly managed to make the boy look and sound like a real sailor. The pair paced the windward side of the deck with Burns talking the most, the little captain listening, head bent in deep concentration. Pearce was not alone in edging closer to eavesdrop, unsurprised that in the telling of his tale, which was naturally of the pursuit and destruction of the *Mercedes*, Burns was allotting to himself a role he had not played.

'Would you listen to that little sod?' Twyman hissed.

Pearce nodded. 'I daresay it's the same story he told Barclay.'

The pacing stopped abruptly, as the small captain, in a piping voice, exclaimed, 'Some of the men from HMS *Brilliant*, men who took part in the action, are aboard?'

Burns looked slightly crestfallen, and Pearce had the feeling he regretted revealing the fact. 'They are, sir, four in all.'

'Then I would very much like to meet them, Mr Burns.'

A moment's hesitation was followed by a look and a call, which sounded almost martial in its delivery. 'Pearce, assemble those *Brilliant*s whom I commanded at Lézardrieux.' There was a very short pause, in which Pearce declined to move, instead glaring at the boy until he added, 'If you please.'

Gathering Charlie, Rufus and Michael took no time at all, for they had all edged close to the quarterdeck. Gherson looked set to step forward too, but Pearce told him abruptly to get back, and in seconds found himself looking down into a pair of startlingly blue eyes, set in a good-looking but quite pale face, and on the receiving end of an engaging smile. The captain wore his officer's hat across his head rather than front to back, which rendered clear his look of indulgent enquiry.

'Captain Horatio Nelson, at your service. You are?'

The reply 'John Pearce,' was unavoidable, given that Burns had used that name, and thankfully it produced nothing but a nod. As this Nelson moved along, introducing himself to the other three with the same pleasant manner, Pearce looked at Burns, who wore on his face a look of deep concern. If Nelson asked any questions, Pearce and his friends were in a position to ditch him, to tell the truth about what he had done, four voices against one would entirely destroy the image he had created with this visitor. But crushing Burns would not do him or his friends any good at all, despite any satisfaction it might give. He heard Nelson ask Michael to describe his part in the operation, and cut across the Irishman to answer.

'It was a joint affair, Captain Nelson, in which everyone played their part in what was a very confusing occasion. For any one man to single out and relate his own efforts would, of necessity, be partial, and quite possibly inaccurate. And I think it is worth reminding ourselves that nothing could have been achieved without the aid of the crew of the *Lady Harrington*, led by Mr Twyman, who is standing by the wheel.'

'Well said, fellow,' Nelson replied; looking at the speaker he did not see the glare aimed at Pearce by Michael O'Hagan. 'I have been in the odd scrap myself, and have found it hard in the aftermath to remember clearly what has occurred.'

For a moment Pearce wondered if Nelson was as much of a

liar as Midshipman Burns; he didn't look as though he could punch a hole in a paper bag, never mind take part in a proper scrap.

'Well, let it be enough to say that I congratulate you all. It is a fine thing you have done and I daresay when the news reaches England it will do much to cheer the folk at home. Mr Burns, time and tide do not wait and I have my orders for the Mediterranean. But let me say before I go back aboard *Agamemnon* that should you ever need a berth, and I have a ship, I would consider it an honour if you would apply to me for a place.' Nelson spun slowly round, taking in the whole deck as he added, 'and quite naturally, I would welcome any man here to join my crew. Good day to you all, and God speed.'

They watched, rocking on the swell, as Nelson's barge made the short trip back to his ship. As soon as he got aboard, men began to swarm up the shrouds to set sail. It was a shock, and an emotional one as, on a command from the quarterdeck, where all the officers including the little captain stood with their hats raised, the entire crew of the sixty-four gun ship of the line gave the crew of the *Lady Harrington* three times three in cheers. In utter silence, with not a shout to be heard but the order to make sail, the men of the warship sheeted home their yards and HMS *Agamemnon* got under way.

'Time we did the same,' said Twyman.

Cornelius Gherson added bitterly, as he looked at the departing man-o'-war, 'Drippy naval buggers.'

They had sighted land from the masthead hours before, and had put up the helm of the *Lady Harrington* to crawl along the long, low Dungeness shore, heading for the South Foreland and the Downs. Twyman had promised to put the five pressed men ashore before they made their landfall. In light airs there was nothing to do, so Pearce found himself on the quarterdeck in front of the wheel, in the place where Barclay would stand aboard HMS *Brilliant.* Pearce thought about the events of the past two weeks; it had been an experience, certainly, almost too much crowded into a short space of time to be credible. He had made friends and enemies. The first he would keep, the latter he would try to forget, for to recall them would require an ongoing hatred he knew to be more damaging to him than to those at whom it was aimed.

The view from this part of the deck was different – he had to acknowledge that fact. Men stood here looked forward, to where the ship was headed, watching the great bowsprit lift and fall on the swell, poetically he thought, as a measure of their hopes. But it was just wood beneath his feet – the same wooden planking that graced the other parts of the deck. What made the denizens of a warship's deck different were their uniforms and rituals – that allied to centuries of tradition. He had learnt that a ship, small East Indiaman or man-o'-war, was a complex affair – that the ropes, blocks, tackles and rigging represented a world of knowledge that could take years to acquire. And then only if what had been learnt passed down from those who had sailed the seas before – and that was before anyone had decided to take these great engines of war or commerce anywhere.

Navigation was a whole other art, seamanship the same: the ability to spot what was going to happen in the way of weather from the run of the sea or the colour and composition of the sky. But much as he admired the competence of those who sailed these ships, who could not but wonder at what they put up with. If accommodation had been tight in the frigate it was more so on this Indiaman; the crew, including the Pelicans, was confined to a tiny forepeak barely big enough to hold them all, so that space could be saved for cargo. Midshipman Burns, now once more pacing the windward side of the quarterdeck, still pretending to be an officer and a gentleman, abrogated to himself half the great cabin, with Twyman using the other half. It was the same on a merchant ship as in the Navy – those with wealth and position acquired more, and the space to enjoy the luxury it provided. Those with little toiled as they were directed – though life was much easier on a trading vessel than a warship – before hauling themselves into cots in a stinking pit, where privacy was unknown and comfort wholly absent.

Idly looking at what ships were passing, going tip and down the Channel, Pearce rehearsed his plans for getting to London and Lutyens' father without risk. The idea was that they would go ashore this very night as soon as it was dark, close enough to Dover – St Margaret's Bay had been mentioned. They would then be able to walk to one of the coach stops between there and Canterbury, without risking the port itself for fear of bounty-hunting crimps. Charlie and Rufus had opted for rural Kent, well away from the metropolis while Pearce himself would go on to London with Michael for company. He would need new clothes, for the coat that he had worn when taken up was torn and useless. And a big hat, one that created shadow enough to hide his face.

'Armed cutter signalling, Mr Burns,' said the master's mate whom Barclay had put aboard. 'Signal is to heave to. They'll be after hands.'

Pearce followed the pointed finger and observed a small

ship, with one great mast dwarfing the hull, beating up the coast towards them.

'Oblige him,' Burns replied, in his squeaky voice. 'Though I fear he is in for a grave disappointment.' Then he made for the cabin, to fetch the papers Captain Barclay had given him.

All the pressed men had been told that it was common for ships to be apprehended once they were in soundings – the point where a lead line could touch the bottom of the sea. It was from incoming merchant vessels that the Navy took most of its crews. The news brought everyone on deck to stare at the approaching cutter, a tiny affair dwarfed by the ship she had ordered to halt, though with gunports that showed she had teeth. Expertly, the man who conned it brought the vessel under the Indiaman's lee and backed the sails, edging on the rudder until the sides touched by the man ropes Burns had seen rigged, so that a blue-coated officer could clamber aboard. As he came on deck, he showed surprise at who walked the quarterdeck – not some flushed full-of-wealth India captain, but a slip of a naval mid with his hat off his head.

'Lieutenant Benjamin Colbourne, at your service,' the officer announced, returning the compliment with the hat.

'The prize ship *Lady Harrington*,' piped Burns. 'Taken by HMS *Brilliant*, Captain Ralph Barclay commanding.'

'Salvage,' barked Twyman, as he had done every time the word prize was uttered.

That raised an eyebrow and a discussion followed in which Burns put *Brilliant*'s case and Twyman that of the Indiaman crew, neither with true clarity, producing on the face of the lieutenant a look of wry amusement.

'You had best make up your mind, gentlemen,' he said finally. 'Your ship is in soundings and therefore I have the right to press some of your crew for service in the Navy. That is if you are salvage; a prize, of course, is different.'

Pearce looked him up and down. Colbourne was tall, well mannered, neatly dressed, but stooped.

'My captain gave me these to cover this very moment,' said Burns, handing over a letter.

Colbourne took it, broke the seal and read it. 'You have aboard, this says, five seamen from your frigate. Captain Barclay intends them for the press tender, and another ship, but writes that any captain intercepting this vessel should feel free to take his men on board.'

'You're wrong,' protested Gherson. 'Those are our papers of discharge.'

'We were illegally pressed,' said Charlie Taverner, a remark parroted by Rufus Dommet.

'I think,' Michael piped up, making more sense of what had happened than the others, 'that you will see we have been right royally stuffed.'

Pearce spoke up last; having listened to the exchange with a sinking heart, he was sure he knew what Barclay had done. 'These men are right. We were illegally pressed from the Liberties of the Savoy on the banks of the Thames. Captain Barclay undertook to free us.'

'Forgive me,' said Colbourne, his voice almost sympathetic, 'but by your garb you are clearly seamen. Those are Navy ducks you are wearing and I can clearly see that your hands are stained by tar.'

'Our shore clothes are stored.'

'Which is as it should be.'

'Would I be allowed to read Captain Barclay's letter?' asked Pearce, holding out his hand.

That occasioned an even more marked lift of the eyebrows, for common seamen were rarely able to read. But the officer passed the letter over. Pearce read the words with a cold sensation in his gut; their names were listed, their rating as landsmen, and the words this lieutenant had just quoted. There was one last chance, and he turned to the confused midshipman.

'Mr Burns, I feel after what has happened and with the glory you will gather from it, you may feel you owe us a favour. Captain Barclay asked me how you had fared, and for the sake of your being our comrade I declined to tell him the whole truth. Likewise with Captain Nelson. I now ask that you return both those favours. Please tell Lieutenant Colbourne that this is some kind of cruel joke.'

Burns looked at Pearce for what seemed like an age, his podgy face showing nothing. Then he turned his back on them all, and began to pace back and forth, quite the little admiral. A look from Pearce to Twyman produced no response – there was no mercy in those eyes, just the avarice of a man calculating an increase in his salvage money. Pearce was wondering whether to produce Lutyens' letter. Would that persuade this lieutenant to desist, or would it – in telling him both who Pearce was and whom he represented – decide him to put ashore into the hands of a Justice of the Peace as a man wanted by the law? He could not risk it.

Colbourne filled the awkward silence. 'Fetch your dunnage, all of you, and get it aboard my ship.' No one moved, until he added, quietly. 'I have the law on my side and I will not hesitate to bring muskets aboard if I have to.'

The temptation to tell the lieutenant to go to hell was strong, as potent as the notion of chucking him bodily off the ship. Pearce was aware that his companions were looking at him, in expectation of some idea of what to do, and once more he felt a slight irritation at being called upon to decide – why could they not think and act for themselves? The thoughts going through his mind were a jumble of possibilities, risks, and consequences, overlaid by the feeling that the Fates were again playing a cruel trick on him – the same trick as they had been playing for the past two weeks. He thought about the near arrest that led him to the Pelican and impressment; the thwarted possibility of escape; Barclay's surprise offer of freedom and now this.

They could not stand against authority here any more than they had been able to aboard HMS *Brilliant*. The law was on the side of the Navy and they were five against that, four because Pearce quickly discounted Gherson. No one on this deck would make a move to help them, one or two from greed, the majority for fear that they too might end up as pressed men. He could not even be sure that anyone but Michael O'Hagan would back him in taking action. But the thought Pearce was left with utterly depressed him; that having fallen foul of a cruel fate and overcome it, he was now being thrust into a situation where he would have to do the whole thing again.

'John-boy?' said O'Hagan.

Pearce turned around and spoke softly so that his reply was for the Irishman's ears only. 'We comply, Michael, because we must. But I swear on your God, Barclay will regret this act to his dying day. I shall make sure of that.'

Then he added, in a louder voice, one that stopped the midshipman in his tracks. 'Mr Burns, we will meet again one day, when I hope you are old enough to allow me to extract the price you must pay for what is an act of pure treachery.'

'Amen,' hissed Michael.

Pearce looked past the boy's pale white face and fear-filled eyes to the low northern shore, to the sandy beach rising in the distance and the wooded hills of the Weald of Kent – beyond that the road to London and the solution he sought. So near, yet so far!

To discover more great books and to
place an order visit our website at
allisonandbusby.com

Don't forget to sign up to our free newsletter at
allisonandbusby.com/newsletter
for latest releases, events and exclusive offers

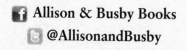

Allison & Busby Books
@AllisonandBusby

You can also call us on
020 7580 1080
for orders, queries
and reading recommendations